The Seventh Earl

Anthony Ashley Cooper
Seventh Earl of Shaftesbury

The Seventh Earl
a dramatized biography

by
Grace Irwin

William B. Eerdmans Publishing Company

Printed in the United States of America.

LIBRARY OF CONGRESS CATALOGING IN PUBLICATION DATA

Irwin, Grace Lillian, 1907–
    The seventh earl.

    1. Shaftesbury, Anthony Ashley Cooper, 7th Earl of,
1801–1885—Fiction. I. Title.
PZ4.I72Sg3   [PR9199.3.I7]   813'.5'4   76-3649
ISBN 0-8028-6059-1

Preface

Where do acknowledgements begin for the experience which has resulted in this book? With Betty Cullen Trewin, a former student, who helped to lodge the idea for the book firmly in my mind? With Lord Mountbatten, whose personal response and direction made the treasures of the Broadlands Archives available to me? With Mr. H. M. G. Baillie of the Royal Commission on Historical Manuscripts and with Miss Felicity Ranger and Mrs. J. Fielden of that staff for their courtesy and help during my two periods of research in Quality House? With the staff of the Hampshire County Archives? With the Tenth Earl of Shaftesbury, who very kindly opened St. Giles's for me to see and has given permission for the reproduction of "The Rosebud" and the Flitcroft dining room?

They should continue with thanks to Mr. Bernard Honess of the Congregational Library for his help with puzzling data; to Mrs. Margaret Wagers for sharing her valuable research; to the Reverend A. Morgan Derham for timely encouragement; to friends and relations for listening, reading, and suggestions.

The portraits of the Seventh Earl and of Minny, Lady Ashley, are reproduced by permission of The National Portrait Gallery, The British Museum, and the Trustees of the Broadlands Archives.

Finally, I am again glad to acknowledge my debt to my friend and secretary Laura Powell for her inexhaustible patience and accuracy in translating my longhand into impeccable typescript.

—Grace Irwin
Toronto, 1976

v

Introduction

BIOGRAPHIES ARE THE THING; biographical novels, not unjustly suspect among those who wish the facts. So every page of this book is capable of annotation, even the first chapter with its seemingly lurid, actually understated, "home and school" background of a future Peer of the Realm. I have done my homework, reading and copying hundreds of pages of the fourteen volumes of Shaftesbury's handwritten diary, as well as dozens of letters, legal documents, and clippings.

Why choose this form? The life of the Seventh Earl spans nineteenth-century Britain and touches every religious, social, political, economic, and international aspect of it. "My Lords," said the Duke of Argyll, "the social reforms of the last century have been due to the influence, character, and perseverance of one man—the Earl of Shaftesbury." Understandably then, his six chief biographies bog down in a welter of Parliamentary and socio-economic detail. But the achievement of the man is less the things he accomplished than their accomplishment under unbelievable handicaps of unpopularity, ridicule, ill health, family agonies, and lifelong financial difficulties. The impression left from our history books of the remote kindly aristocrat, bending from a life of ease to help the poor and wretched, is false. The real Lord Shaftesbury who stands up is a much more human, inconceivably greater figure.

Almost to the end of his life, the Earl opposed the writing of a biography. His diaries, which he often considered destroying, he left for his immediate family. "They exhibit every possible change of feeling, opinion, view, re persons and events, often perhaps on the same day," he said in a memoir opposing their publication, "strong, many hasty judgements, passions, weaknesses, dislikes, affections, on general subjects, private matters; religious hopes, fears, doubts, assurances. I can imagine their reception by the press; the tone of most journals would be of compassion and contempt."

This fear has been realized in the kindly condescension with which most modern biographers play the amateur psychologist, giving labels to characteristics which do not fit into acceptable grooves.

I have—humbly—tried to let that many-faceted, baffling, complex, intense person, Anthony Ashley Cooper, Seventh Earl of Shaftesbury, speak for himself. By cross references from his writings to the writings of his friends and acquaintances I have pieced together, occasionally created, scenes and incidents in which the dramatis personae play out the parts and make conversation of things which were actually said. All the letters are authentic, most of them hitherto unpublished. I doubt if I have put a dozen sentences into my hero's mouth which he did not say or write. I have not done him justice. Of necessity I have merely suggested vast areas of his activity, passed over in silence a hundred interests and causes which he espoused, understated his physical, mental, and spiritual agonies. But I have tried to carry out his expressed and express wish that "the reality be told, be it good or be it bad, and not a sham."

Minny, Lady Ashley
Portrait by J. Hayter

The parish church at St. Giles'
House, with almshouses to the left.

St. Giles' House Wimborne, Dorset

The Pantiles, Tunbridge Wells,
about 1838. From a lithograph by W. Clarke.

The eighteenth-century state
dining room, St. Giles' House

The parish church at the gate of St. Giles'
House where the Earl, Minny, their daughter,
and other members of the family are buried.

The Seventh Earl

SHIVERING, SHIVERING, trying to keep himself from shivering—that was what the bullies liked, to see him shiver; and the Master liked it too, drew out the time as he drew the cane along his hand, testing it, to watch him shiver and try to keep from shivering, drew out the time to minutes so that the pain was almost relief when it came—almost, not quite; it hurt too much. But he must not tell why he could not recite, must not say that Magnus and his gang of bullies had kept him from study, kept him running petty humiliating errands for their night feasts, had tormented him, tortured him when he refused to do things, disgusting things—his mind shrank from framing words for them, though he had heard the ugly words often enough, had kept him sleepless so that his mind could not concentrate at Prep before dawn in the cold dark hall. Even if he could have told, it would have brought harder thrashing—for blabbing the Master would say—and Magnus would get off and take it out on him. There he was now, watching him shiver.

Running, running, and at every turn Magnus with his sneering face, his hard-toed boots, his red, fist-making hands; running—now surely he was safe; it was not Magnus coming towards him, it was Mother!—running to her, choking with fear and relief, flinging himself against the widespread smoothness of her satin panels. An angry cry: "Brat! See, Cropley, he has soiled my gown;" a twist of his shoulder and a sharp slap across his ears with the white many-ringed hand which felt as hard as the bully's. Running again, away, shivering with the pain and shame and repulse, running to the green baize door, his haven—there with arms spread and welcoming smile, Millis. But even as with a convulsive effort which took the last of his energy he hurled himself into those arms, he felt the void, he entered on emptiness, he fell, fell on cold floor, landed in a slender tangle of thin coverings beside his bed.

Anthony Ashley Cooper, half-sobbing, still shivering, but wide-awake now in the black cold room, knew that he had been asleep. It brought him a sense of brief respite but no lightening of spirit, to realize that it had been only a dream. It was *not* only a dream. Every horrid moment, every frantic effort,

1

every baffling of escape, every apprehension of pain redoubled by remembered pain, every hope of relief turned to puzzled heartache, had been his waking experience, and often, except one. And he knew, picking himself up from the chill floor and trying with the inadequate reach of eight-year-old arms, to fold the coverlet so that it might give double protection from the cold—there was no hope of warmth—that he would experience them all, including that one, again and again in the grim foreseeable days ahead.

For Millis was dead. The summer had been desolate without her; but the Park and the woods and the river at Richmond had soothed the pain. He could always forget his troubles outdoors in the sunlight, if people left him alone. His mother too, for the first time in memory, had been indulgent—for her—to his sisters and himself and William when they had crossed her path. Perhaps she missed Millis too. She had been her ladyship's maid, Millis used to tell him, at Blenheim Palace before her marriage. And she had come with her mistress and risen to be housekeeper in the Honorable Cropley Ashley Cooper's household.

But by vacation at Christmas things were different. He had scarcely seen his parents. They had gone away the day after he arrived home, leaving the two babies and their nurses in possession of the nursery. Six-year-old William had taken ill, and any care that was shown in the grim, deserted house was given to him. So Caroline and Harriet and Charlotte played quiet, restless games under the eye of their little governess by day and huddled together for warmth at night. But for him, already marked as eldest son and therefore precluded from any elder sisterly patronage, there was no companionship. His aloneness was more bleak because Millis, though kind and dutiful to the others, had been especially his friend. She had even written a poem to him, very shortly before her death. "To my very dear Anthony Ashley Cooper on his birthday, April 28, 1809." He knew it by heart from:

"O be thou blest with all that Heaven can send,
Long Health, long Youth, long Pleasure and a Friend"

to the signature, "The never ceasing wishes of an old and most truly affectionate friend M.M." He repeated it now, though repetition sharpened the contrast between his chill, ignored, hungry self and the happy state she had invoked for him:

"Let Joy and Ease, let Affluence and content
And the Gay Conscience of a Life well spent
Calm every thought. . . .
Let day improve on day and year on year
Without a Pain, a Trouble, or a Fear. . . ."

Then the lines about Death. Perhaps that part at least would come true. . . .

2

Had the other servants always been so not-friendly, he wondered, burrowing under the covers till he could hardly breathe, and pulling his legs up against the less chilled part of his thin body? Or had he not noticed because Millis had always been there? Certainly he had never before been so hungry at home. He was used to being hungry at school. But now, between the sparse fare of early tea and the still distant prospect of a poor doled-out breakfast, his stomach felt sharp-cornered with yearning for food. He might have ventured down the three flights of stairs to the basement larder but he knew that everything there was under lock and key.

And had he been so cold other winters at home? Perhaps he was bigger now. Still, when Millis tucked him in, the covers had felt heavier. He had asked for more and been told that there were none. And he was too old, they said, to have a fire in his bedroom. Indeed he felt very old. And all alone.

But he wasn't alone, Millis had told him. Never. He was to remember that. "Thou, God, seest me." The words came to him from the verses she had read to him and had him repeat to her. "I will never leave thee nor forsake thee." She would not like to think that he had forgotten. "Lo, I am with you always." "When thy father and thy mother forsake thee, the Lord will take thee up."

The bed was still cold but he had stopped shivering. He tried to think of other verses but the same ones kept repeating themselves over and over. His stomach still ached, but the tight pain about his heart had loosened. Then he remembered something else. He put a hand up under the pillow and pulled down the gold watch Millis had left him. Its deep steady ticking reminded him of her heartbeat the first time she had taken him on her knee after a fall and held him till he stopped crying. He had not known what it was, that deep comforting sound, and had asked. No one had ever held him so before. Now, with the ticking of her watch under his cheek, he remembered that he had not said her prayer. She had asked him to say it every night, and to think of what he was saying. He could not think any more but at least he could say it. Between the words and the beating of the gold-cased heart he fell asleep.

II

Young Lord Ashley, striding up Harrow hill, paused by force of habit at the King Charles's look-out. It was a favorite contest on clear days—and this day was glittering clear—for the boys to see what landmarks they could spot in London, distant across the miles: the dome of St. Paul's of course—even on dull days it sometimes floated clear of the mist—three of the four turrets of the White Tower. He squinted to persuade himself that he could see the mast of a tall ship in the London Pool. Denison had sworn that he could distinguish the Monument, giving rise to a heated argument which had convinced all—except Denison—that the claim was impossible. St. Mary le Strand was another hotly debated object. And St. Clement Danes.

Ashley did not care. It was enough for him that the sun was shining, that birds were singing in the coppice, that the trees below and the fields beyond were green, and that the breeze stirring his thick curling hair was cool enough to exhilarate, scented enough from fresh-made hay-cocks to complete his sensuous delight. He speculated idly on the King's feelings as he had looked his last free look on the London which had rejected him, speculated too on the exact spot where he had watered his horse before riding north to Nottinghamshire to surrender to the Scottish army. On the whole, thought Ashley, he had got what he deserved. His own famous great, great, great grandfather had been a Cromwellian—if later a Royalist under Charles the Second, and then a condemned rebel under James. Since his initial visit to St. Giles's the previous summer, he had taken a great and defensive interest in the meteoric career of that first holder of the title to which he himself was now heir. In fact, when the boys read Absalom and Achitophel, he had defended his ancestor's integrity and consistency against the charges of perfidy and betrayal which the young Tories of his form hurled at him. Whatever the first Earl did, Ashley had countered stoutly, had seemed to him the right course at the time. At least he had been brave—and no party server.

A hail and an exchange of greeting with two straw-boatered classmates passing on the path diverted his mind from its excursion into the past. Almost he turned to join them; but the early summer beauty held him, and the comfortable realization that he was alone by choice. Harrow, especially Dr. Butler's house, had been for the last two years a paradisal contrast to his earlier environment, and he regarded the place with unalloyed affection. Some of his friends returned reluctantly after the holidays. Except for his single sojourn at St. Giles—spent largely in exploring the woodland delights of Cranborne Chase—periods spent at home were still dreadful. His father's stern censure or punishment of himself and the others, his mother's sharp temper, the bickering and coldness which pervaded their encounters, made beginning of term a delight. Fagging for a Sixth Former whose insomniac master frequently called a class at four in the morning might constitute a hardship to some. He had only to recall—he was grateful that involuntary recollection was coming less frequently in nightmares—the unmitigated horror of his first school at Chiswick Manor House to take it equably.

Even the mosquitoes from Duck Pond could not spoil his delight. An idea struck him—why not make that pestilential blot on the landscape the subject of his next Latin verse? What could he use for mosquito? Muscus pungens? He laughed to himself and turned away, ebullient with pleasure. He completed the ascent, passed St. Mary's and sauntered down towards school. A leisurely pace suited his mood. In his fifteenth year and tall for his age, he seldom put forth much effort. Occasional vague aspirations drifted through his mind but they were chimerical and had no association with the winning of school prizes or anything else that meant more than necessary work. Just being alive—and away from home—and at Harrow—was good enough.

"Earth hath not anything to show more fair," he murmured. The uncouth new poet Wordsworth was held in small esteem at Harrow. Impelled by curiosity to pick up his volume of verse in a bookstall recently, he had been thrilled by his apostrophe to Milton and had found this line from a sonnet composed on Westminster Bridge a comfort to repeat when, as now, language failed him.

Where was the noise coming from? It had struck his ears as he came over the hill but it was louder now, unrecognizable as music but with some raucous semblance of a tune. A song was being shouted in snatches by some half-dozen voices, with frequent interruptions of drunken hiccoughs, argument, warning, laughter, and the scuffling sound of erratic, impeded movement. He had heard the song more than once when hurrying past a gin-shop in London.

He stopped as the singers came out of a narrow lane and into view. Five men, a stage removed from stupefaction, were carrying a wooden case on uneven shoulders. A sixth, staggering backwards as self-appointed director, was berating the others for disregarding his orders and being loudly berated by them for shirking the burden. Even as he gesticulated widely to turn the two leading bearers from their drunken determination to go the wrong way, he tripped over a stone and, in falling, took the legs from under the man nearest him. The box sailed over their heads, crashing to the road a few feet beyond. The others, unbalanced by the impetus of its flight and stumbling forward on their companions, collapsed in a shouting, cursing heap, which gradually separated into individual forms, rolling or lying helpless with sodden laughter.

Ashley's fascinated eyes sought the box. The rough top boards held, but a side plank had come loose with a gaping crack. From it a strip of dirty winding-sheet and a grimy stiff-fingered hand protruded.

He wanted to turn away but could not. A few half-grown children who were running along with the grotesque cortege jeered at the men in their ponderous efforts to rise. One, egged one by the others, approached the substitute coffin and poked at the dead hand; then darted away screaming with laughter. Presently the leader, then the others, stumbled to their feet and surveyed the half-wrecked box.

"Thought 'e'd get out, did 'ee?"

"Na, leave 'im be, it'll make it easier for the worms."

The arm was thrust rudely back, the board wrenched temporarily into place, the coffin was hoisted precariously amid loud complaints about the stench from those on the windward side and equally loud guffaws from the others. Then, with a less successful attempt at another song, the bearers and their burden lurched up the hill and passed him on their way to the church-yard.

Anthony Ashley Cooper had not moved. The glory of the day was obscured, the complaisance of his mood shattered. Through his mind came pictures of his uncle's funeral four years before: the procession of mutes, the great hearse, the black-plumed horses, the mourners led by his own father, solemn-faced and head bowed, his own black suit and black-plumed hat and William's, and the coaches in which the new Countess, his mother, sat with the Dowager Countess and her daughter, thick black veils hiding their faces. He heard again the great bell tolling, and the words of the Burial Service. . . . "We brought nothing into this world and it is certain we can carry nothing out—verily every man living is altogether vanity—for as in Adam all die, even so in Christ shall all be made alive—forasmuch as it hath pleased Almighty God of his great mercy to take unto himself the soul of our dear brother here departed—in sure and certain hope of the Resurrection to eternal life through our Lord Jesus Christ—Look, we beseech Thee, with compassion upon those who are now in sorrow and affliction . . ." There were not many, as far as he knew, in sorrow and affliction for his uncle, a quiet man who had greeted him remotely and amiably on their infrequent meetings and who had seemed embarrassed at his brother's brood. But there were tears and dignity and solemnity at his passing. Some of the villagers standing around the church wept and uttered ejaculations about his kindness to them.

What was it Millis had said? "God is no respecter of persons"? Other words crowded upon him from her Bible in which, though with lapses, he still read. "He that oppresseth the poor reproacheth his Maker." "The poor is hated even of his own neighbors; but the rich hath many friends." "Inasmuch as ye did it not to one of the least of these, ye did it not to me."

He tried to move, and with movement shake off the horror and gloom that blanketed him. Somewhy he had to wait, standing there in the empty street which was not empty to his eyes, in the quiet air where wild curses still hung. His eyes saw, clearly as an object viewed in sunlight sears the closed eyelid, the stiff hand flung out as if in appeal, as if in supreme frantic effort to escape anonymity and oblivion.

"Good Heavens!" It was almost physical pain which forced the words from him. "Can this—this obscenity—be permitted, simply because the man was poor and friendless?"

Speech was a katharsis. From frozen immobility, a state in which his mind passively recorded images and words, he found himself consciously praying—half-prayer, half-vow—that whatever the future held, he might be allowed, he might be enabled, to plead the cause of the poor and friendless.

III

"I SEE YOUR YOUNG FAVORITE YONDER. Charming the poor girls as usual. I fear he is a male coquet, the cruellest and most cold-hearted of all things, but handsome and captivating I must admit."

"Nonsense, my dear Lady Holland." Lady Granville followed the direction of her friend's jewelled lorgnette and smiled indulgently at what she saw. "Ashley is anything but a flirt."

"Come, come, I grant it may not be his fault that all the girls fall in love with him, but must he be so charming? Look at him now, all devoted attention to that plain little chit—whoever is she? She will dream of him for days but will she see him again? No. I maintain it was a blessing for all our girls when he made the Grand Tour. And by-the-by—"

"The plain little chit," said Lady Granville, one of the few who could and did interrupt her opinionated friend, "is my goddaughter, Miranda Haise-Jones. I asked you if I might bring her tonight. She has been buried in her father's vicarage in Gloucestershire and has been quite terrified at the prospect of the ball. So to whom should I introduce her but to Ashley? He is behaving like the kindest of brothers. Or, shall I say, as we would the kindest brother always behaved."

Lady Holland's French lorgnette, seldom out of play, focussed again on the set of quadrilles in progress on the salon floor.

"Well—to be fair, he is considerate. I recollect that I entrusted my Mary to his care when she was first out. At Devonshire House I think it was, and very anxious and kind *he* was, keeping her from making a *faux pas* in her dancing. But has he no heart at all? Certainly he has never shown any partiality either before or since his Continental Tour. Yet they do say—"

"I was quite delighted"—Lady Granville seemed determined not to let the other digress—"at the impression he made at my soiree in Paris last year—dear me, almost two years ago I declare. The Hardys and Cowpers were there and Ashley and Denison. But it was of Ashley that the French talked incessantly—'*superbe, magnifique*'—I was as proud as if he had been my own son."

"And certainly prouder than his own mother," riposted Lady Holland neatly. "One seldom sees them at the same place, but when one does she scarcely recognizes him. Or any of the children. I cannot say that I am a devoted mother. But Anne is positively unnatural."

"Ashley is her son though. Look at the grace of the man. He never got that from Shaftesbury."

"Nor much else. Either that man is the most tight-fisted curmudgeon or Lady Shaftesbury spends it all. They say he turned Ashley out of his house when he came back from the Tour—said it was time he set up on his own."

"I cannot say that Lord Shaftesbury is a pleasant man, though capable to a degree as Chairman of Committees—so my husband informs me." Lady Granville was moved from her usual charitable speech. "He seemed utterly unmoved, and Lady Shaftesbury scarcely went into mourning, when that poor boy Francis was pummelled to death at Eton."

"Lord Holland was quite vexed with them I remember. I overheard him say that Londonderry was more upset about his nephew's part in it than Cropley about his son's death. 'In fact,' he growled, 'had the charge of manslaughter been upheld, I doubt if Cropley's tears had outlasted the payment of damages.' So how can we expect the son of such parents to have feelings? Yet—ah, Sir George,"—her lorgnette tapped the shoulder of the assured young man who came up to pay his respects to his hostess—"you are the very one to relieve our minds."

Sir George Clanwilliam bowed again with the formality which he assumed at will. Lady Granville, regarding his pose with unimpressed affection, was suddenly reminded of a dinner years before, when the first course was taken up by vigorous argument regarding this same dandy's habit of sitting in Parliament unshaved, and the previous day having leaned out of his window unkempt and without his neckcloth. Was this disregard of public opinion, Ward had asked Montagu—or had Montagu asked Ellis? she forgot—an evidence of personal vanity? Like his prodigious yawning when bored? Yet he had performed his duties in Berlin most capably.

"Your servant, Ma'am. And my apologies for being late. In what may I perform so pleasant a duty?"

"By settling a disputatious question, Sir George. You were in Vienna not infrequently during your stay in Berlin. And you saw something of Lord Ashley during his prolonged visit. Now tell us the truth of those delicious rumors that he had a grande passion there; that his heart was broken; that he will never love again. For truly it would explain his lack of interest in these girls who dote on him."

"We would not have you betray confidence," interposed Lady Granville as he hesitated, "but it is so tantalizing to hear mysterious hints."

"Such as that the girl was already promised—that Ashley was challenged to a duel—that she was inconsolable—fell into a decline when he left—that Prince Metternich had to pacify her family—that Ashley behaved shamefully—that he behaved nobly. Now what are we to believe?"

Clanwilliam resigned his intention of taking part in the set which was forming. One did not deny Lady Holland with impunity, and Lady Granville had been too kind and frequent a hostess for him to disappoint. He ascended the step of the dais in the great window of the drawing room, drew up a satin stool which had just been vacated and dropped his voice to as confidential a tone as could be heard through the music.

"As to Ashley's conduct, rest assured it was impeccable. As to his passion, there is no doubt that he was deeply enamored. The lady in question is most attractive, part Italian, part Austrian, and very well connected. Many of us, I assure you, sighed for her, but certainly, as long as Ashley was present"—there was a note in his voice which made Lady Holland's carefully arched eyebrows rise sharply—"she had eyes for no one else."

"Then do tell us what happened. Could it not have been a match?"

"Now there we can only conjecture. The lady's religion perhaps—"

"The Earl would certainly frown—but so would he on anything Ashley did."

"I opine that Ashley himself had misgivings. At any event he left her—heart-brokenly we thought. But the lady has recently married, I hear, and no less a person than Prince Metternich himself. And . . ." His gesture indicated the unconscious object of their speculation handing his partner serenely down the long aisle of sundered couples—"You see no evidence of a broken heart. He seems to me quite caught up in his new appointment. And should make his mark in public life. That handsome face makes one forget the mind behind it. Now you will excuse me to pay my respects to Lord Holland.

9

My mother wishes me to convey her regrets. Lady Lyttleton! Permit me to offer you a place you will fill much more gracefully than I."

The newcomer accepted his chair gratefully.

"I am very happy to join the line of duennas. O for Lady Cowper's vigor! I verily believe she has danced every set. Ah well, when her Emily comes out she may feel her age. Have you been in to supper?"

"No. Lord Holland said he would come for me but once he disappears into the gaming room he loses all track of time."

"So they are going to waltz," said Lady Granville with interest. "Little Miranda will not venture. I wonder where—"

"Rest assured, your idol has looked after her." Lady Holland's lorgnette gave her the advantage. "She is standing yonder, guarded by another handsome young man. He looks familiar."

"Why yes. It is Ashley's brother, William. The Sublime and Beautiful they are called. And it is very well to tease me, but my idol, as you call him, is also the best of brothers. He has taken William into his house and is busy finding him a place."

"Who is this paragon?" enquired Lady Lyttleton, adjusting her little scarf above the puffed sleeves of her gown.

"Lord Ashley."

"Oh, the Saint, as I heard him called at Windsor when we were there for the Ascot. You know he will not travel on a Sunday even to please his Majesty. The King was much amused..."

"I see he is not afraid of waltzing at any rate. How beautifully he does it. And—yes, Lady Francis is his partner." Lady Holland was not to be sidetracked. "Now I have wondered about those two. See how well they dance together. I doubt it is not the first time. Henry tells me he is often at Sudbrook. If I were Lord—"

"Come, come, you shall not slander Ashley," said Lady Lyttleton laughing. "It is that enthusiasm of his. He can never seem cool or dispassionate. Why last year Mrs. Fitzherbert said to George Dawson Damer 'Your Ashley Cooper is to marry Lady Bridgewater,' and she's sixty-six if she's a day!"

"You may laugh," insisted Lady Holland when all three had done laughing, "but he might do worse. The old girl is prodigiously rich. And he may be a long time inheriting. Cropley will live to old age if only to spite the children. Then with these scruples of his—he refused office under Canning, because, I understand, Canning has opposed the Duke!—his prospects will not attract the fathers, no matter how those beautiful eyes make the daughters swoon."

"I for one do not blame them," said Lady Lyttleton. "If I were the age of Henrietta or Olivia, I should have swooned myself this very evening. I had a few moments of chat with him. And do you know what about? There we stood waiting to come up the stairs, with all the babble going on and the loveliest gowns sweeping past. And there he stood, gazing into my eyes with his awfully handsome face alight as if he were seeing a vision—"

"Really! But why—?"

"Because he had visited Sir James Smith's observatory last night and seen 'Saturn and its rings, a spectacle worthy of God alone! Man,' he says, 'has not beauty of soul sufficient to comprehend such majestic loveliness.' Oh yes, quite mad, I grant. But a delightful change from the ordinary run of conversation."

Lady Holland laughed, a sardonic throaty chuckle.

"I should love to see his mother's face if he says such things to her. Nor should I blame her. Bad taste these saints show. Dragging their God into polite conversation. Really, what next?"

"I thought you disapproved Anne's neglect of him. In fact it would seem now permanent—of them all, including Lord Shaftesbury."

"That's neither here nor there," said Lady Holland testily. "No matter what I think of Ashley's fanaticisms, I like a show of family feeling. And she makes none. Why Marlborough treats that bastard of his more kindly than his sister treats her legitimate daughters. I believe the Duke would have her presented if he decently could."

"Well," said Lady Granville, "he could not deny paternity. She's the spitting image of him. And by-the-by, have you noticed the resemblance between poor Susan and Lady Shaftesbury's Charlotte?"

Lady Lyttleton clapped her hands with surprise.

"That is why the child seemed so familiar when I saw her at Blenheim. I could not think why. Now I recall. She is Charlotte as I saw her at her wedding."

"She was a happy-looking bride," said Lady Holland. "As much because she was escaping from Shaftesbury's house as because of Henry Lyster I'll be bound."

"I must admit," said Lady Granville, "according to my nephew George when he visited St. Giles's, the Earl was so stern that the girls were afraid to speak when he was in the room. Yes, I think Charlotte is happy. Rowton is a very comfortable seat."

The names provoked another recollection from Lady Holland.

"And what must Ashley do as soon as he visits there? Begin to learn Welsh if you please! Naturally, when the news got abroad the people were so

11

delighted that they held a meeting—don't ask me to pronounce the name of it—and made him a Druid!"

"Dear Lady Holland, anyone would think we three were under a spell. Do you realize that we have talked of no one else?"

"There are dozens of bulls down there at your ball. Why are you obsessed with young Ashley?"

"Because I do not like puzzles. What am I to make of a young man who is all passion, and cold as an iceberg? Who has no affaires, no amours, yet behaves so attentively as to raise any girl's hopes. Whose wit and company are in demand at the Royal Lodge and who dines with the East India Company at taverns instead of keeping such fellows at a distance. Who speaks strongly about the Hindoo practice of burning their widows—can't he leave well enough alone? Who visits Lunatic Asylums on a Sunday afternoon instead of riding in the Park—."

"Ah well," Lady Granville, "it is not that he does not enjoy riding. I've never seen a finer seat. But hush! . . . Here he comes now bringing Miranda."

It had evidently been a great evening for her young goddaughter. From the flat-heeled, satin slippers to the flowered ribbons fastening her auburn curls the "plain little chit" was a triumph of Lady Granville's good taste and her own girlish delight. And of that delight her escort was evidently a chief cause. One of her hands rested triumphantly on the sleeve of his blue frock coat. She was chattering brightly but not nervously, looking up at him with perfect confidence as he steered her deftly around the recent dancers, who were now seeking the dining room with as much vigor as they had expended in dancing. Her small figure made his slender, five-foot-eleven frame look very tall. Against the shifting background of silks and gauzes, of fans and jewel-set tulle hats, there was a statuesque restfulness about his unstudied grace as he came to a stand and straightened from his bow immediately before them. The three women who had been discussing him, all mothers of sons, acknowledged queens of society and connoisseurs of its youth in the Capitals of Europe, thought that it would be difficult to find a more complete beau-ideal of the British aristocracy. The Sublime and Beautiful is certainly the *mot juste*, reflected Lady Lyttleton: perfectly dressed but without either the daintiness or the studied negligence which betrays the fop. He knows he is admired, he likes it, but he doesn't gaze about for it. I really believe all he is conscious of at the moment is that he has just enjoyed a dance, has given a stranger a pleasant evening, and is at our service for supper.

The object of these reflections had the happy faculty of seeming impervious to outward disturbance. Though he had danced every dance and it was near midnight, the white stock carefully folded beneath high collar points above a striped satin waistcoat, and the long white unwrinkled breeches looked as if freshly donned. His face too, though perhaps the thick dark curling hair was a trifle moist where it clung to his high forehead, was marble pale. Fine curling hair, outlining the oval face on either side of a firm, clean-shaven chin, accentuated this pallor. An almost too prominent nose saved his features from insipid regularity. But the eyes, clear English blue under heavy, projecting, white lids and long, dark brows which curved strongly and tapered to enlarge already large sockets as with a frame, those eyes, intense, honest even in mirth, gave the lie to impassiveness, betrayed his vulnerability. It was the glance of those eyes, eager, questioning, trustful, which made him look younger than his twenty-seven years, that and the controlled sensitivity of his mouth. If a Greek artist—Praxiteles, thought Lady Granville, whose vocabulary of classical reference had been reinforced by the rage for Byron's poetry and that of poor young Shelley—had cast an ephebos in English evening dress, there from slight pointed shoes to sculptured clustering hair stood Anthony Ashley Cooper.

IV

Lord ASHLEY PAUSED TO READ the sentence he had just written, before affixing a full stop so definite that it almost blotted his page. He read the whole letter again carefully, the straight, smooth-flowing lines that might result in his dismissal from office. Arbuthnot would certainly not like his refusal to sign the despatch.

He dipped his quill again and signed his name with the flourish which—how wryly conscious he was, even as he did it—concealed a morbid lack of assurance. At least he was acting in good conscience. How difficult for a needy man to be so honest! If he were father of a dozen children could he bring himself to resolve thus greatly? He pondered the question as he sealed the letter and pressed his signet into the wax. Well, he would try to be sparing of animadversion towards those whose needs might cause them to be tenacious of office or any other source of decent maintenance. The reflection should serve to check his tendency to quick, hot judgement.

He rang for his man to deliver the letter to Mr. Arbuthnot. That matter was settled. The other, which was constantly with him, seemed as far from solution as ever. He left his desk, paced the room, paused by the open window, and looked into the mews below. The July evening was warm and he felt a spasm of longing to be quit of the noise and bustle of London and able to roam in solitude. Perhaps a walk in the Park. No, he did not wish to meet people. Except one—the One!

But who was she? And what had come over him that his whole being was recently fused in concentrated desire for a wife, but a wife as much the creature of his own devising as Galatea of Pygmalion's. He had even tried, urged on by the kindly officiousness of match-making friends, to see his ideal in Lord Liverpool's seventeen-year-old daughter. What an insufficient and strange idiot he had been, and how grateful to Providence that his suit had not prospered. The chance of the Duke of Buccleuch's splendid establishment had been much more to Liverpool's taste than the little he could offer. But he had already realized that she fell far short of his imaginary darling.

Sour grapes, many would think. He laughed shortly, paused by the desk in his restless pacing, and picked up a leather-bound book in which for almost four years now he had made desultory entries. It took the place—almost—of a confidant for his loneliness, eased the frantic excesses of his moodiness, served as a salutary, a humbling, a cheering reminder of past escapes, follies, blessings. If anyone, he thought, blushing inwardly as his eye fell on a particularly unguarded entry, were to read the book, he would inevitably be regarded as the quintessence of querulousness. Fortunately no one ever would.

And it was good for him to keep these notes. Things quickly escaped memory and his memory was deteriorating badly. So the diary reminded him of his improved health since a badly deranged stomach had driven him to consult Jephson, the Leamington doctor. The dreadful headaches and concomitant weakness of limbs from which he had suffered for years, were far less frequent. He could not say as much for the low spirits; but his fits of despondency, like his vivacity of heart, were unpredictable and he was learning to regard them as evidence of emotional instability and not to let them affect his activities.

So, at first, he had considered this urge towards marriage. "It is better to marry than to burn," he quoted aloud, and he knew not a little of that burning. But "generally speaking I have stilled the passions"—it was over three years since he made that entry, and its explanation of "An attachment in Vienna. . . . Man never has loved more furiously or more imprudently. The object was and is an angel but she was surrounded by, and would have brought with her, a halo of Hell. I thought the Deity harsh in the obstacles he raised to our union, obstacles in my own mind even."

Two years later Clanwilliam's candid disclosures of her perfidy and wantonness after his departure from Vienna had shattered the "angelic"

14

image but not before passion had cooled. "I find love is not likely to have mastery of my heart and mind," he read. "A man loves fiercely but once; the next time is convenience, or fancy, or plain matter-of-fact. I shall marry, no doubt, but not yet. I feel great kindness towards a select few, towards some, warm and tender affection, but it is a brother's love and probably they would not thank me."

Then his Liebe, his Antoinette, had married, and in spite of disillusionment he felt some return of the "fearfully strong" affection he had entertained for her. After that, perhaps because of the romantic scenery of Wales where he travelled while visiting Charlotte, he had begun to let his fancy invent a creature whom he could love to adoration. But—was it chance or some innate singleness of nature in him?—it was not until the news of Liebe's sudden death that he had begun to look over the girls of his acquaintance with an eye as conscious and discriminating as that of a prospective purchaser: his friends at Boyle farm, Henrietta and Olivia de Ros; Lady Charlotte Greville; his unregretted ten-day infatuation, Lady Selina; and a host of other amiable girls, pleasant to dance or ride with, but lacking either the power to stir his heart or the quality of stimulating companionship.

To shake off the thoughts—he should have gone to Lady Guy's with William after all—he turned the pages of his book, reading at random:

"What a dreadful woman our mother is!" What action or omission of action on the Countess's part had torn that comment from him three years ago? He had made a more general estimate in his birthday meditation that same year. "My mother continues in her hardness; away with her memory! The idea of such fiend-warmed hearts is bad for a Christian soul." It was easy to see why he approached marriage, even while he craved it, with apprehension. Jezebel, Cleopatra, Lady Anne Spencer—how charming and talented and intelligent they and others like them were in youth—and how they had influenced for evil the man who had been allured. His father allured? The idea passed his imagination; but surely something more than a sound business sense—daughter of the Duke of Marlborough must have been a good match for a younger brother with no assurance of succeeding to the title—had existed to generate eight children, particularly when neither parent showed affection for any of them from its birth.

Back to marriage again! He sighed and dropped his glance to a page blown back by the wind.

"It is enough that I am neither gifted, learned, nor profitable. I am only numbered with the crowd; let me endeavour my Duty in that state of insignificance, and in another world, God helping, 'sublimi feriam sidera vertice.' "

"I am too bilious for public life. What I suffer from the brazen-faced insults of that radical party. I am not fit for this accursed effrontery which sneers at every sentiment of a gentleman, and is backed by the applause of others who pretend to Education. Hume's conduct tonight was over-disgusting."

Yet the trouble with himself, he reflected, was that he could not be a party man. Elected because of views which his constituents approved, he found it difficult to uphold those views in public when his private reasoning altered his opinion. "On the Emancipation question, for instance, I am certainly more for the Catholics than I was before, wholly as a matter of policy, but as so little turns upon me I must and may conceal it. My Father otherwise would go mad." He read on:

"Lord Liverpool" (now deceased, *not* Selina's father), "asked me the other night to make a speech upon the Catholic Question. I refused positively to side and state violent opinions for the mere pleasure of a few stubborn and ignorant partisans. What will be my situation without the right of thinking for myself?"

What indeed? Never again he hoped would he make an entry like the one forced from him by honesty when the question came to division in the House.

"I gave a vote 'almost' against my conscience and nothing but a determination not to think prevented its being 'entirely' so. This is in all likelihood the last I shall give. I shall perhaps withdraw from Parliament."

Yet that seemed the sphere to which he was called. He had had a great desire to devote himself to literature—he passed through a period of writing poetry, neither bad nor very good—and, more recently, to science. But every time he seriously considered retiring from public life something occurred to prevent him. Strange too, because he was never more conscious of his inferiority than when some one in power was courting him, working on his vanity. As for instance when Lord Brougham was praising him and setting Warburton and John Smith, those Whig Syrens, to charm his ears with flattery . . . this entry on that very day.

"The time will come when I shall be found not only wanting but contemptible. Even now in Mathematics I was beaten by a man who has not perhaps looked at the Science for a long period nor at any time seriously! I must be a man of uncommon dullness! . . . I care not so much about the wretchedness of my understanding as I am maddened by the ardor of my love for science and true wisdom. I had rather be creeping and contented than aspiring and insufficient."

Yet Canning had offered him a place in the government and after Canning's death the Duke had installed him in office on the India Board. How his aspirations had soared!

16

"India with her hundred millions is the compass of my mind's survey. All petty love of excellence must be put aside, no fretting of mind, no conceited nervousness felt. I must not dread coming down to the level of others. If I am already there the descent is nothing, and why be desirous of appearing greater, when that delusion can be maintained by silence alone? This is the hardest scheme. I ever desired to show myself cleverer than others. If I stop to compare myself with them, either vanity overweening will rush in or else a cruel despondency, arising equally from conceit. What wisdom in saying 'Do what is right and trust to Providence for the rest.' "

A fairly penetrating summary of his weakness, thought Ashley, embarrassed but fascinated by the frankness of his self-analysis. He had not changed. Would he ever overcome this alternate soaring and sinking of spirit?

"Last night I made my first attempt to maintain a long and important speech. Sensitivity and timidity, doubt and heaviness of heart were in me a long time before the day arrived. I prayed most earnestly for aid and courage. Though I did not please myself I found that the House was delighted. Cheering and compliments were abundant. I hastened home to throw myself on my knees in gratitude."

Well and good. But what about his next entry after speaking?

"No man is more despicable in his own estimation than I am. It is truly disheartening to watch the superiority of others. Increased diligence is no cure. I am lost in astonishment when I see men whose lives are passed in the idlest profligacy, who hold reading as cheap, thought as tedious, yet who speak with more boldness, strength, and fluency than I have attained by years of study and reflection. Can I remain in office? I feel hourly a greater fool."

He had remained. Interspersed with his periods of dejection were times of amazed delight at his popularity with various types of people. Perhaps this praise—from the Lord Mayor, with whose wife he had opened the Ball, from the East India Company, from the Speaker, from the King in whose convivial company he had recently enjoyed more hilarious laughter than he had ever before experienced—perhaps it might go to his head if it were not for his inability to win any expression of favor from the man whose approval he secretly most coveted.

"Popular with all men but my father whom I have most studied to please. . . . Not a year has passed in which I have not conferred some favor upon him, not a year in which I have not received an insult, open or implied. He commanded me to leave his home in London and will receive me nowhere else. During four years, except a week in Dorsetshire, I have not broken bread in his house ten times. He asked me to lend him fifteen hundred pounds from the proceeds of the Paston sale. I gave it at once."

17

And he never received a word of thanks. But the unpaternal harshness towards his brothers and sisters concerned him even more. The boys had been refused a home with their father and it was largely by his efforts *in loco parentis* that they were all pursuing decent courses. John, leaving University, was going into Chambers, and even fifteen-year-old Lionel was giving satisfaction as a midshipman in the Royal Navy, under—Ashley had ascertained—a good Captain. Thank God, Charlotte, on whom her father had vented most of his ill temper—the Countess had long since moved her headquarters to Richmond and did not bother with the family—was happily married. If only Harriet, who would make a perfect wife, could find someone worthy of her! It was indicative of her strength of character that, although life was almost unendurable at home, she had refused many offers, offers from men of rank and fortune whose minds she found insufficient! But for both her and Caroline, life with his father was intolerable.

"God in his mercy save me from the errors into which he has fallen. I pray that no family hereafter may endure from its parents what we have endured. The history of Father and Mother would be incredible to most men and perhaps it would do no good if each fact were recorded."

But this last breach of faith in breaking his promise to reopen St. Giles's for the family rankled deeply. From his first visit there as a boy he had loved the home of his ancestors and never returned to it without repeating an appropriate quotation: "Dear earth I do salute thee with my hand." It belonged, it was home, to all of them. And this inalienable right they were being denied. Now if it were his, as it some day, please God, would be, and he had children. . . .

Better get them a mother first! his thoughts came full circle. They always did these days, however much he tried to divert them to other matters: his need to extend his charities, his periodic visits to Lunatic Asylums on which he was preparing a report for the Commission, the Salt Monopoly of India, the appointment of an Astronomer for Bombay, his prospectus for the *Cambrian Quarterly*, the project of studying Hebrew. There was in him again, as he had recorded a few days before, a desperate fit of longing.

"O God," he prayed, with the simplicity of faith which increasing observation and reading and reasoning was restoring in him, "tell me, where is the woman—a wife after Thine own heart, lovely, beautiful, true, the companion of my life and of my mind?"

Could he ask for more? he questioned ruefully. No, but he would not ask for less. He stopped, his conscious thinking strangely arrested by a recollection, an image or the shadow of an image, like an object just beyond the range of unfocussed vision. What or who was it? Someone he had seen recently, seen again, passed without opportunity to pause, half intended to pursue and been diverted. He could visualize no farther. But why should it—she—come to him now? Would he be disappointed or further impressed by acquaintance with one who had left a fleeting, a tantalizing, impression of remote virgin indifference?

V

OF ALL FAMILIES in which to find a girl with an air of fancy-free virginity, thought Ashley, temporarily dazed by his discovery! He turned to Punch Greville, his informant.

"Lady Cowper's daughter, of course! And William Lamb—Melbourne's—niece?"

"Yes. All the men are more or less in love with Lady Emily. She's been the leading favorite in Town. Even old Creevey has passed favorably on her! I cannot imagine that you have not met before."

"I have been about town less than usual this summer. Fordwich's sister of course?"

"Also William's and Spencer's. They call her Minny in the family, I believe, as if there were any danger of confusing her with Lady Cowper!"

"I suppose some distinguishing name is necessary in a family," Ashley said inanely to conceal the turbulence of his thoughts. "Ours has an odd habit—always has had—of prefacing every boy's name with Anthony, regardless of his other name. I expect the idea is that, if I should die, there will still be an Anthony Ashley Cooper to inherit."

If his companion, who knew everyone and everything worth knowing in London, thought that the chance of confusing father and son in Ashley's case was remote, he refrained from saying so. He was presently seized upon by Lady Jersey, who seemed most eager to impart some piece of confidential gossip, and Ashley was fully occupied in watching the latest object of his attention without drawing attention to himself.

He had seen her as soon as he came through the Arcade to the garden, where she was standing beside her mother. The Countess Cowper, before her marriage Lady Emily Lamb, one of the riotous Lamb family, had been

19

overshadowed in youth by *her* mother, the irrepressible and inexhaustible and amusing Viscountess Melbourne. Eighteenth-century Society, which had no false delicacy about bandying a woman's name, had been a bit dubious about Lady Emily Lamb's own paternity, although definite enough in assigning several of her brothers to her mother's several lovers. The daughter had more than her mother's beauty, none of her hardness, but an insatiable zest for giving pleasure to others and to herself. Ashley scrutinized her closely for the first time also. They had met at Lady Granville's in Paris, and occasionally since his return from the Continent, but perhaps because of his own aloofness he had never been one of her many house guests. Now looking at the youthful face, to which the slightly parted lips gave an expression of perpetual zestful eagerness, he deliberately rejected the rumor which made Lord Palmerston father of her children. Still he could not deny that all her family, gay, talented, good-humoured representatives of the Whig ruling class, tended to—his mind sought the most delicate expression—confound the distinction between right and wrong.

And it was to the daughter and granddaughter and niece of these amiable libertines that his praying attention had been directed! Either he was completely deluded and had better tear himself away before it was too late or—God's ways were mysterious.

He ventured another glance at the daughter and decided that God's ways were mysterious. After all, had not he, more than most men, reason to suspend judgement in such a case? His own sisters, domestic, loving, faithful, were the reverse of—he was shocked to have the words come to his mind, but they came—the infernal wickedness of their mother. But how to find out? And—for his mind, once made up, was impetuous as usual—find out with speed. The sort of talk exchanged at a dozen such gatherings would not tell him half of that which he must know.

He had recently been deploring the deterioration of his mentality. It now showed something of the quality which had achieved a first in Classics at Oxford, a feat which still amazed him considering his lack of application at Harrow, and his frivolous idleness for two years with horses and dogs and country society at his clergyman cousin's in Derbyshire. With indolent grace—one did not move quickly—he closed in on his quarry. At almost the same time one of the young men in the chatting group offered his arm to the girl and led her towards the refreshment marquee. Bob Grosvenor, Ashley noted. As they passed close to him she glanced up, neither shyly nor flirtatiously, but with a sunny brightness which seemed to include her escort and all the world. He did not regret her departure. It left his mind undistracted to recall what he had heard recently that might catch Lady Cowper's attention. No amount of interest on the daughter's part, even if he were able to engage it, would avail against the parents' disapproval.

Lord Cowper, handsome, wealthy, taciturn, was nowhere in sight. He seldom was at these affairs. With an air of interest as flattering as it was unassumed, and with an engaging diffidence which his recent rebuff from Lord Liverpool had bequeathed him, Ashley addressed himself to winning the mother's favor.

And her invitation. Surveying the Kentish countryside from the room which he had been assigned in the "place we have taken at Tunbridge for a few weeks," Lord Ashley was conscious of mounting excitement, physical and mental, which threatened the attitude of cool reasonable appraisal he had hoped to maintain. Here he was, her guest, less than a week after their formal meeting. He had spent the previous evening in her society, and the fascination which he had felt from the first had increased and extended to every aspect of her person.

The great moment had come when they were standing in the gateway, quiet under the quiet evening sky.

"How many stars there are!" she had said suddenly almost in whisper. "And when we came out I could see only that great one in the west. I do wish I knew more about them. . . ."

"You can, if you will, Sister," said her brother William who was taking advantage of his eighteen years to stay up late. "Don't you know that our guest is an astronomer? This is your opportunity."

"Are you indeed, Lord Ashley!" she had said eagerly, and not heeding his disclaimer of anything but amateur interest. "Then can you show me Orion? And why did the Romans call Charles's Wain the Seven Plough Oxen? . . . because William says they did. And is it true that the nearest star is so far that it would take thousands of years to reach it?"

And she had followed his explanation with an intentness which indicated genuine interest, thought Ashley, his heart almost bursting with desire to share everything he knew, everything he had, with this lovely girl. But would she care to share what had become his deepest interest? Had she any knowledge—no, that mattered little, he could infuse whatever was deficient in knowledge or practice but—had she any concern for religion? From what he had heard there was little or none in her family. That too he would learn shortly. It was Sunday morning.

She went to Church! After lingering in the hall while the time for morning service grew perilously near, and seeing no one but Lord Cowper, who nodded a perfunctory greeting as he passed, Ashley decided sadly that She was not coming and set out alone to walk the short distance to the Chapel

21

of Grace. The service had scarcely begun when he was conscious of a soft froth of muslin skirts drifting past his pew, and the slim figure which had not been out of his mind since he last saw it slipped into the seat across the aisle just in front of him. Before he could yield to an impulse to join her, young William took the place beside his sister. This was fortunate, Ashley thought after his first disappointment, because he could now see more of her profile. Fortunate too that the great straw bonnet curved back from her face on his side and forward on the other where the broad blue ribbon was tied under her soft but positive chin.

The effect of this visibility, of the rise and fall of long dark lashes, as she followed the service, of the lissome almost floating grace with which she rose and knelt and reseated herself, was to render him almost unconscious of everything else. The stiffness of Lady Selina's movements had jarred him sorely, even in the brief period when he was determined to see nothing but beauty in her. This unstudied harmony of motion and feature acted on him like an intoxicant in spite of his resolution to be cool and sceptical and appraising. And she was so free from affectation! When the incumbent began his sermon she turned to find the shawl which had slipped down, and draw it around her shoulder. She caught his eyes—how could she help it? they had never left her. There was no coyness, no affected surprise, only bright recognition and an inclination of the head so slight that it could divert no one else's attention. Ashley, a careful taster of sermons, could not have repeated a word of the discourse afterwards. Later he might have feelings of shame and contrition. Now he knew only that it was scarcely any time before the dismissal of the congregation enabled him with the utmost ease to move down the aisle beside her, her brother falling in behind them. He found himself praying that this was a prelude to the all-important walk down the aisle beside her . . . to a lifetime of such observance together.

VI

LADY EMILY COWPER, who did not mind—much—being called Minny or Min, since both names were pronounced with affection by those privileged to use them ("All women are a set of little devils—except Minny" was her bachelor Uncle Fred's opinion), became quite suddenly aware that something was happening. She was walking on the Pantiles. The other strollers in that fashionable esplanade were numerous enough to give a pleasant feeling of society, but too few and scattered to interfere with the evening hush or with intimate conversation. She knew that she looked lovely in her saffron silk cloak and transparent blue evening bonnet. If the mirror had not assured her before she left the house—and she knew that by the time she returned home, deepened color and breeze-ruffled curls would have increased the loveliness—she would have seen it mirrored in the eager honest eyes of the man beside her. It was this man who made her aware that something was happening and that, if she did not prevent its happening, the life upon which she had entered on coming out, the life she was finding gay and exciting and delicious, would be disrupted.

She had taken his arm to walk. Now she was conscious that her arm had somehow slipped or been induced farther within his and that he had moved his arm back until his long strong hand rested, not quite closed, over her gloved one. She liked the feeling. It brought a strange flutter to her throat, a delightful, sweet unsteadiness. And the very liking, the very intoxication, warned her to action. She withdrew her arm.

Ashley stopped speaking, and in his look and silence before he forced himself to continue she felt his hurt and vexation and puzzlement. All her life she had hated to give pain. "Minny was born, poor love, with far too much heart for her own happiness," her mother had written fondly to Uncle Fred when her eleven-year-old daughter insisted on getting up at night to look after a sick governess. And she had never wanted to give pain less than now. Her manner, as they walked home, was friendly, her talk confidential. But she did not take his arm again. She had fenced her skilful way through the conversational match, parrying every thrust that would bring home a proposal. It was a game she had played with many since her season began, and Ashley's very seriousness, his dread of evoking a refusal, made it easy for her. But of what use verbal dexterity if she was betrayed by her delighted young body? She must keep him at arm's length—almost literally at arm's length—until she had time and privacy to think things out.

So in the hall they separated, Anthony to scribble his fierce vexation, his agony of uncertainty and suffering into his journal, Minny to dismiss King, her maid who was waiting to undress her, and to sit by the window, looking at the stars he had named for her and facing the first real dilemma of her petted, shallow, happy life.

She did not want to marry yet, perhaps not for a long time. And of course, when she did, she hoped she would love her husband because that was right. Her mother loved her father in a detached, accommodating, dutiful way, considering his interests, even deferring to his rarely expressed wish. She did not sparkle and glow in his presence as she did with her coterie of brothers and their friends, with His Majesty, or especially with Viscount Palmerston. But few married people of Minny's acquaintance did sparkle and glow for each other. Her notorious Aunt Caroline indeed had lavished on Lord Byron the glow which poor Uncle William had missed. And what a wretched end she had come to! It might be better not to glow at all—for any one person. And certainly not to marry him on the basis of it.

Lord Ashley had not mentioned marriage—not in so many words. She had changed the subject, asked a leading question, whenever his talk of what they could do together, of things he would like to show her, of taking her to converse with Sir James South and see his telescope, had come perilously near. But his language and manner were ardent. It was—frightening on so short acquaintance. Bob Grosvenor had, she knew, made a proposal, which her father, after consulting her, had refused at least for the time. And Fred Robinson, Lord Goderich's son, was becoming rather tiresome when they left London. So—occasionally—was Lord Clanwilliam. But she had danced and flirted with them for months! It was little more than a week since Lord Ashley had become conscious of her existence. He had been pointed out to her in the distance—in the King's box at Ascot—as an original, an unattainable Adonis. She had heard rumors of a passionate Italian or Austrian Countess and an ill-starred romance which had left him unable to love again. Then she heard that he was head-over-heels in love with Lady Selina; and subsequently thrown back by her papa in favor of a larger fish!

"Well! Lady Emily Cowper is not going to be taken on the rebound from a pretty little doll like Selina," she told Orion firmly. "And if he can get over the one passion in two months how long will his infatuation for me last?"

Yet—her sense of fair play asserted itself—that charge of fickleness did not sit well on his character or conversation. After all it might be nothing but gossip. And gossip—political and social—was the sole ingredient of conversation in the world of her circle. That was what made Lord Ashley so different from the other men, the older ones who teased and flattered, the younger who chatted trivialities and compliments. He talked of all sorts of things: of conditions in India, of Welsh customs and folklore, of Milton's poetry and of Crabbe, of his friend Sir Walter Scott, of Horace and Virgil and Pliny. He talked of them all vividly so that they became real to her and important as they evidently were to him. More, he talked to her, soliciting her opinion and respecting her questions, as if they mattered, on such subjects as the recent Greek treaty, the advantages of setting up an observatory in Bombay, the

24

advisability of establishing a positive Christian rule in India with complete impartiality and freedom for the religions already obtaining there. He was, she knew, nine years her senior and, as her mother and father agreed, remarkably well informed. But he treated her as an equal, and there was a world of difference between his pleased admiration at her interest and the amused flattery with which other young men greeted her questioning—rare because of it—on serious matters.

Surely, too, if he were a volatile, easily impassioned lover he would have been married long since. Everybody said that all the girls had been in love with him since he left Oxford and that he had loved none of them. The accusations were contradictory!

The knock, light, assured, imperative, was her mother's. Pausing just within the door in the candle-pierced shadows, the Countess Cowper might have been her favorite child's elder sister.

"I saw your light from my room," she said in her deep characteristic drawl, so at variance with the femininity of her girlish face and filmy wrap. "Dear child, pray don't catch cold in that night air. Can you not sleep?"

Emily drew her chair back and placed one for Lady Cowper who sank into it with the leisurely "this is where I wish to be" tranquillity which made her a soothing hostess. She smiled at her daughter and waited.

"I haven't tried to sleep. I was looking at the stars."

"Lord Ashley has been initiating you into his hobby, then?" The relations between them were too direct for any coy approach. "What do you think of your new admirer, Min?"

Minny hesitated. She had always talked freely with her mother. Now, grappling with a desire to talk, she felt a curious reluctance.

"I scarcely know what to think. He is not like anyone I have ever met."

Lady Emily chuckled warmly.

"He is not like *anyone*. You are right, Dear. But how distractingly handsome! '*Si noble si passioné,*' nothing of the commonplace about him as Lady Granville said tonight. And I should add *impassioné* towards you."

Minny was silent.

"Or am I mistaken? During your ride, and your two walks yesterday, and today, and this evening—dear Child you will be quite worn out!—was all the talk of astronomy, mathematics, and the deplorable self-immolation of Hindoo widows?"

The teasing in her voice provoked retort.

"*And* Welsh bards *and* Shakespeare's sonnets and a great many other subjects. I—he," she broke off, "Oh, I don't know."

Lady Cowper was instantly the solicitous mother.

25

"Of course not, Darling. How could you in so short a time? Your father and I are naturally concerned. But he is really too engaging. That is why I suggest that you beware. He is an enthusiast. Bunny"—it was Countess Cowper's prerogative to nickname statesmen and ambassadors—"was at the Royal Lodge recently with him. He says you may be everything today and nothing tomorrow."

"Well—" said Minny stiffly, "in that case—"

"But then Bunny detests the Duke who is one of Ashley's heroes. So I do not attach too much importance to what he says. Apparently Ashley had been carried away by a speech Canning made and critical of him shortly after. And Bunny has never changed an opinion since the days of Pitt—I almost said Walpole. Now do go to bed. Remember, all your father and I want is your happiness. And that," said Lady Cowper, neatly injecting a new ingredient into her recipe for her daughter's peace of mind, "is more than poor Ashley can say about *his* parents. Detestable both of them. Good-night, my Sweet."

VII

"E'EN THE LIGHT HAREBELL RAISED ITS HEAD
    Elastic from her airy tread"
thought Ashley in a daze of joy, but not so much of a daze that he did not make his most graceful leap into the saddle and hope that his superb seat astride the black gelding was a little pleasing to her. If only anything about him pleased her as everything about her pleased him, he thought, taking advantage of the shifting and pawing of horses as the others mounted, to feast his hungry eyes on her. He had anticipated the groom, so that her booted foot rested in his gauntleted hand to swing her up into the saddle of a tall grey mare. For an instant her long-lashed, very-blue eyes had been closer to his than he had ever seen them and the radiance of her fair skin and full lips so near had stirred his senses as palpably as the touch. Every sight of her was a new revelation. In her trim black riding habit with white stock, one hand arranging its full skirts to flow on either side the pommel, she was a different vision this morning. Different but the same. Everywoman, but his, his Emily, his Minny. "O God in Thy mercy, accomplish thus the desire of my heart,"

26

he prayed—the prayer not diverting his attention from contemplation of her, or from careful maneuvering to be beside her as they started. After all, had not the Prince de Lieven on their first ride assigned her to his care? With what adorable severity the stiff black hat enclosed much of the smoothed-back brown hair! Was it a tiny dimple on either side which gave her mouth that irrepressible upward tilt? That—and the color of her eyes—were the most striking differences between the two Emilys. The mother's lips were almost always parted to show small white teeth, the daughter's, as full, as passionate, were firmly, yet reposefully closed.

Their ride began, and Ashley was glad that the wooded paths were wide enough, just wide enough, for two abreast. He had begun the day with prayer—distrait, but calmer than his desperate prayer of the previous evening—to know the best course of conduct to follow. Last night after his rejection—for so surely he must consider it—he had toyed with the notion of leaving for London, knowing all the time quite well that he could not go; considered trying to pique her with assumed indifference, and known, as soon as he saw her this morning, that he was equally incapable of such dissembling.

Was she dissembling? Was the pleasant indifference of today's manner her real feeling? Or was the tenderness with which she had explained her near-refusal to his near-proposal the previous evening, the lack of rebuff when he had repeatedly caught her hand in leading up to it? Ordinarily his passionate delight in riding, the pleasure of well-matched horses, the alternating shadowed paths and vistas of harvest field, would have made him glad of silence. Now he could not bear it. He maneuvered at the next open stretch to put their horses last and slowed them to a walk.

"It is one day more, Lady Emily," he said, trying to keep his voice light.

Her glance was innocent.

"One day more, Lord Ashley?"

"You said last night," he persisted, "that you had not known me very long. I am reminding you that presently you will not be able to say it."

"But it is still true. Two weeks ago we had scarcely met." His heart lifted to realize that she too had reckoned the days. "As recently as last Saturday I had exchanged only a few words with you."

"But this is Thursday. Think of the times—"

"Yes," she said almost petulantly, "and I still know nothing about you."

"Nothing? I should have thought there were different ways of measuring knowledge—that mere duration was not the only criterion of friendship. I suppose your method places me greatly below the level of George Cole whom you have known all your life!"

Emily refused to reply.

"At least tell me," he persisted, "if you *wish* to know more of me."

She shortened rein but he anticipated her intention with a restraining hand.

"I am not bound"—it was almost a toss of the head—"to answer that question."

"Well then I shall take it as given in the affirmative."

"Why now that is acting as a *mauvaise tete*, Lord Ashley."

"Is it?" His heart was in his voice. "Is it indeed, Lady Emily?"

He drew his horse close alongside and laid his hand over her left one as it rested on the pommel of the side saddle. She did not withdraw it and under his pressure the color rose in her cheeks.

"I have no objection—really," she said at last, "to know more of your character. But I am afraid."

"Afraid of what?"

"Of you, I think. You became so angry last night and refused to go in to Madame de Lieven's. They were expecting us and Mama asked why we hadn't gone! I was quite at a loss to explain."

"I am sorry for your embarrassment." Ashley was in agony. "But I *could* not go just then. You saw how I felt, how upset I was. They would have known something was the matter."

"That is what I mean. You should not have been upset. What will people say? It is all so hasty. I never thought of it turning out like this. I cannot—I cannot express my astonishment at finding myself in this dilemma. Lord Ashley, don't you understand?"

The note of appeal melted his irritation at once. But he was honest.

"No. No because I am so sure. But I shall try to be patient. I *must* be patient, you say doubtless. Please, please give me just an assurance that I may hope."

"No," she cried in distress. "That would be tantamount to an agreement. It is out of the question. There are reasons too why you should know me better. We may meet in London. You shall visit us at Panshanger." She ventured a glance at his downcast face and her impetuous voice softened. "Believe me, Lord Ashley, I have no objection whatever to your character *as I see it.*"

They had reached an open stretch of meadow and she urged her horse to a canter. By the time they slowed again he had digested the emphasis of her last clause.

"As *you* see it. Then your objection is to what you hear from others. Please to tell me, dear M— Lady Emily. You are surely too just to keep a— prisoner in ignorance of the charges against him."

28

Was it exercise or the implication of the word "prisoner" that made her color so deep? She met his eyes candidly.

"It is true. I do hear reports that you are capricious, that you are wanting in heart."

"I?" Anthony managed to turn his amazement into a laugh of incredulity. "But, truly, I have always been the victim of too great affection."

"Exactly!" She was unwillingly triumphant. "Your enthusiasm—so I hear—makes you unsteady."

"Do be more explicit."

"Well"—she made her horse trot briefly while she framed the difficult explanation—"it is not easy—to repeat—I know it sounds like gossip. But it is a very short time ago that—they say—you proposed for—someone else, and—"

"So that is it! You refer to Lord Liverpool's daughter?" He checked the horses again. "Then do believe me in this. I made no proposal, only enquiries of her cousin, Lady Cavendish, at which time I discovered her age to be sixteen and considered further steps unsuitable. I admit to a temporary ebullition of social admiration. It was largely inflamed by well-meaning friends who praised her qualities and insisted that she would be a suitable wife. And believe me in this also. I exchanged words with her only three times, and without any confirmation of the feelings induced by her beauty."

"You think she is beautiful?" said Minny quickly.

"I think she is beautiful as I think many women are beautiful, as I think some statues are beautiful, but they rouse no emotion in me, no desire. . . . Nor does she. Nor did she, in her person, only in her idea, suggested by others. You must not—I pray do not—confound an unreal, unbased fancy with deep, premeditated, considered love of excellence such as I feel towards you." He broke off as he caught sight of the rest of the party entering the drive ahead of them. "Thank you for being candid. Promise that you will ask for an explanation of anything else that puzzles you about me."

"Oh I shall," she said. Surely the eagerness in her voice was genuine?

"And I may visit you at Panshanger?"

VIII

THERE WAS NO REASON, Ashley told himself days later, but with complete lack of conviction, for his feelings of utter despair and humiliation. Emily had been as good as her word. Her manner was daily increasing in tenderness. Every tête-à-tête, whether driving, walking, or riding—and why were so many allowed by her parents and assented to by her unless his suit was being seriously considered?—brought franker confidences, more intimate talk. Lady Cowper had assured him in a long and delightful conversation that she and her husband had the strongest inclination towards him,, that Minny thought him extremely handsome, interesting, and versatile; in fact that she was having great difficulty withstanding the temptation to engage herself to him but felt that propriety demanded delay. After all she was very young. And so, counselled Lady Cowper, he would be wise not to hurry the affair.

To this he had agreed. Yet it was not easy when his adored was amiable and heavenly. Never since that puzzling night had she withdrawn her arm. She had in fact taken off her glove on one occasion and allowed her bare hand to rest, passive indeed, but thrillingly warm in his. She had listened with evident pleasure to his protestations of love, esteem, respect. She had promised continued opportunities to prove his sincerity and steadfastness. She showed interest in everything about him, his friends, his letters, his opinions. Yet just when he was wondering and not sanguine about Lord Shaftesbury's probable attitude to his marriage, and determining to disregard any paternal objections, she insisted on going away alone to draw, leaving him to wish dejectedly that religion were powerful enough in him to render him calm and unshaken by such large-looming trivialities.

And tomorrow morning he was to leave for London. She would follow later with her family. Starved for family life himself, he had revelled in the casual, cheerful, independent intercourse here. His beloved was evidently—and with reason, he thought—the apple of her mother's eye. Her sweetness and affection towards her brothers and sister added to his conviction that his love for her was firmly—he could not say dispassionately, but at least reasonably—founded on judgement and careful observation. He liked, though with no suspension of criticism, the whole family. He was very glad that they kept out of the way when he wished to be alone with Minny.

As now. Their last walk on the Pantiles.

It remained in his memory afterwards as a rising crescendo of ecstasy. She seemed as anxious to walk, as ready to hear, as he to say everything which rose in his heart. For an hour they scarcely unclasped their hands. When he urged her not to let their approaching separation, the sights and assemblies of London make her forgetful, she gave the promise he required. When, emboldened by the increased confidence and freedom of her manner, and by the shadow of the lime tree under which they paused, he took off her glove, clasped her hand with unmistakable tenderness, and for the first time called her Minny, she gave him a dazzling glance of wide blue eyes and smiled in acquiescence.

It was small wonder that, when he went to take his leave after dinner, he was completely unprepared for what happened.

"I shall count the hours until I call on Saturday." He hesitated about using her pet name in the possible hearing of her parents and brother. "Dare I hope that you are not indifferent to the prospect?"

Emily had paused on her way to the door. She did not extend her hand, and the eyes which met his were unconcerned.

"You may do as you like, of course," she said coolly. "Really I don't care a fig if you call or not."

She was gone, and his consternation was so apparent that the others made no effort to prolong his abbreviated farewell.

Up in his room he paced the floor in a frenzy of astonishment. What could have come over her? Did she care a straw for him? If so, how, in Heaven's name, could she torture him so? If not, he had been utterly deceived and she was not pure, good, kind as he had thought her. That possibility, that shattering of his ideal, was harder to bear than his own galling humiliation; it reduced him to a state of utter loss. He felt that he would give his life to recall the last ten days.

He went to bed at last, praying and feeling his prayers thrown back upon him. His nine years seniority gave him no emotional advantage over the young object of his adoration. Publicly courted and desperately lonely, outwardly poised and victimized by an appalling sense of inadequacy, with all his friends he had no confidant to unravel for him the complexities of a girl's mind under stress of ungovernable feeling. He was denied the comfort of even suspecting that Minny, to whom her mother gaily, half rebukingly, had already reported his distress, had burst into tears and cried until she slept.

It was belated comfort to hear it several days later from his charming but volatile friend, the Countess Cowper herself. How much of the uncertainty and anguish of the next weeks and months were due to her, Ashley did not know, though he became increasingly edgy and suspicious. On the surface she was on his side. The house in George Street was open to him almost daily during their ten-day sojourn in Town and an invitation to Panshanger established him once more for three weeks under the parental roof. During all

31

that time no effort was made to deny or to interrupt periods, often two hours long, alone with Minny. Only at meals or when they went out in public were they chaperoned.

Yet for every advance he made in his assault on his darling's heart ("I perceived in her manner an increase of affection and confidence;" "I held her hand, nay her arm for minutes together as we talked by ourselves; not only held her hand but interlocked her fingers with mine;" "Her confidence has been redoubled. She entrusts to me the greatest secrets;") he found a corresponding check or regression. The see-saw of their intercourse was to his single-minded masculine devotion incomprehensible. "Am I then wrong to despair?" he asked her, leaning over the piano forte in their drawing room and looking, though he did not know it, so radiant and appealing in his intensity that she recommenced playing to keep her susceptible heart from betraying her. Presently under pressure of his unmoving silence she said, her voice almost indistinguishable above the air from 'Oberon,' "You are wrong to despair," and then with a little laugh, "Oh Lord Ashley, I am sure you have no reason to carry so long a face from what I have said!"

"Not when you tell me of your new doubt, that I may be violent in my temper? And you admit yourself that you have seen nothing of it."

"But it is so important," she insisted, coloring again as she met his eyes. "I feel I must ascertain the contrary. You see, I think of you a very great deal."

"O Minny, my Dearest, can I depend on you, if you do so ascertain that you will not reject me for a mere fancy?"

"Most certainly not."

He continued passionately, "You may like ten men better than me but you will never find one who will love you so warmly or so appreciate your character."

"That is what I fear," was her extraordinary reply, and she rose to rejoin her family so that he was denied an explanation.

Where, where, did these doubts, these reservations spring from?

"I have never heard any man so generally well spoken of," drawled the Countess Cowper, smiling across at him the smile which entranced everyone, from disaffected foreign diplomats to her vicar when, with invariable punctilious tardiness, she swept into church half-an-hour after commencement of service. She was leaning back in the carriage to which Ashley had handed her and her daughter moments before. Minny, "all delights" in a new cape of green velvet and a deep-crowned bonnet, sat beside her, looking with perhaps overstudied interest at the passing scenery.

"You are kind to say so," said Ashley for want of a reply which would sound neither complacent nor insincere.

"Some do find fault, though," proceeded the Countess, extracting the sweetness as unthinkingly as a hummingbird draws nectar. "They caution me: 'he is *so* enthusiastic, he must be capricious.' "

So that was where Minny heard the charge. Ashley felt that something must be said.

"Pray, Lady Cowper, ask your informants to name the friend I have deserted, the acquaintance I have dissolved, the bond I have broken. Surely it is absurd to charge me on a theory if I can contradict their arguments by fact."

"Of course, of course, I didn't attach importance to it," said Lady Cowper negligently. "I have heard too: 'take care! he has a high sense of religion; he is almost a saint.' "

"That last charge I reject out of hand," said Anthony, forcing a laugh. "With all my faults I fear I shall never have the fault of being too good. But I do own the first gladly. Do you not think it is the best security a man can offer?"

"No doubt," she replied in the hearty tone of conviction which he was beginning to mistrust.

He seized the opportunity of drawing Minny into the conversation.

"You are not influenced, Lady Emily, by such sentiments? Is it not the best security a husband could offer for his affection and faithfulness—that he owns a Government above his own whim?"

Her eyes left their study of the passing scenes and met his earnestly. There was a touch of defiance—at her mother?—in her quiet tone.

"Most assuredly it is."

He pressed his advantage. He had wished to make his position clear and now the opportunity had come.

"I have a deep sense of religion. I avow it, but tell me, do you see in me any moroseness, fanaticism, superstitious excess?"

Her brief answer—Minny spoke little to him now when her mother was present—"Oh not a bit" satisfied him for the moment.

So did her tears the next day when he begged her again to end the agony of his probation.

"Indeed, indeed," she said, laying her hand on his, "you are mistaken. It is not a rejection, merely a request for longer time. Am I wrong? The step is so important, so dreadful. There is no one else, I assure you, that I care a straw about. No, I have no abstract aversion to matrimony."

Ashley's love could not bear the tears which encouraged him. When he saw that his urgency increased her distress he laid himself at her feet in a speech which he himself would have thought grandiloquent, had not ardor temporarily suspended his sense of the ridiculous.

"I will ask no promise," he concluded magnificently. "I confide in your honor. I rely upon you. At the appointed time I will put the fatal question. Then, unbound by condition, you will either take me as your husband or—toss me away as a carcass on the seashore."

It was indicative of the state of her feelings that if the alternative struck her as ludicrous, she did not show it.

Indeed his generosity must have moved her, for Lady Cowper informed him later, sealing her promises with the repeated phrase "On my honor," that she knew no one half so qualified to ensure her daughter's happiness; that she would continue to give him every opportunity; that it would all end in their marriage.

Yet two weeks later, though they had been almost inseparable and his feeling that they were made for each other was homed in his heart, she still refused to utter the all-important words. Two events stood out of the blurred recollections of his stay at Panshanger to give him retrospective gleams of encouragement when his return to London found him wretched to a degree he had never before experienced.

One was her appearance, the preceding Sunday afternoon, dressed in a gown for which he had expressed preference—an "old-style" dress she had complained when he praised the simple almost straight flow from the "Empire" bodice to her little kid slippers. She complained too when he said that her bare arms were far too beautiful to need bracelets, but in the evening she came down to dinner with the praised arms quite unadorned. That was the day he told her that all his life depended on her, and, noticing her silence and sadness, guessed unwillingly at the cause.

"Have you had any conversation recently with Lady Cowper?"

"No," she burst out unexpectedly, "and I am astonished. I think she is keeping it till you are gone and then will say everything against you."

"But," stammered Ashley, unable to credit such perfidy, "twice she has assured me on her honor she will stand my friend."

"Well, Lady Granville says just as surely she will not," said Minny, and then loyally trying to defend the indefensible, "You cannot judge her, dear Lord Ashley. She has not your sense of religion, and I—you must see that the people of our circle stand more affected by what is pleasant and—and polite than by what is true."

"Then when she says she wants only to discover the state of your mind—"

"I see how it is. If it all should end by being off, Mama wishes to throw the blame on me."

"But she *said*," insisted Ashley. "'It all depends on Minny. If Minny were to say "I can marry him, I like him better than anybody," then marry him immediately, I should answer!'"

"This is not fair," exclaimed Minny indignantly; "not so. I do not like to use such a word but it is not at all so. It does not depend upon me. Why, only the other day she said: 'I have made up my mind, you must not marry Lord Ashley.' "

"God!" breathed the distracted young man and in the privacy of his room turned the exclamation into a prayer.

The other event was their parting, when in spite of rain Minny insisted on riding seven miles with him. His elation at this sign of affection was subdued temporarily by his astonished discovery, as they neared the milestone where they were to part, that she was humming a tune—a quadrille. True, it was a quadrille to which they had danced the night before but—

"How can you, Minny?" he said reproachfully. "A quadrille—when I am wondering how I can endure leaving you?"

She did not answer immediately and he thought he heard the tune stubbornly but almost inaudibly continued. Then she reined her horse closer to his. The groom was at a discreet distance.

"When I am sorry for any person—or—or anything," she stammered slightly, "I always—that is, my manner becomes more cold. It always has—since I was small. Oh—cannot you understand it?"

Ashley insisted on his i's and t's being dotted and crossed. "You said once that your manner was dramatically opposite to your feelings. You want, then, to conceal them?"

Her voice dropped to a whisper.

"Yes. I do." Then she spoke clearly again. "And you cannot wonder. Mama said on Sunday night 'I told him all depended on you—but it does not and you know it.' I asked her how she could say so. 'Oh,' she said, 'it's better to say so.' But since then," she went on unable to bear the pain in Ashley's eyes—pain, she was beginning to realize, as much for his disillusionment as for his own implied danger, "I do think there is a change for the better in her attitude. And I think it may last."

They reached the milestone. He would have lingered or even ridden part of the return journey with her, but Minny held out her hand and there was no gainsaying its finality. He took it, and his heart gave a great leap. For the first time her hand anticipated his in a pressure of unmistakable warmth.

Then she quickly withdrew it, turned her horse, and rode away. That was in mid September.

IX

THERE WAS NO ONE in the wearing wretched months that followed to give Ashley an explanation of her family's conduct, to tell him that, in considering his suit at all, they were paying him a high personal compliment! His Tory family, his disunited and disliked parents, his father's inhospitality, did not endear him to the easy-going, pleasure-loving Lambs and their Whig circle. Ashley, unused to extravagance from childhood, considered the thousand a year by which the India Board had almost doubled his income great riches; had in fact been stirred to share his new-found wealth in a dozen charitable ventures. This very sort of conscience, were they aware of it, would have increased their suspicion of his enthusiasm. Lord Melbourne, Emily's uncle William, was violently antagonistic to humanitarian schemes. "I am not a subscribing sort of fellow" was his breezy answer to requests for worthy causes.

Lavish entertainment, dress, travel were proper use of money; five pounds to a charitable appeal a bit quixotic. More, the Earl of Shaftesbury's parsimony towards his family, gossip stated, was the obverse side of his self-indulgence where he fancied anything; and while he applied himself diligently to his Chairmanship in the Lords, expenses for his own whims and for his wife's extravagance far outdistanced the income from a now heavily indebted estate.

Still, the radiance and ebullience of spirits, which had made Ashley a young idol of society when he came down with laurels from Oxford seven years before, had suffered little outward diminution through the seven years of family disillusionment, heavier responsibility, and deepening thought. Lady Cowper, half in love with him herself, offset her daughter's whim of rude withdrawal with kind but maddeningly indefinite notes: "Emily has the highest admiration for your character but does not think she feels that love and affection she ought to have for the person to whom she would dedicate her whole life," she had written bluntly, after his return from Panshanger. "I could not let her marry with doubts and difficulties on her mind and a strong desire to remain free another year." And again, "There is no alternative except to wish the thing may be off. If there were a longer acquaintance her good opinion would probably turn into love. But during the time she would feel awkward and raising expectations which she might not realize. She wishes to leave you perfectly free to continue on terms of friendship."

Yet from Chatsworth, where they were enjoying the Duke of Devonshire's lavish hospitality, she wrote with maternal solicitude: "It is impossible to express how anxious we both feel and how grieved at your being alone and

36

comfortless in town—the more I think of you the more I admire your character and conduct in most trying circumstances. Nobody here is fit to compare or indeed to be mentioned on the same day with you."

When, frantic with hurt pride and baffled desire, he begged to see Emily in order to take a final farewell and leave England for unnamed destinations, she wrote sensibly, urging his chivalrous instincts against confronting "the child" with so painful a choice. There was a fruitless interview at George Street (Emily had remained in the country with a cold) as a result of which her mother wrote—for her—quite sharply: "After all the proofs of sincerity and affection it is very unkind and ungrateful to treat me in the cold, haughty manner you did last night or to write the sort of authoritative notes you do. However, I enter into your feelings instead of resenting that my kindness meet with this return."

Her brief annoyance passed quickly at Ashley's apology, written in abrupt sentences of nervous pain: "You are wrong to charge me with unkindness or ingratitude. The manner I had in your presence Thursday evening was not the result of haughtiness. The recollections excited by the room in which we were conversing added tenfold to the agitation of my spirits. I could not be gay and I had nothing to communicate. My language may be urgent. I trust it was not too free; you say it was. . . . You will know how far I have offended or hurt you. Believe then that to the same degree I request your forgiveness. I wrote under suffering. I conceived I had justice on my side; it may have given strength to my words that does not suit the style of addressing a lady. You have promised me an interview Sunday night. I thank you most sincerely—but I confide in you. If Lady Emily cannot come safely on Sunday next, do not bring her, I implore you. Bring her Monday!"

If Ashley could have looked over the Countess Cowper's pretty bare shoulders at a letter received from her brother Fred Lamb, now posted to Vienna, he might have been less surprised at the friendly abstraction with which she later accepted his arm from their carriage to the ball-room at Devonshire House.

"Three thousand a year—at the most—of which a third comes from a place we hope he may lose soon!" Sir Frederick Lamb had exploded. "An odious father and four beggarly brothers! What has poor Min done to be linked to such a fate and in a family, disliked, mad, and the reverse of ours? What the devil is in its favor except his being 'in love' with her and a person you think to be fallen in love with? If the girl had a violent fancy it would be lamented and undergone but to dally and invite it! His love is about as violent as for Liverpool's daughter, and for some other six weeks after Minny turns him off. I can't say how much I admire her; of all matches that have offered

37

this is the least desirable. Ossulston would be forty times better, Bob Grosvenor better, Fred Robinson infinitely better. . . ."

It was fortunate to restore Lady Cowper's balance that Lady Granville, watching him that night as he danced every dance, seemed in good spirits, and asked Minny for only two, said impulsively, not for the first or last time: "How *can* that girl of yours help liking him? If I were twenty years younger! You have spoiled her so perseveringly that she thinks the world is hers. I could wish my Susy so fortunate."

But even apart from monetary and family objections Ashley's personality and character left room for Lamb criticism. A dilettante they could understand. An ambitious politician they could admire. A man who spread his interests from science and mathematics to literature and languages, who endangered his political aspirations by religious scruples and rigid principles, a man whom everyone trusted but no one could comprehend, predict, or sway—that was quite a different matter. As for his quaint reputation for chastity, far from rebuking a circle in which none of the senior members of either sex aspired to the reputation or the fact, such a reputation was deplorable, if at all credited.

His greatest puzzle, however, was Minny. Indeed Minny was at this period a puzzle to everyone but herself. The warring elements within her were so sharply felt and so distinct that every phase of her conduct, which she alternately justified and cried over, seemed perfectly logical. As if the war within were not enough, she had to fight her father's and uncles' cynical disapproval, her mother's uncertain enthusiasm, her young brother's partisanship, Ashley's unremitting siege. It was, she felt, too much to expect of a girl. Especially this girl upon whom, almost since birth, nothing but approval and praise had been lavished.

"May the return of this season for many many years bring with it as much happiness to you as it now does through you to all those who belong to you," her mother's friend, Lord Palmerston, had written her when she was sixteen. And it was a sample of the adulation showered on her by men since childhood.

Last year at the Queen's drawing-room the little Prince of Cumberland, who was thought of as a husband for the young Princess Victoria, had singled her out from all the other beauties and asked to be placed next to her. But she had been just nine when her mother gave a New Year's dance for her—intended as a children's ball—but one at which grown-ups and children danced together. She had been out of her wits with joy, and had danced every dance. And whereas she had officially "come out" a little over a year ago, swains had mooned over her at seventeen, and her beauty and cleverness had been admired and reported by her parents' friends for years. Why should Lord Ashley be an exception? So, with a toss of her curls, she argued in her defiant moments. And would alternately color and shy to the distraction of any male in the vicinity from fifteen to fifty, or lapse into boisterousness and sing some pathetic ballad—Bethgelert was a favorite—at the top of her voice. "Ah *cette terrible chanson,*" said Princess de Lieven to Lady Granville as the strains reached them at their whist three rooms away.

The most exasperating fact, though, was that in her heart she recognized, as truly as Ashley did, their affinity. From some atavistic source she had derived a strain of deep seriousness almost atrophied in the superficial gaiety of her home. This had responded eagerly, tremulously to the depth and range of his outlook. She enjoyed his company as she enjoyed no other. And—for in the conversation at Holland House and Chatsworth and Panshanger little attempt was made to veil the feelings and facts of a "grand passion"—she knew with thrilled resentment what the excitement of his proximity portended, excitement not aroused in her to the slightest degree by other young men.

That was *it.* She was not ready—she did not think she was ready—she did not feel ready—to marry and to have children. Never in her life had she been asked to bear any responsibility nor had she been denied anything she asked for. Though warnings of reduced circumstances as Ashley's wife— subject to the chance of his attaining a brilliant government post or of early succession to the title—meant little to her, they did make her doubt her own ability to manage such a household. And whereas she felt more than equal to other suitors, she was conscious of a strange humility before this burning, yet reverential ardor. She could not bear it if he should be disappointed in her. She was used to cleverness and could, if she chose, imitate her mother's wit. At Chatsworth, when her mind was full of Ashley, she allured Lord Clanwilliam to the brink of a proposal; only his vanity and the rumor of her impending attachment kept him from committing himself. And as a dinner companion Lord Morpeth found her so beautiful and buoyant that he almost forgot his attentions to his adored Aunt Harriet who sat on his other side.

Yet in spite of the sometimes ludicrous behavior to which love reduces the greatest of men, she perceived greatness in Ashley and was not sure that she could rise to it. She wanted time. She needed time to adjust to a whole new concept of life that rose before her from the *obiter dicta* of their private discussions: "God, possessing all happiness in Himself, has shown by His creation that it consists in the communication of happiness to others." "I have a great mind to found all policy upon the Bible, in public life observing the strictest justice, and not only cold justice but active benevolence."

"Obscurity of interpretation is no argument against the Holy Scripture; in no courts of reason have we more than what is absolutely necessary; the rest must be found by deep study." "A broken heart ought not to be regarded by anybody as a compliment. Venus received no victims, only flowers." "The pagan had a glimmering of the real quality of effective atonement, that it should be voluntary. If the victim struggled in going to the altar the priests augured ill of the sacrifice—a grand truth which was known without being understood." "Ideas come certainly through the senses. Let anyone teach his imagination and try to form any new conception whatever!" These were a few of the remarks, pertinent but revolutionary to her thinking, which lingered in her memory from their talks on nature, on religion, on classical authors. No wonder, she thought rather indignantly, that she was scared. No wonder either—this time her indignation was directed at Uncle William and Uncle Fred—that she was flattered. She had always been amused at Lord Melbourne's religious flippancy. His refusal of the Archbishop's invitation to evening service—he seldom attended church at all—"No my Lord. Once is orthodox, twice puritanical," was often quoted by her mother as the acme of wit, as was another comment: "Things are coming to a pretty pass when religion is allowed to invade private life." Now such remarks seemed shallow in contrast to Ashley's undisguised, unapologetic personal faith and his honest, critical concern for sincerity in public observance. "Beautiful, solemn service abominably gabbled by the curate," he said on one occasion, and on another, "he declaimed in the manner of the French éloge." And yet she loved her family and wished him to love them too. It was all most disconcerting!

So, in self-defense, she pursued a course which drove him briefly to contemplation of suicide. The hyper-sensitiveness which, in spite of praise, made him dreadfully susceptible to the least rebuff, the lack of confidence which underlay his public pose of lofty calm, were now accentuated to the point of torment. He felt bitterly the indignity of his position as a dangling if not rejected suitor; but the insult to his pride mattered far less than his baffling anguish that what was his, what had been granted as an answer to incessant prayer, what had become so much part of him that he could not attain any fullness of life apart from it, in fact felt that his salvation was imperilled without it, might be snatched from him by wanton caprice. Days dragged into weeks, weeks into months; the last of October was the time tentatively set as the end of his probation. Then his fate would be decided. He prayed and prepared, with some premonition of happiness, for her decision.

The event could not have been more anticlimactic. Minny, when he called, could not see him. She was in bed with a very bad cough, reported Lady Cowper, who set herself for the next hour to soothe and charm and reassure—without committing herself to any positive assurance—the "most lovable person I ever knew." Finally Ashley, unable to endure more, yet equally unable to reject, face-to-face, that winning, apparently genuine, concern, left the house in scarcely controlled fury. Never, he felt, had a man been so tortured, insulted, toyed with.

Then suddenly—as if in belated answer to the prayers which he had thought unheard—his mind cleared. The situation was unchanged, his heart sore, his puzzlement unsolved; but he was, almost as though by physical force, lifted out of himself so that he could view the situation, the heart, the puzzlement, in a new perspective. For hours he walked, he could not have told afterwards where, not thinking so much as realizing thoughts which, often occurring and recorded, had been theory before: He had called himself "an unprofitable yet overpaid servant," said it was inferior and foolish to question Providence, realized that the Almighty had shown tenderness in creating him for such peaceful times—he thought he could not have undergone Martyrdom. "People talk of being misunderstood, not known, little valued or commended according to their limits," he told himself reproachfully. "Is not God, in every one of the cases, a greater Sufferer? He is absolutely forgotten . . . since the Creation, nay even in His own family, the Jews, He was as nothing. Can we—I—not hold up then for the short space of our forty years?" And, for the first time with sincere acceptance of possible consequence: "God's will be done."

X

EVIDENCE OF CHANGE IN HIM began with a long night of unbroken sleep. It continued in that he stopped making entries in his journal and deliberately refrained from rereading the daily outpouring of his soul already contained in it. He returned with zeal if not zest to his memorandum for the improvement of agricultural knowledge in India, and was surprised to find pleasure in expounding the virtue of the introduction of the potato as a supplementary and alternate article of diet! He followed with interest the heated argument and invective which did not deter Sir Robert Peel from establishing his police force. He heard with delight in December that Sir William Bentinck with a

41

stroke of the pen had abolished suttee, as he himself had been thought mad for suggesting a year earlier. He resumed the study of Hebrew and applied himself to his self-imposed course in critical theology. Scott's Commentaries had opened his eyes some years before to the fact that Dissenters could be good, pious, and highly intelligent. His friend Southey's *Life of Wesley,* unenthusiastic but fair by Church standards, had whetted his curiosity concerning the evangelical revival of the previous century. His recent attachment to the Cowper family had brought their famous cousin, the author of *The Task* and of *John Gilpin,* to his notice; and he sought information regarding that poet's fatal obsession in order to compare his case with the cases of several inmates of the Asylums, which he recommended visiting. He read with alarm and a strange faint sense of personal responsibility the reports of mob rioting and arson in the factory districts.

He did not eschew social life. He held his own in spirited conversation with Luttrell and Rogers and Poodle Bing and Punch Greville on weekends at Roehampton and Windsor and Chatsworth and Sudbrook. He followed the involutions of the international maelstrom and the delicate political maneuverings in and about the Court. Besides, it was an acceptable means of seeing Minny and of being seen in favorable circumstances by her. He attended, by design on the same night that she did, the night of the Princess Victoria's visit, the performance of the Siamese elephant which was drawing crowds to the Adelphi. He made one of the Countess Cowper's party at the new Harlequinade, the Hag of Forest Raven, at Sadler's Wells. And if the courteous pleasure which he evinced with each partner at a succession of Almacks' exclusive balls was different in quality and quantity from that with which he claimed his adored for dances, such was his forced self-control that it was evident to no one but Minny.

For with himself and with her he did not dissemble. "Do you know that I was mad enough a year ago to state that love was not likely to have mastery again over my heart and mind?" he asked her one night—early one morning rather—looking down at the lovely figure which the scandalizing propinquity of the waltz brought within a curved arm's length of his own. He always asked her for waltzes which, introduced to Almacks a dozen years before, were still few on the evening's program. Minny loved waltzing, but only with him, not with others. She found herself now dreamily wishing that the sensuous, entrancing music would never cease. Conscious of this she became deliberately flirtatious. "Have you?"—the dark lashes fluttered maddeningly and the dimples at the corners of her mouth deepened as she raised her eyes, then dropped them before his—"Have you—changed your mind?"

The pressure on the hand in his became almost painful. They made at least three revolutions before he felt his voice under control.

"I also thought—wrote, I believe—that when I married it would be for convenience, or fancy, or plain matter-of-fact. A man, I thought, loves fiercely but once."

"But if you were wrong then, or now think you were"—he had told her about Antoinette—"why may you not love again? Why should this time be so important?"

"If you do not know yet—" he began almost roughly; then, if a man can shrug and continue to waltz, he shrugged. The music sighed to an end. Momentarily they were alone in a corner of the vast assembly room.

"Minny," he spoke on impulse, though the thought had been with him for some days, "I know I have spoken vaguely and wildly of this before—last September when your mother talked me out of it—and later. This is not a threat, nor an effort—as that was, I now realize—to appeal to your feelings. You thought then that I should be going heaven knows where and giving up all my prospects. Now, I may, if I choose, have a post with the Government in Canada. It necessitates giving up any position on the India Board and therefore I have not yet made up my mind. But I feel—increasingly I feel—that it is best for me to resign and go to America. There is nothing to hold me here, except that which might be easier to endure in new surroundings."

There was no flirtatiousness now in her startled eyes. Her lips parted in wordless protest. Then George Morpeth laid a hand on his arm.

"Sorry to intrude, my dear Ashley, but I have been promised this dance. Lady Emily, have you had supper or will you accompany me now?"

She was gone and they did not meet again until the end of the evening. She must have broken from her final partner on some pretext because, when he had handed Lady Frances to Lord Ellesmere and turned after making his farewells, he found her alone at his side.

"Pray, Lord Ashley," she said prettily, "will you escort me to Mama? I am positively swept away in this crush."

She took his instantly offered arm and let him make way for her to the reception room. There Lady Cowper, whose genius for entertaining had given new life to that exclusive social club since she had joined the Committee, was the center of a parting group, a youthful figure in silver tissue, as vivacious as if the evening were just commencing. Minny turned towards him. She looked suddenly small, uncertain, a little forlorn.

"Pray, dear Lord Ashley," her voice was low but very distinct, "if it is on my account do not be so discomposed, and," her voice dropped still lower, "pray do not go to America."

There was a silence between them so deep, so vibrant, that the whole chattering room seemed still. Words crowded, questions, protestations,

43

above all demands for assurance. With the greatest effort he had ever exerted, an effort which gained him, though he did not guess it, far more than it cost, he repressed them. He took her hand, bent to kiss it, looked his passion into her eyes before he turned away.

"I will not go," he said.

XI

"MY DEAR LORD ASHLEY:

I have received your letter and I sincerely congratulate you upon your expected marriage, and upon the hopes of happiness which it affords.

I shall say nothing upon it to anybody. But I saw it announced in two or three newspapers yesterday.

As you have desired me not to mention this circumstance I will not write even to Lady Cowper till I shall have your permission. But if she should know that you have told me, I beg you to let her know the reason for which I do not write to her immediately, and assure her that there is no person who rejoices more sincerely than I do upon an event in which she must feel so much interested.

I beg you likewise to lay me at the feet of Lady Emily, and assure her that she has no friend more sincerely anxious for her happiness than I am. Believe me, ever yours most sincerely,

Wellington"

"The marriage took place at St. George's, Hanover Square, on June the tenth, of Lady Emily Caroline Catherine Frances, elder daughter of the Count and Countess Cowper to Lord Anthony Ashley Cooper, eldest son of the Earl and Countess of Shaftesbury."

"Tell Cox that breakfast may be brought on immediately."

Ridiculous word "breakfast" at this hour, thought Lady Cowper turning from the reception hall to survey her guests with unexhausted pleasure. She was grateful that the sun had shone on a happy bride and would allow the throng to overflow to the portico and garden of their George Street home.

Lord Cowper, who had been straining restively during the last half-hour of greeting—if his noncommittal grunt could be described as greeting—had already disappeared, to his private den she knew, for the sustenance of private potations after so prolonged a period of sociability.

Well, it was a cause for gratitude that he had played the host as long and as graciously as he had. Only affection for his Minny could have kept that kind but unsocial husband at her side through the persiflage of reception-line exchanges. No one would expect to see him again or be particularly conscious of his absence. Some of the guests were already drifting with well-bred but undisguised interest towards the staircase leading to the dining-rooms. The most epicurean would not be disappointed; she had seen to that. Lord Cowper had been quite happy to pay for any quantity or quality as long as he was not required to chat with his wife's friends while they consumed it.

"The world and his wife is here, my dear Emily. No other hostess has your 'flair.' "

She turned to find Lord Palmerston in her husband's place. It seemed quite natural and she was pleased that, although rumor and probability placed him high at the moment in the favors of her friend, the Princess de Lieven, he would fill in as host on this all-important occasion.

He had been the first of her admirers and always the favorite. The Fifth Lord Cowper, nine years her senior and Prince of the Holy Roman Empire, had been a much better catch than an Irish Viscount just down from Cambridge. So Lady Melbourne, who had provided her husband with at least one legitimate heir, felt that a woman as charming and clever as her daughter should be able to have her cake as well as eat it. And Emily, whose aim was to give pleasure, managed to give it to an undemanding husband, as she had to her mother and doting brothers and indeed to all her friends, from Royalty to the elderly tenants of Panshanger among whom she dispensed impetuous, if spasmodic, charity.

She smiled at Lord Palmerston now, preening herself prettily in his approval, and let the smile speak for her. Dorothea de Lieven's long neck, she had noticed and he *must* have noticed, was looking quite stringy, and the yellow of her gown was far too bright for her complexion in daylight.

"It has been too much for Cowper, I see," he continued. "Stood up very well, though, through the ceremony."

"For Minny's sake. Yes, I was proud of him." Her husky drawl grew warm. "Doesn't the child look heavenly, Pam?"

It was a subject on which they agreed. Both surveyed the bride, suddenly in view as the tall form of the Duke of Wellington bent to kiss her hand. Whatever his remark, it had made her shy and color, then look up to meet her

45

husband's glance of pure adoration. Her vivid color, her happy radiance, glowed from the chaste symbolic drift of silk net veil and orange blossoms. Her silk dress, deliberately old-style to please Ashley, flowed smoothly from a high-cut bodice to its slightly outswinging padded hem. It isolated her amid the colorful array of muslins over glazed cambric, printed cottons, striped silks, and Lady Cowper's own lilac satin with its elaborate piping and great wrist-length oversleeves.

"What should you expect, considering her mother?" Palmerston answered lightly. "Ashley is a lucky man. We must do something for him—depending, of course, on how the next election goes."

"You think it may be soon?"

"My dear Emily, if Minny had not made up her mind, she might have had to put off the wedding for court mourning! Then, of course, your guests yonder would be King and Queen."

She glanced at the Palladian window where the Duke of Clarence was deep and loud in good-natured conversation with Punch Greville, while his stiff plain little wife stood, as usual in public, though not, it was rumored, in private, a silent listener.

"News from the Royal Lodge is bad again?"

"The King might die today. Yet he was sitting up yesterday talking with Knighton. The unpredictable rogue could last a month. But I should certainly not lay a wager that this Session will close without a dissolution."

"And a change of fashion! All shoulders covered at court, I expect, if Her Highness has her way. She really is a fright, Pam. Look at that bombazine? And dyed Leghorn of all things! Leather shoes too! Still she is as fond of Minny as he of Ashley. Her wedding gift is a priceless dinner set of Sèvres. So I forgive her German strictness." She dimpled mischievously. "It must be sore tried by his ten bastards! Now we really must go up to breakfast. Melbourne will forget that he is not at home. Look at him! He woke just in time to get to the church and the strain of fasting will be too much for his decorum."

"Shaftesbury didn't show?" he inquired, proffering his arm.

A frown appeared briefly on her smooth brow and disappeared like a guest who has strayed into the wrong room. Her voice almost lost its habitual drawl.

"No. Abominable man! Not that he would have been any asset strutting about. As for Lady Shaftesbury, no one seems to know where she is at the moment. And not the courtesy of a word from either. I have too much pride to care about it or feel annoyed by persons I have contempt for. But," she added as though afraid of protesting too much, "it has distressed dear Ashley. And so I do care."

"I should not worry. He seems singularly undistressed at the moment."
They had reached the group surrounding the young couple and Ashley's
radiant face confirmed the comment.

Within moments and without noticeable management the Countess
had arranged the right people to follow the bridal couple decorously up the
flower-decked staircase and to the long table on a specially erected dais. From
its vantage point she kept an apparently idle but attentive eye on the brilliant
melee as guests helped themselves or were helped by an army of footmen from
the confusing array of silver dishes on sideboards and great tables. She loved
parties and this was a good party: the heads of state, the cream of aristocratic
and diplomatic circles, all wearing Minny's favor, a white flower in silver
leafed lace, the gentlemen on their velvet or satin lapels, the ladies on
corsage or bonnet or turban.

She was startled from her survey by the booming bark of the Duke of
Wellington on her right.

"Egad, Ma'am, as I told him just now, never in my life have I seen a man
more in love than your new son-in-law. I hope that marriage will not cure
him."

XII

BUT WHAT A MARRIAGE! Ashley, in his room at the King's Head in Dorchester, reread the latest letter from his "devoted little wife," with its teasing post-
script "Do you love me?" and felt invigorated for the distasteful struggle still
awaiting him. Surely such letters should offset the debilitating nervousness
before speaking which made him feel unfit for public life and especially unfit
for this contest which his cousin's husband had forced upon him. His recent
elections had been mere routine, distressing enough, and doubly distressing
last year since it obliged him to leave his bride. There had been compensation, though, in her first letter, "I would not have believed that I should have
minded so much your being away two days. Pray come back tomorrow if you
possibly can. It would make me so very happy. There never was such a darling
as you are, dearest Ashley, and I really think I love you more every day." It
had been written confirmation, that letter, of his amazed conviction that six
weeks of marriage had intensified her half-frightened uncertain affection to a

passion almost equal to his. "You have little want of amusement to make the time pass lightly," his new mother-in-law had written to him during their honeymoon at Panshanger. "I send these reports in case you have any time to think of politicks."

He would have been unreasonable in the extreme had those words not smoothed the business of last summer's representation: a few visits to voters, a speech of thanks and assertion of principles at the hustings, a ride through the town on someone's cob. More than that, for election Ashley felt unnecessary and unfitting. He was offering his services, freely, from sheer sense of duty in the more than ever distasteful arena of Parliament. If the electors had no desire for him to represent them, he had even less. The open bribery, the parades, the ribbons, the occasional violence which attended party and personal contests, had never touched him. Only in his first election for the Marlborough pocket-borough of Woodstock, although he and his cousin, the Duke's son, had been triumphantly returned over two rivals, had the candidates addressed a crowd in turn. On that occasion, he recalled his youthful visionary fervor to give himself courage now. John Bull had singled out his speech as "distinguished by eloquence and sound judgement." In his later representations he had been eventually a Tory, for a Tory riding, and acclaimed as choice.

But this election was different. While the Whig ministry hung in the balance over the Reform Bill, a wave of contests swept the country, and in almost every case the Reform candidate had been successful. The Honorable William Ponsonby had been asked by the Cabinet to resign his borough seat at Poole and to stand for the Reform party in the County of Dorset. That pleasant, ineffectual society dilettante, universally called poor Willy Ponsonby or Willy the Fair, having yawned and whispered his way through ballrooms and boxes and country houses for a long nonage, had married (or been married by) the vigorous and wealthy Lady Barbara Ashley. Ashley's first cousin was heiress through her mother to the Barony de Mauley, also to her mother's fortune, and to the huge income from her paternal inheritance of a disposable Durham portion of the Shaftesbury holdings, which had since discovered a rich vein of coal. Her influence and her money were solidly behind her husband's representation, and Ashley, when urged to enter the lists against him, had stated simply that the expenses of a contested election were completely out of the question. The loss of over a third of his income at the fall of Wellington's government in the first year of his marriage had been a minor deprivation, set in the scales against the safe arrival within the same year of his son and heir. But the events conjointly made for a reduced household.

Upon assurances of financial support, however, he agreed to the party's insistence and flung himself into the contest with added vigor to make up for his opponent's five-day lead. So to Weymouth and to Portland, to Corfe Castle and Maiden Newton, to private houses, and to gatherings of freeholders in the Queen's Arms, the Plume of Feathers, the White Hart, and an endless number of Red Lions, he rode, talking informally and speaking to groups with the straightforward simplicity of his convictions and his instinctive knowledge of their bucolic prejudice: that reform was needed but not in the structure of government; that legislative power in the hands of landed proprietors was safer than in that of non-resident, irresponsible, financial opportunists; that open irreligion and revolutionary sentiment was ranged on the side of Parliamentary reform; that laissez-faire, capitalist political economy regarded human beings as subservient to the "great laws of nature" which determined supply and demand.

Then the Ponsonbys and their supporters redoubled their efforts, spent lavishly at the inns on entertainment, offered bribes to the electors, and hired groups of the unfranchised to parade with banners, shout slogans ("Ashley must go! Ashley to the wall!"), and interrupt his few speeches. Ashley refused to retaliate in kind but his committee, without consulting him, became more generous in dispensing drinks and favors; and Minny, as the expected week extended to two, insisted on coming to visit his sister at Crichel, and driving out with Lady Charlotte in her pony-chaise to be seen where, her enraptured husband was sure, no one could see her and not wish him to succeed.

To the amazement, delighted or enraged, of the waiting parties, the unvoting mob, as Punch Greville called them, was from the first on the side of the Anti-Reform candidate. Neither Ponsonby nor Lady Barbara was at ease with the farm laborers or even with the farmers and County gentlemen who made up the number of freeholders. Their attempts at bonhomie were awkward and patronizing.

"She can't help it, poor thing," commented Minny after one of the few meetings when both candidates had been invited to a dinner party in Crichel. "You were right, Dearest, to scold me for calling her a nasty little woman because of her airs at our wedding. Upon my word, referring to your being the 'cadet branch of the family!' But she tries too hard to be affable. And both of them act as if they were at one of her famous masquerade balls—where they would much sooner be."

Ashley began to reply and changed his comment to something of more immediate importance.

"The comfort of having you here, my Pet, even for a few days! You don't know. . . ."

"Don't I? Why do you think I came? I was so disappointed when you said you were not coming back till next Tuesday that I could not help crying.

You'll think me a great baby. So Mama suggested it and offered to take care of Babs and his wet-nurse. You would think this were Mama's election, to hear of her bold operations for you. So I thought: What good fun! For, my dearest Husband, I don't know how it is, I not only love you, but when you are away I hate everybody else. And I can't sleep a wink without you."

Words were no answer to this, though after a few minutes of incoherent murmuring he tried them.

"As for sleeping, I don't—and if I doze I dream of you. I love you more than ever, more than I thought I ever *could* love. It is a great happiness to have one whom I can so completely adore."

"Talking of adoration," said Minny, drawing away from him just enough to be able to look into his face and trace his profile with a fond and tempting forefinger, "I nearly jump out of my skin for joy when I watch you talking to people."

"People?"

"Like the farmer from Brockington, when we drove to St. Giles. And the two who were mending the hedge at Hinton Martell. Or Mossop this evening. And the little woman who gave us a cup of tea."

"But"—Ashley was at a loss—"I just talked."

"Of course. But most men don't know how. They either do an 'Ah my good-fellow, and what are the prospects for the crops this year?'—the mimicry of Ponsonby's voice was remarkably good—"or they are rude. Particularly with tradespeople—"

"Perhaps I have had more experience with them. The best friend I ever had, the only one who really loved me as a child, was of what they would call 'the lower class,'" said her husband. "As for the middle-classes, I recall that several years ago, when I was first asked to dine with the Directors of the East India Company, that silly bray Lord Wallace told me to refuse: 'Keep them at a distance'—his own powers of mimicry were considerable—'Don't let it be known that they have access to you.' What vulgar insolence! If a man be earnest I am proud of his acquaintance."

And somehow conveyed that feeling to others, thought his wife.

"Well—I love to watch you. I wish I could go to Bridport tomorrow with you. Whenever you are away there is something I want to share. Night before last it was the sunset."

"We were never intended to be separated even for a day," agreed Ashley.

But when they were separated, her letters by every post and the relief of sharing his surcharged feelings in his was some compensation.

The contest, eagerly watched and commented on throughout the Country—"I fear Dorsetshire will go against William Ponsonby," wrote Lady

Holland to her son, Henry Fox; and Greville recorded, "It is so severe that they have been for some days within ten or fifteen of each other and, what is remarkable, the Anti-Reformer is the popular candidate"—closed, after an unprecedented fifteen days, with Ashley thirty-six votes ahead of his opponent.

Neither the winner nor his wife, clasped in a thankful ecstatic embrace on his return to their Norfolk Street house, had any idea of the ever-lengthening shadow to be cast by this protracted struggle across the pleasant landscape of their lives.

The cloud came up quickly. Within a month of his election, the bills in for its expenses had accumulated to fifteen thousand, six hundred pounds. Ashley was appalled at the evidence of unchecked waste and implied bribery but trustfully submitted them to his committee. Then the thunderbolt fell. Although the wealthy men of the Party had been approached and heartily endorsed Ashley's nomination, no specific sums had been mentioned and only a small fraction of the needed money had been subscribed.

Still the young couple was undaunted. Emily, who had never had a request ungratified, and Ashley, whose only real concern about money—a growing concern with his growing religious feeling over the last five years—had been how he could give away any surplus for worthy ends, were quite sure that the grateful Tories, hopelessly outnumbered in a House packed with Whigs and Radicals, would rally to his support. Peach in London and Henry Sturt in Dorchester, with his other agents, put the case in urgent letters; but as usual, the incentive to give money for an end already gained was less compulsive than when the issue was in doubt. Such contributions as came could not be said to flow in; they merely trickled.

At this juncture William Ponsonby, backed by Lady Barbara's fortune and goaded by her pique, announced his intention of entering a petition against Ashley's return. If this were allowed, the whole battle would have to be fought over again.

Ashley decided to intervene. Pride had prevented his personal canvass to raise money for his own relief, but this new threat demanded action. Confiding in his hero-worshipping friendship and the Great Duke's former patronage and hospitality, he first essayed a letter to Wellington:

"I think it my duty to inform you, not only as the head of the party to which I belong, but also as having taken so great an interest in the struggle for Dorsetshire, that if Mr. Ponsonby should present the petition I do not intend to resist it, however feeble, nay despicable, may be his claim, as indeed my Counsel assert it to be.

My Election expenses are still unpaid; indeed, even the amount nominally subscribed has not as yet been placed in the Banker's hands. I have before me, in consequence, the prospect of debts and incumbrances which no economy or exertions on my part will enable me to discharge. Under such circumstances it would be dishonorable in me to incur further expenses.

I am, my dear Duke, with great respect, yours very truly,

Ashley."

This letter was dated November 30. The heading "December 1" on the Duke's reply indicated that there had been no prolonged searching of heart in his hero. The letter bluntly repudiated the title of "head" of the Tory party and any responsibility for his young friend's predicament. Cold water thrown over his head could not have shocked Ashley more than the implications of the final paragraph:

"I am very sorry that you should find yourself under the necessity of retiring, in case Mr. Ponsonby should petition. I did everything in my power to support you. I did even more than I promised.

Believe me, ever yours most sincerely,

Wellington."

After this disillusioning rebuff a cool answer, without a subscription, from Sir Robert Peel left him almost indifferent. Not so Minny, or Lady Cowper, whose efforts on behalf of her Tory son-in-law caused the raising of many a Whig eyebrow. Almost daily letters from Brighton, where his wife and child had been taken by her mother out of the London fog, warmed his chilled spirits with their loyal fury.

So on December thirteen:

"So sorry, Darling, to think of you in London in the midst of all your troubles.

Mama heard from the Duke. He was sorry that he was not well enough to see you and Mr. Peach. I think he feels rather ashamed."

And on the fourteenth:

"It is so shabby of the Tories. They can look out for the Petition but not help your expenses. Mama has not heard from William Bankes or the Duke. What do the Dorset people say—Henry Sturt and Mr. Farquarson? What Mama wishes is that you would take money from both parties under *plea of Petition* and devote part of it to election expenses. My uncle said he would on no account advise you to venture a sixpence on the Petition. I am so vexed that your worry is still going on. Do come down, my own Pet. There are parties every night. We dined last night with Mr. Brooks Greville, then went

52

to Mr. Bradshaw's where there was some very pretty music. What do you think of the company I keep? Babkins sends a slobbering kiss. I long so, Darling, to see you again."

And on the fifteenth:

"It is too vexatious, the state of your affairs. Mama had a letter from Mme. de Lieven about it. The Duke of Cumberland asked about you and hoped you would not give up your seat hastily. Upon my word the conduct of all these people is outrageous! Take care they don't involve you in the Petition and leave you to pay it. There is no news of the Duke of Wellington.

Do come down Monday. Is Saturday impossible? The weather is so heavenly, if you were here I should be perfectly happy in spite of our circumstances. Take *great care* of yourself, my Pet. All the people of the Pier think that Babkins is my little *brother* and call me Miss. I do everything I promised you, Darling. I get up and breakfast with Fanny early."

Again on the sixteenth:

"My dearest Husband. I don't know what to think about your affairs. I begin to be afraid they are nearly hopeless. Mama is indefatigable. She goes on writing the most *violent* language right and left. She has written to Lady Jersey to see what she could do. Upon my word Sir Robert Peel's conduct is quite atrocious and scarcely credible. I can't but think they will all feel desperately ashamed of themselves when they find that they have lost your seat in the House but that will do no good. However I hope, Darling, that you will go on bearing it as well as when I was in London. Do come down for a day. If the House adjourns Tuesday, couldn't you come Wednesday and stay till Friday? What do you think, Dearest? Pray tell us if Mr. Peach has heard anything from Dorsetshire. I am by no means for your defending the Petition if you can't get any of your election expenses paid. What a ridiculous idea: to pay expenses necessarily incurred by being County Member, and interest of the money you must borrow—out of two thousand a year. Darling, don't make yourself unhappy. Mama thinks you have a better chance of getting some of the money back by remaining in Parliament. I think the chance so small it would not be worth it. If when they think your seat depends on it they won't give a farthing, how much will they give when it is secure? Good-by, dearest Love. I hope you love me and are not angry with me for thinking I could be very happy if you were out of Parliament for a little while.

God bless you, dearest.
Your devoted little wife,
Emily Ashley."

53

He was not to be out of Parliament. On December 20, in a terse letter to agents and committees he refused any share in either the labor or expense of defending the seat against Ponsonby's petition and left the matter in the Party's hand to do exactly as they pleased. They pleased to resist it. But the decision was long pending, and Parliament opened with Ashley unable to take his seat.

March the tenth found him at Norfolk Street, deprived once more of Minny. Lady Cowper, pleading ill-health and need of her daughter's company, had taken her off again to Brighton.

"My dearest Child," wrote Ashley, "It makes me so wretched to say I cannot come to you, but really my affairs look so ill that I am unwilling to leave London in such a state of uncertainty. Peach is everlastingly engaged on my behalf and I am apprehensive of his feeling that I do nothing for myself and throw everything on him. He has perpetual suggestions to offer me. One or two others less kind would think I had no consideration for their trouble so that I enjoyed my own pleasure.

But you will soon be here I hope, dearest Love. The house is a dungeon without you and even Babs occasionally seems to think so; he always breakfasts with me—you will be delighted to see his health and beauty.

Ponsonby's great object is to make a series of frivolous objections and exhaust the money which might otherwise relieve me. This cannot be helped. I must submit to the evils which await an insolvent debtor. God be praised, I have done nothing to disgrace my character, though much to diminish our happiness.

I am much better to-day, indeed quite well. (Babs has just been here on his way out. He looks *too* heavenly.)

My Pet, I am so careful of myself. I always dine at home. Yesterday to my horror (though, poor fellow, it is a shame to say so) just as I sat down, Cole came in; so I was obliged to feed him, but he was very grateful.

Pray come back as soon as you can. Give my love to Mum and do return without making me wait longer than is necessary for Mum's health.

God bless you,
Ashley."

A week after this letter, decision was given and his election was triumphantly confirmed. But although the Duke of Cumberland and a few others made contributions, individually generous, and Ashley converted every feasible asset into cash, he was obliged to saddle himself with a loan of seventy-five hundred pounds at an interest which must either eat into his income or grimly augment the principal.

Still—he had won the seat in a spectacular contest. Money for his needs had always been forthcoming. His wife's family offered a permanent country home at Panshanger and they had more invitations to dinners and country houses and balls and entertainment than they cared to accept. True, he deplored the state of the country. Radicalism and violence were increasing. The election necessitated by the passage of the Reform Bill was sweeping a different breed into the House of Commons, where he felt less and less at home. But he was respected—in his dejected moments after an attempted speech he did not know why—in the Party and his approval sought. If it came into power in the relentless see-saw of measures and ministries, there would certainly be a place for him with emolument not less, perhaps much more, than he had received on the India Board.

His relations with his father, briefly pleasant, were becoming less cordial. Lady Cowper's diplomatic tactics after his marked absence from the wedding—no one had expected the Countess to attend!—had won a grudging apology, and Minny had charmed him into an awkward and heavy gallantry. It was amusing that he always asked her to dine at Grosvenor Square when her husband, his son, was out of town. There had been one visit to Panshanger with his daughters Caroline and Harriet, which had been almost relaxed. He had also parted with an additional one hundred pounds a year allowance. But he had never forgiven Ashley for his speech on Catholic Emancipation and his reputation as a "Saint," and was transferring his attention to William, whom he could dominate, and to his recently acquired bride. Ashley was thankful for small mercies and had ceased to expect anything in that quarter.

As for great mercies—he had Minny, "the wife of God's own gift," for in everything she supplied his need, made up for his deficiency, compensated for his frequent disillusionment. When the maneuvering and tricks of politicians sickened him, her refreshing honesty healed; when a new scandal broke and most women of his acquaintance indulged in cynical or unperturbed comment, Minny carried with her an atmosphere of innocence and purity which emanated, not from ignorance, but from an instinctive bent towards rightness. Her premarital flirtation had been a social game. Heart and mind and body satisfied in her husband, she went to school to him and, like a bright pupil, on occasion instructed her teacher. For there was nothing mawkish about her new piety, nothing vapid in her sweetness. Her comments on politics were alert, on people occasionally sardonic, usually kind. They came out in a delightful mélange in the letters she wrote, again from Brighton, to cheer him through his December election.

"We dined at the Pavilion, as the Court Journal says, 'a galaxy of beauty.' And are particularly asked to dine there again tomorrow. It's rather a bore. I sat next to Miss Bagot and made her acquaintance which I liked. Lady Sydney looked so pretty. We are going to Petworth Saturday or Monday—so of course it will be Monday as Mama *se jouhait ici beaucoup*. . . . Ten long days before I see my love! . . . Lady de Ros is living here *en famille* and trying very hard to get my uncle to marry Olivia. . . . So sorry, my darling, I forgot to give you some blue pills to take. . . . Henry Greville says that the only question put to candidates here is whether they will vote for the Queen's income being reduced from fifty to fifteen thousand pounds! . . . Brilliant sun and the look of the pier makes one jump out of one's skin for joy. I wish to heaven you were here. . . . Lady Chesterfield's child is frightful with very light eyes like Lord Chesterfield's, but turned up at the corners like hers. . . . Fordwich has a madman opposing him. He says he is King of the Jews and Gypsies and comes to the Hustings in a crimson velvet suit and cloak lined with white satin. His creed is 'the rich should pay taxes and the poor eat roast beef'. . . . I had a letter from my brother Bill. He says Lord de Gray's old front tooth dropped out, the only one he had. . . . Babkins is the admiration of the town but grows so wilful there is hardly any managing him. *So violent. It is astonishing how like his father he is!*

Good-bye darling!"

To him also—and only to him—stray comments showed how far she had come from satisfaction in frivolity. "Hyde Villiers died suddenly. There have been so many sudden deaths. I cannot understand the way in which people go on neglecting such happenings. Mama goes on thinking of nothing but going out gadding right and left. . . . The effect of this dreadful cholera is that we can't be absent from those we love for an hour without most intense anxiety. . . . what a fancy to seize Mama today! She would come and read prayers with Fanny and me!"

But it was the quality of sunniness, glinting and permeating, at which he warmed himself. It was shadowed only by his absence, and he would have been a poor lover indeed to prefer unvarying contentment to such expressions as found their way into every letter:

"My darling love:

Thank you a thousand thousand times for your kindness in sending a letter by the coach today. I was so enchanted. It was such an agreeable surprise after the blank I had expected. . . . It is almost wrong to doat as I do on you. It makes me *so miserable* even for a day. I can't bear my room without you sitting in the arm chair . . . without you I dislike everybody and take no pleasure in anything. Think of me as I think of you—every five minutes."

56

No wonder he found everything flat and dull unless she was by him or he knew her to be near. After his starved childhood, his careless but homeless youth, his increasing loneliness, he had a home. What was a load of debt and a reduced income to a man blessed by such a wife?

XIII

"BUT, SIRS, YOU MUST give me time for consideration." As usual when in doubt, Ashley felt that he was stammering. To the man whose proposal had reduced him to the state of astonishment, doubt, almost terror, he looked quite composed, though half a dozen years younger than his thirty-two. Sir Andrew Agnew, who had made the introduction, opened his mouth to speak, then waited.

"There is no time, Lord Ashley." The Reverend G. S. Bull was gentle but insistent. "It is well known that Lord Morpeth intends to give notice this session of his measure which will defraud us of our Ten Hours Bill." He paused to see what effect this would have. "You know in what a maimed condition the proposal for eleven-and-a-half hours received the Royal Assent. Mr. Sadler thought from your letter to him—"

"I know. I know. I was astonished and disgusted on reading the evidence taken before his Committee, 'our white slave trade' Mr. Southey calls it. And I felt that I must offer my services since he had not been returned to Parliament. But only to proffer a petition or do any other small office! Not to head the movement. I have nothing but zeal and good intentions. My knowledge of the situation is fragmentary and second-hand. I am, I assure you, the last person to achieve such an objective. My ability in speaking and in debate is puny. Almost any one else would be more certain of success."

"There is no one else," said Mr. Bull bluntly. "And by that I do not for a moment mean that I accept your estimate of your ability. You are perhaps unaware of the reputation you enjoy for disinterested humanitarian service, for benevolence, above all for Christian character and integrity. This we covet, this our Bill needs, both in your dealings with the operatives and in your presentation to the Commons."

Ashley hesitated. The appeal touched his most sensitive spot. But he held out.

"Tomorrow—yes—tomorrow morning, Gentlemen, I will give my decision. I must have a night's respite for reflection on a matter so important."

And consultation, he thought as he walked up the Hill past Buckingham House towards Park Lane with the long free stride of a man who enjoys walking. He had sought out Peach and Scarlett as he left the lobby and acquainted them with his difficulty. To his surprise both of them strongly urged him to adopt the question. Their assurance of support and confidence armed him where he had felt lacking in armor.

There was great need of prayer, however, and—though he fought free of desire for 'Sortes Divinae' as a type of superstition—he felt that reading the Bible might, as it so often did, clarify his thoughts. And there was Minny.

For he was not deceived, as he went on with steady pace, pausing only once to gaze over the Park at a vista with its own beauty of budding tracery even in the saffron and gray of an early February twilight. He knew that this decision placed him at the crossroads; that whether crowned with success or failure, his adoption of such a cause would put him outside the pale of his class without identifying him with any other. So far, especially since his marriage had swept him into pleasant relations with the Cowpers and their set, he was accepted there, and—to himself unaccountably—considered a young man to be reckoned with. True, his disillusionment with the Duke made him less sanguine of advancement should he regain power. True, his first love of Peel's honesty and truth was giving way to saddened realization that principle weighed less with that capable statesman than policy. Tact and diplomacy were native to Ashley, political chicanery always remained an alien concept. Yet both men still seemed to think highly of him, consulted his opinion, requested his support. If he went on as he was, a life of amiable family enjoyment, political influence, general prestige, seemed assured. The other way—he fought down the sense of destiny which had been with him since the implications of Mr. Bull's proposal had sunk in—was unknown, uncertain, unpleasant. Whatever his own views, Minny should have the choice.

She was waiting for him in the nursery, where Accy must have an evening visit with his father before going to bed. A habit which had begun from Ashley's searing recollection of childhood loneliness and Minny's equally clear remembrance of childish importance had grown into a delightful episode of every day. In their child as in every other aspect of their life together, Ashley thought gratefully that no man had ever enjoyed greater happiness in his married life. It would not be fair, he said to himself, to ask his wife to sacrifice the little he could give her. She took enforced economies so gaily. This little house in New Norfolk Street was the smallest she had ever lived in, and the paucity of their staff—her maid King and his man, Accy's nurse, a cook, a housemaid and a boy—must make the Countess Cowper raise her brows—never, be it said to her credit, in front of him. Fortunately one of her mother's carriages was usually available for her. He made light of his own longing for a horse to ride.

They went to dinner and he held her chair, observing how gracefully she slipped into it in spite of being eight months advanced in pregnancy. It was not the least of God's mercies to him that childbearing seemed less difficult for her than for most women. Her first accouchement had been brief and—though he still suspected her of trying to spare his feelings just as she made light of her headaches and other ills—not very painful. Now with her second a month away she looked younger and more radiant than ever.

"What has happened to distress you, Ashley?" she asked suddenly.

He looked at her incredulous. The sweet had been removed and dessert was on the table. Through the courses he had maintained a steady flow of what he thought had been interesting conversation. Seldom had he exerted himself more strenuously to be companionable. She saw his amazement and was pleased at her astuteness.

"Do you think you can deceive me by telling anecdotes? Or passing on gossip about Mrs. Fitzherbert or Lady Holland, as you never do when we talk. When there is no trouble on your mind you do not work to keep me entertained. So you had better tell me quickly."

He waited until they had gone to her sitting room, where he drew a chaise longue near the fire and stood by the mantel, watching her as he gave a brief summary. She listened thoughtfully, her eyes fixed on the flames. She said without looking up:

"Have you thought it over?"

"I have thought of nothing else since it was suggested."

"But why—why ask me as if my agreement is so important?"

"Because it is. Because I cannot agree unless you assent. My Child, don't you understand? This may—almost certainly will—change the whole course of our lives. This is not a Party measure. Some Tories will support me because they detest the mill-owners as a class, some Whigs because they are sworn to reform. Many, even of the radicals, will not, because they dread anything that will interfere with the economy, or because they are theorists about laissez faire and oppose what they will certainly consider limitation of the freedom of the individual. I shall be considered by some a traitor to my class, by others an envious meddler. There will be those who detest 'humanitarians and philanthropists' as hypocrites. My father will repudiate me completely—

just when you have won him around to civility. You know your Uncle William's opinion even of Abolitionists. Your family will wish they had never let you marry me—not for the first time." His laugh was more wistful than sardonic.

"Ah now, that is unfair!" said Minny warmly. "Mama thinks so highly of you that she was quite annoyed when the Duke's chance to form a ministry came to nothing. 'It is my special joy to see Ashley's radiant face,' I heard her tell Lord Palmerston. Papa likes you and Uncle Fred came quite round even before the wedding after I told him that if I was not to marry you, I ought not to have had anything to do with you. And in spite of his talk about the 'inconvenience' of your principles, he is much taken with Fanny's disdain for the young men she sees at Mother's. At fifteen she shouldn't be considering marriage at all, but she insists that she want a Hero—some one she can look up to. 'Like Ashley?' said Uncle Fred and laughed when she said: 'Oh, if only I could meet some one like him!' But he did not dissuade her."

"They are always very kind to me—and if chiefly on your account, that is only natural. But so far I have done nothing to arouse the opposition which this Bill will arouse. You know what economies you already endure because of my election debts. The least I can do is to put myself in the way of a well-paid post. So far I seem to accumulate those which demand expenditure of time but bring no financial return. . . ."

"Like the Lunacy Commission—" murmured his wife.

"But to do that I must be a good Party man. And this Bill will endear me to neither party."

"Come and sit here." Minny moved her feet, around which her husband had tucked an afghan, but her gesture brought him to a seat where her outstretched hand could rest first on, then within, his. "My dearest love, you know far more of this than I. Tell me—do you feel certain in your own mind that this Bill is right?"

"Right—yes; but it is only a beginning," said her husband. "The more I learn the more appalled I become. That too is a reason for hesitation. For if I espouse this cause I can take nothing on hearsay. And to see with my own eyes—as I must—will take me much from you. And to be separated from you even for a day is almost unbearable."

In answer to her unspoken invitation he leaned over to kiss her; then almost immediately resumed:

"But sometimes I can hardly bear to look at Babkins and to think that thousands of children in this country, a few years older than he, are condemned to an existence to which we are too kind to condemn adult slaves.

60

The heathen who sacrificed their children to Moloch were a merciful people compared with the Englishmen of this century."

"Then there is only one thing to do," said Minny very quietly.

"But the consequences for you, my Pet—"

He never forgot his wife's face, its childlike earnestness, the unwavering courage of her eyes, as she interrupted lightly.

"I would be a very poor pupil of my Lord Ashley, if I have not learned more than that from him these last three years! And I'm not being heroic. I know you, dearest Love, and I dare not face what would happen to you, or to me, if I set myself against something that you feel to be your duty. You did not seek this. It has come to you. You cannot turn back. So we—" she linked her fingers with his in a gesture of complete and defensive union—"shall go forward. And, never doubt, my Husband, it will be to victory! Consequences? We must leave them. They are not our concern."

XIV

SHE HAD NEVER DISOWNED HER WORDS, though now, almost ten years later, she recalled the youthful bravado of their utterance with some wonder. How ignorant she had been of the vicissitudes into which their decision would lead—*through* which, rather, for her unbounded confidence in her husband refused to accept any setback as final, any checkmate as game. If only Ashley felt the setbacks less intensely, were not so vulnerable to ugly attack—but then he would not be her Ashley.

Last month's further postponement of his Ten Hours Bill had affected him as deeply as a personal bereavement. He could not feel partially or at a distance. The children and laborers amid whose wretchedness he talked and walked—when they had toured the manufacturing districts together, he would not let her go with him on his investigations—were never far from his consciousness. Even now, she knew, he was probably estimating the number who could be fed from the inevitable waste of such a dinner as this. As for the children in the collieries! She had inadvertently glanced over some of the correspondence from members of the Commission which he had impetrated two years ago, and he had begged her to put the horrid details out of her mind. But she knew that he could not put them out of his; for, true to his principles, he would give no evidence on hearsay, he would descend the dangerous mine shafts, see the gruesome dank tunnels, the naked crawling women, the pitiful unchildish children. Across the gleaming gold plate of the great dining table at Windsor she met his eyes and thrilled with a rich suffusing warmth to see the serious face, though bent attentively to Lady Lyttleton's conversation, light up, as always, in response. Deeply satisfied, she turned back to Lord Palmerston, whose last remark had set off the train of memories. She was glad that her new stepfather had handed her in to dinner rather than her Uncle Melbourne. That debonair worldling, still youthful at sixty-two, had been assigned to her sister Fanny, recently married to young Lord Jocelyn, now seated at Minny's left. Lord Melbourne's long protectorate of the young Queen, at once fatherly and romantic, gave his manner an assured freedom to which none of the others present aspired. His notorious laugh had hooted more than once above the hum of subdued conversation, and Fanny had smiled or blushed at the causative remark. But the Queen, whom he had often made laugh immoderately, looked down the table at him indulgently, and young Prince Albert, who still found his wife's mentor sympathetic and helpful, relaxed a little from his stiff shyness.

This was very well, thought Minny. She had always been fond of Uncle William. But she no longer admired—if she ever had—his opinions and attitudes, particularly where they derided and opposed those of her husband. Some perverse streak made him keep his most careless and profane remarks, his indifference—real or assumed—towards any benevolent scheme, for his conversation in Ashley's presence. "There, Madam, is the greatest Jacobin in your Majesty's Kingdom!" he had said to the Queen in his laughing way, the last time they were at the Palace. And even in his talk to her there was a constant cynical belittlement of "piety" and "philanthropy" which all her efforts to keep on neutral subjects had not availed to silence. As for his comment on Ashley's speech regarding the Climbing Boys: "Why the hypocrite dislikes his own children!"—Minny thought she could *never* forgive him for that! Her mother, injudicious as ever in reporting, had—by accident probably—repeated the remark in Ashley's absence during one of her infrequent tirades against her son-in-law's "religiosity," and had been almost cowed by her daughter's shocked and furious repudiation. Her Ashley—who could scarcely bear to leave even the youngest of their six darlings at home when they travelled, and who spent part of every morning reading and talking and doing lessons with his boys!

Lord Palmerston, on the other hand, had always put her at her ease, even when she had known that Society in general assumed that her mother was his mistress. Minny was glad that Ashley and she had not joined her brothers and sister in opposing the marriage. Impervious and daring, stormy petrel of the Foreign Office, darling of the ladies during his long bachelor years, he was now making her recently widowed mother radiantly happy and—to Minny the important thing—showing an increasing admiration for her husband and his interests. No affection for her would sway that independent mind. The lack of a pronounced organ of veneration in him was a probable root of the constant unease with which he was viewed in safe, sane, diplomatic circles.

> *"Hat der Teufel einen sohn*
> *er ist sicher Palmerston"*

was already a refrain in Prussian circles. And to all cautionary reprimands he turned an assured insouciance which made him as dear to the British public as he was detested by Metternich and Guizot.

He was still waiting for her reply and she gave it.

"Ashley finds it very curious to be fighting your battles with such gusto. He doesn't wish the government to go out yet because he feels he will obtain more from the Whigs than from the Tories."

"No Party man—that's the trouble with him." The handsome face smiled impishly at her. "If I dare claim any affinity to a man as superior to me morally as your husband, it is that I let people know where I stand, once I know myself! No good is ever gained by unjust concessions. You don't stave off war or stop demands by yielding to urgent demands, however small, from fear of war. The maxim of giving way to have an easy life will lead to your having life without a moment's ease."

A sentiment which inspires what people call his "gun-boat" policy, thought Minny. Aloud she said demurely:

"Do you expect to have ease? Ashley said to Mr. Bull when he undertook the Factory Bill: 'Talk of trouble! What do we come to Parliament for?' "

" 'A hit, a very palpable hit!' " Palmerston paused to help himself to salmon and Minny glanced down the table with feminine interest in dress. She was glad that she had not left her front hair in the sleek, looped-back braids of the Queen's fashion. Instead she wore hers in soft rounded ringlets under the evening bandeau with its lace edge, because Ashley liked them. The Queen's black damask, with its low-cut corsage accentuated by white lace ruching, set off her beautiful young shoulders. Minny's own throat and shoulders rose from the silver lace flowers edging the pale rose taffeta which had been made for Fanny's wedding. Her mother, happy to be out of black, wore a gown of the new Jaquard flowered net. Her young sister looked bridal in white organdie with fresh flowers. The same age as Victoria, she had been a favorite lady-in-waiting since the Coronation when, doubtless at Melbourne's suggestion, she had been one of the train-bearers. Her choice of a Tory bridegroom had not pleased Victoria overmuch. Still, was it partly a concession to her that several of her husband's Tory connections had been included in this Ascot party? More likely it was Prince Albert's good sense, for the tottering condition of the Government made Victoria's girlish partisanship of the Whigs dangerous and unbecoming. Odd that the Tory Ashley had always been a favorite! But no. Only the most ignorant or bigoted could think of him as swayed by Party, in spite of his adherence to what he conceived to be Conservative rule and Conservative principle.

She wondered what subject was holding Lady Lyttleton engrossed. She approved Lady Lyttleton only because of that influential dame's approval of her husband; for she felt intuitively that the approval did not extend to his relatives by marriage or even, in genuine cordiality, towards herself.

"A very sensible and highly-principled man," Lady Lyttleton had written, and someone had quoted the letter to Lady Holland who had quoted it to Lady Palmerston who had quoted it to Minny, "who married a beautiful wife and taught her all the good she could not learn from her mother, so that from being a flirting, unpromising girl she is grown a nice happy wife and mother."

Well that was damning with faint praise! In her heart Minny conceded it to be true. She *had* learned everything of vital importance from Ashley, whose perfections as a mentor were matched only by his perfection as a lover. But although she was aware of her mother's limitations, thoughtless as an animal on spiritual matters as long as she was in a bustle of social activity, she resented any outside criticism. As for herself it was one thing to admit that she *had* been a flirting, unpromising girl, quite another to have someone else say so. The Lady's unconditional admiration of her boys only partially overcame her resentment.

"But in spite of occasional trouble in the House," continued her stepfather, having dealt adequately with the fish course, "Ashley is achieving success of a rare kind. His influence is gradually pervading the whole atmosphere of society. His interests are certainly varied! And his powers of persuasion are extraordinary. From complete indifference—ignorance rather—he won me over at one dinner to see the political and financial possibilities of this Jewish scheme of his. And with Bunsen's arrival in England next week there is little doubt he will carry it through."

"You know how Ashley regards it," said Minny, smiling to soften any implied rebuke. "Political and financial advantages do not even enter into it with him."

"Quite so," said Palmerston comfortably. "So I shall render unto Caesar for him. If, that is, we manage to ride out this Jamaica storm. Whereas if Peel is asked to form a government, Ashley will most certainly be offered a post."

"It will need to be a more suitable offer than the last," said Minny indignantly. She remembered where she was and dropped her voice. "I do not care to speak hotly, but to confine a man of my husband's stature to a Court appointment! And how unfair to appeal to his patriotism and love of the Queen till he could scarcely refuse! Just to tie his hands politically and in a department where . . . what was it he said when he told me of it? 'I could exhibit nothing good but my legs in white shorts.' Shameful! And the more shameful," she went on laughing ruefully, to make up for her lapse into anger, "because he is showered with appointments which take endless time and energy but to which no salary is attached!"

"Talking of Sir Robert Peel," the Duchess of Sutherland suddenly and startlingly interrupted from Palmerston's right, "though I detest the man I cannot speak too highly of his Peelers. I hear that though there were 20,000 gathered at the dreadful fire this morning, the crowd was managed so admirably that there was no untoward incident."

"An ill-fated place, Astley's theatre," commented Palmerston. "This is the third time it has burned. Well do I remember the second. It was in '05 for I had just come down from Cambridge."

The interruption gave Minny an interlude of chat with her new brother-in-law, young Lord Jocelyn, back in England from service in Chusan. His swift siege of Fanny's uncertain heart had culminated in their April marriage after a brief engagement. He was an impetuous, likeable youngster, handsome in his dress uniform which stood out, brilliant, even among the embroidered waistcoats and jewelled buckles and studs of the other men's dress. Fanny, who had been looking for another Ashley, had not, she herself conceded, found that *beau ideal* but the nearest to it. The fact that he and Ashley had struck up a friendship reassured both sisters.

"She hazards something, but less than in taking any other of the mass of young gentlemen who after London life are candidates for matrimony," Ashley had commented to his wife. "There are materials in him to be worked to good purpose."

They were all hoping that he would win a seat in the next—uncertainly forthcoming—election, though from different motives: Ashley felt that to be in Parliament would keep a naturally restless temperament from the temptation and mischief of society; Lady Palmerston, to whom Lord Roden's estates in Slieve Donard seemed far, wished to keep Fanny for a good part of the year in England even if the arrival of children should release her from the Queen's

65

service; and Minny hoped that he would provide vigorous support in the Tory ranks for her husband's darling projects.

"Are you betting on the favorite tomorrow?" he asked half-teasingly. The Queen's band, which had been playing Mozart in deference to Prince Albert's taste, had struck into the more timely rendition of John Peel. Minny shook her curls in mock horror.

"Sir, you forget my husband. He is here and will attend the races only by royal command. Not that he considers racing wrong; for that he doesn't," she went on defensively, "nor do I. But he deplores—as I do—the results and consequences of it. He has met too many people ruined by betting. And he regrets that his presence may be thought to condone it."

After this exceptional dinner at which a hundred guests had sat in St. George's Hall, there was—unlike the usual rather long-draw-out evenings at Windsor—special entertainment. Mademoiselle Rachel, fresh from her sensational success in Racine's Andromaque, standing on an impromptu stage made in the embrasure of the great window, gave three recitations from Bojazet, Mary Stuart, and Andromaque. So it seemed earlier than usual when, at eleven, the Queen and her Prince left the assembly and a general punctilious exchange of good-nighting began. Minny, suddenly tired, made her farewells pleasantly brief and wished Ashley would do the same. She wondered, as a wave of irritation swept her, if she could be pregnant again. She had found herself saying almost sharp things to him recently, when his enthusiasm for the subject of the bishopric in Jerusalem, over which her own feelings were tepid, had struck her as extravagant. But pregnancy usually went lightly with her and seldom affected her temper. In fact—recollection brought saving gratitude back to her mind and face as she stood waiting—she had danced so blithely at the Queen's ball in her eighth month of carrying Lionel that she had almost borne the child the same night, and her life and his had been feared for. That had taught her a lesson! And she knew by experience of Ashley's stricken face at any unkind remark from her that she must control her occasional impatience. He *depended* so on her. Ah, here he came!

Not quite. On his way to her he met Lady Lyttleton, who had paused to pick up the Queen's fan and reticule. Minny saw him take her by both hands and noted the surprise and pleasure of her face at his farewell, though they were too far for her to catch what he said.

Husband and wife were silent as they passed through the lengthy series of corridors to their rooms. Minny was about to pull the bell-cord for her maid when Ashley stopped her. For a long moment he held her at arm's length, surveying her with utter delight before catching her close to him.

"Darling Min,"—she wondered if Fanny's young husband sounded as ardent—"this is what I have desired every time I looked at you this evening. Have—"

"Oh, come now," but she made no attempt to leave his arms, "you seemed quite happy at dinner with Lady Lyttleton."

"Of course," said Ashley, surprised. "If I cannot sit beside you, I find her much more agreeable than the younger ladies. Particularly when she speaks as she does about you."

"Ashley, she doesn't really like me. She does approve of the way I dress the children! But we never have anything to say to each other. What on earth do you find to talk about so earnestly?"

"Oh" . . . He kissed her again, gently removed her lace-flowered bandeau, ruffled her curls with his face against them and released her as an aid to clear thinking, . . . "the character of St. Paul came up—I've forgotten just how. I doubt if she had ever thought of him as a man, as a living individual. She was quite interested in the possibility that he had been married. It had not occurred to her."

"I'm sure it hadn't," said Minny amused. "Are you going to tell what she said about me?"

"I trust it will not puff you up and make you 'behave yourself unseemly'. No? Then if I can quote her accurately, she spoke of the 'immense pleasure of looking at Lady Ashley before whom *all other* women look muddy and dirty and old ' " He knew his wife's loyalty too well to add, "her young sister is, I think, barely pretty, begging the world's pardon."

"Well!" Minny was temporarily speechless. "All I can think of is your phrase 'that's a good 'un!' "

He did, thought Minny gratefully, looking with careful self-criticism in her dressing-room mirror while King arranged her hair for the night. All through their married life he had been equally delighted to marvel at her himself and to pass on compliments from others. She remembered the ball in Rome when a Frenchman had asked to be presented to *Mademoiselle* Ashley. "You looked heavenly tonight," he had commented in telling her, and then rather guiltily: "Is it very wrong to be so entirely proud of, and happy in, one's wife's beauty?" A few moments later he had arrived at a satisfactory answer: "No, for God pronounced *all* that He had made 'very good.' And there is *nothing* of all His handiwork so pretty or so fascinating as my Min."

But that was after four years of marriage; the day after tomorrow, tomorrow almost, was their eleventh anniversary, an occasion which he never let pass without spoken thanksgiving, no matter how many affairs and burdens pressed upon him. Minny sighed with pure gratitude and went into the adjoining room to see the lovely sleeping faces of Maurice and Evelyn in the faint ray of their night light—"their beauty is most striking; and not wonderful considering both parents," the same Lady Lyttleton had commented to Lady Palmerston. Then she rejoined her husband with a passing feeling of pity for her mother, her sister, the Queen, and all other women under the royal roof.

XV

"WHO SHALL BE LORD STEWARD? Who Lord Chamberlain? Shall I propose Lord Liverpool for the Stewardship? I need your advice on this whole matter of Court appointments."

The staccato rain of sentences stopped abruptly. Sir Robert Peel plainly expected answers. Ashley, taken rather aback, looked at the strong, handsome face of his Chief and saw nothing to account for an intuitive feeling that his manner had changed. He suddenly recalled the Duke's words at Melbourne's triumph on the occasion of the Bedchamber crisis: "The trouble is that I have no small talk and Peel has no manners." Yet from Ashley's days as a fledgling Parliamentarian, Peel, then already a veteran and Wellington's Home Secretary, now for years the undisputed leader of the Tories in the Commons, had treated him with respect and as much warmth as his notoriously cold reserve was capable of showing—except presumably in private relationships. Was that unbending hauteur, he wondered, the result or the cause of his unique status: the first man to become Prime Minister from a father and family whose wealth was acquired by trade?

"It would set my mind at rest," Peel recommended as abruptly, when no answer was forthcoming, "and be greatly to the Queen's liking if you would fulfil your promise of '39 and accept an office in the Household—Treasurer for instance?"

"My promise, Sir Robert?" Ashley was astounded and indignant. "If I recall, I told you then that the triviality of any court appointment was repugnant to me—that only an unqualified assurance of its necessity for the good of the nation and the Party would make me consent to it."

"And as I told you then"—Sir Robert waived the interruption—"your character is such, you are so connected with the religious societies and religion of the country, you enjoy so high a reputation, that you can do more than any man to assure the moral tone of the Court. Remember that the welfare of millions of human beings depends on the moral and religious character of this young woman."

With the change from brevity to rounded periods, his voice made Ashley think of Disraeli's description of it as one of the two perfect things he had known. It almost exercised the hypnotic effect with which it played upon the House. Not quite.

"The situation has greatly altered since then," he countered firmly. "The Queen has gained in maturity and in popular favor. She has a child, and a husband quite capable of taking care of her. Besides, you misunderstand the Court."

Had he been tactless? Peel stopped shuffling papers, rose and stalked to a window overlooking Whitehall, but remained silent. Ashley explained his point with the unselfconsciousness of a man who had been socially involved at Court since his majority.

"A man, however high his rank in social life, is placed according to his official position; the Queen cannot, consistently with etiquette, admit me in a subordinate station to intimacy and confidence. I should be of no more value for the purpose you name than any of a dozen others."

"Ah yes, but it would be desirable to exhibit a high morality. We should display a contrast to the bad appointments of the late Administration at Court." The tall figure in its cutaway riding-coat was still turned away. "What shall I say to the Queen if she proposes your name?"

"I should then, of course, confer with you on the best answer to return to her." Ashley realized suddenly that he was *tired*, and that, although he had not expected much from the interview, he was depressed by the gratuitous insult, as he felt it, of Peel's offer. He thought of the ten weeks since Melbourne's dissolution of Parliament in June: ten weeks spent in exertion for the Party and the country, with only a few days—and those not free of business—for his family. He had spent days at Leeds in vigorous but vain support of Jocelyn's candidacy; travelled to Salisbury in an equally futile effort to secure a seat for his brother John; gone to Dorchester where he himself was easily returned as County Member. He had shuttled from Broadstairs, where Minny was holidaying with the children, to Panshanger, to London, and for a series of meetings to inspect factories and to encourage disheartened operatives in Manchester, Leeds, Bolton, Ashton, and Huddersfield. He had undertaken to prosecute the mill-owners at Stockport, on behalf of a poor girl whose body had been mutilated and broken by unprotected machinery. This and another case in which he stood to lose hundreds of pounds—which he did not have—he had won without loss, to his great relief and gratitude. The sufferers had been recompensed and the workers convinced that the law did not operate against them. But it had all taken its toll. And now he was being offered a less important office than he had held six years before, and the same one that Peel had expressed shame for suggesting two years earlier. It struck him suddenly that this time there was no word of regret or apology. That was the difference. A majority of ninety-one at the polls had made him a much more confident Prime Minister than he had been with none.

"Sir Robert," he said, rising as the other returned to the desk. "I should like two minutes of your time for a matter upon which any decision of mine must hinge. What will be your attitude and the attitude of your government to the Factory Bills?"

"Surely, Ashley, the question is irrelevant to our present decision. Every man must not run his own hare when we have the large issues of government in our hands."

"It is not irrelevant to me," said Ashley. "I have run my hare, as you call it, for ten years and across difficult country. Do you know that the master-spinners in Manchester have declared their resolution to oppose any Bill that I can bring in? No human power therefore shall induce me to accept office and allow myself to be put in a position where I may not be equally or better placed to advance this cause. When I made a similar answer to your proffered position in the Queen's household two years since, you pooh-poohed the notion that you could not easily, once you formed the Government, adopt the Ten Hours Bill. In that three-day crisis nothing was settled. I am asking your word now that you will support it at the next Session."

"I do not even know the present position of the Factory question," said Sir Robert coldly and forestalled his companion's obvious desire to supply the information. "I can talk about it with you another time. Meanwhile I urge you to make no rash decision. Consult others of your friends, consult Goulbourn and Graham. Now you must excuse me. I have an appointment."

The coolness of his parting was noticeable. It left Ashley burning with things he had no chance to say, things he should not have to say for himself. His fourteen years in Parliament; his debates and proposals; his prominent involvement with the most important undertakings of the day; the services he had rendered the Conservative cause, even in the generally acknowledged influence by which the country had resisted all agitation on the Corn Laws during the recent election: this to be henceforth employed in ordering dinners and carrying a white wand! It was a plain, cruel, unnecessary insult. It would have been far more kind to have been left unnoticed altogether.

But that, Ashley realized shrewdly, was impossible. The general assumption that he would be given a post when the Tories came into power had caused great uneasiness among the operatives, who distrusted Peel. It was to hobble him that Sir Robert, under guise of flattery, was attempting to put him out of the way in the Palace. A colleague so independent that he did not bow to the obvious political dicta: "We must concede part of our principles to preserve the remainder;" "there are two sorts of truth, both convenient, one for the opposition, one for the Government;" in fact who considered such statements "time-serving balderdash," and said so, was bound to be troublesome.

His first impulse was to talk to Minny. He repressed it, still smarting from a recent unexpected rebuff. The incident was over and his wife had recalled her words in a burst of penitent tears. But it was scarcely a week since his exuberance at the support by King Frederic William of Prussia for the Jerusalem bishopric (what Palmerston had called his "Jewish scheme") had provoked her to petulant anger: "You din this perpetually into my ears and it sets up my back against it, always talking of 'how wonderful, how wonderful!'" Ashley had always admired her power of mimicry; he had winced at its exactness and had left the room angry and hurt. His Minny, whose dear smiling face made everything shine! He acknowledged the weakness of his undulating moods and was determined not to give her—so soon—another instance. Better to preserve the calm aloofness for which he was known in Parliament. Possessor of "the palest, purest, stateliest exterior of any man seen in a month's perambulation of Westminster," he was glad that the reporter, who had proceeded to describe him in meticulous detail—for he was presently in great favor with the Press—had been unable to see beneath that exterior. Very unstately, he thought, were the violent periods of digestive disorder which at times almost prevented the delivery of his speeches and which did keep him, more often than not, from impromptu debate. But he would reserve his immediate comments for his diary. And he would—having given his word—discuss with one or two unbiassed friends, Henry Corry perhaps, Jowett, and Seeley, the Prime Minister's suggestion.

He had scarcely time to consider advice before a second summons to Whitehall. Peel renewed his proposition, totally disregarding any difficulties on the score of the Factory Bill. Ashley patiently and stubbornly cut through his presentation of the Queen's needs, preferences, wishes, to force a statement of the Government's intentions.

"This is a great Ministerial measure," was the reply he at last elicited. "It will require the deliberation of several Cabinets."

"It is no novel one," said Ashley without heat. "It has been discussed in

71

the House frequently over the last ten years. It has in fact carried the West Riding and other places in the General Election—."

"But it cannot," Peel pounced on a pause, "become a subject of discussion before the spring. You may take office now and reserve the right to enter on some other arrangement then."

"And meanwhile," said Ashley, "convey the universal impression that you are favorable to my views. From your own point of view it would be far less injurious for me to decline now, saying that you are undetermined, than to declare on experience that you are so hostile to the working-classes that I could not continue with you. A resignation demands stronger reasons than a non-junction."

As you very well realize, he thought. Peel's next words took him by surprise.

"There is a wide difference between an office in the Household and a political appointment."

"But in the four-month interval I must remain quiet. I could not marshal forces, collect evidence, gather material for an explosion in the House."

"No, there could be no agitation. But I wish you would take other things into consideration—your unblemished reputation, the need of such men about Court. If I believed you preferred civil office I should, of course, make arrangements to that end."

Ashley stood up. The situation was becoming farcical. No slightest suggestion of a post that was his due, as long as there was a remote chance of his being shelved on the Palace! Then when the principle had been established that any office must be rejected, a flourish of appearing to propose what could not be accepted! It was too much for his straightforward nature.

"Sir Robert," he said, pointedly ignoring the last remark, "consider my position. I have for ten years told the Government (being in strong opposition) that they know the rights and interests of the working classes, that they were indifferent to their welfare, and were ignorant of the wants of human nature; that the question was vital and concerned the permanency of the social edifice; that I would never allow it to be tainted by party; that I should push it under all circumstances, whichever party was in power. Can I now, because my friends hold office, withdraw or modify the principles I have declared to be sacred? Not only would such a change of conduct involve total ruin of character, but at this moment I am, no doubt unworthily, the representative of the whole aristocracy. If I deceive the operatives, they will never believe that there exists a man of station who is worthy to be trusted. And I should be deprived of that very public morality to which you—ostensibly—attach so high a value."

72

There was silence in the room while the two men measured each other with fair appraisal but without sympathy: the elder to whom change was always abhorrent, yet who changed his convinced policy under the slow cumulative pressure of circumstance; the younger, who saw that his course was excluding him from political power, patronage, sorely-needed income, yet was incapable of changing it.

"I suppose I must convey a negative to the Queen," Peel said at last. Then with an unexpected surge of—what was it? regret? admiration? he shook Ashley's hand very warmly. "I have never in the whole of my public life experienced half so much pain as in your refusal of office."

The interview was over. Ashley, always easily moved, found his emotions cooling later, when he discovered that he had been discussed for a variety of civil offices, including the Secretaryship for Ireland, but that Peel had thought him "impracticable" for them all.

Yet the refusal which he had written after the first interview, and the decided negative of the second did not keep the Prime Minister from two other abortive attempts to make him yield.

Meanwhile Ashley had made his position clear in a letter to Mark Crabtree, Secretary of the Yorkshire Central Short-Time Committee.

"In answer to your inquiry, I have to reply that office was tendered to me by Robert Peel. Having, however, ascertained from him that his opinions on the Factory Question were not matured and that he required further time for deliberation, I declined the acceptance of any place, under circumstances which would impede or even limit my full and free action in the advancement of the measure which I consider vital, both to the welfare of the working-classes and the real interests of the Country."

XVI

APPROVAL OF HIS ATTITUDE, expressed in private letters and conversation, as well as in almost fulsome praise by the *Herald* and the *Standard*, tided Ashley over the inevitable reaction of flatness when the rightness of his stand faced the dispiriting prospect of continued financial struggle. He was ashamed to find himself almost regretting his surrender, a few months earlier, of an annuity paid to his wife from Lord Cowper's estate. Old Mr. Henry Cowper had left Minny some four thousand pounds, and she had agreed with her husband that the conditions under which her father had made the additional provision no longer existed. Together they had overcome her brother's generous but not prolonged resistance. Now he wondered if his insistence *had* been caused by a strict sense of honor, or by the pride which made it painful for him to accept a sum which he felt beyond his proper share.

Fortunately there was little time or space in his crowded life for such speculation. Fortunately, also, the next months provided several periods of rare exuberance. In November his dream of "reviving the episcopacy of Saint James" was realized. Dr. Alexander, Professor of Hebrew and Arabic at King's College, after considerable opposition because of his Hebrew origin, was consecrated as Bishop of Jerusalem. Two weeks later he set out for Syria in the Admiralty steamboat which Ashley had bullied from Peel "to carry back to the Holy City the truths and blessings which we Gentiles received from it." The whole affair stirred in Ashley a sense of poetic rightness: the first episcopal benediction from Hebrew lips in seventeen hundred years, the beautiful voices of Hebrew children singing praise to the Messiah; the "truly Catholic" collaboration of the Lutheran and the Anglican Church in the venture.

Then, as an auspicious omen, the instigator of the Bishopric, the King of Prussia, was invited to stand godfather to the infant Prince of Wales. The warmth of that good man's reception by the populace and press was as gratifying to Ashley as the monarch's marks of friendship to himself. The King enquired publicly concerning the possible success of the Factory Bill, issued Ashley a warm invitation to visit him in Berlin, and, when the Jewish Society presented an address of welcome, asked the Society's venerable president, Sir Thomas Baring, who had written "such beautiful words. I never heard such beautiful words." Informed that it had been composed by "the noble Lord on my left," the King said, lapsing into the language familiar to both, "*Cela en rehausse bien le prix á mes yeux.*"

These moments, and the diplomacy and arrangements preparatory to them, weighed in the scales against Minny's threatened miscarriage and intermittent ill-health; against the government's hostility to the Factory Bill and the consequent change of attitude in many former supporters. "The very men who patted me on the back, praised my exertions, rebuked the apathy of the Government (while we were in opposition) now look black and cold. I am in the right, Peel in the Treasury," he summed up. "Meanwhile wrong, oppression, mutilation, death, are in full liberty—millions of infants are consumed—cotton is everything, man, nothing."

But he could not let disillusionment degenerate into bitterness and lessen his diligence in the unpaid tasks piled upon him: his position on the Ecclesiastical Courts Commission; his work for Drainage and Ventilation bills; his labor, continued now for fourteen years, for the mentally afflicted; his personal inspection, at the instigation of Southwood Smith, of unspeakably filthy areas in central London. Undramatic, unspectacular, unrewarded, the work for the poor must be done.

Then in May the Commission, set up two years earlier on his own motion to enquire into conditions of children in mines and collieries, at last published its report. The Home Office tried to keep it secret but it came "by a providential mistake" into the hands of members; and though for a long time the Secretary of State prevented its sale, he could not prevent publicity of the gruesome facts, brought home by gruesome eye-witness illustrations of children, naked to the waist, crawling on their hands, dragging burdens of coal along wet passages, or climbing with coal baskets strapped to their foreheads up steep ladders—"the height and the distance traversed in one journey by an eleven-year-old girl carrying a hundred weight exceeds the height of St. Paul's Cathedral"—facts which sent a shudder through the nation.

One month later, after every attempt to sidetrack the motion, after the exercise of every trick of privilege, and after adjournment and a state of alarmed debate at the second attempt to assassinate the Queen, Ashley brought in his Mines and Collieries Bill. It proposed to exclude from the pits all women and girls, all boys under thirteen, and all parish apprentices; to forbid employment of enginemen under twenty-one or over fifty and to appoint inspectors to ensure that the terms be put and kept in effect.

For two hours the House listened to him in silence broken only by bursts of applause. "Only be strong and of good courage"—the words came forcibly to his mind as he stood at the table about to begin speaking; and his resultant ease was evident in the masterly and unfaltering progress of the address to its simple and inspired but not unbarbed conclusion:

"But here you have a number of poor children, whose only crime is that they are poor, and who are sent down to these horrid dens, subjected to every privation, and every variety of brutal treatment, and on whom you inflict even a worse curse than this—the curse of dark and perpetual ignorance. . . . Where is the right to inflict a servitude like this? Is orphanage a crime? . . . Let apprenticeship be abolished on the spot; let every existing indenture be cancelled. Undo the heavy burdens, and let the oppressed go free. . . .

"Is it not enough to announce these things to an assembly of Christian men and British gentlemen? For twenty millions of money you purchased the liberation of the Negro; and it was a blessed deed. You may, this night, by a cheap and harmless vote invigorate the hearts of thousands of your country-people, enable them to walk erect in newness of life, to enter on the enjoyment of their inherited freedom, and avail themselves (if they will accept them) of the opportunities of virtue, of morality, and religion. These, Sir, are the ends I venture to propose; this" (in pointed reference to Ward's accusation that the Noble Lord's principles, carried out, would restore the barbarism of the Middle Ages) "is the barbarism that I seek to restore."

The effect on the House and the country was enough to justify Ashley's prayer that he might not be exalted overmuch: members moved to tears; praise from press; Cobden won, not to agreement in policy but to a new appraisal of his suspect philanthropy; even Joseph Hume touched; Sir James Graham's assurance of Government support to carry the measure; the Queen and her Prince deeply concerned; the tide of encouragement running so strong as to implant a hope that his Ten Hours Bill would be swept through on its crest.

Then the anticlimax for which he was never—quite—prepared. His diary became a chart of the slowing pulse of support. The coal owners, pleading the misery of unemployment for the children if the Bill should carry, tried to have the suggested employment age reduced to ten and to have the Bill referred to a select committee, thereby delaying action. Apparently well-meaning religious men deprecated such sweeping reforms; conceded the exclusion of females under thirteen, suggested a law to make the miners wear clothes: "nakedness was certainly wrong." Deputations from the coal-owners wooed the House of Lords in anticipation of the Bill's arrival there. Members of the Government in two divisions in the House reneged their implied support; Peel and Graham kept silent, voted for the Bill the first time but disappeared before the second count was taken; Gladstone and Knatchbull voted against him.

One month after the original motion, with Palmerston, his father-in-law, persistently needling the government on their lack of sincerity, Ashley heard the glad fiat "that he do carry the bill to the Lords."

But this was preliminary to another month of anxious and humbling work. The coldness of the coal-owning peers to this measure was a match for the coldness of the mill-owning Commons to factory legislation. Seven otherwise friendly lords refused to take charge of the Bill for him. Finally Lord Devon became its sponsor and remained steadfast, while the Duke of Wellington spoke contemptuously of the Commissioners who had brought in the Report, and Lord Londonderry, with continued and determined opposition, described the conditions in collieries, the anxiety of women to work there, the happiness of the young employees' lives, in terms almost lyrical. Other speakers made pointed references, as had opponents in the Commons, to the wretched housing among underpaid agricultural workers in the South.

In the face of this attack, and to avoid consigning the Bill to a select Committee, Lord Devon softened some of its stringent demands. His concessions and the state of public opinion, which still ran high, persuaded the Upper House to a grudging approval. The same week and almost the same day at the end of July made Ashley father of a healthy daughter and (his greatest legislative success hitherto) of a mutilated but immeasurably healthy Bill.

XVII

"WHAT A CAVALCADE of brats and nurses!" commented Ashley. Minny and he stood at the front entrance of St. Giles's Wimborne, under a gray October sky, watching the unloading bustle of the old family coach and laden wagons. The two of them with Accy, baby Mary, and her wet-nurse Anne Carroll, had arrived from Bourne half an hour earlier in the barouche.

"Yes. I asked your father if it would put a strain upon his health."

"And he said?"

Minny bent down and held out her arms as five-year-old Lionel broke away from his nurse and ran to her. It was only four days since they had been reunited with the younger children after her three-month sojourn at Carlsbad to drink the waters, and the small ones regarded with tearful suspicion even so brief a separation as this migration from Bourne. Over the child's curly head she smiled up at him. " 'I thank you. My health has endured before through circumstances as trying.' " The imitation of Lord Shaftesbury's brusque voice was astonishingly accurate. " 'I doubt if they will seek my company and I shall certainly not seek theirs.' " She straightened with Lionel clinging to her skirts and dropped her voice. "He scarcely overwhelms one these days with his hospitality!"

"No. It is a matter of wonder to me that he extends it at all. You are very gracious with his ungraciousness, Darling. But I cannot disguise it, I do enjoy being here. And for so many years I was exiled that I rejoice with fear and trembling."

That "fear and trembling" expressed one's usual state of uncertainty regarding his unpredictable father, thought Ashley the next day as he walked with the children to his favorite post on the Downs. In the four years since their unexpected reconciliation, Lord Shaftesbury had blown hot and cold. That first holiday he had put himself, as the phrase was, to sixteens to find ways of giving them pleasure, had allowed his eldest son complete freedom to plan the gardens, had accompanied them to Church and been host at Christmas to most of his children and their families. (Lady Shaftesbury had been permanently at Rosedale House in Richmond for many years and nobody felt her absence as a loss.) Since that time he had periodically issued half-peremptory, half-grudging invitations which Ashley desired and felt obliged to accept, even though the relaxed and increasing friendliness of the Palmerstons at Broadlands created an atmosphere with far less strain. The Earl's recent illness had taken much of his energy and, as long as they kept off the subject of Ashley's Parliamentary activities and religious interests, conversation with him was safe. Fortunately for the Ashleys, there was plenty to talk about in their recent trip and, as the Earl barked out reminiscent comments on every place mentioned from Antwerp to Heidelberg, their exchanges had so far been free from acrimony. Besides, the old man was pleased—or at least less annoyed—that Ashley, six years too late in *his* opinion, was about to send Accy to school. According to their grandfather, Francis, Maurice, and Evelyn, now seven, should be shipped off too. But Anthony was expected at Bembridge on the isle of Wight at the first of the month. In fact this may be our last family walk, thought Ashley.

"Father, we're all racing to the pond to see how full it is." It was Francis who usually took the lead in any project.

"Be sure you stop short of it! What about Vea and Edy?"

"Oh they'll probably win. Look at the handicap we're giving them. Say: Get ready, set, go, for us, Father, will you, please?"

Ashley watched Accy carefully leading Evelyn and his little sister about a quarter of the distance to the green dimple of their goal. An idea of racing with them crossed his mind but fleetingly. Exercise he certainly needed and was glad of the daily ride which his lack of horses denied him in London. But he found himself easily fatigued and had been disturbed recently by a strange buzzing in his ear, intermittent but unnerving.

He shouted the required signals and his children took off, Accy almost instantly gaining and establishing the lead.

" 'Primus abit longeque ante omnia corpora Nisus
Emicat et ventis et fulminis ocior alis.' "

he murmured, watching his young Nisus with wistful pride. For in spite of Anthony's sweetness of temper, and in spite of his own watchful, prayerful, daily intercourse with him even during the last three years when the elder boys had been under a tutor, there was an incalculable element in his eldest which caused him unease. The uncontrolled "passions" of his babyhood had been subdued, but the intense susceptibility of feeling which he had shown at the age of three had continued. It was he who first noticed and told his father about the wretched black object huddled in the alley behind their London home and had followed with great concern the long and successful struggle to rescue the little chimney-sweep from his brutal master. It was he who set his brothers the example of giving unasked contribution towards the Jerusalem bishopric. More recently, overhearing his father describing a distressing case of poverty in the village, he had come in private with a sovereign—more than half his school capital—and insisted tearfully that it be used for the wretched family. Now he was alternately elated and depressed at the prospect of leaving, even for so short a time as remained of term before the Christmas holiday. Surely no cause for anything but parental rejoicing? Yet—Ashley watched the distant figures now playing an irregular but rollicking game of leap frog—there was an instability about the youngster, a tendency to respond instantly to the newest influence, a lack of determination, a readiness to be pleased with everything of outward attraction. God knows he probably inherits it from me, thought Ashley, though only half-convinced Francis had been from babyhood more independent; Evelyn was already more studious and determined. As for eight-year-old Maurice, whose bouts of ill health made him more slender and scarcely taller than his sturdy younger brother, he had a disposition of almost angelic gentleness. Individually and together they were a beautiful group. Amazing the differences of feature and expression in six children in spite of the double inheritance of blue eyes and dark hair. Little Victoria and young Lionel were still at the golden-brown stage. No one could fail to recognize relationship, no one could mistake one for the other.

He missed Minny who had been kept at the last minute from taking the walk with them. Even if she were quiet, her presence was a buffer against the disturbing thoughts which crowded in upon him, now that the diversion of the children was removed. And their conversation while walking was always interesting, soothing, sometimes inspiriting. He needed it now to clarify his mind on a topic which could not be put off much longer and yet would bring him into disfavor—serious disfavor, a general disfavor was the norm—with his father.

He took off his tall hat and ran a hand through still curling dark hair. The breeze, almost like sea-breeze, was pleasant to his forehead, and his eyes were rested by the far spaces of undulant downs. They tired easily these days,

79

and his brief plunge on his return from the continent into the accumulation of letters and papers had caused a sharp pain over them which he had never known before. He could almost wish for the life of a country gentleman. At least he would not attract the hostility and adverse comment—what on earth had he done to be so disliked?—of so many opposing individuals and groups.

He broke off the thread of his thinking, ashamed. What had he to complain of when he compared his happy home and the praise which had been showered on him this last year—together with much obloquy—with the contempt and ridicule faced by, for example, Rowland Hill, whose biography he had recently completed. And he had thought he could despise calumny and violence—what a rosebud, he thought in disparagement, compared with the oak-like strength of such a man!

It was reaction, he knew, the sudden realization, after his enforced but pleasant travelling, of work facing him. Minny said it was constant disillusionment because, in spite of his statements and his settled belief in the fallen state of mankind, he retained a naïve hope that it would disappoint his pessimistic expectations. Why should a man who believed Scripture expect that wealthy men would be pleased to have their methods of obtaining wealth condemned?; that poor men would prefer one who counselled peaceful means and patience to a rabble-rouser who urged them to take the law into their own hands?; that a nation rejoicing in victorious aggrandizement would welcome such an unpatriotic and scathing speech as he had made on Britain's guilt in the Opium trade? The curious circumstance was the instant effect of his speeches on the audience and often on the press, compared with the opposition and criticism and vituperation in speeches and editorials and letters, signed and anonymous, which immediately succeeded. Was he, as someone had suggested, the conscience of England? And was the sequence of acquiescence and hostility man's normal reaction to the prickings of conscience?

Even to think such thoughts made him blush inwardly. If he confided them to his diary it was to sort out his confusions, as he could with no confidant. Not true, that. For Minny—God eternally bless her; she will be thirty-three next week, yet when I met William Cowper's wife, a noted beauty and twelve years her junior (poor soul; it is still incredible that she has gone so distressingly after less than four months of marriage!), I thought her incomparably less attractive than my beloved. She has been all that I desired, infinitely more than I deserved.

His thoughts, as usual when he thought of his wife, had strayed. He could not confide his depths of gloom to her because it was the one thing that made her sad. Her sunny joyous spirit bore her own burdens of illness, of anxiety for the children, of financial retrenchment, with such a lilt that it was unfair to load her young shoulders with the weight of his mercurial temperament. She became—for her—infuriated by a statement of his deep-felt inadequacies; his passionate love of applause, linked with a feeling of inferiority to almost every other public man in those respects which make for the fulfilment of political ambition. Hardly a man in the House was less able than he to do the smallest thing unprepared. And he labored under the insuperable infirmity of being unable to speak at all unless on conviction. He could say nothing but what he felt and—he admitted wryly—his feelings frequently got the better of him. So his language had been criticized as too strong, when he found difficulty in finding words strong enough. Ah well—if he acted on his present conviction there would be more strong language from his opponents, and soon!

XVIII

"THE FAME OF THE NOBLE LORD whose health I have the honor to propose is not restricted to this county, nor this country. His efforts and manifold activities have won attention and acclaim in the United States and in many countries of Europe . . . indeed India and the Levant have cause for gratitude to him. He has given a new direction to man's thoughts, turned them into a deep-flowing channel of duty to the poor and of moral obligation. We are honored that he has consented to take the chair at our Agricultural Dinner. Your presence in such large numbers shows and will show our chairman that this prophet is not without honor, even, or especially, in his own country. Gentlemen, the health of the illustrious Member for Dorsetshire, Lord Ashley."

Good for Bob Grosvenor, thought Ashley, as the heir to the Marquis of Westminster clinked glasses above his head. His reception had been cordial, the dinner excellent. Almost two hundred landed proprietors flanked the long, convivially disordered oak tables in Sturminster Town Hall. Now, the customary cheers over and glasses recharged, the faces turned towards him were cheerfully, benignly expectant. How good, how easy, to bask in the warm friendly atmosphere. He had been rebuffed so frequently of late in his efforts to obtain signatures among the nobility for the Oxford Petition against Pusey-ism that he shrank from incurring further criticism. Much more pleasant—would it not ultimately advance his cause by strengthening his popularity?—to indulge in jovial, complimentary reminiscences of his earlier acquaintance with Lord Grosvenor; to relate a few amusing anecdotes; to flatter their national pride with a derogatory tale or two about the heavy field and construction labor at which he had recently seen women employed in Austria and Bohemia; to sit down amid applause, and return home without further antagonizing his father.

But there was his conscience.

"References to my influence outside my own country," he said, after the conventional opening remarks, "are more flattering than founded. Your welcome, but particularly your unprecedented numbers at this dinner, is in heartening contrast to the last dinner at which I took the chair. I had accepted the Presidency of an excellent London charity on the assurance—you have heard the sort of thing—of the immense service I should render. I went—it was the thinnest company and the smallest collection for many years past! So much for the 'influence' of which I hear so much and feel so little. Here in Dorset the relationship is different. I am one of you. This is my home."

He paused for a moment to let the mild applause run its course. He remembered to raise his voice, against which the charge of inaudibility had often been laid. He was surprised by the emotion which had caught at his throat when he mentioned St. Giles's. Many of his audience were living on ancient ancestral soil. Few could say, as he could, that their estate had never changed hands by purchase since the Norman Conquest. The actual house was scarcely two centuries old, but on that site his ancestors or their connections by marriage had lived for almost eight.

"Because of this," he resumed, "it is my grief, as it must be yours, that the County of Dorset is now in everyman's mouth—every paper, metropolitan and provincial, teems with charges against us; we are within an ace of becoming a byword for poverty and oppression. . . . Gentlemen, are we prepared to look these charges in the face, discuss their justice, repel what is false, but correct what cannot be gainsaid? Do we admit the assertion that the wages of labor in these parts are scandalously low, painfully inadequate to the maintenance of the husbandman and his family, and in no proportion to the profits of the soil?"

"If this statement could be denied," he said in answer to a scarcely audible murmur, "then it could also be easily disproved. If not, the reproach *must* be instantly rolled away."

"I do not pretend to give advice," he spoke with preventive frankness, "as to the precise mode of doing these things. I am not sufficiently practical or conversant with the hiring or payment of labor." As Cobden should know, he thought bitterly, instead of charging me publicly with dishonesty; or as Harriet Martineau could easily have ascertained, or for that matter, the well-meaning correspondents who are perplexed about the state of our schoolhouse and other of the buildings on my father's estate.

"But this I know: that if a larger self-denial, an abatement of luxuries, a curtailing even of what are called comforts, be necessary to this end, let us begin at once with the higher and wealthier classes—it must be done."

It would, he admitted frankly, have been easy to suppress the real situation but the consistency of his principles was at stake.

"You ought to know and reflect on these things; and I ought not to be lynx-eyed to the misconduct of manufacturers and blind to the faults of landowners.

"Set yourselves to mitigate the severity of the Poor-law . . . begin a more frequent and friendly intercourse with the laboring man—we have lost much in departing from the primitive simplicity of our forefathers; respect his feelings; respect his rights; pay him in solid money. I say it again, emphatically, pay him in solid money, pay him in due time; and above all, avoid that monstrous abomination which disgraces some other counties but from which, I believe, we are altogether free, of closing your fields in the time of harvest; give to the gleaner his ancient, his Scriptural right: throw your gates wide open to the poor, the fatherless, and the widow."

At St. Giles's the candles in the gilded Chippendale chandelier threw irregular shadows on the heavily gilded cornices of the large dining room. Although it could easily accommodate forty persons, the Earl used it in preference to the smaller refectory even when, as on this December evening, only three sat down to dinner. In this Ashley found almost the only subject on which he agreed with his father. Harmoniously proportioned, spacious yet comfortable, it was his favorite room.

Francis and Maurice and Evelyn, at Minny's sunny insistence, had been allowed to come down for dessert and crack some walnuts—a dubious favor under their grandfather's frowning scrutiny. In fact his whole bearing had been more than usually austere during the meal and Minny, finding her brightest chatter met with heavy silence, was about to excuse herself with the children earlier than usual.

Just at that point Francis, experimenting with the wooden mallet, hit his walnut askew and sent it in a beautiful arc to rest neatly in his grandfather's claret glass, fortunately empty.

"We must take you up to Scotland to learn golf, Francis," said his mother rising hastily. Ashley sprang up to pull back her chair. The three boys, without taking their fascinated eyes from the Earl's face, stood silently and waited. "You will allow us, Sir? Say good-night to your grandfather, boys." The three blue-velveted figures bowed gravely, long curls hiding the faces of the younger two. Evelyn, Ashley noticed, was stiff with inward laughter. "It is long past their bedtime," the bright voice went on, not leaving a second's silence. "It was very good of you to let them come down." She allowed her eyes to meet her husband's for a moment as he handed her the fringed silk cashmere shawl which had slipped from her shoulders. The glance conveyed, like magic, love and fun and sympathetic reassurance. Then, with a slight curtsey to the Earl and an affectionate gesture to her sons, she glided to the door.

The footman closed it behind the little procession, then stirred the log in the fire beneath the white marble mantle. Symonds, the butler, tactfully removed the claret glass with its captive walnut, and poured port. At a curt dismissal, both men disappeared. Ashley, reseated opposite his father, was thankful for the long table between them. This after-dinner ritual, rigorously enforced, was seldom a relaxing period. All through the meal he had been uncomfortably aware that it would be less relaxing tonight than usual.

He tried to summon a feeling of filial reverence as he waited, and admitted to himself that there were few grounds for it. True, the Sixth Earl looked his best sitting down and under his own roof. There, leaning forward with his arms folded on the table, the candlelight kind to his large cold eyes and thin cold mouth, he showed less than his seventy-five years. Standing or walking he was undignified to awkwardness, as brusque in movement as in manner. This very brusqueness made his speed and efficiency proverbial in dealing with useless discussion and in passing bills through Committee in the Lords. Used to expecting and obtaining submission once he had given his judgment, he found opposition intolerable. And in this son with the still hopeful youthful face, he encountered, in spite of deference and readily given acquiescence on all minor matters, a hard core of opposition which remained utterly unmoved by threat or displeasure. It almost maddened him.

Ashley, for want of employment, drew the nutcracker towards him and placed a nut carefully in the hollow.

"I shall try not to repeat Francis's feat," he said, poising the mallet judiciously. "I doubt it will travel so far this time."

"Nice condition the table or my waistcoat would have been in if I hadn't finished the claret! You're far too lenient with the brats. Mollycoddled by their mother too! They should be at school, I've told you often enough."

You have indeed, thought Ashley. Aloud he said:

"Do not forget the cost of schooling, Sir. It is much less expensive to teach them at home."

"Hmph!" Any mention of expenses annoyed the Earl. He turned it adroitly now. "If expenses worry you, I suggest you cease making speeches which would increase yours a hundredfold—if any one paid attention to them."

Ashley was silent. Ever since the Sturminster dinner he had felt his father's anger growing. That was just the trouble. Attention, far too much to suit the old Earl, was being paid to his speech. It had made "a deep impression," Grosvenor told him, on his hearers, and had been reported at length in the local papers. The *Times* had tried to find fault; the *Herald* had been kind. But the local reaction had been a disappointment, if not a shock. He had spent a few days in London crowded with the business of preparing his protest Memorial for Oxford, with exhausting investigation for the Lunacy Commission, with the delicate matter of forming a visiting society for the East End, including laymen and Dissenters, without clashing with the Bishop and Puseyites, one of whom had recently declared he would rather the people should starve than receive relief through any but Established Church sources. He had ridden to Richmond to visit his aging mother, now greatly softened in disposition. Then he had returned to St. Giles to find landowners and farmers there cold, if not hostile.

"This Lord must expect," the Examiner observed in a not unfriendly article upon him, "if he go about telling everyone plain truth, to become odious to everyone." And not least, Ashley felt, to his father. He thought, as he often had thought, that, except for the benign safeguarding law of primogeniture and entailment, he would certainly be disinherited by now.

"Meddling in matters you know nothing about," growled the Earl. "Bad enough to hear of a son of mine as a 'philanthropist,' a 'saint!' Catering to the pusillanimous sentimentality of a crowd of vaporizing idealists! Publicity-mongering I call it. But stick to the mill and colliery owners if you must meddle. I daresay they squeeze every penny they can get. And the poor devils who work for them never get out in the fresh air—not like our people. Spend all their lives in it, good natural labor. No comparison. No comparison at all."

Ashley cast about for an opening.

"The charges made against us—"

"Exactly. And you substantiate them. Foul your own nest. Excite the people. Another Cobbett! They are content enough till some one stirs them up to extortionate demands. They have no complaints."

85

Ashley thought of a newly planted tree in the avenue maliciously cut in two the previous month.

"It's your own throat you're cutting, not mine," his father continued with a certain grim relish. "They're not easily put down, once they're up."

"But they must live—" for a moment he thought the Earl would emulate the French aristocrat and fail to see the necessity. Instead he deliberately finished his port and, without summoning Simmonds, jerked his head peremptorily towards the sideboard. Ashley filled the glass and as a gesture replenished his own.

"An excellent year, this port," he ventured as a digression.

"They do live," resumed his father without thanks or comment. "Get on very well—I don't know how—on six or seven shillings a week. Their wages can't be raised. You have no experience of keeping up an estate. Ignorant as a babe unborn of the problems."

A bit exaggerated, that statement, thought his son, but pragmatically true. Yet it was not altogether his fault. Only in the last few years had he and his family been allowed at St. Giles's. Every effort to acquaint himself with his future duties—even attendance at the local meeting of Justices or Board of Guardians—was jealously misconstrued.

"Oh it's very easy to point out the fact that some of the cottages need repair. It's a different matter—as you'll discover some day; don't think it will be soon!—to find a remedy. I can't afford it. I've been engaged all my life, trying to abate the mischief. These things cost too much."

His voice was actually plaintive. Nine hundred pounds for a hothouse last year, Ashley did not say, six hundred for game, eight hundred for a farmhouse which was wholly unnecessary—surely these sums would go far? He knew the futility of speaking. Defense or opposition would exasperate his father without accomplishing any good. His position in the house was tenuous enough. He dreaded another open breach. Even more he dreaded the closed state of his father's mind to the slightest suggestion that *anything* he did could be wrong. "Open his eyes, Lord," he prayed, "and if they are blinded by the god of this world—who am I to say?—shine on him with Thy glory in the face of Christ Jesus."

The prayer reassured him, though in the Earl's grunting ungraciousness when the subject was changed to his recent illness—it was difficult to find a safe ground of conversation—there was no indication of softening. But repeated prayer and silence would surely have effect.

"Of course they will," said Minny as he made the comment, closing the Bible in which they had been reading together. "Mother asked Lord Mahon,

86

when I was at Broadlands, if it was not wonderful that you succeeded in everything you undertook."

"Lord Mahon might have had an answer if he had been at the Blandford Agricultural Dinner last night." It had been his first local public appearance since the Sturminster speech and there had been a marked chill in the atmosphere. His presence had been almost ignored, his acquaintances polite but guarded. Blame for a recent malignant attack in the Manchester Guardian on conditions of agricultural labor in Dorset was evidently laid at his door. He knew that he should be impervious to personal slights. He knew that he was not.

"It's your health that makes these things depress you, Ashley," said Minny, touching his cheek with her hand as she passed his chair to place a sprig of holly back in its vase on the table. It was Christmas Eve and the children had been allowed to decorate their nursery and their parents' sitting-room. The rest of the house was under the Earl's express taboo. "Dr. Coates would not have advised as he did on Tuesday without cause. And you had been in pain for weeks but would not consult him."

"Until you drove me—literally—to Salisbury. My Pet, it is ungrateful of me to complain of any treatment elsewhere, when your treatment of me is unfailingly kind. And don't think I am unaware how much you would prefer to be at Broadlands for Christmas."

"I thought I was concealing any preference. No. I should not care for Broadlands unless you were there."

"And St. Giles's was spoiled for me without you a year ago. Ah well . . . if my father's anger grows we may not be invited here for Christmas again! Meanwhile as long as I have you—and the kids—but above all, you, it will be a merry Christmas."

Yet he could not put out of his mind when he rose the next morning, the thought of those who, even that Christmas day, had been forced to rise at four to undergo their suffering toil in mills and factories. His heart revolted at the mockery of a law which could not be enforced in spite of vigilance. He knew, yet told himself as if he did not know, that the victims gained nothing by his suffering. But the pain of their pain had become palpable to him as his nerves, his stomach, his head, his eyes, testified. He made a special effort to conceal it, if not very well from his wife, successfully from the children, to whom, after he and Minny had returned from Sacrament, he devoted the day.

Fortunately the weather was unnaturally beautiful with the sun and temperature of April; so the glades and woods behind the house and along the stream were a substitute for Sherwood Forest, offering sanctuary to a band of very young outlaws, the smallest of whom showed most inappropriate terror at the sight of deer.

"Have you been taught the rules of boxing yet at Bembridge?" Ashley asked when they had returned to the house. Accy was showing his brothers the correct way to hold a cricket bat, for that game had made astonishing progress in favor in the past few years.

"No, Sir. There are some fights, of course, but they are not according to rules."

"All the more reason for you to know them," said Ashley cheerfully. And much to Minny's surprise, he took off his coat and laid it across the balustrade. They had gathered on the wide lawn outside their bedroom window far from the Earl's apartments.

"Do you know how to box, Father?" asked Accy. Francis regarded him with awe.

"I am—or rather I was—a very good boxer, I can tell you. It is called the noble art of self-defense, and if you use it only as such it may be of immense benefit to you and to any one you need to protect. Now watch. Accy, put your hands so—Francis, you too. I think I can take on both of you."

The lesson was a great success. Presently Accy and Francis squared off in approved fashion. Young Evelyn—called Old Edy because of his precocity—clamored for instruction but Maurice, after trying with mounting excitement to follow his father's orders, suddenly left the improvised ring, flung himself by his mother and buried his head in her lap. Francis and Accy each took their young brother on, while Lionel and Vea shouted and jumped ecstatically at the side.

As a result, Ashley hoped and Minny thought, the boys listened with even keener interest to their boxer-father when later, in their sitting-room, he read the passages in Luke's Gospel regarding their Saviour's first Advent, talked simply and feelingly about its purpose and significance; and, as he almost always did these days, urged them to pray for His Second Coming, as the cure and conclusion and compensation for all the wretchedness and suffering and injustice in the world.

"You said once that we had some great pictures of the Nativity at St. Giles's, Father," said Francis in the silence that followed. The younger children had been taken off to the nursery supper and to bed. "Would—would this be a suitable time for you to show them to us?"

Ashley hesitated. Such a procession, if met by his Father, might provoke the old man's most sardonic comment. Then he stiffened. It was, after all, his home.

"You'd really like to see them? How many wish to come?"

"I wish to be included," said Edy with dignity. Minny decided to rest before dressing for dinner. So Ashley led the four boys downstairs and through rooms hung with tapestries, through the yellow Drawing-Rooms to the Panelled Hall, and finally to the Library in search of the pictures in question: Pannini's fine Nativity against a background of Roman ruins; its companion Adoration of the Magi; Parnegiano's Nativity, and a small oval of the Virgin and infant Saviour by da Vinci. But so many questions arose regarding the likelihood of the scenery, the conventions of the artist—Edy was sure the baby would catch cold, Francis gravely questioned the architecture of the stable—that the demonstration turned into a lecture, with Ashley telling the story of Leonardo and promising to take them someday, if he could, to see his great works and those of Michelangelo in Florence, Milan, and Rome.

"And what, pray, is going on here?" rapped a familiar voice. Their grandfather stood in the doorway.

"I am showing the boys some of your collection, Sir," said Ashley diplomatically.

"Yes? Well. All the good art is not by foreigners. Too many Englishmen think it is. D'ye draw, boys? Has that tutor of yours or your mother taught you to draw? Hey? Anthony?"

"We have drawing lessons quite often, Sir. Usually with Mama." Accy was his grandfather's favorite, if he could be said to have a favorite.

"Ye do? Then I'll show you something. Come." His orders were customarily obeyed in the House of Lords and there was no question of them now. After a quick glance at their father they fell in behind the old Earl as he led the way, with his ungainly but still quick step, up the dark stairs to his candle-lit dressing room. They had never been in it before and glanced about with eager curiosity, as he led them over to the west wall, and held a candle sconce close so that they could see what hung there. It was a framed sketch, executed in chalk on paper, of a boy about the age of Maurice. The young face which looked out directly, if rather wryly, at them was not familiar, yet they had a sense that it should be. But it was so strikingly, so boldly done, the lines so sure and revelatory that if one of the eyes had winked—for the eyes seemed to have light behind them—they would scarcely have been surprised. Lord Shaftesbury was at least not displeased by their interest.

"There. What do you think of that, ha? Can any of you draw as well?"

"Of course not, Sir." Francis was polite but nettled. "This must have been sketched by a great artist."

"Who is it, Grand—Sir?" asked Evelyn.

"Ah, that's the question. Who do you think, young Anthony?"

Accy glanced at his father who was standing just behind the Earl, and thought he saw the answer in Ashley's scarcely perceptible movement.

"Is it—is it you, my Lord?"

The others gasped; but their grandfather's pleased chuckle confirmed the unlikely guess.

"Good eyes, young Anthony. Yes, I was that boy. Remember as if it were yesterday. And you were right too, youngster—you Francis. It *is* the work of a great artist. One of the greatest. Sir Thomas Lawrence."

"But," said Accy while Evelyn squeaked with excitement, and Maurice's eyes widened, "he has just finished painting Mice and Edy. Grandmother— Mama's Mum—had him do it. And didn't he paint Mama when she was small? You don't mean *that* Sir Thomas Lawrence."

"And why not? There hasn't been another Sir Thomas Lawrence that I know of. Certainly his father was no Sir. Kept an inn, that's what he did. At Devizes."

"But—" the boys were puzzled. There was some mystery in this. Their grandfather was greatly pleased with himself and was concealing something. But what? All men over fifty looked old to them; but surely the urbane, white-haired master whom they had met during sittings at Cambridge House and at Panshanger was not a grown man when their grandfather—they took another look at the lively face in the portrait—was that age—not more than nine or ten.

"But you'd like to know when he did it, hey? Well, I'll tell you. He is younger than I am. A year or so, at least."

"But then," it was rude to interrupt and usually with his grandfather, unthinkable, but Accy was incredulous, "then he would be just a boy."

"And a little boy," his grandfather nodded. Ashley, to whom the story was familiar, stood back in the shadowed room, thankful that Christmas had briefly mellowed his father and hoping to get his brood away before they made any remark to incur his whimsical wrath. "Never a lesson in drawing did that youngster take. Down at Devizes it was. I had stayed the night at the inn with my father and mother. At breakfast in came Lawrence, the innkeeper. 'If it please me Lord and Lady,' he said, 'I have a boy with the gift of drawing. If you and his young lordship would have no objection, I'd like him to do a portrait of his young lordship.' My parents had some time on their hands and said he could please himself. So he brought in the boy, a bright young brat, with his chalk and paper. And in a very short time he presented that to my mother. That boy is now Sir Thomas Lawrence. Now clear out," he said, lapsing into his normal brusquerie. "Time to dress for dinner. And I daresay, as it's Christmas, I'll have to put up with you."

The boys left the room in silence, and in silence clustered around their father along the dark hall to the far wing. Only when they came to the welcoming light and warmth of Minny's room did Evelyn express what was uppermost in their minds.

"Father, was Grandfather really a little boy like that once?"

Ashley swung him up on his shoulder.

"Of course, Old Edy. Weren't you listening?"

Evelyn looked very old for his years, but his round eyes were very young.

"Then I could look like—like him some day?"

God forbid, thought his father. May He use this experience to prevent it!

XIX

January 1, 1844.

A week later Ashley paused over the date in his diary. He was not feeling cheerful and thought it rather a pity to soil the first page of a new year with raven-like croakings. Even his family must weary of them. Repeated attacks in the press and in letters made him wince, even though the contradictory bases of the attacks discredited them before any impartial tribunal. He knew that there was a leaven of personality in his reaction; he knew that injury to his reputation, tarnishing of his public image—favorable publicity had been his strongest weapon against the stubborn opposition in the House—greatly abated support for his causes. And they—his causes—had become so much part of himself that he could scarcely distinguish where personal hurt left off and disinterested anxiety began.

Not least painful of his puzzles was the degree to which his support came from infidels or non-professors, his opposition from religionists and declaimers. He paused to reflect whether he could be right when so many "pious" people discouraged him.

"They read and study the Bible—as I do," he murmured; "they pray for guidance and light, ask, and surely obtain, grace to judge aright. They must make (is it so *in fact?*) their conduct the subject of fervent supplication before and after they have resolved to weaken my efforts. What can *I* do that *they* do not? Do they too ask Almighty God to 'prevent us in all our goings?' If it be so, I am indeed gravelled."

He set the book aside, took from his desk a separate piece of paper, made two columns and wrote under the heading 1843—Past:

Education of the Working Classes clause: Speech a personal success, clause abandoned—opposition from all sides overwhelming.
Opium Trade Bill—temporarily withdrawn—speech a personal success.
Field Lane Ragged School—for discovering which, thank God.
Repeal of Colliery Act—defeated, Laus Deo.
Oxford Petition—hostility aroused, apathy among nobles, support from county families and middle classes.

And under the New Year?

The Ameers of Scinde—protest at our dealings.
Metropolitan Commission on Lunacy.
Ten Hours Bill???

He would not then have believed, pessimistic as he sometimes considered himself, that on January 1, 1846, the last item would head his list. Yet it did—but with a difference. He had carried it to all intents and purposes almost two years before, in three months of unbroken struggle against the Government's Twelve Hours proposal and another month of increasing support for his own Ten Hours clause. He remembered the intense enthusiasm which greeted his initial two-hour speech, and his support in the debates. He remembered the disapproval which had greeted Bright's ugly attack and insinuations against him. He relived his amazement that Peel and Graham, failing by skilful maneuvering, had succeeded by blunt threat of resignation in bringing the Party to rescind its vote with an overwhelming majority against him. The sarcasm of the *Times,* the ugly name-calling of the *Globe*—"ranting, ambitious, hypocrite, Prince of Canters," the "Jack Cade" jibe of Sir James Graham reflecting the *Examiner*'s spirited cartoon; under these his head was still high but bludgeoned.

To the Government's bait of office—the Lord-Lieutenancy of Ireland with almost unlimited powers in respect of the Church, not directly offered but suggested in the line of public duty, and undeniably tempting in view of increased financial difficulties—he was by habit immune. After all he had a record of refusing office on principle from the days of Canning's ministry! Since then, of offers from both parties, as when Palmerston suggested that he be Undersecretary of State in the first year of his marriage to Minny, he had found only one which he could accept with clear conscience. That brief period of his Lordship in the Admiralty had passed with Peel's first Government ten years ago, almost before the Ashleys had moved into the Whitehall house! But for the Ministers to stoop to suggest that he betray his cause to save the Ministerial face and that he instruct his friends to cease their efforts while he himself put up only a token resistance!—if Ashley had had any illusions regarding the state of fallen man, they disappeared when Jocelyn relayed this message to him.

"Thou shalt not go over this Jordan"—the phrase had rung repeatedly in his ears since he had used the allusion, not really crediting its possibility, in a defiant rebuttal of criticism of his bill. He had been called "a government prophet."

"Well. It is not difficult to foretell what Bobby will do," he said, though aloud only to Minny who came in at that moment. "The reverse, always, of what he said and did when in opposition. But he succeeds in humbug. He gives one thousand pounds for public walks in Manchester—and stakes his political existence on the perpetual refusal to allow people time to enjoy them. I am sorry, Dearest," he added contritely, "but my heart is so full that it is my great relief to disburden to you. You should have discouraged me when we were first married." He did not say that there were a hundred agonies which he still kept from her. "Or you should not have come in just now."

"Ashley, Darling!" His wife, a slightly fuller figure in her voluminous brown walking dress, paused at the mirror to adjust the veil of her hat under her chin, and came over to his chair. She put her hands on his shoulders, then as his arms went around her in instantaneous response, she drew his head against her breast and held it till the painful throb in his temple relaxed and he lost himself briefly in her protective tenderness. "Must we go over *that* again? Upon my word, if you begin keeping things from me now—And I know that we must talk on the Corn Law question. But I brought you to Brighton for your health. And it was so—what is your word?—ungo-outable yesterday. Today is beautiful. For dinner we are to have the turkey your sister sent from Rowton. Can't we walk first and talk upon the Downs as well as here?"

The glory of the day, the blue of the sea, were grateful to Ashley's country-starved senses. For the last two years he and his family had been summarily barred from St. Giles's. The offense of his Sturminster speech, of his whole public life and his philanthropic connections, had increased with the passage of time. Occasional meetings with his father, even on his recent visit because of the Earl's sudden illness, had been barely civil. The Palmerstons had been hospitable as usual and he was grateful for the open house at Broadlands. But "Mum's" insatiable desire for society usually ensured the presence of other guests. So, even though she had drawled "Ridiculous" to their assertion that the ménage involved with eight children—including a month-old baby—would be an imposition at a Christmas party likely to include one or two Foreign Ambassadors, several Cabinet Ministers, and assorted friends, the Ashleys had refused the latest invitation.

In consequence they had spent Christmas in town for the first time in years; but Minny, who loved the sea, had insisted that they leave London for Brighton at New Year. She usually had her way even when her choice of locale was not his. This time he was glad to agree. Concern for her languor since the child's birth—she had been confined to a couch all Christmas day with a terrible headache—and desire for the children's enjoyment, were joined to a secret hope that he might be able to get rid of his latest and undiagnosable annoyance, recurrent periods of roaring in the ears.

This walk was her first lengthy exercise since the arrival of their third daughter and she took it slowly, leaning on his arm.

"I believe you are thinner," she said suddenly. "Dearest, you are taking Dr. Cotton's tonic, aren't you?"

"Faithfully. Ah, but the Ten Hours Bill would be the best tonic of all! And I could have it, Minny. I am sure this session will see it through, but—." He broke off with a puzzled movement of his free hand.

"Go on, Darling."

"As if you need to hear it!"

"In a sense I don't. In another I do. We must be very sure we are doing right."

He smiled down at her. His smile came much more rarely than it used to, and the fine bones of his fine face were more prominent. He misses his riding so, she thought almost angrily. If only he could afford a horse. It would be such a good diversion for him, working night and day as he does.

"I know you will do right even if it breaks your heart," she said to start him from his silence, "but I like to have my answers clear and ready for—"

"For Mum. I know. And for people like Lady Nancy who told me at Harcourts' that she heard nothing but abuse of me from morning to night."

"And Lady Francis asks information to battle her guests who—who—"

"Who revile me. Yes. My letter to the electors of Dorset seems to have started a hornets' nest. How they buzz! The League hates me as an Ultra-Protestant, the High Church thinks me abominably low, the Low Church several degrees too high; the mill-owners, because I am no longer represent-able as doggedly opposed to a revision of the Corn laws. . . . Complete it with the Church regarding me as *persona non grata* for working with Dissenters, and

94

Exeter Hall criticizing me as being insufficiently theological and fiery—!" His laugh was a bit forced.

His wife's voice, very low with intense feeling, shocked him.

"It is awfully hard for me not to hate them when I think of what you have done, what you have given up—"

"Don't," said Ashley. "I love to hear you praise me. I lap it up, but . . ."

"And you should. With these horrible letters coming in—you don't show them all to me, I know—and every newspaper spreading lies—lies that are ridiculous to those who know you, lies that are contradictory. If there were any truth in them I shouldn't mind—" She broke off as Ashley suddenly stopped and swung her to face him, catching both her hands. His face, radiant with laughing surprise, looked years younger.

"My Child,"—the name of their early marriage slipped naturally out— "thank you for that! Oh thank you! I've said it so often—and not until I heard you say it did I realize how ridiculous I was."

"I am happy to be helpful—always—even if in being ridiculous," retorted Minny, "but just how—?"

Ashley dropped her hands and ran the risk of scandalizing any polite society by putting his arm around his wife in public. Fortunately, polite society had chosen to promenade on the still fashionable Chain Pier and no one was in view but their five boys, who had far outdistanced them.

"My Pet, of course you see. I wonder how many others, Christians through the ages, have said just what we have said, feeling virtuous and not realizing how completely they are gainsaying or ignoring the express words of our Blessed Lord."

Minny's face lighted suddenly in comprehension.

"You mean: 'Blessed are ye—' "

" 'when men shall revile you and persecute you and say all manner of evil against you *falsely* for My sake.' We are not to care as long as it is false. We are to rejoice and be exceeding glad. A counsel of perfection far beyond me, I fear. But if for His sake—" He paused. "I was once—it seems long ago now—in danger of the woe pronounced upon those of whom 'all men speak well.' Remember, Darling? The favorite of the news? Extracts from one hundred journals wafted me through all degrees of praise. There is little danger of that in these days! This last year or so has been most damaging to my reputation! But"—his face sobered, though still with joyful soberness— "what is it all compared with God's undeserved mercy to me?"

She held his arm tightly and they began to walk again.

"You know," he went on, "a great part of my difficulty is realization of the difficulties in which I place you and the children. But so far what I have had to do—give up, you call it—for conscience has been personal sacrifice; and I count you and our darlings as part of myself in it. Now, more than that is at stake—and I confess to you, Minny, I am desperately puzzled."

They noticed what until then they had been too absorbed in each other to notice, that young Francis had left his brothers and was walking beside them.

"Please, Mother. Please, Father," he said as they stopped. Don't send me off. Let me listen."

Ashley looked down at him, adjusting his mind once more to the fact that, at nearly thirteen, the slim youngster was as tall as his elder brother. In every other respect he was and had been from babyhood more mature, more independent, with greater control of his emotions, with far more power of application to study.

"Oh that Francis might stand before Thee," he had prayed on occasion when Accy's consecutive periods of frivolity, indifference, and short-lived, over-passionate remorse increased the anxiety which his parents had shared about him since his seventh year. And there was evidence that the prayer was being answered. True, during his terms at Bembridge he had proved himself—what was the new word?—"normal" enough by neglecting to write home. But he had shown fortitude even two years before, in grappling with his deep-seated fear of firearms and accompanying his parents and the impervious Anthony and Evelyn to witness a naval review and mock engagement. And in recent vacations he had shown much concern about his father's work. Evidently he followed the newspapers with avidity. Especially heartening and spontaneous was his new interest in their daily Bible reading. His comprehension and comments, his father thought, would shame seven-tenths of adult confessors. He was waiting now, with eyes, Minny thought, very like Ashley's in their earnestness, for his father's answer.

"Why should you not? It is a family matter," said Ashley, and was touched to see the full young face compose itself in an expression of deep gravity, and the stride adjust to keep pace with his own.

"You know what the Corn Laws are, Francis?" he resumed.

"Yes, Sir. They were passed in 1815 to protect English agriculture by imposing a tariff on all food imported from foreign countries."

Score for Mr. Millington or your Bembridge master there, thought Ashley. Aloud he continued:

"We needn't go into the conditions in the land during and after the Wars with Napoleon. Suffice it that those who believe agriculture to be the backbone of our country felt—many still do feel—that such tariff is necessary.

96

I was brought up in this school of thought and my electors in Dorsetshire took my views for granted. I do not think they ever questioned me on the subject. I was elected as a Protectionist. As for the Party, we have been summoned every Session to make a plain unconditional resistance to Repeal. Now what do you know of the doctrine of Free Trade and those who hold it?"

"Free trade," said Francis, glancing at his mother to see how he was doing, "is the theory that goods should be allowed freely from one country to another to—to compete in an—is it open?—market. I'm not quite certain what that means. But those who hold to Free Trade"—he was now on sure ground—"are the manufacturers and mill-owners who make vast amounts of money by employing people in their factories and would like them to be able to buy bread cheap so that they will not demand higher wages."

Minny laughed.

"Take Francis to meet Mr. Bright, Ashley! And Mr. Cobden."

Ashley had laughed too but returned to the argument. "I fear, Francis, that those gentlemen would retort, as they have been retorting for some years, that the landowners—we, if you like,—wish to keep up the price of British bread so that we can make higher profits at the expense of the poor. And they have been saying 'Tu quoque' about the wages that our southern agricultural laborers are paid—especially," he added ruefully, "in Dorsetshire."

Francis glanced quickly up at him, but waited.

"Now whatever the original justification for the Corn Laws, I have for some time felt that it had ceased to exist. And, as you must have heard, a circumstance has lately arisen which has made the whole question of Repeal urgent."

Francis nodded.

"The potato blight, you mean?"

"Yes. And the consequent appalling shortage of food in these islands, especially in Ireland. With this crisis upon us, to keep needed food out of our country or to let it in at a price which prevents the needy from buying it would make the Government most unpopular. Therefore it will not dare continue to preserve the Laws intact. Some form or degree of Repeal is inevitable."

"Then why shouldn't they repeal them?"

"I think they will. I am sure they intend to do so at the next Session of Parliament."

Ashley paused. This was the part difficult to explain.

"When a member is elected to Parliament, Francis, he is responsible to those who elect him. That is my belief, though many haughtily repudiate what they call the principle of 'delegation.' Sir Robert and his Party, as I said, have always stood for the Corn Laws and against their Repeal. They came into power on that understanding. There is no shame, indeed there is great credit, in honestly changing one's mind and admitting it. That is why I wrote a public letter to my own electors indicating my change of mind. But many, if not most, of the Whigs have for years stood for Repeal. Even Lord Melbourne expressed his altered views five years ago. They have promised it to the country. To my mind, if Sir Robert and Sir James Graham have decided that Repeal is necessary, it would be honorable in them to resign and let the Whigs bring in their measure. For there will be opposition. It is not as though every one were convinced of it. Sir Robert will depend on the support of Radicals and Whigs as well as on some of his own Party."

"I see," said Francis slowly. "But you are not in the Government, Father. You are not responsible for them."

"Only for myself. True. Though I am a Tory I have voted against the Government and on occasion for the Whigs when they were in power. And I would vote against the Party in this issue if I believed their measure wrong. But as I am convinced that it is right, although I feel that they are wrong in clinging to power, I should by conviction have to vote with them. And what would my enemies—let us say my detractors—make of that?"

Minny began to speak but broke off to let her son reason the matter through.

"It would look—you mean—as if you had changed in order to keep in favor with the Government? But you haven't. You'd be voting as you really think right."

"And I could justify such a vote before God," agreed his father. "But Francis, I have entered into relations with men and I must observe them, though it be to my own detriment. I cannot make promises at the hustings which I fail to keep in the House. You see, when I said I was responsible for myself alone, I include my character, my public reputation, the principles I maintain, the language I have held. And you know—my poor family, you can scarcely escape knowing—that my reputation is that of a 'religious' man."

Francis flushed and clenched his fists as at some memory. His father was suddenly reminded of his almost unknown young brother after whom he had named his second boy. That Francis had been little more than two years older than this Francis when he had paid with his life for standing up for sixty rounds against his seventeen-year-old boxing antagonist at Eton. Ashley shuddered and laid a protective hand on his son's shoulder. He knew what had caused the flush.

"I see that you have read some of the comments: 'saint,' 'humbug,' 'canting hypocrite,' 'liar,' " he said dryly, "and you will doubtless hear more. I shall be accused by the High Tories of broken faith even if I leave the House.

98

But if I remain in it I shall indeed give 'occasion to the enemies of God to blaspheme' and say, 'After all, your religious men, when they are tried, are no better than any one else.' Many would say, many more would think it. Whereas if I resign—"

"They cannot suspect you of a dicker with the Government as they did—so unjustly—when you allowed your Bill to be withdrawn a year ago," said Minny, with heat which she seldom showed before the children. "To accuse *you* of all people of being a tool of the Cabinet!"

Francis had waited his turn.

"They will have to admit that you would sooner give up your seat than—"

"Your integrity," said Minny very quietly.

But at what cost, thought Ashley, turning to look out to sea so that they should not see the pain in his face. All my beloved projects, all for which I have sacrificed everything that a public man values, all that I had begun, all that I have designed. "Nearly my whole means of doing any good will cease with my membership of Parliament," he murmured.

"But you must resign?" It was a question, but it confirmed his resolve.

"Yes I must, Dearest."

"Then how do *you* know that your whole means of doing good will cease?" asked Minny. "Or that God may not bring greater good out of this?"

Her husband turned to Francis.

"Young man," he said, lightly because he did not feel lightly, "I can ask nothing better for you in this world than that you be granted a wife like your mother—capable of every generous self-denial and—what is better—prepared to rejoice at it. May all you children inherit her spirit!"

"And not tire so quickly." Minny turned the compliment with the smile which covered pleased embarrassment, "and the thought of that turkey—fresh mackerel too—tempts me home. Call the other boys, Francis dear."

"Accy! Mice! Edy! Bava!" The shout brought the four on the run.

Anthony, his winning face flushed with exercise, came up and linked his arm affectionately in his mother's. Eight-year-old Lionel seized her other hand. Evelyn was deep in an argument with Maurice—a one-sided argument, for Maurice was not heard to reply except in unconvinced monosyllables—about the habits of some birds they had seen on the Downs. Francis had not left his father and shoved the younger boys off when Edy would have made him the arbiter.

"Would it distress you,"—oddly observant for a boy of his age, thought Ashley—"to explain something else to me?"

"Why 'distress?' "

"Because"—Francis flushed again; that quick heightening of color was inherited from his mother—"I hate to refer to horrid things that people say and I know they hurt you. But, Father, I understand why some people don't like your speeches against the Opium trade, and particularly when you accuse the British of injustice to the Ameers or of 'shedding more heathen blood in China and India in two years than heathen have shed of Christian blood in two centuries' "—he did not mention the anger several schoolmates at Bembridge had relayed from their homes regarding this statement—"And I understand why the factory and colliery owners don't like your exposing the dreadful things that go on. I can even understand people who have never seen a poor chimney-sweep being angry at you for trying to make them use machines to clean their chimneys."

"Well, then," said Ashley encouragingly, "it seems to me you understand a great deal more than I did when I expected that, as soon as these abuses were pointed out, redress would follow. What do you still not understand?"

"Why *religious* people oppose you. Why all Church people don't help you. Why—how—clergymen can write to you as they do; how they can say the sneering things they do about you in the *Morning Post* for taking the Chair at the Ragged Schools' meeting. I heard Mama tell the Duchess of Beaufort that the Tractarians must have a pug-dog snuffing you out wherever you go, and that it was strange anyone of their elegant tastes and habits should bother going into such districts as Broadwall. And things about you mixing with Dissenters. Are Dissenters not Christians? Some of the boys at school seem to think they are worse than heathen. Or frightfully low class. Only servants go to Chapel, they say."

It was a complex question. They had reached the outskirts of the town and the house which Colonel Wyndham had lent them was within sight. Ashley decided to answer the central problem. His first remark seemed irrelevant.

"Whenever we discuss people who do not agree with us, particularly other Christians, Francis, we are in danger of self-righteousness. Man in his fallen state is desperately evil and habitually self-deceived. It is easy to have the will to do good when one has not the opportunity. With the opportunity one often loses the will. And if I had the capitalist's temptation to acquire great wealth, how do I know that I should not do as he does? So I must remind myself, when I am tempted to—and often do—pass harsh judgments on professing Christians. I mean, among others, good kindly friends of ours who waste vast sums in unnecessary luxury while the people committed to their charge can obtain neither the cleanliness nor the privacy of swine."

He paused. He had been accused of violent and strong language in his denunciations. He decided that it would not harm his son.

100

"People talk of my mixing with 'dangerous classes.' Indeed! Dangerous classes, Francis, are lazy ecclesiastics of whom there are far too many, and the rich who do no good with their money!"

He returned to the question. The two were sauntering now, stretching the distance between themselves and the others. "As for the Tractarians, what do you know of them? I should think a good Evangelical like your rector might have mentioned them in Catechism or Religion classes?"

"Occasionally, Sir. They are named from the Tracts in which they set forth doctrines contrary to the teachings of the Church of England. They are also called Puseyites after one of their leaders, Dr. Pusey of Oxford."

"Who is a distant cousin of mine. Did you not know? A godly man for whom, humanly speaking, I entertain much affection. And there are many such. But I loathe their doctrines and regard their growing influence in the Established Church with horror. Some have already gone over to Rome. I would all had, for I regard a convinced Papist with more respect than these men, who hold ordination in the Church of England and repudiate, as I heard Mr. Ward say in Oxford, not one doctrine of the Roman Catholic Church, and set aside the Thirty-Nine Articles to which they have subscribed. They would bring us back to forms and ritual; they deny the right of private judgment and the sole authority of Scripture; they fail to declare the doctrine of Salvation by grace through faith; they practice auricular confession as essential and teach the substitutionary doctrine of the Mass; they set up again a mediating priesthood instead of proclaiming the priesthood of all believers—" Ashley remembered his son's age but, as he paused, the young eyes met his, not puzzled and evidently waiting for more. "We can discuss their tenets again. But to your question: they detest me because of my share in presenting a Petition to Oxford protesting their teaching there. It was announced in France recently that seven college chapels at Oxford were in readiness for High Mass to be performed on their altars! Shades of Ridley and Latimer! Also they dislike me bitterly for other reasons. They were, on the whole, active in opposition to our setting up a Bishopric in Jerusalem: first because they claimed there already was one—that of the Roman Church— and secondly because we worked in conjunction with the Lutheran Church in Germany—heretical because a product of the Reformation. And finally—" Father and son paused, looking down to the pier to finish the conversation— "they and many others disapprove that I work with Dissenters, both ministers and laymen. And in that attitude," admitted Ashley, "but for the grace of God, I should still be agreeing with them."

"You mean you usen't to approve of Dissenters. But you do now?"

" 'Approve' is not the word I should choose. There are thousands whom God 'approves' and my approval matters little. We are creatures of prejudice,

101

Francis, and one of the hardest things for us to do is to let God deal with our prejudices. God forgive me, I voted as a young M.P. against the repeal of the Test and Corporation Acts! I was twenty-five when I was astounded to find that a book which opened my mind, as to a flood of light, was the work of a Dissenter."

"But," said Francis with an obstinate set to his chin which was again absurdly reminiscent of Minny, "shouldn't there be one Church? And wasn't it the Dissenters who made the Government withdraw the scheme for free education of poor children? I remember because you made your speech about it just before my birthday and people were still calling and congratulating you on it. And I couldn't understand why you referred to it afterwards as another failure. But wasn't that wrong of them? To refuse to let all those children have a chance to learn?"

"Even there—as I know by the protests which poured in, from the Wesleyans as well—fear of the Tractarian influence in the Church was to a great extent responsible. And their fears were not groundless though I deplored them. No, I deplore schism and disunity. But I have found a unity possible with those who love Christ which is far more important than fighting about establishments. So often, all the combatants end by getting their share of the nutshell but losing the whole of the kernel."

The swift, appreciative smile which lighted Francis's face left it quickly. "But, Father, they called you a renegade and a schismatic for appearing on the same platform and working in committees with them!"

"Yes. It is sad that so far only one Bishop and, because of the Bishops, no clergyman in London, has dared to do likewise." Ashley, about to enter the house, faced his son and put both hands on the slender shoulders. He spoke with intense earnestness.

"I conceive myself acting in the Spirit of the Bible and the Church of England in which I was baptized and hope to die. I believe that I am violating no law, precept, principle, or prayer. But if the conduct I pursue be at variance with the doctrine and requirements of the Established Church, I shall prefer to renounce Communion with that Church to abandoning these wretched infants to oppression, infidelity, and crime."

There was a moment before he relaxed his grip and turned. Without a word Francis seized his right hand and pressed it hard in both his. They smiled at each other and entered the house together.

XX

BEFORE THE END OF THE SAME MONTH Ashley became, after twenty years in Parliament, a private citizen. One thing was his to do before his withdrawal: taking advantage of the turbulent atmosphere created by Peel's *volte-face* on the Corn Law, he reintroduced, with freshly gathered information, his Ten Hours Bill. Roebuck, Escott, and his inveterate enemy Bright opposed him; Lord John Manners, Mr. Wakley, and John Fielden, on whom his mantle would soon be cast, supported; the evening ended with the First Reading. The following day he applied for the Chiltern Hundreds, and walked from the House with the extraordinary sensation of being an outsider.

He had predicted to Francis that his action would be misinterpreted. It was. In the House, Protectionists cheered Lord Bentinck's charges of tergiversation, broken pledges, betrayed faith. The Press embroidered these terms with harsh, misleading comments. Outwardly their victim preserved the same calm under attack as under the warm approval of his Ten Hour colleagues and the unalloyed praise which followed his speech of explanation at Dorchester.

Less than a week later an offer was made at which he could not help feeling gratified. A few persons, including, to his amazement, Sir Robert Peel and Sir James Graham, contributed two thousand pounds towards the expense of his reelection. They assured him that acceptance would entail no obligation; but he felt—was it pride or integrity?—that some fettering of independent thought and action was inevitable, and accordingly wrote a grateful but positive refusal.

Not pride but penury, however,—and the grim specter of his still unpaid and interest-accumulating debt for the election expenses of fifteen years before—made him decline the next proposal to fight the County Purse, which was backing a Protectionist candidate in Dorset.

But there was no question of leisure. Wherever he turned, Chairs and speeches faced him. Misrepresentation of his motives in resigning from Parliament made a tour through the industrial districts imperative. So to Manchester, Preston, Ashton, Bolton, Oldham, Bradford, Halifax, Huddersfield, Leeds, and back to London, in—barring Sunday—as many days, with inspections, meetings, and speeches at every place . . . "the pertinacious, unwearied revolution of a steam engine," he thought, except that he was not unwearied. He found it monstrous, difficult to make a fresh speech every night, and to Minny he described his speaking as "sticky" in spite of the general enthusiasm and approval of the operatives. It was difficult especially

103

to "soft sawder" the masters and yet encourage the workers; in an effort to be conciliatory to avoid all exciting topics; in order to attain the desired end, to leave out, in fact, all the stark reasons for it!

There was some satisfaction, on his return, to read an address composed by the Assembly of the Free Church of Scotland in praise of his efforts for the poor. It served briefly to invigorate him for the anxious period of waiting while the Second Reading of his beloved Bill hung in the balance, evoked the determined opposition of the Government, and, in spite of warm espousal by Lord John Russell and a brilliant oration by Macaulay, was defeated by a small majority. During the debate Ashley hung around restlessly in the lobby. To sit silent under the gallery and hear points raised which only he could—but might not—refute, was too painful.

But he seemed to have more business than when he was a Member. Chairman of the Lunacy Commission, he had to make repeated visits to smaller and larger asylums, to particular cases drawn to his attention and often requiring days of examination and inquiry. Now that afternoons and evenings were not taken up in the House, he set himself to another investigation for which he had long tried to make time. Four years earlier he had helped to found the Laborers' Friend Society. Two years after its founding he had been chairman of a meeting called to rename it "Society for the Improvement of the Laboring Classes." As a result of his speech, which received wide favorable publicity, the Prince Consort had accepted the Presidency. The living conditions of London's poor which Ashley had uncovered—dredged up would, he felt, be a better word—were appalling; but so far little had been done to improve them. Now he began a series of walks through Broadwell, Lambeth, St. Giles, and Whitechapel, entering one wretched house after another, controlling the nausea which almost overcame him at the filth and accompanying stenches. He knew that his arrival, like that of a being from another world, excited notice. His concern was so heartfelt that it did not occur to him as strange that he was not resented, that people spoke freely to him, that children clustered around him wherever he went. His companions of these perambulations, Dr. Southwood Smith and Morrison of the City Mission, silently remarked it; though far less removed in social status than he, they felt and evidenced a constraint in visiting, in talking, in accepting occasional pitiful and repellent hospitality, quite different from Ashley's immediate and apparently effortless communication. He shrank from nothing and often shamed them, by his assumption of their equal willingness, into exploring places from which they scarcely expected to emerge alive or uncontaminated.

Goaded by his discoveries, he addressed an influential audience at a meeting of the Society with an account designed not merely to startle but to impel action. That action was the erection of a Model Lodging House as the first step towards the demolition of places which his most powerful language failed to describe: "alleys choked with squalid garments and sickly children . . . pavement, if any, broken and bespattered with dirt of every hue . . . rags and bundles stuffing the window panes of the houses, passages blackened by the damps arising from undrained and ill-ventilated recesses . . . in a hostel offering 'Lodgings for Single Men' . . . the *parlor* measures eighteen feet by ten. Beds composed of straw, rags, and shavings are arranged all in order—but not decently according to the apostolic precept. In this room there were twenty-seven male and female adults and thirty-one children, with several dogs (for dogs, the friends of man, do not forsake him in his most abandoned condition); in all, fifty-eight human beings in a contracted den from which light and air are systematically excluded. . . . In the upper room, measuring twelve by ten, six beds hold thirty-two individuals (these bearing little resemblance to Alexander the Great, Cujas the lawyer, or Lord Herbert of Cherbury, whose bodies, we are told, 'yielded naturally a fine perfume') . . . up an ascent more like a flue than a staircase, four tiny compartments are all full.

"It has been asked once, 'What is the best method of protecting against depredation a barrel of small beer?' The answer was 'Place alongside of it a barrel of strong.' On this principle the Society has determined to act; and we shall now sketch the triumph of the superior barrel."

This address, condensed into an article for the *Quarterly Review*, roused interest in a wider public, as did an article on the children for whom Ragged Schools were designed: "bold and pert and dirty as London sparrows but pale, feeble, and sadly inferior to them in plumpness . . . in Lambeth and Westminster especially, the foul passages are thronged with children from three to thirteen. Their appearance is wild; the matted hair, the disgusting filth that renders necessary a closer inspection before the flesh can be discovered between the rags . . . visit these regions in winter and you are shocked by the spectacle of hundreds shivering in apparel that would be scanty in the tropics, many are all but naked; they line the banks of the river at low water seeking coals, sticks, corks—for nothing comes amiss as treasure-trove.

"Many a pestilential search and many a sick headache will prove to the disgusted enquirer that a large proportion of those who dwell in the Capital of the British Empire are crammed into regions of filth and darkness; here they are spawned and here they perish. . . . We penetrated alleys where air and sunshine were never known, the walls damp and slimy; flowing before each

105

hovel a broad, black, uncovered drain or a stagnant pool; touch either and the mephitic mass will yield up its poisonous gas like the coruscations of soda water. Some few have a common bed for all ages and both sexes; but a large proportion lie in a heap of rags more nasty than the floor. Happy the family that boasts a single room to itself and in that room a dry corner." And in praise of the Ragged School teachers, "Ladies and gentlemen who 'walk in purple and fine linen and fare sumptuously every day' can form no idea of the pain and the toil which the conductors of these schools have joyfully sustained in their simple and fervent piety. . . . Surrendering nearly the whole of the Sabbath, their only day of rest, and often, after many hours of toil, an evening in the week, they have plunged into the foulest localities, fetid apartments, and harassing duties. We have heard of schoolrooms so closely packed that three lads have sat in the fireplace, one in the grate with his head up the chimney; frequently the female teachers have returned home, covered with the vermin of their tattered pupils. All this they do without hope or recompense, of money or of fame; and many a Sunday School teacher will rise up in judgment with lazy ecclesiastics, boisterous sectarians, and self-seeking statesmen. God has made these children immortal beings and no system will receive His blessing that does not recognize their equality with ourselves."

But in addition to speeches and such articles—by the proceeds of which he paid the expenses of a Ragged Evening School in Romsey—he wrote innumerable letters seeking to raise money from the wealthy for the beloved projects, on four of which he had circulars printed at one time. The contrast between fifty pounds from "the richest man in the world," the five refused, on plea of poverty, from one of his friends, who was spending four thousand on a ceiling preparatory to entertaining the Queen; and the thousand pounds put at his disposal year after year by an unknown Evangelical, Miss Portal, or the hundred regularly given by an equally unknown Mrs. Kennedy of Exeter, struck him as incongruous. He went in person to wealthy homes in Lambeth and Southwark, praying the occupants to support a Ragged School in their district; and drew barely twenty pounds from twenty homes with an estimated income of two hundred thousand. He seemed to write to the four corners of the earth and brought in two hundred pounds where he had calculated on five hundred. At his Ragged School meetings, collections always fell short of demands and often of the expenses involved. The influence of which he heard so much seemed nonexistent to him when, at seven-tenths of the meetings at which he presided, the attendance reminded him of the scanty stalks of grain in Pharaoh's dream. However he asked himself one question: Is the cause right or wrong? If right he must continue in it and trust God to prosper it.

Meanwhile the Ten Hours Bill was to be presented in the next Session and Ashley found himself laboring as hard for its success as though he were still in charge. Another tour of the manufacturing districts enabled him to supply John Fielden with the latest facts, for enemies of the Bill were sure to pounce on last year's evidence as out-of-date and worthless. And when in the Session of '47, the long process of Parliamentary procedure from late January ended with its final passage through the Lords in June, his joy was deepened by the gallant rallying—how different from the earlier sessions!—of the bishops in its support!

Even the croaking of a Member for Glasgow who met him in the Lobby, "The mischief you have done is incalculable. If you are alive in three years"—was there a note of hope in his voice?—"you will be the most unhappy man in the Country," could not diminish his elation.

The summer after he quitted the House, Minny insisted that they go to Switzerland and Germany, pleading her own health as there was no other way to make him consider his. Ashley had long since renounced his wistful desire to lead the life of a country gentleman; but his concept of duty did not entail the sacrifice of family relationships. Cheerless memories of his own childhood were not needed to stimulate the delight which he took in every one of his children—he never got over a faint amazement at his ample paternity—and the care over them which he shared with his wife. He recalled the bleakness of a home which his parents' frequent absence made more tolerable than did their chilly and irascible presence. His boys should never, he had determined, find him too preoccupied to feel for their concerns. He had often snatched moments while sitting in the House to write them at school, involved them in his projects when they were willing, and planned vacations and expeditions.

So now they took the four older boys to the Continent. He walked with them and read and commented pithily on the sights they saw, whether the dungeons and oubliette in the castle at Baden, the monument to Marshall Saxe in Strasbourg, or the "dried Count of Nassau and his daughter," as he called the four-hundred-year-old carcasses on show there. After less than a month they were forced to return by Maurice's frightening and unaccountable languor; but their forced return was brightened for him by reunion with the smaller children who had been left at Ryde.

The following Easter vacation, as Minny's labor was approaching, he took the children in his personal care to Brighton. When she was delivered of their ninth child, a fourth daughter, he tore himself from her after a week to visit the children. He tore himself from them—five-year-old Mary clung and would not leave him—to return to his darling, for she was uneasy to be alone in what both felt to be a dismal silent house without "the kids." On their return to London he took the boys to hear Faraday's lecture on astronomy; went to install Francis in Dr. Butler's house at Harrow; walked in the Park with Lionel and Mary; interviewed a succession of young men to find a suitable tutor for Anthony. On holidays he found himself elated or depressed in direct proportion to the number of children they took with them ("to Ryde with all the kids") or left behind (Galloway House—"the children haunt me. I cannot endure absence from them"). It was good that such moods lifted quickly as long as Minny was·with him. Her health suffered less from nine confinements than from the fogs of London. But the sight and smell of her beloved sea usually effected a swift cure.

Fortunately for her, the Palmerstons' affection, the social life of Cambridge House, of Broadlands, of Panshanger, made up largely for the economies which their increasing expense levied upon an unincreased income. Rugby for Anthony and Harrow for Francis took four hundred pounds; nurses, tutor, governess, and Ashley's mounting and irreducible charities made further inroads. Prince Albert's admiration of Ashley's work ensured the continuance of Royal favor. So invitations to Windsor, Osborne, and the Palace, although each visit increased Ashley's thankfulness that he had been spared a place about Court, kept them in the milieu to which they had been accustomed from the days of the Regency. Minny still was at home in it with quasi-political chatter and international gossip. She was, in fact, a source of considerable and valuable information to her husband; and conversation with her after her sallies into the social world, with or without him, never lacked spice.

It was any interruption of their family Sundays that Ashley found most trying. The Queen before her marriage had played in the corridors at Windsor with Anthony and Francis. She approved the upbringing of the Ashley children and occasionally summoned one of suitable age to play with hers at the Palace. But when Lionel was once invited on a Sunday afternoon, Ashley allowed him to go from pity for the "amiable, secluded, moped-up, overworked, little Prince of Wales," but courteously requested her Majesty in future not to intrude on their Sundays together. Only illness ever prevented Minny from taking the Sacrament with him, and after the children's bedtime, their evenings of reading and talk were guarded by both from intrusion. The amours of other women in their circle, less frequent and more discreetly conducted now than formerly with an eye to court censure, the affaires of other men, the casual, cynical speculation on the parentage of various members of families: these might have belonged in a different world.

Yet there were solitary reaches of his being, a brooding introspection, which he could not or would not inflict upon his wife. Years after his marriage he had resumed his diary; but what had been a recommended discipline for keeping account of forgettable events became increasingly more: a safety valve for the intensity of feelings kept publicly in check; a score in which he beat out the music of his swift impressions and slow thoughts; a breviary of his daily prayers; a confessional through which he sought the release of assured absolution. Here he recorded not only the succession of daily activities, personal, social, political, but his own comments and, more particularly, a chart of physical, mental, and spiritual experience.

This record eased the strain of repression since much of it would pain or infuriate Minny if communicated to her. She never could *bear* his self-depreciation, his conviction of poverty as a public debater, and of recent years as a social figure. The truth was that most of his life, all his real interests, now lay in so different a sphere that he never attended a fashionable dinner party without being convinced that he was inferior to the whole company. The witty, often brilliant, conversation on books, music, affairs, flowed past him. Once a constant reader, he now looked at a book "as a donkey looks at a carrot and like the donkey was disappointed." Unlike the donkey's, *his* time was preempted by correspondence, chairs, engagements on behalf of the needy. These were not suitable subjects for conversation. And he felt— Minny thought absurdly, but was silenced when Lady Grey remarked one evening that he had lost all his former spirits—that he had lost, too, his vivacity and imagination.

He could not, as she did, lose himself in the occasion. Dining at the Palace, he was appalled by the amount of ornamental pastry—as much ornament as on the towers of the Houses of Parliament! To carouse on superficialities when famine stalked in Ireland and when, a stone's throw away, Londoners eked out an unspeakable existence, made society painful to him. Guest at a shooting party at Frognall, he asked himself if it was wise or right to expend so much money on such things; less tactfully he asked his host the rate of wages and the house-rent for one of his workmen. Even relaxing in the pleasant hospitality of Broadlands, he found himself estimating that the mere waste of food and fuel in every such large establishment would feed and warm fifty families. The thought haunted him especially in winter: the luxurious recklessness of "easy" people who burned and ate as though no one wanted fire or food but themselves!

Was such vicarious pain more self-indulgence? he wondered. At least he tried not to inflict it on others. And he tried not to judge. He knew from experience how difficult it was to make servants economize. His own had grudged their share in the day of fast and humiliation when the savings on the house-books went to the Irish relief fund. He himself had taken some bread and cocoa in the morning and the same in the evening but interdicted only meat and puddings from the household menu. But they had grumbled freely, and still more when he forbade the purchase of potatoes because of their scarcity. "It's all right for my Lord and Lady; but poor servants should not be refused their little comforts." Ashley marvelled at their lack of feeling for their poor brethren. He had no illusions about the innate virtue of any class!

The question of his return to Parliament hung fire for over a year. Then a deputation from Bath offered to pay all his expenses as candidate against his old antagonist, Mr. Roebuck, who had held the seat for fifteen years. Prospects, scarcely fair to begin with, gloomed as opposition strengthened. It was an unexpected slap in the face to have Lord John Russell candidly admit to him that the Government's first choice was Lord Duncan, their second, Roebuck. The Press, except for the *Standard, John Bull,* and *Britannia,* were against him. The *Times,* the *Bath Journal,* the *Spectator,* the *Morning Chronicle,* vied in derogatory contradictions: he was—somewhat to his amazement—accused of "sneering at Protestant principles, half-Puseyite, half-Papist;" listed as a mountebank with the notorious minstrel Mr. Cochrane; called a "tool of the present ministry" and "a pretty fellow who resists all improvements." Even *Le Journal des Debats* in Paris charged "the Apostle of Philanthropy in detail" with "indulging in personalities and a bitterness of language not understood in France!"

Ashley, like King Hezekiah in his difficulty, "spread it before the Lord" and went his determined way. Capital arrayed on Roebuck's side poured thousands into display. Ashley refused to allow banners, processions, music, or ribbons, nor did he ask a single vote. During the week which he spent in Bath before the nominations he walked about freely, though once mobbed and once struck. By advice he did not go unattended, since there were rumors of men hired to accuse him on oath of offering a bribe, if they could find him speaking to anyone without a witness.

So it was with surprise that he found the crowd at the hustings good-humored, except for a score of paid hecklers; that the freethinker Roebuck's speech contained few of his previous terms: "subservient tool," "miserable helot," "sovereign contempt," and, of course, "hypocrite;" that towards the end of his speech, cries of "Ashley forever" became frequent; and that, when the votes were taken, he was at the head of the poll, well above Lord Duncan, and almost two hundred above Roebuck.

The justification of his person and his principles in the mode of electioneering cheered him through his anxiety at the state of Ireland, through his incredulous tension at the unrealized belief of his friends that he might be sent for by the Queen to form a ministry during the government crisis that

110

November, through his unceasing labors on the Lunacy Commission. When after fright, dejection, and a sense of failure, his first speech, during the debate for the admission of the Jews to Parliament, received prolonged praise as "clear, logical, powerful, closely reasoned, masterly"—he could not see why, almost felt as if people were making a joke of him—he closed the year with fearful optimism.

XXI

"How STUNNING, FATHER. Absolutely stunning. Going to sea! How perfectly jolly."

Ashley looked at his son with a mixture of pain and relief. Accy's reactions were never predictable except when he was the recipient of a gift, but there was no doubt that his father's announcement had delighted him. The handsome, amiable young face, so anxiously scanned, so thoroughly known, its expression alternating from indolent vivacity over a new neckcloth or an accordian, to polite imperturbability under question, advice, or rebuke, was now aglow. The morning sun, striking across it as they strolled along the Royal Crescent towards the Circus on their way to the Abbey Church, could have disappeared and the impression of sunshine would have remained.

"You will be away a long time, Accy, once your ship sails. Three years."

"Think of South America! And Australia! What is the ship's name, Father? Oh yes, the *Havannah*. Do they know yet when she's due to sail?"

He need not have feared, thought his father, that the idea of separation, which struck such a chill to his own heart, would dim the brightness of the prospect for the boy. Love of home was his chief—in Ashley's more pessimistic moments he feared his only dependable—virtue. But his mind was like a mirror, retaining an impression while the object was near, becoming blank when it was removed. And the near, the immediate object, as usual, was obliterating everything more remote.

"When shall we buy my uniform, Father? What will it be like? Shall I be called Midshipman? Midshipman, the Honorable Anthony Ashley Cooper?"

Clothes, of course! It was less than two weeks since he had been billed for seventy-five pounds for Accy's clothes after giving the boy forty pounds towards settling the debt. He controlled a sigh.

"We shall see about your uniform when we go back to London. Portsmouth, I think, is the place to purchase. I dread telling your mother, Accy."

This will tear her apart, he said to himself. Minny had been unwell with a cold, too unwell to accompany him on this journey to address a meeting in his Bath constituency. He had brought Accy along to keep him out of mischief in London and to try—as he had done before the election and on his last tour of the mills and factories—to awaken his interest and to instil a sense of responsibility. His hopes were fleeting but persistent. And it was a chance meeting in the Pump Room with his friend, Captain Price, that had led to his decision about the boy.

"Oh, Mama will be ever so pleased," said her firstborn airily. "I shall write from every port and give her all sorts of exciting news. Wait till old Edy hears, and Francis. Mice wouldn't like it, of course, and Francis would sooner stay at school. But Edy will be mad keen to come too. Is there gold braid on the coat, do you think? How long will it take me to become a lieutenant?"

I wish I could be as sure of my darling's feelings, the undercurrent of Ashley's thought ran on as he gave perfunctory answers—Accy did not really require replies nor pay much attention to them, for the same questions recurred as they walked and he rattled on. Men cannot feel as women do. We take things in the gross, they in detail. So if his long absence seems too dreadful for me to contemplate, how will his mother bear it?

"The question is rather what we shall do if he remains?" Minny, still pale from recent influenza and shaken after Accy's exuberant news-breaking, surprised her husband, not for the first time, by her straightforward practicality. "He is well into his seventeenth year and we have been assured that there is no point in leaving him at Rugby any longer—no remove for two years! If you obtained a tutor who could manage to prepare him for Oxford, what would he do at Oxford? Consider what reports all his tutors have given us. According to Mr. Hames, he spent most of his time at Sandfield last month, when he could be found at the lodgings, thinking up excuses for postponing lessons! He has no taste for learning." The subject of the discussion had dashed off to tell his brothers and sisters. Vacation was nearly over and he would be gone long before Francis came home again for Easter.

"No. And the University would give him ample liberty for the one pursuit in which he is not apathetic. He would be as far removed from our influence as in New Zealand, and would spend his time at the turf, the green-room, the gambling table."

"Sending him abroad would be even worse. No, whatever you decide, the next two years in England would be a loss of time and money. At eighteen he will be more set in his idleness than he is now. I'm not excluding our prayers for him, Ashley dear." He had come to fetch her from Broadlands and she had been gazing over the frozen lake from their sitting-room window but came over to the settee beside him when she saw the distress of his face. Not for the first time she was the comforter instead of the comforted. "I believe and we shall go on praying, 'continue instant' as you say. But—"

"Was ever more care expended on any child? Well, perhaps this will be the channel of God's answer. Of all services the navy is the most likely to infuse the desired qualities. He will be removed from 'man-about-town' temptations and placed under control and discipline. Perhaps I had no right to form bold hopes and designs for him—that he should complete much in the House of Commons and become a model landlord."

"And who knows that he will not?"

"True. At sixteen I showed little inclination to exert myself. Nor did I really apply myself to work until I went up to Oxford." He did not mention that without exerting himself he had won several prizes at Harrow; and repressed the recollection of yearning for his parents' approbation, and of the indifference with which they had packed him off to Yorkshire and apparently forgotten him for two years.

Certainly there was no question of forgetting Anthony. A train of bills and complaints would keep him in mind even if the exasperated affection he inspired were less. He had a remarkable quality of putting everyone in a constant fidget, exciting all affection, giving no comfort. The next two months required a series of Anthony services superimposed on the full calendar of his father's duties: a day to Portsmouth and back for the purchase of a uniform; another to Sheerness to enter him on the *Havannah,* there to meet and be reassured by his liking for Captain Harmingham; calls, enquiries, correspondence, to find and engage a suitable Chaplain for the ship; Anthony's confirmation in the Chapel Royal by the Bishop of London; a week later the boy's first Communion in St. Saviour's, Chelsea.

Meanwhile all Europe was in ferment. Almost overnight, Revolution in France drove Louis Philippe to England. The provisional government declaring "France for the French" expelled all English workmen from their jobs, in some cases at the point of a bayonet. Six thousand refugees, turned out of their homes in Paris and in the provinces, denied public relief, their savings withheld by the banks, claimed Ashley's "spare time." Committees, funds, agencies, raised at his instigation together with Lord Palmerston's cooperation, cared for these unfortunates.

113

"Political Economists and men of the world vote Lord Ashley a bore," commented the *Times*, "but there is none of them who would not rather have twenty speeches from him on Humanity than one circular from Ledru Rollin."

"No thinking man concurs with Lord Ashley," said the *Chronicle* largely, "but it is a very good thing in these days to have a nobleman who brings forward the distress and needs of the people."

It evidently was. Amid riots and disturbances in Trafalgar Square, in Glasgow, in Edinburgh, in Liverpool, his working men, beneficiaries of the Ten Hours bill, remained tranquil. In Manchester alone, several thousands of the operatives enrolled themselves as special constables to keep the peace. But the menace of Chartism grew, with its slogans of "Down with the Ministry," "Dissolve the Parliament," and its plans to converge on the capital early in April in a monster demonstration. It was an inevitable echo of the insurrections which, as Ashley noted, "go off like popguns in Lombardy, in Berlin, in Vienna." The fall of Metternich had about it an apocalyptic finality which seemed to presage general doom. To meet the alarm, the Duke of Wellington was entrusted with the military defense of London, a quarter million citizens were enrolled as special constables, Downing Street was barricaded. Cobden and Bright in Parliament made no effort to repress their republican aims.

Ashley, in committees all morning, in the House in the evening, with a dozen other claims on his time, had scarcely a moment to eat, drink, or sleep. He was daily deeper in financial difficulties and bought nothing for himself for, as he wryly recorded, nine children could not be clothed, fed, and schooled for a trifle. In fact his condition, as Minny protested, approached that of a brat in a Ragged School. But his son and heir, waiting at home for winds favorable for his ship's sailing, began to regret the career he had so joyously anticipated.

"Must I go to sea?" he asked his harassed father, who had at Minny's insistence stopped to have luncheon at home. His voice had the hurt tone, his eyes the wistfulness, which since babyhood had wrung their hearts, even when their heads restrained them from granting his immediate plea. It was significant that neither his mother nor father showed much surprise, and did not answer immediately. Maurice squealed with astonishment.

"Why, Accy! You've talked of nothing beside! And you were so pleased with your uniform."

Accy glanced down disparagingly at his trim white trousers and blue frock coat.

"A career is more than a uniform," he told his young brother loftily.

"Mamma, I met Dick Jervis's brother in the Park today. You remember Dick Jervis who shared my study last year? His brother is an Ensign in the Guards. Now they *have* a uniform—all scarlet and black and gold. And I'd be right here in London, not thousands of miles away from you all—" There were tears in his eyes.

Ashley was silent. That afternoon, almost immediately in fact, he had an appointment with Toynbee to inspect another district of courts and alleys where the filth and misery and savage indecency were tenfold more painful to him because their presence was un-Christian and anti-Christian in a professedly Christian city. The mental image of the pitiful waifs spawned there, contrasted with the physical presence of his petted, complaining son, brought a recurrence of the noise in his ears which had distressed him with increasing frequency for some months. His whole frame seemed to vibrate like a Jew's harp, and a buzzing like that of ten thousand bees made him helpless to do anything but attempt to control his agony. As through a waterfall he heard Minny's bright voice—filigreed silver it called to mind— still bright in spite of rebuke.

"Don't be absurd, Accy. Do you think the time and trouble and expense your f— we have been put to, is to be forgotten at your whim? Even if you had not entered into solemn covenant with the Royal Navy! I'm afraid you have too much time on your hands. You may help Mice and me send invitations this afternoon. We are giving a tea party for the poor city milliners."

That was Saturday. On Monday Lord and Lady Ashley, with Maurice, Evelyn, and Lionel, escorted Anthony to Portsmouth and put him—all smiles and charm and full of promises to write regularly—on board the *Havannah* in preparation for almost immediate departure. Ten days later a note posted off Plymouth announced him as being fearfully happy in shipboard life.

It was like a gleam of sunshine to close an uncertain, stormy day. Out of sight, with Ashley, was anything but out of mind, and his eldest son continued to be a constant object of prayer. Despair at the boy's infrequent writing was occasionally chased by delight at a newsy, affectionate letter, succeeded by a still longer period of silence. Yet there was a much-needed relaxing of tension from the very absence of constant harassment. It was easier to pray hopefully for a son under distant supervision and employment than to have hopes raised and dashed by alternate promise and failure to perform. Accy's father and mother, never at odds regarding their children, were conscious of relief and time to attend to the claims of the other eight.

Maurice, their delicate, thoughtful twelve-year-old, asserted his claim with unexpected force the Easter Day after Accy's departure. Walking home from church he suddenly fell in the street, foaming at the mouth and exhibiting, for the first time, symptoms of epilepsy. The next week two more fits occurred; and, although the doctor said that the evil proceeded from the stomach, not the brain, and that the boy was too cheerful and sparkling for an habitual epileptic, he predicted a suffering and inactive life for him. Evelyn, who had for a long time played elder brother to his senior, gained steadily in maturity. As well as evidencing deep thought and profound concern to help Ashley—he was proud of the title of private secretary which his mother gave him—he provided a certain long-faced hilarity in looking after Maurice and devising amusement for his younger brothers and sisters in their spare time. So the next year when, a term late, he departed to Bembridge school the loss was almost palpable. "The house is dismal without you;" wrote Ashley, "we all feel your absence a real affliction." Meanwhile young Lionel had trouble with his eyes; seven-year-old Mary and five-year-old Constance were taken to Scotland and left briefly under treatment in Edinburgh for undiagnosed respiratory troubles. Vea, entering her teens, was at the in-between stage, pretty, but quiet and outshone by the more boisterous personalities of her brothers.

But the one of his family who gave Ashley the greatest joy and had not caused him a moment's real uneasiness was Francis. Since their talk on the Brighton cliffs the bond between them had strengthened until, apart from his wife, there was no one whose companionship afforded him greater pleasure. What the boy lacked in experience he made up in interest and readiness to learn. A good, thorough student, he won praise and affection at Harrow. His father, still smarting under the almost uniformly bad accounts of Accy at school, found solace in the enthusiastic report of Francis's tutor—both by letters and when he accompanied the Queen on her first visit to Harrow. Less brilliant than either Evelyn or the precocious Lionel, he achieved distinction in his studies by resolute application, and progressed without wavering to the sixth form.

This same application during vacations made him a quick and valuable assistant in any project, but particularly at the voluminous correspondence regarding Ragged Schools in which the boy took great interest. He was also a young, but avid, theologian and never met his father after an absence without a store of questions which indicated the searching seriousness of his private Bible reading and Chapel attendance. He had asked for confirmation at Harrow and took the Sacrament with his parents at every opportunity.

His unfailing encouragement and increasing promise were a steadying reassurance at a time when Ashley felt his own physical resources at their lowest ebb. He had temporarily outridden the storm of political and social vituperation which had vilified his name during the Corn Law and Factory

Bill disputes. But the demanding tasks thrust upon him, in addition to his work and speeches in the House and the burden of his increasing financial difficulties, threatened him with physical collapse.

"You must rest or decay, be more moderate or utterly disabled," said Dr. Latham bluntly, when, after a "not very merry" Christmas, six months of unpleasant symptoms—and Minny—drove him to consultation. "Your over-toil and anxiety and sensitiveness to the subjects you handle have shaken you in every part."

But how to rest? From what to refrain? Ashley, terrified at the prospect of useless inactivity, tried prayerfully to find a *via media*—and kept on as before. The strange sensation of being very long and very light—alternately a telescope and a feather; the feeling of levitation, "as hollow and bright as a soap bubble;" periods when the least application of thought and the smallest excitement made his head and body ring like metal; these he would not allow to deter him from any important engagement. But the dreadful roaring in his ears, sometimes intermitting a week, then returning with increased strength to a daily assault, became his normal state. Even on holiday in Scotland "in good health" the very stillness made the noise intolerable. "God sanctify it, if it is my 'thorn in the flesh,' " he prayed humbly; then plaintively, "I wish that the noise would leave off me!" and frantic under an unbearable onslaught, "Oh God have mercy!"

Meanwhile the looming threat of Charter day collapsed like a pricked balloon. But the Queen summoned Ashley to Osborne to advise on the condition of the poor and the working-classes. The immediate result, Prince Albert's inspection of house after house in the poorest part of London and his speech as chairman at a crowded meeting of the Laborers' Friend Society, was an unqualified success. Ashley, who had bluntly advised the Prince to disregard Lord John Russell's repeated efforts to dissuade him, was glad. He knew whose judgment would have been blamed if the occasion had been a failure. But this was only a minor cause of his rejoicing. Prince Albert's evident sincerity and the excellent speech of his own composing gave a shattering blow to revolutionary sentiment—"If the Prince goes on like this," was the Socialist reaction, "he'll upset our whole apple-cart." And the brightest aspect to Ashley was that perhaps he could trade on this increase of his own reputation for good judgment to win support for other weighty projects.

As, for instance, his scheme for emigration. His proposal to the House that a number of boys and girls from the London Ragged Schools be allowed—as a reward for good conduct—free transport to the colonies, to begin a new and unhampered life there, had the result which so often attended his reasoned and eloquent pleas: there was great interest in the

117

House, much Press approval, showers of letters in praise, a token grant of fifteen hundred pounds; but the labor, the planning, the rest of the expense, left to him and to a small group of devoted helpers.

So expeditiously did they work that a month-and-a-half later he gave a tea party for the first group of happy ex-street arabs. These successful "candidates for emigration" had passed the tests imposed: they were in sound health; had attended a Ragged School regularly for at least six months; they were able to write a sentence from dictation, to "do" simple addition, subtraction, multiplication, and division, to read fluently, to repeat the Lord's prayer and the Ten Commandments with comprehension of their meaning, to answer a few easy questions on the life of the Saviour. They had also been taught in an industrial class, or showed competent knowledge of some handicraft or practical occupation. Now washed and brushed and neatly clothed by funds contributed largely by Miss Portal, Lord Wriothesley Russell, and Ashley's sister Charlotte, they were on the eve of departure for South Australia. That location had been selected for the first trial because of its plentiful opportunities for employment.

From juvenile emigration to adult, from amateur or potential pickpockets to professional burglars, was a natural step. "I'd jump at such a chance," was the immediate reply of a notorious thief, when Ashley's friend, Thomas Jackson, told him of the emigration scheme.

News circulated among others who, like him, visited that City Missionary for advice and help. Accordingly a letter, painstakingly written and signed by forty prominent members of the illicit professions, courteously begged Lord Ashley to visit them. And early in July, the evening after he had bidden his first young hopefuls God-speed, he met a group which showed him what, but for the grace of God through his efforts, ten years more would have made of them.

He could not tell how many men turned to greet him with uncouth enthusiasm as Mr. Jackson ushered him into the room which he had obtained for the meeting, a low, narrow room in the Minories. His own estimate was close to three hundred, but he later learned that the number was nearer to four.

Their dress varied from the black coats and white neckcloths of the "swell mob" to rags clothing half-naked bodies; their state, from the evidently successful to the down-on-their-luck who had not tasted food that day. Lord, what a spectacle! he thought, as he faced them from behind the uncertain wooden table which gave a semblance of parliamentary order to the proceedings, and suddenly realized that one thing was common to them all: when they left his presence it was to go or return to their lawless work.

Characteristically, he had no self-consciousness. That was reserved for those in whose presence he had moved from birth, and whose judgment of him was affected by his departure from their concept of obligation to a caste. These men were his brothers, and he could not repudiate his responsibility as their keeper. It did not occur to him that their crimes, their conduct, their language, made his first action incongruous. He was there in the name of Christ. He reminded them of the fact simply, opened his Bible and read slowly, clearly, without comment, Luke's account of the penitent thief. There was a brief interruption, during which some latecomers, who were not immediately recognized by the doorkeepers, were put through a public cross-examination to make sure that they belonged to the fraternity. Then Ashley asked Mr. Jackson to offer prayer, and the proceedings were duly launched.

"Men, you have the advantage of me," he began on an impulse, "You know who or what I am. You have invited me to come here. I feel we shall talk more freely if I have an equal knowledge of you." He turned to Mr. Jackson, "Sir, can you suggest a method by which I can distinguish the situations, the occupations, of my hearers?"

The thieves' missionary was equal to the occasion.

"His Lordship wants to know the particular character of you men, so that he can deal frankly with you. Those who live by burglary and the more serious crimes will go to this side of the room"—he indicated with his left hand—"the rest of you to this"—he raised his right.

Came a scuffling and shuffling as of a small army rising. When a rough count was made, about two hundred had identified themselves as burglars and serious criminals, and a fierce-looking gang they were. The pickpockets and shop-lifters, as more respectable members of society, were herded to Ashley's right.

"Now at least we are on plain terms with each other," he said directly. "I am here to be your friend, if you wish it and insofar as I am able. But you will help me to this by telling me what I cannot learn any other way: how you live and why you have turned to your present means of livelihood."

Whether it was the unforced courtesy of his address or the evident concern in his honest eyes—perhaps the tall frame, spare to emaciation, and the lack of ornament in his well-made but well-worn clothes—man after man accepted his invitation. The resultant addresses, graphic, picturesque, touching, and completely uninhibited, interspersed by his question and uncompromising but friendly comment, made it clear that these men were dissatisfied with their life and would willingly break away from it. But how?

"How can we leave off stealing? No one will employ us. We're not that fond of dodging about, m'lord, I can tell you."

119

Ashley outlined his scheme for emigration and the entire company cheered repeatedly.

When he asked how many would avail themselves of it, the cries were deafening. Then one man rose.

"But will you ever come back to see us again?"

"Yes, at any time and at any place, whenever you shall send for me," he said instantly and was touched by the deep murmur of gratitude.

Mr. Jackson rose to conclude the meeting. He was interrupted by a thin, poorly dressed youth who had listened intently but taken no part.

"Just one thing, Sir. His Lordship has said we must make a fresh start and stop stealing. That's all right and there's many a one of us would like to. What I want to know is, how are we going to live till our next meeting? I can't answer for the other blokes but I ain't had food today. I must go out now and steal some or starve. What other way've I got?"

Ashley was silent, appalled. The magnitude of his task and the feebleness of his power lay like a weight upon him. His first impulse—to take the man home and feed him, as he had done many another—was, he knew, madness. This was no isolated case. The murmur of assent, the waiting stillness that ensued, indicated that he spoke for many, in some degree, for all present. And if, with impractical philanthropy, he emptied his house of food tonight, what of tomorrow, and the day after? He prayed desperately and was glad that the question had not been directly addressed to him.

Thomas Jackson was not happy with it either. He could not, by conviction, tell them to continue stealing until they could afford to be honest; that would be to limit the power of his God. His own life of self-denial and service among them took all taint of cant from his words. Yet Ashley, blaming himself for lack of faith, was conscious of fearful discomfort when the missionary urged them to cast themselves and their condition upon God in prayer.

"He can help you. He alone. And He will, if you put your trust in Him."

I know it is true, thought Ashley. I know cases of such intervention and provision. But, Lord, these men are not capable of exercising faith, while their bodies are starving. Thou hadst pity on the multitude because they had nothing to eat. That which is natural comes—it is Thy word—before that which is spiritual. Lord, I believe. Help Thou mine unbelief. And strengthen me to help these souls for whom Thy blood was shed.

One of them had risen.

"My Lord and Gentlemen of the Jury," he said, obviously using a term of respectful address which had become familiar, "prayer is very good, I'm not denying, *but it won't fill an empty stomach.*"

"Hear, hear!" came the general response, and Ashley's sympathy was with them.

It did not limit itself to thought. He enlisted the interest of the same dedicated group who had assisted him with his emigrant children. Mr. Farrer, Wriothesley Russell, Mrs. Kennedy, and Miss Portal again were generous. Letters to ship-companies, letters to the colonies, visits to members of the government—he was hurried, hurried by day and by night. But the recollection of that strange meeting never left him: those wild, fierce, timid, yet hopeful faces peering at him through the shadows. And their concern was very evidently sincere, in the efforts they made to see him again and to avail themselves of the opportunities of improvement which the City Mission and the Adult Ragged School classes put in their way. So, before the first of November, thirteen of the same men had set out to begin a new life in Canada. By the next year almost three hundred of the group had either emigrated or found other means of livelihood.

In all this activity, as in his persistent efforts on the Board of Health— another unpaid and unrewarded post—and his scheme to have the parishes of London subdivided so that the masses of neglected poor might be brought within the scope of religious attention, the deep, bright interest of his Francis was unfailing. His hopes for Accy persisted, with little encouragement from his spare though lively correspondence. Gradually and reasonably they were transferred to his second son; and their communion through letters and close association in vacation time became increasingly happy.

XXII

ASHLEY, STANDING at the stone balustrade of the balcony, was reluctant to go in for dinner. It was almost seven and the blossom-scented evening air was as restful to him as sleep. The Park at the end of Brook Street tempted him as always with the idea of a walk instead of an evening's work. May had been an unnaturally cold month till now and a busy one. Chairing and speaking at the May meetings this year had been unusually difficult because of his physical debility; and fees for the previous week of ten guineas from doctors and surgeons did little to soothe his nerves.

A few nights before he had attended the Queen's concert, one of the season's most brilliant affairs. He had been thankful for a night's respite from the noises in his head and had been able to control the trembling in his body, even, he hoped, from Minny. That remarkable woman, in the seventh month of her tenth pregnancy, mingled happily with the guests, supplying the bright occasional conversation of which he felt himself incapable.

He could wish himself less conscious of the same weakness in his public address. His opening remarks as chairman of a stupendous Ragged School meeting in Exeter Hall had seemed heavy and hobbling. After roaring to the four thousand there, he was hoarse in speaking at the next night's meeting, admirably chaired by Prince Albert, for the Servants Provident Institution. But—

The sound of running footsteps from the direction of Grosvenor Square diverted his gaze from the Park and a saffron sky in the west. A man in livery with hasty news—he recognized one of Palmerston's staff—was bringing a message. Ashley signalled to him and he stopped below.

"Message from Lord Palmerston, m'lord. He instructed me to say that some one took a shot at Her Majesty just now—but to say no harm's done, m'lord, and they caught the fellow."

"Stay!" Ashley re-entered the house, ran down the stairs, opened the front door and questioned the messenger, to forestall the chance that Minny hear a garbled and terrifying version from the servants.

As they sat at dinner, he acquainted her with the meager account which the man had relayed.

"She was driving down Constitution Hill after the official birthday celebrations."

"Of course! Fanny suggested that I go but I don't care to be in crowds. Dear, was Fanny with her?"

"If so she was not hurt. Nor was anyone. That much Palmerston was anxious to tell us, for fear we should hear exaggerated rumors."

"Thank God. But why should anyone try to harm her? It is senseless as well as wicked."

"At the risk of sounding sententious I should say that all wickedness is senseless! But you are quite right, Darling. Strange that the profligate George the Fourth passed through a life of selfishness and sin without a single proved attempt of anyone to take it. Whereas this mild and virtuous young woman—"

Minny glanced at him quizzically.

"If I'm not sadly mistaken, you have spoken to me of her Majesty in less flattering terms on occasion."

122

"As when she fails to attend prayers at Windsor, and yet expects the staff to show devotion."

"Or when you disapprove her attitude to the little Prince and her absorption in Albert."

"True. But none of this contradicts my description. And she is the more amazing if we consider her antecedents and—" he was going to say 'early advisers,' but remembering that Minny's uncle was the most influential of them he broke off suddenly. "At any rate, you know that I am an ardent Royalist, my Pet, and I thank God for her escape."

It was ten o'clock the same evening. Minny had gone to bed, and Ashley was engaged in his never-ending task of clearing away part of his accumulated correspondence, when a letter was handed in to him. Scarcely glancing at the address, he broke the seal, expecting further information regarding the Queen; then recognized the handwriting as that of Mr. Werner. The Master of their son's house at Harrow, he had written briefly to acquaint his parents that Francis was suffering from a severe attack of cold and influenza and had been bled. There was, he felt, no great cause for alarm; the boy was having the best of care from Mrs. Gay, the housekeeper, and from the school physician. But as a precautionary measure—.

Francis smiled happily when they entered his room. The sudden lighting of blue eyes, unnaturally large and dark against the clammily white skin, gave his face an ethereal radiance, and Minny faltered at the threshold. It was her only sign of weakness and she fought it down gamely, even when the heat of his hands and of his face under her kiss made her eyes burn with restrained tears. All the boy's failing and fitful strength was in this embrace. He clung especially to Ashley, and for the first time his father realized the power of the bond between them and what he stood to lose.

"I am so glad you have come!" was all he said at first.

"And I shall stay until you are right as rain," said Minny, breaking an emotional silence. "I am here as your nurse. And a very good one too. Now what is the young master's first request?"

"Mamma, I am so glad if you will stay. But the younger children? How will they manage?"

"They can manage very well without me, with Vea and their nurses and Mr. Middleton. You are our chief concern now, Darling. Is there something—anything—we can get for you?"

"I woke feeling very thirsty. But don't bother. I'd sooner have you here. And probably I'll just get thirsty again." But his mother was already out of the room and Francis tightened his hold on Ashley's hand. "Will you read to me,

Papa? Mrs. Gay is very good but she has all the other boys to look after, and I've caused enough trouble through my incaution and neglect. Do you know that she sat up with me all last night? But I want very much to hear you read again."

There was no need to specify the book. Ashley read what he was requested to read—unusual choices for a boy: the seventh chapter of Revelation and the twenty-fourth of Matthew. Francis interrupted with faint but eager questions and heard his father's tentative answers with evident satisfaction. Minny came in with fresh water while he was reading, and afterwards the three prayed together.

Dr. Latham, summoned hastily from London, concurred with the treatment, and ordered a fourth bleeding. The next day Francis was so weak that he asked Dr. Hewlett if he was in imminent danger, and received the grave affirmation with a smile. Until the sixth day of his illness there was little variation in his condition and no reason for hope. It was not an ordinary attack of fever but a positive conflagration. Yet on Thursday a change came and continued, so that when Ashley prepared for his ride back to the city, there was for the first time high expectation of recovery.

Ashley's spirits, always volatile, soared. Minny, usually cheerful, was pensive.

"Of course, I rejoice," she said, trying to reassure him. "But, O Darling, I do it in fear and trembling. He seems so—so ripe for eternity that I feel God must intend to take him. I've never heard, never seen, such calm confiding hope, such readiness. He said to me the first day: 'I fear I shall be numbered among the fearful,' but he seems now to have passed completely beyond fear."

"Yes," said Ashley defensively, "but he is talking of coming home. And planning—bless him—to be of help to me while he's there 'in return for all the trouble and expense I have caused you.' What a boy!"

What a boy indeed, he thought, as the fresh air and the long trot of his horse brought him their customary quieting. How I wish that Accy were as fit for life or death. Accy! He turned his mind, after an instant's prayer, from the gnawing thought that months had elapsed since their last letter, though news of the *Havannah* came to them regularly. The keen, emaciated face of his second son, so recently, so constantly, so anxiously scanned, crowded out the dimmer image, and fragments of their conversation kept recurring:

"Read to me about the forgiveness of sins." Whatever the special cause of his deep conviction that he was totally unworthy of the joys of heaven, his father was grateful that he had been able to reassure him with the free and full mercy of God in Christ Jesus. "Above all," he had urged him to bear in mind, "God *is* love. Human love is capable of great things; what then must be the depth and intensity of Divine love?"

124

"I want to thank you for having brought me up as you have done," Francis had then said earnestly. "I feel all the comfort of it. . . . I owe my salvation to you. . . . Yes, to the grace of God I know, but you were made the instrument. . . .

"What a futile thing a death-bed repentance must be. I feel that I have been reconciled to God, but what could I have done, lying here, to make my peace with Him, if I had not before been brought to a knowledge of the Truth?

"Dear papa, give me your blessing." Ashley had felt, without conscious sacrilege, like paraphrasing John the Baptist "I have need to be baptized of thee, and comest thou to me?", but he had given it. Now it would appear that the danger had passed. Strange—and disquieting, for years had given him a great respect for his wife's intuition—that Minny was not more hopeful.

The near assurance of recovery suffered a lapse that Sunday. It was a day of fearful and agonizing anxiety. Ashley attended the school Chapel service and was amazed that one hundred and twenty boys took Communion. In his day, he remembered, none of them had even dreamed of it. All the rest of the time the parents spent either in the bedroom, or on instant call outside it. Ashley stayed all night. The morning brought a much better account and what the physician called, "symptoms of permanent improvement."

His ride home that night and his visits on the following days were comparatively cheerful. Francis accepted the renewed prospect of recovery as tranquilly as he had faced the imminence of death. During the morning he discussed the Second Coming of Christ with his mother; and with his father in the afternoon the latest schemes for Ragged children and for London sanitation.

Thursday, the last day of May: Ashley, who had suffered a bludgeoning return of noises since the previous Sunday—like a thousand railroads in his head—rode out to the peace of Harrow-on-the-Hill and to the cheer of finding Minny elated and Francis talking with much of his old vivacity.

"See how steady my hand is now," he insisted, when his mother firmly refused to allow him to get up. "I shall be able to write dozens of letters for Papa, once I come home. And perhaps Maurice will be better if I am there to talk to him."

"Steady on, Francis," said Ashley, smiling with pleasure and with relief at a temporary cessation of the roaring in his ears.

"He wants to run before he can walk," said Minny, ruffling the curly hair which looked less like a brown halo now that he was raising his head and moving it with some vigor.

"But Papa has so much to do," protested Francis. "I heard Mrs. Gay talking to the gardener about the cholera. Has it reached London yet? And how can *anyone* oppose your drainage bill?—or whatever it's called. Don't people see—?"

"Don't fret, Francis. Your father will persuade them," interrupted Minny and, to change the subject, "We have been talking about Dr. Cummin's calculations that the end of this age is one-hundred-and-sixty years closer than was previously possible."

A strange consideration, thought Ashley, to cause such evident joy to a sixteen-year-old. But there was no question either of the genuine pleasure or of the reasoning behind it.

"Think of the poor people, the children, who suffer every year—" He pressed his father's hand when Ashley's wince showed how constantly their image was before him—"in spite of all you do, Papa. And multiply it by one hundred and sixty years—and cancel those years out. 'Even so, come, Lord Jesus.' I remember when you first taught us to pray that. I didn't realize then what it meant. I suppose I don't now, but a little more. Mamma," he said with a complete change of manner, "I feel hungry. Do you think they would let me have something more than broth—and gruel? I know I must be thankful for it, but truly I never wish to taste gruel again."

Half-an-hour later Ashley was in Mr. Werner's study. They had discussed the most suitable time and day, subject to the doctor's approval, for removing Francis to Brook Street. Lady Palmerston would send her carriage. Even with the present sanguine reports of his progress, there was no question of his return by the end of term; and Mr. Werner had suggested a year's convalescence and then a tutor to prepare him for the University.

Ashley ordered his horse brought round and decided to glance in at Francis once more. If he were asleep Minny would have told him. In any event he could spare her another descent and ascent of the stairs. The darling would never spare herself regardless of her condition. Ah, there she was—his impulse to save her had come too late.

It was not his wife. Mrs. Gay stood at the threshold, winded and white. He did not need her pitiful gesture and inarticulate sob to take him up the stairs with long unexercised speed and into the room where his wife was standing at the bedside of their unconscious boy. He did not see any one else. And she, without a word, without turning, stretched out her arm as he came, put it around him, and drew him close around her. So, together, they watched him die.

XXIII

"YOUR LETTER," wrote Minny to the Duchess of Beaufort on the ninth of June, "gave real pleasure to dear Ashley and myself in this, our very heavy trial. . . . It would be in vain to say that the loss is not heartbreaking and to Ashley the greatest deprivation of sympathy, interest, and affection, for he was almost as much interested as he is in all the objects in which Ashley loves to work, but daily our sources of comfort become greater from the assurance that he is now enjoying the blessed presence of his Maker, and singing the praises of his Lord and Saviour. . . . My health has not suffered seriously. My nerves are much shaken—that is the most I can say of myself at present. God bless you, my dear Duchess. Ashley begs me to give his love. He is not quite well but I trust that after the effects of the shock are over he will get right again. He has borne this, as you will readily believe, with the hope of a Christian, sorrowing, yet rejoicing. . . .

> Very affectionately yours,
> Em Ashley."

Her husband's assessment of his condition after the lapse of four months was confided to his diary.

" 'The thing that I greatly feared is come upon me;' and the very effect I anticipated from the death of one of my children has been produced. It has left me equal to business, with life and energy and sympathy with important interests as warm as ever; but it has thrown an alloy into all enjoyment. Nothing has its former flavor. Two objects are constantly by day and by night before my eyes: I see him dying and I see his coffin at the bottom of the grave . . . the pain ceases and then begins anew. Every trifle makes me expect some sad intelligence—a knock, a footstep, a letter, an unusual expression of countenance. The truth is that the shock I experienced on being summoned in a moment to attend his death-bed, having left him not half-an-hour in, as we all believed, returning vigor, was far deeper than was then felt."

But this was private. Even Minny, to whom in this crisis he paid heartfelt tribute as a "true, enlightened follower of her Redeemer," was kept, as far as he was able to keep her, from bearing the burden of his agony. In spite of her brave serenity, it did not escape him that she was wasting visibly— "how dearly she loved her precious child"—and they were both upheld by "comfortable" talks about him with each other and with the questioning, grieving children.

So by November she was able to write to the Duchess at Cholmondoley

Castle with some of her former breeziness. That old and constant friend had found an acquaintance who interpreted handwriting, and had sent her analysis of Ashley's, with a kindly impulse to divert his wife: "He is a man of considerable ability and he possesses a very accurate mind; taste delicately refined; there is a dash of sentiment about him, a fine appreciation of the beautiful, and high culture of the arts. He has peculiarly warm and tender domestic feelings and is occasionally rash in making friendships from an unsuspicious and generous confidence of temperament and character. There is a delicate perception of the humorous about him; a little pride of birth. There is a noble, self-denying benevolence in the character which should achieve great things for his generation."

"I am quite amused," Minny commented, "at the character the Lady has drawn from Ashley's handwriting; it is so marvellously accurate. I really think in the smallest details that it is as if she knew him intimately. I much wonder if it is chance or whether there is a regular system? The passage you have marked about being inclined to form 'friendships' easily is to a certain extent true; perhaps friendships may express too strong a feeling, but it is curious how often I have appeared to myself cold and suspicious in suggesting doubts and cautions as to motives, and how reluctant Ashley has been to admit them.

"The other passage 'pride of Birth' is perhaps also too strong but at the same time I think he *has* a strong sense of the great advantages in this country, *if rightly used,* of birth and station.

"We are going back to London tomorrow. We have been staying a fortnight with Ashley's sister, Charlotte Lyster, in Shropshire, where Ashley has been riding, which always does him more good than anything, and I think he is on the whole very well, though I do not consider him quite fit to go to work again which he is now going to do, as he has a measure to prepare connected with the Board of Health regarding Extra-Mural Interments, which will require much sifting and evidence.

"Maurice was better for his treatment at the Hague. The pleasure and excitement of seeing all his brothers and sisters has thrown him back a little. We have not heard from dear Anthony since June—we daily expect a letter, have heard from the Captain that he was quite well last May. Ashley hears from all parts that there could be no better appointment than Dr. Oliphant, a pious man, a good parish priest, the reverse of a Tractarian; it was necessary as consolation for the appointment of Dr. Milman! We are thankful the government has named a day of General Thanksgiving. I hardly say I hope to see you in London—it is so foggy and unpleasant.

Your affectionate friend,
Em Ashley."

Events of the period between the two letters had amply justified both Ashley's praise of his wife and his diary entry that he was equal to business, "though mirth seemed to him interred in Francis's tomb."

For fourteen-year-old Maurice, who had loved and admired Francis intensely, responded physically to the stunning blow of his death much as his father did mentally. His fits increased in violence and frequency. By July he had eight in a single day. One of these occurred when Ashley was walking with the younger children in the Park. He sent the others away and sat beside the boy as if he were just lying on the grass. When the spasm passed, he was able to help him walk by degrees across the leafy stretches of Park Lane and the short distance along Upper Brook Street to number forty-nine. Then Vea began to sicken, and the doctors recommended a change of scene and air. Fortunately her uncle William Ashley and his wife Maria were on their way to the Hague for a holiday and offered to take the children for medical consultation there. The other children were sent to Tunbridge Wells for Minny's confinement. On the eighth of August, with her customary ease of delivery, which, however, seemed miraculous in view of recent strain, she gave birth to a son.

Ashley, going down to take the news to his kids, found eleven-year-old Lionel so sick with stomach disorder that he was fearful to tell his wife. Little Mary presently caught the sickness and, when Minny joined them a month later, the baby also developed alarming symptoms. Mercifully the lesser sicknesses passed. But the consensus regarding Maurice—that if he were separated from the family, and had no study or society, his health might be improved by the age of twenty—faced him with the sad prospect of an uneducated and narrowed life. The boy's game spirit almost broke their hearts. When he found himself stammering badly, he tried to disguise his inability by singing his sentences and pretending it was a joke.

Vea's weakness continued in spite of the treatment of special physicians. Ashley, adding hundreds of pounds for medical expenses that year to his already large indebtedness, noted that hers alone mounted to three hundred.

"Fears within" were assisted by "fightings without." He endeavored in July to obtain further grants from the House for his Ragged Emigration programme and failed; but the publicity given by the Press increased private support on which the scheme had now to depend. His public failure there depressed him less than reports of bad behavior of a large majority of the pupils in one Ragged School, and of bad conduct in a group of his Emigrant girls on board ship. It did not lighten his spirits to pay a visit to Harrow Churchyard and there find the new gravestone soiled and mutilated, a large part broken into slivers. There was no way of finding out if it had been the act of senseless vandalism or of personal hostility to himself. He was grateful that none of Francis's schoolmates, all on vacation, could be implicated. And Mr. Werner's request that friends be allowed to put a tablet to the boy's memory in his House was some comfort. So he duplicated the gravestone and concealed from Minny an occurrence which would have distressed her.

The roaring in his ears and trembling of his whole body were so constant now that no new shock could aggravate them. Two hours of healthy comfortable sensation were so rare as to be recorded with special hopeful thanksgiving in his diary.

Miraculously the cholera, which entered London early in July and raged for two months unabated, did not touch him or his household. Yet during the whole of that time he remained at his unpaid post as Chairman of the Board of Health and worked unflaggingly. Since they spent their time investigating the filthy conditions by which the epidemic spread: the overflowing cesspools, the condemned water-supplies, the crowded unsanitary cemeteries, the intra-mural burial places, it was more of a miracle that he should escape contagion by the disease, which was carrying off steadily mounting thousands. But, though all who could were fleeing the "City of the Plague," he stayed with Chadwick and Smith at their steady, unpopular work.

His efforts to obtain a day of fasting and humiliation for the plague were unavailing, but September seventeen was declared a day of prayer; and from that day, he noted with thankfulness and without surprise, the cholera fell off rapidly. Not until a month later did he allow himself the brief holiday with Minny at his sister's place in Shropshire.

His numbed emotions did not prevent him from feeling it incongruous that Oastler and Sam Fielden should be reviling him as a traitor to the Ten Hours Bill at the very time when, almost incidentally, he began a fight on behalf of the working-man, which was to make him again the most derided and detested public figure in the Kingdom. For in October the Post-Office decreed regular labor for all clerks on Sunday; and Ashley, seeing thousands of workers deprived of their one day of rest, found himself overnight at the head of the resistance. Failure for the moment spurred him to continued effort in the next Session. But his brief triumph over his government, and the success of his resolution—for three weeks Sunday deliveries of mail were halted before determined opposition achieved its repeal—visited upon his head the torrent of abuse and ridicule peculiarly due any conduct which could be tagged as pious. Bigot, fool, fanatic, Puritan, were the mildest terms employed in the Press. "It requires strong shoulders or an ass's skin to bear the strokes," he said ruefully, quite conscious that the latter term was the choice of his foes—"those aristocratic people who missed having their gossip at their country houses every Sunday morning." The letters of grateful joy which he received from postmasters and messengers could not be made public, nor the unexpected reassurance that "no real inconvenience had arisen anywhere." So another brush stroke was added to his caricature as a legalistic killjoy. Ashley's appreciation of style made him concede with wry admiration that a series of sardonic attacks in the *Times* was done with a very clever and light hand. Custom was steeling him to abuse; but he realized how deadly to his efforts well-written abuse could be.

XXIV

THE SEVENTH EARL OF SHAFTESBURY caught himself in the act of signing the familiar A, and practiced the unfamiliar S, feeling strangely self-conscious as he transferred it to a letter. Fifty years old, father of nine children, of necessity a man of city duties and Parliamentary business, he was suddenly in a new world of land-management, farms, rentals, repairs, water-course disputes, manorial rights, for which long expectation had given him no practical training. Even his beloved Saint was different, now that the complications and unknown intrigues of its management devolved entirely on him, who had been never more than an occasional, and recently only an overnight, visitor. He had dreaded his father's death, especially as it entailed his removal to the House of Lords. Yet if it had come ten years earlier he might have faced his responsibilities with the vigor which the last decade had sapped. As might Minny.

A wave of longing for her swept him. She had stayed in London with the younger children, while Evelyn and Lionel came to attend their grandfather's funeral. Nothing could be right until he saw her again, could bring to her bright, wise, penetrating attention the disclosures, not unexpected but devastating, which lawyers and executors had made to him these last few days. Fortunately no woman was less mercenary, less disturbed about comparative poverty than Min. Had she been other—.

The uncertain sunlight, finding the library window, went further and discovered the marble bust standing in its recess. He rose and went over to it, gazing with a transferred surge of tenderness at his wife, her youthful loveliness frozen into marble at the very threshold of their marriage. His strange

131

father—to insist on having the bust made during that halcyon period of Minny's favor with him, stranger to insist on keeping it here during the years when she, with her family, was barred from the house! The rounded shoulders, half-bared by classic drapery, the young breasts, the almost-seeing eyes, the lovely mouth—to her adoring husband less beautiful than the wife of twenty years from whom a day's separation tore him. He put his hands in the cluster of ringlets, then kissed the unresponsive lips. Like a dear ritual the gesture comforted him. He passed a sensitive finger down the slight tilt of her nose as he liked to do with the one which screwed under his touch, kissed the mouth again gravely, and returned to his littered desk.

"It cannot be said that I anticipated much or aspired high, but I find possession far short of anticipation," he told Minny a week later. He had in the interval been up to London by Rail Road, back to St. Giles's, and, after closing everything there for the time, had returned to town. This was the first opportunity to talk with her at any length. Even then it was only after a long and difficult meeting of the Board of Health that he had seized on a spare hour at five o'clock to walk with her in Kensington Gardens.

"You say your father endeavored to make you some compensation for the past? At least he left nothing away?"

"No. And except to my mother—there, I feel it was pride, certainly not love; he would not have the Spencer Churchills say that she was impoverished—and to Harriet, who had had nothing previously, there were no sizable bequests."

"Then—I am not being sanguine, Ashley—but surely there will be considerable revenue from the estates: Dorset, Purton, Swine. Have you not also manorial rights in Shaftesbury?"

"Yes, which, I think, I must sell to the Duke of Westminster. Darling Min, you have lived so closely these twenty years—what do we estimate our spending income to have been? scarcely more than nine hundred pounds—I should be so glad to say that our economies, our pressing economies, were over. And not to spend money on ourselves. Merely to 'provide things honest in the sight of all men;' especially," his voice was vibrant with longing, and in response she pressed the arm on which her hand rested, " 'to owe no man anything but to serve him in the Lord.' But that is exactly my point—and my pain." He broke off. "I seem never to bring you good news, Dearest. And you must be very weary of bad."

"In that case perhaps we should sit down," said Minny quaintly. "Then I can bear it better."

They found a bench by the Serpentine and sat, he gazing into the quiet water and she watching the bent dark head, the tense averted face. Though

132

he had not told her, she knew the signs which spoke of acute physical discomfort, the "roaring in the ears" which seldom ceased entirely but which intensified to an agony at times of stress. His words came slowly though he was considered one of the most rapid speakers in the House. Now he seemed to be rehearsing the facts for himself as much as for her.

"I have debts of one hundred thirty-three thousand pounds." He paused to let this sink in. "One hundred thousand pounds of that is my father's; the rest is mine, as you know—particularly that wretched election debt which has accumulated interest since '32. I believe my father's intentions were good; but all his resources were dissipated. Everyone lived upon him"—"except you," murmured Minny—"and he upon posterity. You would not believe the instances of deceit, of treachery, of embezzlement, which have come to light—too late for redress. His great defect was self-satisfaction, and self-confidence. He could not believe that anything he did could be wrong. So he spent where he would and, when he had no money, he raised it by mortgages—twenty-seven thousand pounds on Dorset, fifty-four thousand pounds on Swine, ten thousand pounds on Purton, notes elsewhere."

"But"—Minny remembered financial matters discussed at home— "surely there must be a good income from the Saint and from the other estates. And there is always timber."

There were things he had hoped to conceal from her. She had an amazing faculty of putting her finger on them.

"I find that my father has sold every small life-hold he could for cash. So income there is cut off for perhaps thirty years." He loved Minny for her silence at this disclosure, and was emboldened to go on: "Also he has cut timber at the Saint to the value of one hundred twenty thousand pounds; so that all I have is the thinnings worth about five hundred pounds a year." A lover of trees, he found their wholesale destruction harder to forgive than the financial loss. "And"—there was a horrid relief in making a clean breast of it—"as you know, by law no money can be drawn from the estate for a year. So every penny I spend, and spend I must, will be borrowed."

"What shall you do?" asked Minny as tranquilly as if he had been deciding between two conflicting engagements. Her husband thanked God silently for her before he answered.

"I shall sell everything I can without impoverishing St. Giles's. It is madness to go on with undiminished landed property for the sake of dignity, and end in bankruptcy. The manor rights in Shaftesbury, the estate in Dorchester, will realize enough to cancel much of the debt. I must sell the plate except for the heirlooms. My father bought it—cousin Barbara has most of the family silver—and it is fit for someone with a clear twenty thousand pounds a year." He did not mention his estimate of their probable income as little more than three. "The house stands in great need of change and repair. William and John and my sisters want it for open house to the credit of the family; Car already has plans which might interest you. But I will not spend a penny which belongs to Ragged Schools or my London charities—nor take it from the improvement of the conditions of the peasantry. There is one source of money which I should feel justified in expending on the mansion since it belongs to the mansion."

"That is?"

"The sale of pictures, many of them bought by my father, who delighted in pictures. You must decide what you wish to keep, Darling, but a fraction of the number, so Lyster and Pilk tell me, should raise the five thousand pounds needful for repairs."

"Well," said Minny brightening, "that is very good. But"—for there was no corresponding lightening of his face—"that is not all. What is really distressing you?"

Ashley raised his head and she saw the look in his eyes—the haunted look, she called it—which was there when he had tramped through the dens of Whitechapel or when he returned from visiting the Potteries or when he heard of some new case of cruelty to his Climbing boys or—

"The whole condition of the estate," he said in a tone of intense feeling in which disgust, anger, and desperation were mingled. "I have had no time to look far. But the few cottages I inspected right in the village are filthy, close, indecent, unwholesome. If the people were not cleanly, we should have had an epidemic. They are stuffed like figs in a drum. And I have criticized others."

"You have had no opportunity to right things," protested Minny.

"Till now. And now no funds to seize it. But I *must*, Darling. I must borrow more money, for if I do not correct these abuses I dare not call others to account. And the pity of it! Vast sums wasted on useless luxuries which he never even enjoyed, or taken in fraudulent transactions by unscrupulous sycophants. Then the church looks like a ballroom. What is called a school is a disgrace—Bright's supporters arraigned it ten years ago when they sought to distract attention from the factory conditions. Worse, there are fifty children, at least, at Pentridge with no school at all. And the vast areas there, at Purton and Woodlands—I must secure a Scripture reader at least for them . . . and for Hinton Martell. The people are as ignorant of God as the heathen to whom we send missionaries."

He did not tell her of his discovery that the "trucking" system was rife among his farmers or that he had ridden over to give the richest and most tyrannical of them an ultimatum: "Either you shall pay in money or quit your farm," he had said, realizing as he did so that the vacant farm would increase his problems. And when Farmer Davis claimed truculently that he had managed his farm without interference from anyone for nigh on a quarter century, he had agreed passionately:

"And I knew your abominable system ten years ago, but I was tongue-tied then, perforce. Now that I am master here I will not allow the poor to be oppressed."

He had won the first round. But there was nothing in the farmer's sullen acquiescence to set his mind at rest. Perhaps he might sell the Edminsham farm. It was in sad need of repair, two miles from the mansion, isolated in the midst of other land, and had no sporting advantages. Then there was the recurrent litigation about the watercourse near Cousin Sturt's property. Rental for the three water mills there barely cleared at one hundred pounds. Sturt had suggested that he would be interested in possession.

He became aware that Minny was waiting in the reposeful silence which always stimulated his thought. Unlike many women she did not give advice if she had none to offer. He tried a more cheerful vein.

"I shall manage. God has not raised us to this position and left us to ourselves. I could wish we could afford—in time and money—to live there. I walked the wide and lovely gardens early the other morning and longed to have you with me. It is just the sudden accumulation of business and responsibility which weighs one down—less heavily though, since I began to talk with you."

Minny's smile reflected the glow in her heart. Her husband's gratitude—he never took her for granted—went far to repay her for being the cause of it.

"Have you decided to take your seat?"

A duck waddled up from the Pond and squatted beside them. The slanting sun burnished the iridescence of its neck.

"Almost. Harrowby writes that my Lodging House Bills will be through the Commons shortly. He suggests that there would be grace and right in my taking them up in the Lords. Nor does the malignancy against me there seem deeper than in the other place."

"Darling, that is not quite fair. Think how many have expressed their sorrow and sense of loss. 'No one can supply your place.' 'You have left a gap.' Mum says Pam reported Sir Robert Inglis's tribute to you yesterday in the House as the finest thing he had heard—and very warmly received. I'm so glad he informed them that when you weren't there you were 'enjoying no luxurious ease—seeking to lighten every form of human suffering.' I think those were his words."

"Yes. Did she tell you of Mr. Williams's attempt to forestall the motion?

'When only five hours is given for twenty bills it is too bad to occupy our time praising Lord Ashley whom nobody blames.' Now that is 'damning with faint praise' if you like. I am sorry," added Ashley, contrite at the reproach in Minny's face. "That was less opposition than I should expect. And Inglis's generous words that my career had been 'Christo in pauperibus' more than compensate. To answer your question and *not* to be superstitious, I feel that Harrowby's suggestion and the conjunction of my Bills may be the sign that there is still work for me in Parliament. But O, so much to do out of it! Which I cannot, will not abate."

"Could you, could you not"—she knew the answer but essayed the question—"while this other business presses, not of your own choosing, abate a little—for a time only—of your city work? With the Board of Health, for instance, where you get no credit, but only blame."

"While hundreds die and thousands live, right here in Tindall's buildings, Gray's Inn Lane, in conditions which cry to Heaven for the wrath of God. I walked there yesterday with Southwood Smith, Darling. Ah, Lord, are we a Christian people? A people at all? It is scarce a question of caring for others. Do we care even for ourselves? Instinct alone ought to make us better."

The duck, not finding the place equal to expectation, wobbled to its feet and departed with ungainly deliberation. Minny too rose and stood in front of him, her mature figure in its conventional mourning at variance with her vivid play of expression as she tried to find the right words. "Dear Ashley, what I wish you to know—only surely you know already—is: Do not worry about me, that is, about position and luxury and the things we cannot afford. What does any of it matter compared with—for instance—our loss of Francis, or our concern for Maurice or our anxiety about Accy? If God answers prayer for him, if we can keep the other children and each other, I want for nothing. You—I am well aware—suffer the anxiety, the embarrassments, the unremitting labor. Mum and Lord Pam see to it that I have all the society I could wish and too much—except your society of which I could ask more. You know you shouldn't kiss your wife in the Park—conduct unbecoming an Earl, I'm sure Her Majesty would consider it. So Darling, remember, I knew when I married you—I was told often enough—that I was marrying a difficult person. And have I ever tried to dissuade you from doing what you thought was your duty?"

"Go forward—and to victory." Ashley recalled the bright assurance of her encouragement almost twenty years before. "No, darling Min. And not only so, but without you I should not have dared embark, and I could never have continued on such a career. If ever a woman was the gift of God's choice and the undeserved answer, far beyond my prayer—"

136

"There, there. I didn't intend to ask for praise. Or did I? But set your mind at rest about me. Remember the *Times'* sneering at your 'restless philanthropy,' and your reply, that if you are rest*less* it's because everybody else is rest*ful*. I'm sure it will rest little enough."

Nor could it. He took his seat in the House of Lords, forcibly reminded of Isaiah's description of the arrival of the King of Babylon in Sheol: "Art thou become as one of us?" A little confused by such comments as: "A Statue-gallery or a dormitory;" "You'll find it very different from the Commons—no order, no rules, no sympathies to be stirred;" and "You must rouse them;" "Give them business to do;" "In some measure popularize the House;" he spoke on behalf of his "Inspection and Registration of Lodging Houses" Bill, which Dickens later told him was the best law ever passed by an English Parliament. Its complement, urging the erection of Model Lodging Houses, was passed by the Lords only to suffer mutilation in the Commons. All his speeches for the short remainder of the Session were well-received, even languidly cheered, whether the majority were with him as in the Jew bill, or against him as in the case of the Chimney Sweeps. When the Queen closed Parliament in early August, the Seventh Earl, wearing the robes of the First Lord Shaftesbury, was the center of "enraptured" interest. His admirers would scarcely have recognized him two hours later as in plain, almost threadbare, garments, he took the Chair of a meeting for a Ragged Dormitory.

Meanwhile throughout the summer he travelled back and forth to St. Giles's with and without Minny and any available children. I cannot live as a hermit, he told himself in extenuation of the added expense. He managed with unwilling diplomacy to get rid of the butler and the housekeeper, who had tyrannized over his father and battened off him, so that he grudged the legacy and annuity which he was compelled by the will to pay. Daily he marvelled at incongruous evidence of his father's fearsome domination of his children and his plasticity in the hands of servants and flatterers. Symonds, the butler, he suspected, had acquired influence and popularity among the young bloods of the village by countenancing gross disorders in the public taproom. Ashley firmly put down the brawling at the Bull by enforcing a nine o'clock closing time. His persistent veto of the trucking system threw a second wealthy farmer into a towering passion in which he resigned his farm. Ashley accepted the resignation and prayed for the swift advent of another and better tenant. Meanwhile the claims of the Great House on attention became pressing so that repairs were no longer a luxury. Rats broke through a wall and invaded the new housekeeper's bedroom. Even an untrained eye could see the danger.

"Tell you what I'll do, Ashley," said his sister Caroline, "if you will let Minny and me go ahead with plans for the house, I'll build you four new cottages. I was talking last week to that man at Christie's. He was quite agog that you had a Karel du Jardin. Italian landscapes are all the thing. Mr. and Mrs. Browning have brought them very much to the fore, I believe. I told him of your grand one signed and dated by Paul Potter but didn't hold out any hope that *it* would be up for sale. The Dutch painters interested him too—van der Heyden and van der Meer and Jan Miel. So you can realize money there whenever you wish. Do allow us. It will be good fun for Minny."

And for me, she might have added. The Lady Caroline Neeld, Ashley's eldest, though not his favorite sister, had grown closer to him during recent years. The three girls—Car, Har, and Char as they called each other—had been driven by the severity and lovelessness of their early environment to a mutual defensive alliance which neither marriage nor separation dissolved. In the days of Ashley's despairing suit for Minny, Harriet had interrupted her own marriage preparations to visit Lady Cowper and plead her brother's cause. Charlotte, the youngest and first married, had made Rowton Castle a home and haven for her family. Perhaps it was her interest in his Ragged Children which had communicated itself to Car, or perhaps it was the heady feeling of moving freely about St. Giles's without falling under her father's forbidding eye and caustic tongue. At any rate it was, both Minny and Ashley felt, a triumph of character that she had not allowed the public shame of her marriage to overwhelm or to embitter her. A wealthy husband leaving his wife quite literally at the altar—though after and not before the ceremony— had been even in jaded social circles a nine-days-wonder. He had successfully eluded all attempts to bring them together by fleeing from one watering place to another and finally to temporary exile on the continent. Ashley and Minny, on their postponed honeymoon tour of Italy with her parents, had come, in the winter of thirty-three, to the hotel in Rome where Neeld was staying; and his departure the following day had been the subject of much comment. Such treatment might well have driven a weaker mind to distraction. But the blood of the Marlboroughs and the Ashley Coopers rose to the challenge. The woman who, in her twenties, was cowed to silence in her father's presence and, in her thirties, was the talk of a town which seldom had a stranger non-sequitur for speculation, refused to allow either gossip or her father's baffled fury to quell her spirit. Joseph Neeld finally bought his illicit freedom—what had persuaded him to barter it in the first place remained his secret—and Lady Caroline found a husbandless marriage, a town house, and independence, considerable improvement on her spinsterhood. She had

138

lived down the persistent report of having given birth to a child in Florence, a report which had gained acceptance less because of evidence than because it alone made sense of the extraordinary circumstances. Fortunately her heart had not been involved and she had soon become able to treat it as a jest, referring in her letters to Harriet to "my Joe" without embarrassment and without rancor. Now in her mid-fifties she had become a partisan of her brother's philanthropy and gave sporadic aid to his charities. Physically she resembled him, the prominent nose and heavy-lidded eyes which were handsome in his face, rather forbidding and unfeminine in hers.

Ashley's face lighted with his customary mercurial rise of spirit at her suggestion. He looked suddenly years younger.

"Car, would you do that? The cottages, I mean?"

"I have named my condition. Minny and I go ahead with the house."

"Yes, yes. If the pictures will pay for it." He winced slightly. On his journeys to Italy as student and young husband, on their two later holidays to the Continent, he had delighted in the art treasures of every city—his early diary recorded his independent criticisms. In London he was kept far too busy to follow his bent; but second only to his delight in the scenery of any mansion at which they were guests, came his interest in its paintings. And latent in his mind, when possession of St. Giles's seemed imminent, was the consciousness that, though small, no mean collection of pictures awaited his will-o'-the-wisp leisure. "If it isn't necessary to put up the Paul Potters and the Van Meer de Jonge I should be glad. And there is a small da Vinci I would leave to the last and the Rubens self-portrait. Oh well," he dismissed the wistfulness from his voice. "Whatever Minny and you decide is best. But the cottages!" His face lighted again. "Car, I cannot tell you what a load it will take from my mind. The world will at least see one good intention—and that is of high importance when, like me, a party has been a great professor of religion."

Evelyn, whom they still called Old Edy on occasion, even though he had attained the great age of fifteen, had come into the room with Lionel on the last words. He scowled—ferociously for him.

"Everyone knows that you are more than a professor, Father."

"Both Houses would profit by a few more members with my son's sentiments," Ashley observed to Caroline, "to say nothing of the daily Press and the *Punch* cartoonists. I'm afraid you are sanguine, Edy. The world passes light judgement on everyone else; the worst criminals are more exempt from harsh criticism than those whom it loves to pillory as 'saints.' And unfortunately, pretenders to piety give plenty of cause by their backslidings and

139

shortcomings. But your dear aunt has saved me from immediate disgrace, boys. And I thank her most heartily—and thank God who put it into her heart."

He repeated the thanksgiving for this clear gift many times during the days when, in spite of his mounting horror at debts, he was forced to add to them. Otherwise he would be shamed publicly, and, still more poignantly, in his own eyes, for rating other landlords on the filthy immoral dwellings of their tenants. Because of his father's sale of life-holds many of these were out of his control, but the discredit and blame—his enemies would see to it—would be his. But where the responsibility was his, more cottages, repairs on the better existing ones, a school for Hinton Martel, another at Woodlands as well as the one already being erected at Pentridge, teachers for them—the catalogue was unending. To live there, he estimated, would cost eight thousand a year.

So he must leave the management of the estate, improvements, drainage, and building, in capable hands. Waters was highly recommended as steward of his affairs. Then he could see by visits that his plans of rewards for care of gardens and allotments, of evening classes for the young men, of cricket clubs in summer with the matches to be played in the Park, and of celebrations like Harvest Home with bread, cheese, meat, beer, games and general cheer, be carried out.

And—understandably—now that he had come into the title, people assumed that he was a rich man and wrote to him in all the fervor of meritorious need, as to one blessed with abundance. Ashley had for years, and deeply against his proud grain, been a mendicant for his causes. He wondered afresh as, in agony, he answered No to worthy pleas, after giving far more than he should out of his borrowing, how the wealthiest men in the world— railway magnates and other millionaires—felt when they neglected his requests altogether. His own pain at refusing brought on attacks of water-brash and what the physician called hysteria. Why must he feel so intensely with every case of distress? Useless to accuse himself of sentimental self-indulgence in suffering. Minny had given him writing-paper with the Greek inscription of his favorite prayer, "Even so, come Lord Jesus," on the envelope and he sent the prayer with every letter. But until that consummation, he could force his mind to accept the incurable mass of human suffering but not—never— his heart.

"Scripture states that there will be poverty," he retorted with heat when a cynical bishop tried "the devil's own trick," as Shaftesbury reminded him, of counter quoting the Bible. "It nowhere justifies in a Christian land a mass

140

of foul, disgusting, helpless, blasphemous poverty which is by no means irremediable."

Fortunately his spirits were as easily raised as depressed, although the
causes and duration of exaltation were not as numerous or lengthy. When
"out of the blue" as Minny gratefully described a communication from a death
bed, they each received a gift of a thousand pounds from an aged clergyman, a
relative of the Lamb family, and later another thousand to be used for the
education of their sons, they rejoiced as if their financial troubles were ended;
and each independently made several thanksgiving offerings for the bounty.

Almost concurrently, the son whose education at Harrow was then their
largest expenditure gave his parents a shock. Evelyn had been, in his peculiar
way, as helpful in assisting his parents as Francis, though more boisterous and
unpredictable. He was, Minny once remarked, the administrative rather
than the meditative Ashley. He had "organized" his brothers and young
sisters into a committee to fold his father's circulars, reported local news items
with understated accuracy, acted as messenger between his parents and the
servants, even written letters for Ashley in painstaking copperplate, assisted
at St. Giles's in the examination and sorting of papers. Always beyond his
years, he had, before his ninth birthday, composed a prayer with precocious
evaluation of his own character and, when his mother inadvertently came on
it, asked if he could use it:

"Give me grace to love Thee and obey my superiors; to govern my
temper and love Thy service; to study the Bible with avidity and care. I beg
Thee, Lord, help me pay more attention to prayers and *not refrain* from going
into the *most filthy cottages* when I enjoy the privilege to be one of God's
ministers." Since then he had not shown the overt piety and love of religious
discussion which had brought Francis close to his father. But his interest was
keen in all family affairs, particularly in his father's political activities . . . and
Ashley, indeed both parents, wrote to him almost as to an equal.

His school record was good—he had gained his name at Harrow the year
before—if not that of a model boarder. Mrs. Rendall, wife of his house
master, complained that he would not take his cod-liver oil! But this defec-
tion of duty and other charges of negligence and carelessness did not prepare
his parents for the news that a "coarse" word, flung out in defiance of a
remonstrance—the actual word was not reported and the original cause and
complications were not clear—had brought on him heavy punishment. The
severity of it, a public caning, ostracism, forfeiture of privileges, seemed out
of keeping with the gravity of the offense. Ashley did not doubt that the result
would be beneficial, but he was always concerned with justice, no less when

his own son was the victim. Accordingly, after ascertaining the facts, he wrote to the Headmaster to remonstrate. Dr. Vaughan upheld his position, and a correspondence, sharp on his side, firmly courteous on Ashley's, ensued.

Meanwhile both parents wrote to Evelyn. His mother's letter, characteristically much stronger than his father's, castigated him for his sinful carelessness. Ashley's rebuke lay in the changed tone of his address.

Before

September 25, 1851.

"Dearest Edy:

Bava writes in high spirits from Norfolk. He likes the masters and boys. We hear that the *Havannah* now arrives at the last of December. I am sorry. I hoped Accy would be spared the follies and temptations of a London season. I fear his easy temper and readiness to yield."

October 22, 1851.

"Dearest Edy:

I saw the kids yesterday. Maurice is fairly well. We had a grand audit dinner before leaving The Saint. The farmers dined in the salon, fifty-two of us. Miss Rose cooked the feast and we had excellent entertainment. All the brats appeared after in the gallery and savaged the company. When you come to the Saint you must see our hollow brick machine."

After.

October 27, '51.

"Dear Evelyn: This will teach you, I hope, to abstain from coarse and offensive language. But you have been severely treated. I shall write to Dr. Vaughan.

You are reckless, volatile, easily betrayed by temptation to be unmindful of your duty. You have a good disposition and a warm heart. Some disgrace comes to me by your use of foul language. Many will say: 'see how he brings up his children.' "

October 29.

"Dear Evelyn:

I am sorry Mr. Rendall still gives you an indifferent character. I am sending it for your inspection. Please return it. This causes great pain to Mamma and me and fills us with astonishment. You promise so fairly. We are quite at a loss to understand. I can hardly believe that the temptations you meet require a very mighty effort to resist.

142

Pray let us know   [a neat touch, and he knows I'll recognize it, thought Evelyn with wry relish] if the gravestone is in good order, unbroken and clean.

Your affectionate father,
S."

The correspondence with Dr. Vaughan—a good man but proud and to a great degree insolent, or so Shaftesbury summed him up in his Diary—reached an amiable compromise. The prospect of Accy's first homecoming in three-and-a-half years superseded it and underlay the busy surface of Shaftesbury's thought with alternate swell of hope and sink of fear. A long letter, hinting at others which had miscarried, was, like all since the death of Francis, tender, unselfish, filial. Two bills which came almost on the same mail alarmed Ashley with their threat of added drain on his slender resources.

XXV

THE HAVANNAH docked at Portsmouth on the fourth of December. Now at last, thought Ashley, he would know. Would his heir bring honor or disgrace, joy or sorrow? The telegram had indicated that he was on his way to London and his parents waited until midnight in expectancy.

It was six in the morning when Ashley, who had not slept, and Minny, who had, were roused to welcome their son.

"Dearest Mamma, Papa!" The vigor of his embrace left them breathless. Subconsciously they had expected the weedy schoolboy who had left and momentarily felt that a stranger had invaded their dressing-room.

"Accy, dear"—Minny held him at arm's length. "Surely you have grown. You look like a young giant."

"Just filled out, I think, darling Mum. See, I'm not as tall as Father yet."

Nor was he by an inch. But the splendid, uniformed figure, the eyes more blue than ever in the healthy tanned face, the spontaneous smile: "there never was such a beautiful creature as our Babkins"—a sentence repeated in her proud young mother's letter to the proud young father came to their minds. Surely their prayers had been answered.

And his whole demeanor buoyed up that hope. "While I am here I am

143

ready to make your wishes my own," he replied simply, when they asked him what he wished to do while on leave. "I cannot say how grieved I was not to be here to comfort you in the death of Francis. I wept bitterly when your letter arrived—so many months later—for my loss, but more for yours. And poor Maurice! Where is he now? May I see him? I feel that I have years—indeed I have—to make up with you."

Ashley was happier that night than he had been for a long time. The whole day had been a crescendo of delight. Accy had brought beautiful gifts for every member of the family, extravagant, his father might have thought, had the idea not seemed ungenerous. He had played with baby Cecil, made himself an elephant for four-year-old Edith to ride; performed sleight-of-hand tricks for Constance and Mary. Serious six-year-old Conty held herself a bit aloof, but nine-year-old Mary trotted around after him like a willing slave. He complimented and teased his "grown-up" sister Vea out of her shyness, wished that Evelyn and Lionel were home, played the accordion and guitar and sang for the children at nursery tea, and protracted the dinner hour until after ten with graphic description and well-told lively stories.

"Darling," Ashley said, dropping the curtain and turning away from the fog-blanketed window as his wife entered from her dressing-room, "I've been thanking God for the change. Have you ever known such improvement? And he is a most entertaining speaker. He inherits your charm."

Minny drew him down beside her to a sofa in front of the fire. A bedroom fire was a luxury she insisted upon, even on less chill nights.

"You forget, m'lord Shaftesbury, that when we met you were a favorite week-end guest at the Royal Lodge, and elsewhere in great demand. Whatever Punch Greville thinks of your philanthropy and religion—and there I fear he's just looking at his own wasted life, poor fellow—he never found you a bore. Nor does any one else. I become annoyed when you underestimate yourself."

"Underestimate? Did you ever know a man to respond to kind words and flattery as I do?" He laughed suddenly, happily. "Remember for instance how my bristles went up at the prospect of meeting a blue-stocking Tractarian in Miss Strickland? And my becalmed spirit and altered opinion when she spoke gloriously of my public exploits? Darling, I'm far too susceptible of fuss and civility. Proteus was stable compared with my vacillations."

"Nonsense," said Minny. "Your spirits rose because you were on holiday in Scotland. I remember your comments on the bracing air and the indescribable scenery. Inverary was like living in the bottom of a teacup with lovely edges, you said—a perfect description, my poetic husband. And you laughed more than—" she broke off.

144

"Than I have since? True. I have not felt much like laughing. Until today at Accy's yarns. Ah, back to Anthony, Pet. After all our fears, to find him simple, dear, affectionate—"

Minny turned from gazing at the fire and gave him a long, enigmatic look. Her lips parted, emphasizing her very slight resemblance to her mother, but she did not speak. She stood up, the full folds of her blue cashmere peignoir flowing from her shoulders, and when he rose, she turned and put both arms around him in a tight, protective embrace. Then she drew his face to hers and kissed him with passion and tenderness. When they drew apart he saw tears in her eyes.

"I love you, Ashley," she said. "I hope—Oh I pray God I may never hurt you and disappoint you."

That was all her answer.

Several days later Ashley thought he understood. Accy had accompanied him to St. Giles's on necessary business. The boy had wanted the whole family to go. When the expense of the railway journey was urged against it as they were all going down for Christmas, he had suggested that they hire a coach—what a lark—which he would drive. Overruled, he submitted with good grace and made a charming chatty companion, full of anecdote, question, and opinion.

His mother had told him of his aunt's tentative suggestions for alterations and when they reached St. Giles's he was aglow with interest. Ashley, who had left the plans, perforce, to his wife and sister, was amazed at his retention of detail.

"You mean there will be a tower here," he said, pacing it off in front of the North room, "and, of course, one to match it on the south side. Then the main entrance will be here—with a grand set of steps—and the Oak Room will not be cut up as it is now. Will the door become a window, Papa, and the pillars be taken away?"

"I expect so. Your aunt—"

"That will make a grand passage room. It will be an excellent house. Shall we have guests for shooting? It is ample enough for large parties. I wish I had not to go to sea again. I'd like to settle down as a country gentleman."

This was an opening for his father to tell him, succinctly and sparing the late Earl's memory as much as possible, of their financial position. In the library, where Accy exclaimed over pictures and furniture, Shaftesbury showed him papers and accounts to document the situation which, as his heir, the boy should understand.

"By economizing and living away, by selling parcels of land which do not diminish the estate, I trust that you will come into its possession in good

145

condition and free of debt." He shuddered slightly. "What I would give to be free of it now," he added in an undertone.

He had no cause to be afraid of disturbing Accy. Over the boy's face, politely turned to him across the desk, had come the glazed look with which he had usually heard parental remonstrance. As his father fell silent, he rose and went again to the great window. The faraway look in his eyes was replaced with excitement.

"What jolly stables!" he exclaimed. "Papa, shall we keep hunters? We have room to keep racers too. We might raise a horse for the Derby, who knows? There's pots of money in racehorses. Finchly tells me his brother cleared thousands of pounds in one year. Of course, we'd have to get a good jockey."

Accy, Accy, will you be childish to the end of your days? thought Ashley, and bit off a dry and cutting retort. He took his son over the gardens, the almshouses, the village, pointing out what had been done, what needed doing, in hope that sight would impress where words failed. After all, he told himself, the boy was not yet twenty-one. It was natural that he should be stirred, after seven years, at the sight of the ancestral home which would some day be his. He had, at least, a feeling for the place. Natural too for him to revel in being saluted by the villagers with his new title "Lord Ashley" and being referred to as "the young lord". After forty years it sounded strange applied to someone else.

The boy behaved well when they visited the cottages too, but his relief when they emerged was patent.

"Phew! Father how do they stand it? Imagine being crowded into a place that small."

"I do imagine it," said Ashley, drily—day and night he might have said. "And that is why I am borrowing thousands from the Hand-in-Hand so that—"

"Of course, they are used to it. It doesn't affect them as it would us. By the way, Papa, when shall we be moving into Grosvenor Square? Before my leave is up, I hope!"

I travelled on the Continent and fell in love with Liebe and danced at Almack's and visited the Pavilion when I was years older than Accy, Ashley told himself fiercely. But I had not his upbringing, the love and prayers which have surrounded him since his birth, his knowledge of conditions of the poor. Unwillingly he tried another tack.

"You live in a world apart in the navy, Anthony. You would be astounded at the growth of democratical and republican talk and agitation in England. Not among people at large but among those who will aspire to be their leaders. Extension of the franchise—a just thing if it were done wisely, but not as they plan it—eventually universal suffrage, and the secret ballot, are their immediate aims. But the grand enemy is the hereditary landowners. At every opportunity the mill-owners and manufacturing and Rail-Road magnates attack hereditary aristocracy. Unless we demonstrate our concern for our people, unless we show that privilege entails responsibility, unless we work sacrificially and untiringly to improve the condition of those entrusted to us, we shall not long be left in possession of our estates—and we shall have brought it upon ourselves."

"As the French aristocrats did, you used to say." Accy's mood changed quickly. He seemed impressed. For half an hour he was sober, asking intelligent questions about the new schools and cottages, though shifting the conversation carefully when the question of finances recurred. Then they crossed the little bridge over the Allen and if the sight of a great trout lying still behind a rock in the clear brown water—for the weather was like May—made him forget the problems of a landlord in excited and reminiscent fishing talk, Ashley could not help feeling indulgent.

So his leave passed in a see-saw of delightful hope and exasperated disappointment for his parents.

At Christmas, their first entire gathering celebration at St. Giles's, he behaved impeccably; took the Sacrament with his parents in the morning; contributed vigorously to family entertainment during the day; showed no restlessness during prayers, when his father included Francis in their fellowship by reading appropriately from the fourth chapter of First Thessalonians; joined in the general dismay when a message arrived to say that Lord Palmerston had resigned from the Government; listened without impatience while Evelyn, with a grasp of events which made him seem the elder of the two, explained the niceties of that political situation.

He was shocked at the haggard and old appearance of Maurice, concerned but obviously ill-at-ease. With his grandmother, his aunts, with Palmerston when they visited Broadlands, he was all deferential charm and winning gaiety.

In London after the New Year, his father took him, through unknown and unimagined scenes within easy walk of the Palace, to visit the inmates of the new Ragged Refuge made possible by Miss Portal's unfailing generosity.

Ashley, who had for days been enduring several attacks of pain in his head, giddiness, water-brash, and faintness, had attended a five-hour session of the Lunacy Commission—he could not give up his work—the previous day, and that afternoon a tea party for one of his Ragged Schools in Lambeth. So it was now with tense anxiety that he watched his son's reactions. Oh for some one to carry on his work, his uncompleted work! Accy rose to the occasion. His attitude to the superintendent and to the children was modest and instinctively correct. His burst of genuine grief and horror on their walk home made his father underline the first part of a recent entry in his journal: Accy, *great darling, much to love,* much to fear.

The fear, in fact, was due chiefly to omissions; to vagueness when his prospects on shipboard were discussed; to evasiveness regarding money matters; to occasional absences for which he never volunteered explanation; to his confirmed habit of smoking, though he confined it at home to his own room.

On the third of February he departed to board the *Britannia,* bound for service in the Mediterranean; on the fourth came an influx of bills for extravagant expenditure, including a demand from one of his messmates for payment of a long-standing loan. And he had assured his parents that all his accounts were settled!

A letter of unlimited contrition at his mother's rebuke for this was balanced by another from the Admiral to Shaftesbury, stating that Anthony was backward in his duties and wholly indifferent. So the see-saw continued.

XXVI

"THIS IS THE LAST EVENING I shall ever spend in this house," wrote Ashley pensively from forty-nine Upper Brook Street on the sixth of February, "I cannot leave it without regret. I have passed many happy useful hours here—certainly more happy, probably more useful, than ever again. I am now in the vale of years. We had outgrown the dwelling. It was too strait for us. But I shall never have any place like my own little room."

He was left alone to mourn, for his children were in the country and Minny, to avoid what she felt would be a dismal evening, had gone off with her mother to the opera. She had begged him to come. "There is no point in your moping at home," she had said, for her almost sharply. He was glad that she could go and enjoy herself. But he felt sentimentally—he hoped it was weakness and exhaustion—like indulging in regret and self-pity. "I am in the vale of years," he repeated aloud.

If he was in the vale of years, his active interests were a steadily rising peak. There was a multiplication of causes which claimed his presence, his patronage, his effort, for their inception and success. Those who wrote to him with requests which amounted to demands and wrote insulting letters if they were not met, would have been astounded to know that he could not afford a secretary and that every answer, as well as almost every appeal, must be written by his hand. Those who saw him walking steadily through the streets, and with apparent aloofness to Westminster and in the chair of the May meetings, and in the reception rooms at Windsor or Osborne or the Palace; even and especially the children and young ruffians who crowded, but never jostled him in the schools and clubs and lodging houses, could not know the agony of spirit which alone forced him to continue despite his bodily agonies. Nor how, he confessed to himself, he would enjoy a ride on fine evenings in the open carriage he did not, would never be able to, afford.

For it seemed a period of frustration on every side. Almost twenty years of labor for the factory hands—and the Ten Hours Bill, cunningly evaded by the shift system, was keeping thousands of children and women at work or exposed to vice during their irregular and unpredictable respites from five-thirty in the morning until eight-thirty, and often later, at night. Several years before, a Government proposal would have corrected this evil by setting six-to-six limits on the working day, but added two hours to the week's total. His proposal that this measure be accepted had earned him, from the leaders of the working-man, the title of traitor, Judas, tormentor, trickster, "our pretended friend." Yet when his father-in-law, now restored to the Government in the Home Office, passed the Bill through Parliament he was showered with praise.

Meanwhile the Board of Health, attacked on all sides, continued its unpleasant, incessant labor to the hour of its predictable doom. Their efforts and success in combatting cholera, providing pure water-supplies and adequate sewers, abating air pollution, and introducing compulsory vaccination, had not made them popular with a populace which disliked interference. On this essentially English trait, those who stood to lose financially by the Board's activity were not slow to make capital. The newspapers took up the enraged cries of Dissenters, offended by the Extra Interment Burial Bill; of civil engineers, whose services had been replaced by more able and cheaper workers; of the College of Physicians, jealous of the success and efficiency of Poor Law medical officers; of Parliamentary agents, mourning their reduced fees; of Boards of Guardians, whose selfishness and cruelty to the suffering poor had been exposed; of water companies and commissioners of sewers, whose methods and plans had been superseded; of undertakers, smarting at

149

the scheme to provide decent burial for the poor at a moderate price. The *Times* referred to the Board as an "arena for noblemen given to speech-making and philanthropy" and again to "noble philanthropic amateurs who know nothing of the state of the people for they never visit them." A *Punch* cartoonist depicted a small, howling John Bull squirming in the firm grip of a caricatured Board of Health, which was trying to wash his face.

The "unpardonable activity" of the Board constituted its sin. Besides, of the three on the Committee, only Dr. Southwood Smith was—comparatively—without enemies. Edwin Chadwick had antagonized many by his dry, incisive manner and his ruthless cutting of red tape. Shaftesbury wistfully recorded of himself that he often urged people not to place him at the head of enterprises. "I am sure on many occasions I do more harm than good. I heard from Scott of King William Street that many of his acquaintances at the newspaper offices refused to give his lectures a notice because the whole thing was a 'Shaftesbury movement.' " He tried to retire from the Chair of the Board but was not permitted.

So when, amid unnecessary cheers, the Bill dissolving the old Board was passed, Shaftesbury gave a dinner party for his unappreciated associates, seventeen in all, and saved his wry comments for his diary.

"Five years of my life and intense labor and I have not received even the wages of a pointer: 'that's a good dog' . . . rewards in the service of the public are like a monkey's—more kicks than ha'pence. I may say with old George the Third, on the admission of American Independence: 'It may possibly turn out well for the Country but *as a gentleman I can never forget it.* ' "

The House of Lords was not the least of his frustrations. The news of the Country, he felt, was made in the other place and had to be learned here secondhand. Here a few minds were being influenced, there the pulse of the nation was stirred. It was vain to hope to be an effective man out of the Commons, the real repository of power. Though he gained a kindly hearing for his Chimney Sweeps, the Bill was thrown out later in the Commons. His Juvenile Mendicancy bill, the best to his mind that he had ever framed, likewise received summary treatment.

Of his sons, Evelyn flourished at Harrow, and his speech in French and English was the object of general admiration on Speech Day. Perhaps the presence of young Lionel goaded him to effort. That youngster was put on his arrival in the highest form accorded a newcomer and within three weeks was promoted to the Fifth Form, "A thing," as Edy wrote his parents with jubilant generosity, "unparalleled in history." From the eldest came affectionate letters, unwearied promises, flying visits en route to the Baltic and to the Dardanelles, unpaid bills, and the news that he had lost his promotion by his own neglect and unseamanlike character. His uncle, Lord Cowper, would have given it, and the Admiralty confirmed it; the ship's book made it impossible.

Perhaps Ashley's greatest frustration came in the realm of the spirit. That God had called him to His work he could not doubt; he knew. That God alone empowered him in answer to constant prayer, he also believed. But that the work should be thwarted, the victory postponed, while uncounted thousands—sweeps, pottery-workers, needlewomen, milliners—suffered and died from exhaustion of which his exhaustion kept reminding him, and from hunger which often prevented any enjoyment of his food, and from cold which made him deplore his own fire: that was the insoluble mystery. For God is Love—this too he knew; it was the cardinal fact of his theology. "He is wise, I am a fool" was the confession to which the recurring inward argument reduced him; "What I do thou knowest not now but thou shalt know hereafter" was the text on which he fell back, never without conviction of its truth.

In spite of overt hostility from Puseyites and Neologists, and covert criticism from Evangelicals, he was chosen as President of the Bible Society. He wrote persistently to Napoleon the Third, protesting measures repeatedly taken against Protestant Churches in France and her domains; he was invoked to intervene when Francesco and Rosa Madiai of Florence were sentenced to five years at hard labor in the galleys for reading the Scriptures with friends in their own house. By stirring up vigorous disapproval through Reformed Europe he ultimately won a grudging repeal from the Grand Duke, while from the other side of the Atlantic he received a request from Mr. Barnum's agent to arrange for "these interesting people to exhibit themselves across America in one of his shows." Mr. Barnum, he was assured, would act liberally by these good people!

Less enviable was the notoriety which he achieved in America, as well as in England, for espousing the cause of the American Negro slave. At a dinner and reception in Grosvenor Square for Mrs. Harriet Beecher Stowe he made table- if not bed-fellows of the Archbishop of Canterbury and the godly flaming dissenter, Reverend Thomas Binney. He himself wrote the Address to the Women of America signed by ten thousands of the Women of England, which brought a stinging *tu quoque* reply from ex-President Tyler's wife. The association of his name with the anti-slavery cause provoked in one Southern religious journal a bitter attack on "the unknown lordling, Lord Shaftesbury," who had never been heard of "when the noble Lord Ashley was fighting for the English slaves in the factories and mines!" It was well that he could laugh, as letters and articles flooded the *Times* concerning the hypoc-

151

risy of interference with American slavery, when slavery flourished among the poor in England.

His most approved contribution at the time to public affairs was, of course, bitterly attacked by his Quaker Peace League critics, with Bright and Cobden in the fore: critics who had hailed as a hero Kossuth, "a man embrued with blood," who had clearly stated that nothing would serve his purpose but an armed convention of all people and a universal massacre of tyrants. The contribution was a brilliant, lengthy answer to a Manifesto by the Czar which charged that England and France had ranged themselves by the side of the enemies of Christianity against Russia which was fighting for the Orthodox Faith. Shaftesbury's speech in the Lords, enthusiastically received and relayed, was sent in letter form to Czar Nicholas himself. A proud and discerning letter from Evelyn delighted him as much as all lavish praise from outside.

A month later, to the utmost astonishment of the man who had never received any public honor except the freedom of the tiny Scottish town of Tain, Lord Aberdeen begged to be allowed to submit his name for a vacancy in the Order of the Garter.

"I do wish you would accept it," said Minny when he showed her the Prime Minister's letter. "It is a just acknowledgement of your deserts."

"And if I do it may be considered a *payment* of them. In which case I should be told that I was never disinterested in my labors. And if I later appeal for Government aid they will feel that they have done enough to oblige me."

"Nonsense!" said Minny. "The Ribbon is very little—but I crave it for you, darling Ashley, because other men have had so much more recognition for so much—oh so much—less labor."

She had slipped her arm around his shoulders as he sat at his desk and he responded by turning his head against her breast.

"Once I should have cared greatly. Now I do not, at all. But I should accept it to please you, my Pet, if it were advisable to take a step by which nothing can be gained and something may be lost."

"What can be lost?" said Minny mutinously. "Mum says—"

"It would in some degree lay me under an obligation to Aberdeen," interrupted Ashley who knew too well what Mum would say. "And I cannot be bound to the Government by party ties. Another minister may succeed Aberdeen at any time, and I can prosper in such difficult undertakings only as I am on disinterested terms with them all. Then, such an honor inevitably excites envy. Ignorant and malicious persons would decry all public virtue and say that 'every public man has his price.' Yes, Dearest—" he forestalled her counter-interruption. "You observe that Aberdeen himself says that honors of this description are usually conferred from very different motives.

Many people would be offended and consider the value of the decoration lowered."

Minny was momentarily speechless. He took advantage of her generous rage to take both her hands, kiss them, then push back his chair and hold her at arm's length, smiling into her indignant eyes.

"One last argument—even if you can answer the others—but one which you may not tell Mum or anyone lest it be thought the sole reason: I simply cannot afford it. The fees for regalia, waits, singers, gratuities, College of Arms, amount to one thousand pounds. Even if I had, or could command, the sum, I should have to devote it either to the children or to my people. How could I spend it so on trivial personal vanity, when at this moment people are asking for payment of their debts and I am unable to satisfy them?"

To that, Minny well knew there was no reply. Both parents knew, and avoided the painful subject, that Ashley had borrowed exactly that amount recently to pay off Accy's accumulated debts. Her determined efforts to give him respite by taking him to the Continent—which she greatly preferred for holiday to either Scotland, his choice, or the seaside, and could justify in that Europe was much less expensive than England—had succeeded recently twice; but only when his doctor ordered him to Ems to drink the waters, and when the chance of seeing Accy before a hazardous voyage took them to Nice . . . and on both occasions he had combined business with relaxation. For her and for the children he would provide any decent pleasure within his ability. On himself he would spend no more than was absolutely necessary.

XXVII

"IT IS GOOD OF YOU to spare me this time, Lord Shaftesbury, when you have so many important interests." Dr. Hector Gavin took a glass of wine from his host's hand and ventured to move his chair a little nearer the fire. "The climate of the West Indies has made me less fit for a January like this in England."

"I am sorry that you have had difficulty finding me at leisure." Shaftesbury stood on the hearth, one long forearm resting along the high mantel. "Apart from the relaxation of chatting with one of whose work I have heard nothing but praise, it is pleasant to hear kind words about our late, generally unlamented, Board of Health."

"My staff and I in Jamaica had frequent cause to be grateful to your findings. And never fear. The Board's efforts and its members will yet be recognized at their true value."

"Perhaps; not, I think, in our lifetimes. I have never known a wrong by the public redressed so that the sufferer could enjoy reparation.

'Nations slowly wise and meanly just
To buried merit raise the tardy bust.'

Forgive my pessimism. I fear that accounts from the Crimea are rendering me gloomy. Our poor fellows there are decimated by disease, cold, and hunger. Raglan's staff—especially his Quarter-Master and Adjutant-General—are incompetent, ignorant, obstinate. They prefer red-tape regulation to the lives of the soldiers. But that does not excuse me for forgetting my hospitality." His smile of apology deleted the grave to grim lines from his mouth.

"Such gloom requires no apology, Lord Shaftesbury. I share it. Surely the political upheaval is a sign of wide-spread public dismay." Dr. Gavin's fine eyes blazed from a thin face, burned coffee color by the tropical sun. You'll pardon me for saying so, my Lord, but I'm one of the many who feel that we should not be in this pass if Pam—Lord Palmerston—had been in the War Office. And that he should have been asked to form a government as soon as Aberdeen went down. All this dithering with Lord Derby and Lord John Russell while, as you might say, Rome is burning. Of course,"—it was his turn to be apologetic—"I am speaking as an outsider and from hearsay. I am not alone in wishing that your lordship could be in the government at this time, if only to clear up the mess at Scutari. 'A man who does more than talk,' I remember one of the papers saying of you."

"In one of its kindlier moments," said Shaftesbury, but remembering his earlier lapse he spoke lightly without bitterness. He did not tell his stranger guest how nearly his wish had been to fulfilment. In fact his present relaxation was the aftermath of two days' tension during which pressure had been brought to bear on him by Palmerston, by Lady Palmerston, not least by Minny, to accept the nominal Duchy of Lancaster and its "without portfolio" Cabinet office. The offer had been put in the form of a personal request. The Queen's three choices had been unable to form a government. Palmerston, summoned by his unwilling Sovereign, had felt the need of a disinterested and capable supporter. It had been hard to refuse; the stirring of spirit inevitable with a chance of official recognition and power warred with his deep conviction that his real work lay elsewhere and that his beliefs would bring him into constant conflict with his colleagues. He had prepared a

154

highly provisional acceptance, when violent opposition by the Whigs to their small share in the Cabinet had forced Palmerston to a more politic appointment. Shaftesbury was doubly relieved because his acquiescence had pleased Minny without involving him.

He listened now and responded while Dr. Gavin talked, but with a part of his mind curiously detached, as though waiting for an idea, conceived by a chance remark of his companion, and drifting just beyond the circumference of his consciousness.

The talk inevitably centered on the dismal subject of cholera, doubly dismal to him, as Fanny's husband, Lord Jocelyn, had fallen a sudden victim to the London outbreak five months before. Its appearance among the troops in the Crimea had been the last straw on an unendurable casualty rate—men dying, as Lord Raglan dispassionately reported, at the rate of a regiment a day. Shaftesbury's mind, long trained to glean useful items from every encounter, noted and stored fact, figure, and anecdote from the physician's experience as Government Commissioner for the prevention and care of the disease in the West Indies.

More: by the time he had to terminate the interview—suddenly drawing from his pocket the large gold watch, his legacy from Maria Millis, glancing with a start at its bland white face, exclaiming, "My dear fellow, I am so sorry. I have an appointment with the Bishop of London in less than half an hour"—the idea had been born.

"February Fourteenth. Have been running about to stir up Prelates and Ministers to a day of prayer. Tried unsuccessfully to see Panmure on sanitary arrangements for Crimean Hospitals, but all in vain. A 'Philanthropist' is always a bore."

The two enterprises were to his mind equally necessary, the second and younger fearfully dependent upon the first. Almost as a sign, he felt, success in the spiritual was granted to encourage him to persevere in the temporal. The cool scepticism, the politely veiled ridicule, which had greeted his plea during the Irish famine and the worst ravages of cholera were, if not converted, at least suppressed by the threat of national disaster and loss of international prestige. Plainly the Bishop of London, the Archbishop of Canterbury, Mr. Gladstone, and Lord Palmerston, willing to take plague and famine in their stride, felt that only God could solve the riddle of mismanagement, stupidity, and negligence, which had caused the Charge of the Light Brigade and the cold fact that, though England was sending out stores equal to five times the demand, neither sound nor sick officers or privates were obtaining one-twentieth of their needs.

Once the day of prayer had been granted, Shaftesbury set his mouth with determination which hid from everyone but his wife his sense of outrage, his dislike of suing, his personal grief; and pressed past excuse, subterfuge, and delay to an interview with the Secretary of State for War.

The Second Baron Panmure had never, Shaftesbury thought as the two men faced each other over a forbidding official desk, agreed with him in principle or politics, nor given him any help in his work in or out of Parliament. He well remembered the Whig's defense of the Whig government when, as Fox Maule, he had countered Ashley's impassioned appeal for the Factory operatives in '38, and prophesied the evil results that would ensue if children were thrown out of the labor market. But then John Russell and Daniel O'Connell and Roebuck and Graham had opposed him bitterly on the same subject and changed their attitudes. And the present situation was one in which no Secretary for War, however Whigly obstructionist, could feel secure. He wasted no time in preliminaries.

"The war proceeds, the army perishes, judgements arise out of our personal childishness. We are silly beyond the silliness of a boarding-school," he began with impolitic vigor. "Miss Nightingale and her thirty-seven helpers arrived early in November and, in spite of heroic efforts, have been impeded on every hand. They will themselves fall victim to disease unless something is done. We shall have a national disaster unprecedented in English history."

"And you have a suggestion to avert it?"

Shaftesbury brushed aside the insult of the cool, enquiring tone.

"I have: A Sanitary Commission must proceed with full powers to Scutari and Balaclava to purify the hospitals, ventilate the ships and exert all that science can do to save life. War—this war—is inevitable. But that thousands upon thousands should die, not from their wounds, but from dysentery and disease, the result of foul air, and preventible mischiefs—this is intolerable."

Lord Panmure did not speak for a moment. He had never had sympathy with Lord Ashley's reforms and philanthropies. He had none with Lord Shaftesbury's continuing activities and viewed his enthusiasms and personal commitment as in bad taste. He had shared the prevalent dislike of the Board of Health and rejoiced in its demise. But he could not deny that the man had a way of getting things done; that he acquainted himself at first hand with the facts; that, if he espoused a cause, he let no personal, party, physical, or financial consideration stand in his way. If he, Panmure, were to continue in the position in which Lord Newcastle's ineptness had caused a government upheaval, some action was necessary. But short of dismissing Raglan and his staff—and who was to succeed them?—no plan had occurred to him. For all

156

his slowness and lack of imagination, Panmure had a former good record in his present office for six years, during Lord John Russell's Cabinet; but there had been no such crisis as that which now confronted the nation. Nor had a brilliant journalist like William Howard Russell been at the scenes of the comparatively petty squabbles then settled by Palmerston's alternating bluster and compromise. Russell *was* on the scene now. For the first time in English history authentic commentaries from the front were being published in the *Times* and devoured by grief-stricken, puzzled, and increasingly impatient readers.

He made a sudden brilliant decision.

"Will you undertake the arrangements?"

"I?" Ashley was startled. Success he had prayed for; but a responsibility of such magnitude when he already needed twenty-four hours in a day—

"Who else? Or who better?" said Panmure almost testily. "Your work on the Board of Health has made you familiar with people and details that none of us knows. And, as you say, speed is an essential factor. Lord Palmerston will certainly approve whatever you require."

Shaftesbury's decision was equally swift. His financial difficulties, his pendent Bills and their preparation, his family arrangements, must wait. On his answer depended, under God, the lives of pitiful uncounted souls involved through no doing of their own in war, souls "for whom Christ died." On his answer also depended the success or heartbreak, perhaps the life, of that strange dominant woman whom he had met and for whom he had felt instant sympathy, at Mum's, before her departure for Scutari. But he pressed his advantage.

"On condition that I be allowed a free hand for instructions and that the members of the Commission be given a free hand when they reach Scutari."

"Of course," said Panmure.

"It will not be *of course*," riposted Shaftesbury sharply, "when they run foul of the stupid hauteur, the bureaucratic officialdom which sacrifices lives rather than false dignity. The men must be preceded and accompanied by letters which will enable them to override petty interference, to cut red tape ruthlessly." His brain was working at its old speed. He scarcely knew if the details were being produced by the moment or emerging from the background of a month's occasional brooding. "They must proceed by Marseilles. A screw steamer from that place will cut the voyage by half. Letters should be direct and couched in the strongest terms to Lord Raglan and Lord W. Powlett; also to Lord Stratford de Redcliffe. The Commissioners should have the power of hiring, on their own account, such numbers of workmen as they may find necessary. If, upon giving a plan, they are met with any delays, however

157

short, sent from one department to another, their shins broken by a succession of official stumbling-blocks, they will be useless—indeed ridiculous. They might as well remain at home. We cannot trifle with time. A pestilence might ravage the troops while a score of functionaries were writing to each other to ascertain whose business it was to attend to it." He broke off with a quick smile. "And here am I giving an example of what I decry. So I reiterate: The authorities must be instructed, with no loophole for evasion, to carry into execution, without delay, whatever the Commissioners declare essential."

Panmure had little imagination but enough to call up a picture of the military gentlemen in question when "strong" letters required them to hand over authority to a group of untitled laymen. He came to another decision.

"When I asked you to undertake the arrangements," his tone would have been pompous but it was difficult to be pompous to a man whose inherent dignity never stood upon itself. "I meant that I leave everything in your hands: that includes such letters as you see fit to write, such instructions as you give the members of the Commission. They will be issued from the War Office and have our full authority."

"Thank you, Panmure." Shaftesbury rose. He felt none of the embarrassment with which his next words filled his companion. They were completely sincere and, to his thinking, necessary. "God bless you. And He will bless you, as will thousands of men and their families, for what He has moved you to do today."

"Quite mad," murmured Panmure as the door closed after Shaftesbury's quick, purposeful exit. "But I hope he is right. And I hope it works. If it doesn't, Pam will have his saintly son-in-law to blame."

This was, however, the sort of enterprise for which Pam most admired his saintly son-in-law. He cordially seconded Panmure's permission and was grateful for the selfless efficiency and energy which Minny's husband was displaying in his anonymous and unrecognized task.

His choice of Commissioners was prompt and happy: Dr. Sutherland of the General Board of Health; Dr. Hector Gavin, the unconscious seed-ground of his project; Mr. Rawlinson, a Civil Engineer; Mr. Newlands, the Chief Inspector of Liverpool; three sub-inspectors, and an assistant engineer. That he persuaded them to surrender personal comfort and, in at least one case, professional emolument for a hazardous expedition, was a triumph of his own contagious dedication. That the Commission was actually despatched less than two weeks after his interview with Panmure, confirmed the truth of a brief journal entry:

"February eighteen. Busy, very busy about Sanitary Commission. But the work is Herculean. We have neither time nor strength to do it in merely human power. May God 'prevent us in all our goings.' "

With them, written in Shaftesbury's own hand, went their instructions.

"On your arrival at Constantinople and Balaklava you will put yourselves instantly into communication with Lord W. Powlett and Lord Raglan respectively; and you will request of them forthwith (according to the official directions they will have received) full powers of entry into every hospital, infirmary, or receptacle of whatever kind for the sick and wounded, whether ashore or afloat.

"You will inspect every part of such infirmaries; ascertain the character and sufficiency of the drainage and ventilation, the quality and quantity of the water supply, and determine whether the condition of the whole is such as to allow, by purity of the air and freedom from overcrowding, fair play and full scope to medical and surgical treatment for the recovery of health.

"You will call to your aid, for this purpose, whether as witnesses or as guides, any of the officers or attendants that you may require.

"The result of your inspection and opinions, together with a statement of all that it is necessary should be done—whether in the way of arrangement, of reduction of numbers in the wards, cleansing, disinfecting, or of actual construction, in order to secure the great ends of safety and health—must be laid, as speedily as possible, before Lord W. Powlett or Lord Raglan, as the case may be, or such persons as may be appointed by them to that special duty, and you will request them to give immediate directions that the works be completed.

"As no time is to be lost, you may reserve your detailed and minute reports, and give, in the first instance, a statement only of the things to be done forthwith.

"The Engineer Commissioner will be expected to conduct the inspection along with his colleagues, and to devise, and to see executed, all such structural arrangements as may be declared indispensable.

"You will examine the modes whereby the sick and wounded are conveyed to the transports or to the hospitals, ashore or afloat. Much suffering and mortality have been caused by the want of jetties for the embarkation and disembarkation of the patients. You will see that a remedy be applied to such a frightful omission, and that there be no recurrence of these disorders.

"You will take care that, so far as is possible, all evil influences from without be removed, so that the air inhaled by the inmates of the hospitals be not contaminated. It is reported, for instance, that the hospital-ship in the harbor of Balaklava is as much surrounded by dead carcasses as though it were in a knacker's yard. This, and everything everywhere approaching to it, must be remedied at once. As a necesssary consequence, you will order peremptorily that the dead be interred at a sufficient distance from the hospitals. You will give directions both as to the time and mode of interment, consulting, of course, the convenience of the constituted authorities.

"Should any new hospital or receptacle for the sick be decided on, while you are on this expedition, you will examine it and state all that must be done for health, decency, and comfort.

"You will not interfere, in any way, with the medical and surgical treatment of the patients, nor with the regulations prescribed to the nurses and attendants.

"Upon your arrival at Constantinople you will determine, among yourselves, in what way you can best carry on your operations; but it seems desirable that, after the first inspection, one Medical Commissioner should be almost constantly in Scutari and another at Balaklava. The Engineer Commissioner would be more frequently in motion, to inspect the various works and maintain the communication between his brother Commissioners.

"It is important that you be deeply impressed with the necessity of not resting content with an order, but that you see, by yourselves or by your agents, instantly to the commencement of the work and to its superintendence, day by day, until it be finished.

"It is your duty, in short, to state fully, and urge strongly for adoption by the authorities, everything that you believe will tend to the preservation of health and life.

"You are empowered to institute, both at Scutari and at the camp, such systems of organization for sanitary purposes as may be considered essential to carry your plans into effect.

"The camp must also come under your immediate and anxious attention.

"You must consider, and apply, with the least possible delay, the best antidotes or preventives to the deadly exhalations that will be emitted from the saturated soil whenever the warmth of spring shall begin to act on the surface. . . ."

The scope of these orders which continued with explicit directions about the cleansing of the harbor and the transport of the sick impressed Lord Palmerston to such a degree that his letter to Raglan might have been dictated by Shaftesbury himself.

"The Commissioners will, of course," he wrote from long experience of balky officialdom, "be opposed and thwarted by the medical officers, by the men who have charge of the port arrangements, and by those who have the cleaning of the camp. Their mission will be ridiculed, and their recommendations and directions set aside, unless enforced by the peremptory exercise of your authority." Here Pam's cocky smile indicated admiration of his own diplomacy. It was Raglan's underlings, not Raglan himself, who would be recalcitrant! "But that authority I must request you to exert in the most peremptory manner, for the immediate and exact carrying into execution whatever changes they may recommend."

"That," said Palmerston jauntily, affixing his signature and the imposing seal, "should assure Raglan of our temper. Now, my dear Shaftesbury, I shall seize the few minutes we have left to warn you that I may be calling upon you at any time to reaffirm your acceptance of the Duchy."

"My acceptance?" Ashley turned from the window in 10 Downing Street where he had been calculating on a pad the probable cost of additional medical supplies, requested by Miss Nightingale and more likely to arrive at their destination if they accompanied the Commission. Not for him or anyone connected with him the confusion of stores decaying at Varna which were intended for Scutari; the damnable carelessness which had sent consignments of boots all for the left foot; the mismanagement which left tents standing in pools of water for want of implements to dig trenches. "I thought you considered it a qualified refusal, and in any event, the matter was settled."

"On the seventh. This is the twenty-second," said Pam flatly. "Gladstone, Sidney Herbert, and Graham resigned yesterday over Roebuck's Committee of Inquiry. Carlisle is becoming Lord Lieutenant of Ireland. So Lancaster is vacant again. I wished you for it then, I wish it now. Think it over," he added, rising hastily to avoid argument. "I expect Clarendon any moment. Pray see to this despatch for me, personally. It must reach Raglan well before the Commission arrives. Emily will be in touch with you tonight."

Also, he might have added, but did not, the Duke of Cambridge who represented, in flattering terms, the views of Royalty on the matter of his joining the government. Shaftesbury stated honestly what he had already objected in his letter to Palmerston: the difficulty of being a member of a government which took an official stand against him regarding further endowments to Maynooth, admission of Jews to Parliament by alteration of the oath, the opening of museums and the Crystal Palace on Sunday. He stressed above all the necessary surrender of occupations to which he was devoted. "I have injured no one but myself," he said when His Royal

Highness departed, courteous and baffled. "He thinks me a fool, a fanatic, an impractical ass. However I have brought no discredit to my public profession of religion though I have closed the gates of office against me forever."

He reckoned without Palmerston, without Lady Palmerston, without Minny, who, in the country, was informed by her mother of the situation.

"I do *beseech* you not to refuse," she wrote. "Think how much more weight everything has coming from a Cabinet Minister—all you have said to the Emperor about the persecution of the Protestants; it will have tenfold weight when he knows that your position in England is such as to have a seat in the Cabinet."

Touché, thought her husband, under a barrage of calls and notes from well-wishers advising him to be advised. Lady Palmerston urged the Queen's disappointment in his refusal of a place in her Household, in his refusal of the Garter, and presumably his refusal of a place in her Government at this crisis, in which she had plaintively exclaimed to Clarendon: "Lord John Russell may resign, and Lord Aberdeen may resign, but I *can't* resign. I sometimes wish I could." Her list of his admirers, from Henry Stanley who had written her from Athens, to Charles Villiers and Sir Benjamin Hall—he wishes my hands to be tied so that I cannot oppose him on Sunday amusements, thought her son-in-law—left him less impressed.

But were these the signs that he asked God to show of His will: their urgency, the recurrent opportunity, the possible chance of increasing influence with Palmerston, who had for the first time consulted him seriously on the appointment of bishops. "The views, hopes, and fears of the country, and particularly of the religious part of it are as strange to him as the interior of Japan," Shaftesbury wrote on the twenty-eighth of that month to Evelyn who was studying in Geneva. "Why, it was only a short time ago that he heard for the first time of the grand heresy of Puseyites and Tractarians!"

No satisfactory candidate for the vacancy—he had no reason to doubt Pam's word—was to be found. Minny was still at the seaside where she had taken Mary, who had been ailing since December. He would have given much to talk again with her, having no time to write. By the Herculean effort required he had set everything in train for the departure of the Commission; but he was not leaving the completion of arrangements to chance bungling.

At that point a note, obviously scrawled in haste, arrived.

"My dear Ashley—

Palmerston has three people waiting for him and two in his room, so that he could not write a line now, but he will satisfy you entirely upon all the points you mention.

And he is very anxious now that you should put on your undress uniform and be at the Palace a quarter before three to be sworn in.

Pray do this, and I am *sure* you will not repent it. Palmerston is Very anxious to have his Government complete and as there has been so much delay, he would be very anxious that you could, for the Queen's sake, appear at the Palace to be sworn in a quarter before three.

Yours ever Affectionately,

E. Palmerston."

He had never felt so helpless. He seemed to be hurried along without a will of his own, without power of resistance. It struck him suddenly as a bit humorous that the notoriously unpunctual Pam, and Mum who, when the Queen visited Panshanger, Broadlands, and Brocket, had repeatedly, and with impunity, kept her Majesty waiting—no one else dared—should doubly insist on the exact time. No other lightening of spirit was vouchsafed him.

Moving like a man in a trance, he ordered a hack, dressed, and went down on his knees with a confused prayer for counsel and wisdom.

He heard the heavy knocker. It must be the carriage. He rose from his knees, took up his sword and hat, and was leaving the room when the butler appeared.

The note written in pencil contained one line:

"Don't go to the Palace. Palmerston."

Relief swept over him like a wave. The mental exercises, the nice calculations, the terrifying prospect of endless unproductive meetings in which principle would be compromised to expediency—the sacrifice that he had been almost ready to make because it seemed to be required—this was not demanded of him. How he did not know, but Pam's hand, like Abraham's, had been stayed.

On his knees again he was conscious of the incongruity—Pam as Abraham required some adjustment—but the simile persisted. Some "ram caught in a thicket" had been found, presumably a willing ram. He had been spared for the little people, the shepherdless sheep, the unsensational or unpopular causes which no one else would take up: "small works compared with political and financial movements—a Lodging-House, a Ragged School, a Vagrant Bill, a Thieves' Refuge;" and, if God so honored him, for the defense of the freedom of the Gospel.

Later he was pleased to hear that the sacrificial ram was his friend, Lord Harrowby.

163

XXVIII

IN THE CONFUSED AND HUMILIATING tangle of military episodes, divided command, deaths, appointments, counter reappointments, petering out of hostilities, and a dictated, but far from glorious, treaty, Shaftesbury's share in the war remained anonymous. Yet the result of the Commission—the startling drop in the casualty rate from forty-two to two-and-a-half percent—gave luster to Florence Nightingale and her heroic nurses which she was not slow to share.

"That Commission of yours saved the British army," she wrote to him simply. And later, accompanying a copy of her Report to the War Office:

"It is strictly confidential and has not been presented to the House of Commons. But as Lord Shaftesbury has, for so many years, been our leader in sanitary matters (as in so many other wise and benevolent things) it seemed to me but right to send him a Report which contains so much of what was done by himself, viz. the work of the Sanitary Commission in the East, although I can scarcely expect that he will read it.

> I am, dear Lord Shaftesbury,
> Yours very faithfully,
> F. Nightingale."

And again,

"Dear Lord Shaftesbury:
Always remembering that to you first we owe the giving of sanitary hope to our poor army, I should have ventured to solicit your acceptance of a copy of the report of our India Army Sanitary Commission. But . . .
I should be proud indeed to be called upon at any time for information by you.

> Your faithful servant,
> Florence Nightingale."

"If we be told," said Shaftesbury in his Presidential address to the Social Science Congress in Liverpool, "that spiritual remedies are sufficient and that we labour too much for the perishable body, I reply that spiritual appliances, in the state of things to which I allude, are altogether impossible. When people say that we should think more of the soul and less of the body, my answer is that the same God who made the soul made the body also. It is an inferior work, perhaps, but it is His work and it must be treated and cared for according to the end for which it was formed—fitness for His service. I maintain that God is worshipped not only by the spiritual, but also by the material creation. Our great object should be to remove the obstructions which stand in the way of such worship. If St. Paul, calling our bodies the temples of the Holy Ghost, said that they ought not to be contaminated by sin, we also say that our bodies, the temples of the Holy Ghost, ought not to be corrupted by preventable disease, degraded by avoidable filth, and disabled for His service by unnecessary suffering."

"To expound the Word of God," he wrote bluntly to the Archbishop of Canterbury, "to offer up prayer whenever and wherever he pleases, to ten or ten thousand, is a right inherent in every Christian man. The clergyman has it antecedently to his ordination—it is higher than a right, absolutely a duty. He cannot give it up. No law, form, or condition, civil or ecclesiastical, can take it from him."

"There is no slight amount of mischief arising from the long detention of young people of both sexes in shops and warehouses."—so ran his address to the Young Men's Christian Association in Manchester—"It lowers the physical system by over-toil and it lowers the moral taste and appetite, leaving only the desire for what is most stimulating and sensual. Therefore I see the immense value of what is known as the Early Closing Movement. All who concur with me in opposition to the opening of places of amusement on the Lord's Day are bound to advocate giving a good half-holiday on Saturday and supplying them some form of recreation on that day."

No one could accuse him of mincing words in his repeated forensic efforts to obtain decent lodging houses.

"There is a mighty stir now made on behalf of education and I thank God for it; but let me ask you to what purpose it is to take a little child, a young female for instance, and teach her for six hours a day the rules of decency and virtue, and then send her back to such abodes of filth and profligacy as to make her unlearn, by the practice of one hour, the lessons of a year, to witness and often share, at first against her will, the abominations recorded? . . . People . . . hear the long catalogue of bastardy cases and then cry out, 'Sluts and profligates,' assuming that, when in early life these persons have been treated as swine, they are afterwards to walk with the dignity of Christians."

Pursuing these public pronouncements the Seventh Earl of Shaftesbury had no hesitation—in fact had little time for hesitation—in turning from his Religious Worship Bill to bills for his poor Chimney Sweeps and for the dressmakers and milliners, whose wretched lives had been a heavy burden to him since he had drawn public attention and some voluntary solace to them a dozen years earlier.

Thousands of these women were working in London and in every large city fifteen to eighteen hours a day until, useless from consumption or impaired eyesight, they slipped into statistical oblivion. His inclusion of every woman rich enough to have a fine gown—"Darling, that means me!" said Minny, stricken—as "*particeps criminis*" did not endear him to either middle or upper class.

The Conventicle Act, still unrepealed, had been invoked within the last two years to prevent Bible reading or prayer with "more than twenty people outside the household." It was called a dead letter by those who resisted efforts to expunge it; but its latent menace had already become patent when Shaftesbury and his supporters began Sunday evening services, first in Exeter Hall, then in the theaters, for thousands of the poor who could not be induced to church or chapel. His passionate efforts to ensure complete freedom of religious exercise were successful (thirty-one votes to thirty) in spite of the legislative maneuvering and opposition of Tractarian peers, led by Lord Derby and the Bishop of Oxford.

"That every man should have a perfect right to worship God when and how he pleases, in his own house, with his neighbors, in any number, and at any time; that this should not be a mere privilege but a right unless it can be shown that public morality or public safety be endangered by it," was his demand. As for power to be vested in Bishops or "Licensed" curates—or "permission" to open and close such permitted meetings with prayer (but not offer prayer in the middle!)—it was intolerable. "Permission to pray?" he exclaimed. "It may as well be said that I am to have permission to breathe the air!"

This liberty he was equally prepared to grant to other religions, regardless of what he considered their falsity or error. So, when after the Sepoy mutiny he advocated a Christian Government of India, he set forth the terms clearly. "We must declare that it rests on Christian principles, has Christian views, will go forward in Christian action. The Government must declare that it will never directly or indirectly, by itself or by others, use force or bribery or any illicit mode whatsoever, in order to turn the natives from their faith. You must give to them precisely the same rights and liberties in matters religious that you claim for yourselves. If the Government gives all due countenance and protection to the Christian missionaries, you will call upon the Government to declare that they will allow to the Hindoos and to the Mahometans precisely the same liberty that they claim for themselves."

XXIX

"THERE, ASHLEY. SEE! VEA IS NEXT."

Ashley recalled his mind, which had strayed from the formal glittering procession in the Queen's Great Hall at Windsor to a far different queue he had seen that afternoon, of twelve hundred tattered mortals patiently lining up for soup in Ham Yard. His eyes found his daughter Victoria—just as her name was announced—beginning the slow glide in which she had been gaily but carefully schooled by her mother, along the crimson carpet and up to the dais where the other Victoria sat. Charming in the white silk gauze gown which Lady Palmerston had insisted on as her gift, with her mother's bracelets, and with the plumes set in their tiny tiara moving at one with the proudly held head, she reached the two gilded chairs. The Queen and her Consort, with whose daughter she had played as a child, allowed their formal smiles to become almost personal as the girl dipped to the floor in the required deep curtsey.

"*That* is the best one so far," whispered Minny, her pressure becoming almost painful on his arm as she waited for the most difficult moment, the backward descent from the Royal Presence.

It was made beautifully. The next name was called.

The next debutante received the polite attention of monocles and lorgnettes. Minny relaxed her tension but left her arm in his. Ashley forgot his cares temporarily in her evident delight. One of her most captivating qualities was still her unimpaired enjoyment of every pleasant thing she saw or heard: another person's beauty, color in sea or sky, the expression on a donkey's face. He knew that she attached no more importance to such a social occasion than he did; but such occasions were for enjoyment, and she enjoyed. He was glad that he had not let fear of public opinion deprive Vea of this opportunity.

The ceremony was over and they were passing from the Presence Chamber to the Drawing Room. She seemed to read his thoughts.

"I think we were right. After all it is five months since dear Maurice died. She was always wonderfully kind to him when they were together. The child should have some diversion when she can."

"Yes. Though I am afraid coming out 'into the world' too often calls girls to idleness and dissipation—and injury to health."

"Not Vea," said Minny certainly. "She is your daughter, remember. And if *I* hadn't come out would I have met the husband who called me *from* idleness, dissipation and injury to health?"

167

There was no arguing with her, even if he had been inclined.

"I only hope, but doubt, the child can be as fortunate," she went on lightly. "Doesn't she look lovely, Ashley? Her hair draped *á l'imperatrice* is so becoming."

"Not as beautiful as her mother."

"At her age? O come, you have forgotten."

"Never. And I do *not* mean at her age. I mean now."

Fortunately at that point they were interrupted. But Ashley held to his statement. Victoria resembled him rather too much for girlish beauty, he thought. She had not the *charm* of his "little Min," was more shy and reserved, but intelligent, sincere, warmhearted, with qualities which would make her an excellent wife and mother. Would God all the girls eventually find true pious faithful husbands! He knew the services that could be rendered by spinsters—the inestimable Miss Portal was an example—but his daughters would not have her independent means. Besides, for women of their class marriage was the safest, happiest state. "I wish you boys were all girls," Minny had written recently to Evelyn, almost petulant in her anxiety about Accy in the Baltic. But Ashley in spite of that anxiety did not echo her plaint.

Six months later he was inclined to agree. Edy was giving a good account of himself at Cambridge, and Lionel nothing but satisfaction at Harrow. The memory of Maurice was dear, and because of his arrested development and dreadful weakness, his death, which had occurred before his parents could reach him in Lausanne, had none of the poignancy which still twisted Ashley's heart at the thought of Francis. But Accy, his first-born, his hope, the heir to his title and to the estates which he was agonizing to restore—only that they might be handed over to money lenders, wasted in riotous living!

The young man's most unnerving characteristic was unpredictableness. If I could give up hope, Shaftesbury thought, knowing that he could not and would not, I could resign myself to his loss. Yet once and again it flared up and burned, bright if not steady. After Captain Seymour's humiliating letter regarding his total disregard of discipline and his long history of debts to messmates and steward—with hints of trickery and deceit—after reports from Portsmouth of his low connections there, he had left the navy and come home, quiet, amiable, indifferent and, if no comfort, at least no active trouble. He found his way about London, was often still in bed at midday, had his name linked with one of the most coarse and loose young ladies in the fashionable world. Yet he went willingly enough with Evelyn to hear his father address the operatives at Manchester, was a model of behavior at his uncle Fordwich's funeral, took the chair at a dinner in place of the Duke of Argyll, behaving as well and simply as his father could ask, went off with an embassy to Russia and returned to charm his parents' guests at St. Giles—an overflow of Lady Palmerston's entertainment of foreign diplomacy including the Persignys, the Russian ambassador, the Portuguese minister and their wives.

But on November 15 he left Grosvenor Square at noon. At one-thirty Ashley's lawyer, Burnett, arrived to report that he had been arrested and was being detained in a bailiff's house. The details were not clear. Some fateful attraction at Portsmouth had lured him to obtain a loan by fraudulent means. Ashley wrestled with his heart and his conscience—or was it, he asked, his pride? and obtained five hundred pounds to rescue him. One more effort to save the name from public taint, he told himself.

The expressions of contrition and sorrow, the affecting and penitent language, the declaration that he had received a real lesson, induced his father to trust—at least to pray—that lasting benefit would ensue. Had hope deferred made Min's heart sick? he wondered, when she looked at him strangely after Accy made his abject departure from their room—he had stayed away at his club two days in shame—and said, not for the first time:

"What is it about him, Darling? He is not defective in the usual sense."

Anything but defective he seemed four months later when, after his father had made sundry other vain efforts to obtain a nomination for him, he went to Hull and won the seat there without bribery or treating. Or when he was clapped and cheered in company with his father at the Anniversary of the Ragged School Union and spoke with simplicity and good taste. Or when, shortly afterwards in St. George's, Hanover Square, he married Harriet, only daughter of the Marquis of Donegal. His parents heard her praises as good, steady, right-minded, and were glad to be impressed by her demonstrations of affection and lively, but sweet, temper on their few meetings. They thanked God as they sat in the church of their own joyful union, and took fresh courage. After all he was just twenty-six.

Twenty-seven when his first child, a daughter, was born, with Minny remaining in the heat of London to take a mother's place for Harriet's confinement; the relationship was still amiable . . . twenty-eight—almost— when he decided to abandon Parliament and, to his father's alarm, went to request the Chiltern Hundreds . . . scarcely twenty-nine when the steadily decreasing pleasantness of Harriet's attitude to her husband's family disappeared in a scene of spitefulness and ugly, wounding language from which it never re-emerged whole.

"I think we can understand," said Minny, who had been less hopeful and therefore less surprised by the scene than her husband. "She has vast energy and no desire for usefulness. To marry your heir was an achievement. It must have been galling to learn his financial position, to have to curb her social ambitions."

"We never gave her—I never gave her father—cause to expect more."

"No—Accy probably did. Poor boy! He told Fordwich—it was just after he left his ship—that you gave him a thousand a year. Fordwich who was giving young Fordwich only six hundred and Henry three—exactly as you were to Accy and to Edy—was naturally taken aback. So we have no idea what glowing stories she heard. And for some one without religious feelings, our household and reputation—"

"You mean mine."

"Ours," she insisted, "cannot be congenial. The very contrast between her frivolous idleness and our four darlings, going twice a week to help the young cripples at your orthopedic hospital, must be galling. She could scarcely bear to hear them praised, and took refuge in mimicking what she called sanctimonious philanthropy."

"Well!" he said almost bitterly, "it isn't as if I exercised any domestic discipline. In spite of my entreaties that the boys attend prayers, not one was present at St. Giles's even on Christmas. And as I would not have them dislike me and the house—it is their home!—I will not exert authority."

She knew how hurt he was and how concerned because of the bad example set to their servants. She said:

"They are feeling their independence, Dearest. It is not popular to be Evangelical and they are just down from University. They do respect you and your views—in spite of their cigars!"

"And their Neological talk. Though when Harriet goes to church she takes Anthony to hear a Puseyite!"

"They are young and this appeal to the intellect is new to them. Believe me, they will return to the profession they once made. And they are most proud of you. Consider Edy's letters from America, his interest in your success over the Religious Worship Bill."

Shaftesbury conceded that point.

"The truth is that I expect too much. It is unwise. Evelyn passes few hours in our society and I feel a personal slight. Whereas it is natural for young men to find their parents prosy. They are just as they always were, except that modern powers of locomotion have extended the number of houses to be frequented. New amusements to be pursued have added activity to their restlessness."

"You would be unhappy if they stayed at home more from courtesy," said Minny.

"True. And, bless God, Evelyn and Lionel are good, honest gentleman-like lads. So, under other influence, might Accy be."

170

" 'I am weary of my life because of this daughter of Heth'!" said Minny, smiling to soften her quotation. "I *am* sorry that she truckles to rank and fashion, but was insulting and contemptuous at the Saint to our county neighbors. *That* distresses me more—because it displays meanness—than her coarseness of action and speech."

What grieves me most, thought Ashley, is that her influence has robbed Accy of his single unspoiled quality: respect and affection for his mother and love for his family. Dreadful—God avert it—that if I am cut off, they will be in no small measure dependent on this couple for protection and comfort. All their movements seemed—he dared not say were—calculated to injure his reputation, directed against the public stand which he had taken. Her most talked-of "rag," sitting on the box of a drag to Goodwood, had been on a Sunday. Anthony, in a condition approaching diphtheria, and severely warned by the doctor of excess in wine and tobacco, had got out of bed and gone to a stag party at the Chester races. The two seemed driven by a desperate resolve to eat, drink, and be merry. Aloud Ashley said, with a none too successful attempt at lightness:

"Ah well. Driving to Ascot on a drag and playing at Aunt Sally on the race ground does indeed put her in a different class from the county. I doubt a girl in a tradesman's shop would condescend to it. She must be drawing heavily on her own resources to pay her extravagance. But their poor child can seldom see her parents. God's Spirit alone can check her—"

"But He can," said Minny with that practical simplicity which often made him feel that his own faith was merely theoretical. The recent vulgar—it was the only word—tirade had been in no small part directed against her, perhaps in jealousy of the bond between mother and son. Yet without the slightest insipidity she was placable. Somehow or other, it seemed to him, her heart could not retain the impression of an affront or a harshness. As he, in his excitability, had often had cause to know with gratitude.

XXX

24 GROSVENOR SQUARE,
LONDON, SEPT. 10, 1861.

"Dear Mr. Haldane—You will have heard from the papers that nearly a week ago my precious child entered into her rest."

Ashley threw down his pen and pressed his hands against his temples, closing his eyes as if to shut out the sights—the sounds rang constantly in his over-sensitive ears—which the sentence recalled, the month of agony, the last week of ineffable horror. He had thought it might ease his mind to share it with someone who would sympathize without personal distress. Vea, Conty, Edith, and Cecil, who had been present at the last, needed diversion, not reminder. To Minny, who had risen above even his adoring estimation of her in the eighteen months of her attendance on Mary, he must show nothing but strength and faith. And take her away to recuperate.

But he loved his friends and felt their individual loss keenly. An odd assortment they had been and were, from the old Duchess of Beaufort to the gentle, saintly Bickersteth; from Dean Law to Lord Harrowby, from Sir James South to Elizabeth Fry and the city missionary, Roger Miller, whose untimely death in a railway accident had been an irremediable bereavement. From his exuberant post-Oxford days with George Morpeth and Evelyn Denison he had enjoyed the give-and-take of stimulating male topical conversation, and still craved it in the narrowing social circle forced by his widening humane and religious interests. Alexander Haldane had come—intruded, the Scottish barrister and editor had termed it—into his life, just at the time when the loss of Miller, Francis, and Bickersteth trebled his need. His support by articles in the *Record*, his almost daily encouraging presence in the visitors' section of the Lords, his calls, letters, suggestions, and stimulating talk were a lively antidote to many discouragements. So—he had written several times since leaving to visit his native Perthshire—this letter was due as well as therapeutic.

But he could not continue, could not write freely. Not even to this mature fellow Christian of his own age, any more than to his beloved Minny, had he the right to voice the agony of doubt and questioning through which he was passing. His profession demanded an outward attitude of unqualified faith in the will—in the love and goodness of the will—of God. The fightings and fears within should be talked out—groaned out—to his Lord alone, not aired to increase the difficulties of others and to suggest smallness in the consolations of God.

How he had longed during those last awful days to see evident consolation granted to the child—and had not seen it. He had prayed from the first indications of serious illness; and none of his prayers had, seemingly, been granted. It was natural for a girl to cling to life; but he had prayed that her hold on it might mercifully weaken, as her eighteen-year-old body waned and lightened to its twentieth year, and bones protruding almost through the white young face advertised the unremitting approach of death.

He broke off, contrite. How dare he say that prayer had not been answered, when he had been given strength to continue month after month his work for displaced laborers, for the middle-class insane, for the irrigation of India, for the efforts of Garibaldi, for the Sunday theater services? And he had been sustained during his six-month separation from his darling wife while she remained at Torquay with Mary. How dare he, when she too had been sustained almost until the end in her incomparably more difficult role, a heroic blend of judgment, tact, skill, sympathy, and affection, which seldom allowed her a night's uninterrupted rest, and at least once had kept her for twenty almost unbroken hours at the bedside. And even the brief collapse, when the doctors had given up hope, had been quickly replaced by outward serenity for her daughter's sake. The bond between the two had been beautiful to see.

But unavailing. What was Bishop Hooker's prayer? "Since I owe Thee a death, Lord, let it not be terrible; but Thy will, not mine, be done." So he had prayed on her behalf. And God's will had *not* been his. Except—his frantic mind took comfort—she had not rebelled in word. Her gentleness had astonished him, in such trials as he had never seen or heard of.

"Her faculty and love of teaching children were Heaven-sent; her appearance in the infant school closed all eyes and ears but to her; and truly did that inestimable girl deal out to them the Bread of Life."

So his letter to Haldane continued. But why, his inner turmoil persisted, why had she not been granted—not, at any rate, discernibly—the comforting sign for which he had prayed, of her acceptance in Christ, her Saviour?

"I am punished for my sins," she had shrieked in a paroxysm of choking. Surely one so young, in the eyes of man so innocent, hardly ever had suffered the like. She prayed audibly and asked them to pray. Yet her cry of "Speak to me. I cannot bear silence," was alternated with "Pray do not speak. I cannot bear the sound of a voice," as though her whole nervous system lay bare to terror and suffering.

And at the end. Would he ever efface from his mind, from his sight, from his ears, the writhings and unparalleled chokings of that terrible death? He had suffered acutely with thousands of unknown, nameless children, women, men. This was a child of his begetting, the Baby who had strained at parting for a last sight of him, and would not let go his hand when they were reunited. And he had prayed—a foolish prayer, perhaps, but he was hypersensitive to the sunlight and yearly felt sad when the twenty-second of June marked the waning of its strength—that she might go out in the bright day rather than in the darkness and solitude of the night. Her last agony had come at twenty-past-three in the morning!

173

" 'What I do,' said our blessed Lord, 'thou knowest not now but thou shalt know hereafter.' " His favorite text—how often he had used it, how near desperately he clung to it—continued his letter. "We submit in faith, being assured that, as God is absolute and perfect wisdom, absolute and universal mercy, He was not unfaithful to Himself in this particular."

But a positive horror was upon him. How he wished that God might reveal to him, before the time when all things would be known, His purpose in such awful severity.

Now he had spent time enough in self-indulgence. He finished and despatched his letter, and turned to the business which had to be settled before he could take Minny to the Continent and arrange a healthful month for the children.

He put resolutely from his mind some misgivings about Conty. The doctor had feared that her lungs might be affected. Of all his children, she alone had reached her seventeenth year with no period of rebellion, self-assertion, natural but distressing estrangement of mind, if not heart, from her father. The others had in turn become—temporarily in some cases, he hoped in all—lukewarm, though not actively opposed to works of temporal and spiritual usefulness. Constance, without priggishness or unchild-like piety, took a zestful interest in them. No. The doctors had often been wrong. Vea had overcome her adolescent delicacy. Now that the strain of Mary's illness was over, Conty too would recover.

XXXI

"THE RIGHT HONORABLE, the Earl of Shaftesbury, K.G." Minny read with relish the address on the envelope her husband held out to her. "Darling, I'm so glad you accepted the Ribbon this time. I hear constantly that it is doing good—giving prestige to your opinions and attitudes. They have been attacked often enough—"

"But—"

"And it is good for the children. Evelyn and Lionel are still bursting with pride. Whether you like it or not, such things carry weight. How pleased precious Mary would have been."

"Well—she has better things to please her now, the darling." Shaftesbury changed the subject abruptly. "Of course, you recognize the hand? We should, both of us. I can never forget his tact and generosity in insisting not only that I accept the Garter, but that I incur none of the expenses. I am convinced that he defrayed them from his own pocket."

"So am I. It's just like Pam. Now my lovely little horse, now pheasants—always on the plea that it gives him pleasure."

"As it must have done to see me preceded by waits, singing boys and flower strewers—each at a moderate fee!" said her husband. "To say nothing of the Garter itself—seventy pounds for that alone—and the banner, helmet, sword, crest—another one hundred and thirty."

"How do you know?"

"By error a receipted copy of the itemized bill was sent to me. That is only a small part. Pam was embarrassed—a rare thing for him—even more than I was."

"What is he writing about now?"

He sighed and shook his dark head with a quick gesture of distaste.

"About his concern for the state of my affairs at St. Giles. In much the same vein, only more urgently, than in his long and ambiguously phrased letter of last year. About which I did nothing, feeling that he was over-suspicious. Now I greatly fear he has reason, as the French say."

Minny's bright face shadowed as she read.

"But Mr. Waters was most highly recommended!"

"And I was so grateful to leave the management at the Saint in experienced hands that I have overcome my discomfort at the expenses and considered any doubts either ignorant or unworthy," said Ashley. "Now I fear I must investigate. But the waste of time, my Pet! Apart from the money."

"Let us be thankful," said Minny who could always remember a cause of cheer, "that Evelyn and Lionel are both in positions. 'Ah yes—our two younger sons, one Treasurer of the County Court of Dorchester, and private secretary to Lord Palmerston, the other a partner in Pinto, Percy and Ashley'. . . . I admit the association with trade has caused some eyebrow-raising but Bava carries it with such an air—"

" 'His Lordship,' " his father quoted the family nickname. "Yes, I am thankful that they require little from me just now but a home."

"What shall you do," she made a gesture with the letter, "about this?"

"I have already asked Burnett to go down and investigate. His firm has, after all, been in complete charge and I have acted steadily on their advice. Perhaps I am over-apprehensive."

He was not. The disclosures, and the muddled confusion delaying disclosure, which his trusted lawyers reported to him over the ensuing weeks, were worse than his most pessimistic fears. As rot, showing small on the outside of a fruit, grows and branches and reveals nothing solid at the core, so the investigation dug away but could not isolate or trace the insidious corrosion of peculation, trickery, and direct fraud. In August Ashley concealed the dismissal of his mismanaging manager under a kindly pretense of voluntary resignation. At that time he was aghast to reckon his loss over twelve years at twelve thousand pounds. A year later the estimate had risen to fifty thousand.

By this time his lawyers were urging him to enter a lawsuit against Waters for embezzlement, to recover twenty-seven thousand pounds for the debt of which they were able to obtain direct evidence. At first the suggestion was dismissed. Vengeance and desire for it was abhorrent to him. But he believed in the reign of law. He consulted the New Testament and decided that St. Paul's strictures on Christian versus Christian before worldly judges was inapplicable in this case. He had been inclined to excuse and pity Waters as inept and led into excess by his association with racing and betting men. But evidence was piled on evidence, recalling puzzle after puzzle in his steward's always plausible dealings: the delay, breakdown, and inefficiency of his brick-making machine; bills out of the blue for eight hundred pounds on "farm repairs," never carried out; an annual three thousand pound interest appropriated; loans from the Land Improvement Society for Drainage disappearing without trace. Deep anger mounted within him. Precious time and energy was being stolen from current matters of vast import—his impassioned protest at the brutal rape of Poland; the collection and presentation of evidence for his Chimney Sweep Act; the welcome and entertainment of a Garibaldi deeply interested in his housing project. And the money—all borrowed in addition to his inherited debts to advance the condition of his people and remove the stigma which his opponents would gladly attach to him as an iniquitous landlord—this had gone. The sum seemed likely now to mount to seventy thousand pounds, and the work was not done or done so poorly that it had to be done over again.

"He *must* have some of it left. He *cannot* have spent it all. My only recourse is to law," he said at last, tapping the last legal communication on his desk with a nervous fury of resolve.

Evelyn, who had come down to the Saint, opened his mouth but let his mother speak.

"Will it do any good, Darling? In view of the difficulties it will involve? You look so pulled now—doesn't he, Edy?—I cannot bear to think of your tangling with lawsuits."

176

"I doubt very much," contributed Evelyn, "if a man like Waters has retained enough to make it worthwhile."

His father looked at him. Through his mind, as a succession of past scenes to a drowning man, the last twelve years passed in review: association with need upon bleak need; agony of want and filth and consequent vice and apathy and crime; individual faces and masses of tattered, huddled figures; his efforts with courageous, devoted, unpaid assistants to minister to them; chair after chair of meetings to raise funds; innumerable letters and calls—at one time standing outside the Lords buttonholing any likely contributor for a pound—and all the time feeling shame that his own contributions, though made at the sacrifice of luxury and personal requirements, were far smaller than any but a few intimates could understand; humiliation at his inability to provide an attractive dowry for his daughters, or—yet—a respectable settlement for his sons. And what seventy thousand pounds could have done!

"Worthwhile or not worthwhile," Edy had never heard such anger in his father's voice, "it is bare justice. Justice I demand." He turned abruptly away.

The room was very quiet after he left it. They watched his tall figure stride down the path and stop to lean against one of the great stone urns, gazing over the autumn garden to the long avenue of interlacing trees. Minny had followed her son to the window and stood with her arm around him. At last he spoke.

"I've never seen Father like this. I remember how strongly he felt when he was tricked out of giving his vote against abolition of capital punishment—how he opposed Ewart's motion. I was only a kid but it impressed me because he is so kind, and a good many for the Abolition aren't concerned at all about people as he is."

"It is his concern about people and the dignity of man that makes him wish to retain Capital punishment," said his mother with insight born from years of study of her husband's apparent paradoxes. "He is, as you say, tenderhearted. He is not sentimental. And he has a passion for justice."

"Well—I know he has a hot temper. But he is usually so good—about things happening to him particularly. Now he seems almost beside himself."

"I have seen him like it only once before. It suddenly came back to me when he strode out like that, as if it were yesterday." Minny shivered at the recollection. "Again it had to do with justice. Did I never tell you children how your father prosecuted the postilion?"

"Never." Evelyn welcomed the relief. "When did a postilion fall foul of him? Poor chap. Or was he?"

"No. It was long before you were born. Papa and Mum had taken us with Accy—we left baby Francis at home—for a holiday to the Continent. It was

177

the autumn after your father had taken on the Ten Hours Bill. They offered to look after Accy in Milan and your father and I had a delayed honeymoon in Italy." She smiled a little with happy recollection. "Actually the only spoiling incident happened on our way from San Marino to Loretto. One of the lead horses fell and lay as though dead. I still cannot bear to think how the driver treated it, especially the postilion, who seemed quite mad and foamed at the mouth with rage. Ashley would not let me look but I heard the man cursing and the sound of the whip. Then he kicked and stamped on the poor creature's mouth and side and eye. You can imagine your father! We were alone on a lonely mountain road. He ordered them to stop; he threatened them with the law. It was all I could do to keep him from using physical force on the three of them, and they looked like brigands. Well—Ashley reported it at Loretto, had only a regretful shrug from the postmaster, went from commissary of police to secretary, to president, and finally, after a great deal of delay and inconvenience, succeeded in having the cruel brutes imprisoned, though for only three days."

"The germ of his project for a Bill to Prevent Cruelty to Animals! Is there anything he won't fight against?"

"No wrong thing," said his mother proudly. "Believe me, if he prosecutes Mr. Waters it is not from personal animosity, though he has been deeply hurt. It distresses him more than you will ever know to find himself mistaken in his estimate of a man. Unless, as rarely, the man turns out better than he believed. Then he is always delighted."

Evelyn bent and kissed her.

"I shall go and talk to him, though I doubt if I can change his mind. But I greatly fear that no good will come out of legal proceedings."

How right he was, even his father admitted, when by Christmas, Waters, on the daring advice of a lawyer, brought a counter-suit. And when, shortly afterwards, a farmer, whose invalid agreement with Waters had been repudiated by Shaftesbury, brought another suit which, like the former, went into Chancery.

Meanwhile his confidence in the lawyers was also being undermined. No amount of legal terminology could cover up a deplorable record of inefficiency bordering on fraud. In complete charge of his affairs, they had taken a yearly fee of one hundred pounds to audit his accounts; and the accounts had never been audited. Later in the case, Vice-Chancellor Kindersley was to cry in disgust: "Does this man presume to call himself an auditor?" They had advised him to have an estate account at the Provincial bank where Waters could draw drafts. Now he had reason to doubt if they had ever examined the pass books. Waters, he found, had never kept any account of the vast sums obtained for drainage and land improvements. The lawyer now told him that his steward's accounts were in such confusion that their clerk had put the papers away in disgust. "No doubt!" said their astonished employer, reminding his informants of their constant reassurance that the accounts were "satisfactory" or more recently "not what I could wish but you will perhaps sign"—as, pressed by affairs and confiding, he foolishly had done.

He had replaced Waters in '63 by Mr. Turnbull and, after several years of the latter's careful administration, concluded sadly that, if he had been steward from the beginning, he might have saved eighty thousand pounds and have twenty thousand to hand. In '64 he hired a new lawyer, who proved dependable and skilful through the miserable, expensive, protracted Chancery proceedings. During that period Shaftesbury apologized mentally to Dickens for having considered Bleak House grossly exaggerated.

It was a new phase of humiliation for the proud spirit which, thirty-five years earlier, had chafed at insulting language from Radicals. The County squires who made up the Grand Jury at Dorchester, afraid of being charged with favoritism to their Lord-Lieutenant, treated him with scant courtesy. He was "detained, badgered, vexed, insulted," and the case was transferred to London on the appeal of Waters' lawyer, that it should be tried on neutral ground.

Ashley's straightforward mind boggled at legal equivocations. In spite of his own clear conscience in this instance, he was always ready to question his own motives, his own character. His puzzlement grew beneath the barrage of Waters' virtuous claims, a judge's praise and judgment in his favor, the support of the Spectator and the Saturday Review—nothing is as good copy as a prominent Christian in the law courts—vicious anonymous letters, one so fearfully blasphemous and obscene that he could not show it to anyone. He asked himself if it could be possible that his ex-steward was innocent. And, "if so," he asked his diary, "what am I? Can I be awfully deceived?"

Fortunately, Mr. Waters was unable to maintain any of his fluent falsehoods under examination, and his refusal to answer a large proportion of the questions asked him raised Ashley's hopes. They were dashed again when decision was given upholding the farmer, Lewer. Appeals and counter-appeals dragged months into years. Perhaps the greatest blow to his self-esteem, confirming the delight which his opponents felt in his difficulties, was the information that some fellow Peers had taken a subscription (with single contributions as high as two hundred pounds) to enable his unfaithful steward to continue his litigation. Mercifully, the Lord Chancellor declared against Waters, and his trial for embezzlement was finally set. At this point the wretched man declared himself bankrupt and his lawyer, Lord Portman, suggested that Shaftesbury withdraw proceedings against him.

There was nothing to be gained by continuing. Ashley, in spite of his passion for justice, many times regretted being drawn by his original lawyers into prosecution. So after five years he had the wry satisfaction of being thanked in court, through Counsel, by the embezzler for his forbearance.

But if Waters was bankrupt, his ex-employer was nearly so. The lawsuits had added five thousand pounds to his indebtedness. His mother, having passed the age of ninety, died in '65, and the price of the Dowager house at Richmond went almost entirely in assigning ten thousand pounds as Evelyn's fortune. He then, with deep regret, sold Swine, his cherished Yorkshire property, for one hundred and twenty-five thousands pounds—to discover later that his friends had driven a hard bargain—and grimly recorded its use:

Payment of Mortgages to Hand in Hand—eighty-eight thousand pounds.

Payment of money lent free by

five friends—twelve thousand pounds.

Payment of Insurance Office—nine thousand pounds.

Residue—sixteen thousand pounds.

To Lionel—eight thousand pounds.

Investment in Iron Works for Cecil—five thousand pounds.

XXXII

IN THE SOMBER FINANCIAL LANDSCAPE two gleams of light had cheered him, less by their practical ministration than by the encouraging kindness which prompted them. At the blackest depth of his initial discoveries, a letter from Palmerston to Minny enclosed five thousand pounds: "I must be allowed to pay my half of your son's start in the world"—apparently with reference to their outlay for Lionel's partnership. And a year later, when the suits had gone into Chancery, his non-conformist friend, Samuel Morley, together with four others, insisted on making him a loan of twelve thousand five hundred pounds without interest or security. He had accepted with gratitude and relief; it was with equal relief that he was able to insist on its repayment out of the proceeds of Swine.

Now—July of '68—he emerged from the long nightmare. "I have been an unhappy, unskilful, but not unfaithful steward of my estate," he wrote to his sister Caroline, reporting on the progress of house alterations for which she was paying. "But I am hoping for such clearance that within the next two years no tradesman will be waiting for his bill. I have reduced the stables, gardens, game, to the lowest point. Thanks to Mr. Turnbull's honest efforts there will presently not be a bad cottage. Many of them are first rate and the peasantry sit at easy rents."

But he was always on the verge of subsistence and longed to be free of debt with longing that sometimes burst out in passionate utterance.

"God bless you," he wrote affectionately to Morley. . . . "And keep you out of debt!" It seemed to him the acme of personal happiness. "I could live perhaps on a pound a week," he confided to his diary. "Others must be otherwise maintained or ruined socially. What a painful, degrading, heart-wearing thing is debt! Our blessed Lord suffered in all points as we—except, as far as we know, from debt!" As far as we know—the thought arrested his murmuring.

He took stock of the situation. They had been eventful years. He had not allowed, as far as he could help, his legal troubles to affect his personal and political and philanthropic work. He had pressed with considerable success for legislation to curb the brutalities of agricultural gang labor for children. He had, fifteen years after he conceived the idea, obtained the use of the fifty-gun frigate, the *Chichester*, and later of the *Arethusa*, to be fitted up as training ships for homeless boys. He had opened the Farm and Shaftesbury Schools and Fortescue house to train other such boys for agricultural labor or migration to the colonies; he had established similar training refuges for girls at Sudbury and Ealing. . . . He had made himself more abominable than ever to Tractarians by seeking to stay the tide of Ritualism with his bill on Clerical Vestments. He had taken vigorous part in opposing the "Neological" or Higher Critical attitude towards the Scriptures expressed in such publications as *Essays and Reviews*, Seeley's *Ecce Homo*, Rénan's *Vie de Jésus*, Bishop Colenso's *Pentateuch*; while with customary large-mindedness he protested Bishop Gray's effort to defrock that offending clergyman, though the book he "loathed with the utmost abhorrence." Similarly he grieved and exasperated the predictably orthodox by refusing his vote to an effort to exclude Dr. Jowett from the Chair of Greek at Oxford because of his Neological views. "Heaven knows how I loathe his theology," he wrote frankly, "but we should not put him down by dishonoring his Chair." And

181

with equal pursuit of truth, regardless of its source, he disconcerted his Evangelical brethren by recommending warmly that they read "Lectures on the Prophet Daniel" by Dr. Pusey. "A man of greater intellect, of more profound attainments, or of a more truly pious heart than Dr. Pusey, it would be difficult to find in any Christian nation."

Small wonder that he had been summarily and publicly deposed from the leadership of the Protestant party, with perhaps half a dozen letters of regret and appreciation of his services, countered by such statements as: "Protestants want another sort of man." "You are too well known." "Your opinions are extreme." "You suit no one purpose." The announcement was, he admitted, another mortification to his self-love; he tried to take comfort in the fact that it saved a world of trouble and responsibility.

At the other end of the scale he had been again pressed, this time by Lord Derby, to accept a seat in the Cabinet as Duke of Lancaster—and refusing, had been tentatively offered the Home Office or the Presidency of the Council.

In his family? Lionel's business venture—no blame to him—after three years turned out disastrously. The firm declared itself bankrupt. Evelyn balanced the scale of good and bad by marrying Sybella, daughter of Sir William Farquar. The addition of "Sissy" to the clan proved an unqualified joy; and the arrival of young Wilfrid, the next year, contradicted Shaftesbury's prognostication in an hour of gloom that the family name would die out. So far Anthony's children were girls. Their relationship was still distant but the young Ashleys had established a home in Wimborne St. Giles, and his heir gave frequent indications of turning into a model landlord, popular with his people, and capable once again of spasmodic bursts of pious feeling.

Dear St. Giles's! It was perhaps Ashley's only marital trial and the only point on which he allowed himself secret criticism of his adored wife, that she did not share his love for the home of his ancestors, at least to the extent of wishing to spend much time there. Long residence, because of expense, was impossible; even a few weeks of house-party at Christmas or Easter required an outlay ruinously beyond his means. But surely in the summer? Yet it always seemed to him that they scarcely arrived before Minny had plans, or had accepted an invitation, to go elsewhere. "The girls need the sea-air." "You must drink the waters." It did not occur to him that a country-house constantly reminding its chatelaine of debt was less than cheerful, even to the cheer-loving, cheer-dispensing Minny. There she was surrounded by buildings in the process of renovation; she saw the walls continually being shorn of their finest paintings; the beautiful new entrance hall was unable to welcome the guests for whom it was designed. Even the splendid bust of her

182

husband, which four thousand Manchester operatives had presented to her in a touching ceremony, and which had been erected under the eye of Noble, the sculptor, seemed to give a symbolic loneliness to the unused surroundings. So for their family Minny preferred Broadlands and Brocket, and chose holidays on the Continent, largely because only in isolation from England could she compel her husband in any degree to relax.

"In fourteen years we have spent only two summers—partly—in Dorset," he once ventured to remonstrate. "That is but little."

"I think it's quite enough," she had said with unexpected tartness, which he ascribed to a visitation of her "special pains." But he did not try again. With the constant carking cares to which she was subjected because of him, it was as little as he could do to accede to her wishes.

For the cares were very real. The boys, out in the rough-and-tumble of the business and political world, escaped much of the depression which carping and slurring articles in the Press caused Minny and the girls. Constance was particularly affected by sensitivity of feeling; the chest symptoms which had caused her parents alarm were never wholly absent. "Coming out" in her state of health had been out of the question. Edith (Hilda to the family) had made her eighteen-year-old bow to society. But Vea was now thirty. Other girls far less attractive were sought by eligible suitors "it must be something in my personal character and career which has operated perniciously on their prospects," thought her father sorrowfully. "Probably my public and social life has averted young men and their parents from near connection with me."

But one event during that nightmare quinquennium had, by its emotional impact, dwarfed the importance of all other personal matters: Lord Palmerston had died.

"He is the peg driven through the isle of Delos," Shaftesbury had written a few months before; "Unloose him and all is adrift." But how true his prophecy would prove to him personally he had not expected. His mother-in-law had revolved with her husband around the center of all political movements. "Stay! We must have a party," had been her husky drawling answer to every diplomatic conundrum. No one would ever know how many had been solved at her famous Cambridge House assemblies. Now that glittering orbit was arrested, that unstinting devotion objectless, the pivot on which her social and political importance turned was gone. Lady Palmerston, now Countess Melbourne, mistress of Broadlands and Brocket, mother and grandmother, still had many interests. But the main interest of her life, her inheritance from the governing Whiggery of another era, had come, with the last representative of that era, to an end.

183

But why, her son-in-law asked himself, should he feel it so personally and intensely? Why should a sense of age which had certainly not come to him with the death of his father, nor recently with that of his mother, be upon him now?

Because Pam had been *"Ultimus Romanorum"*? Because in his jaunty, alert, eighty-one-year-old frame he embodied the England of muddle-headed, instinctive, dogged individualism that refused to be set in a mold, or to be bound by inexorable precedent, or to take itself and its dignity with massive seriousness? Because of all the men who had been in the government from his boyhood Pam alone remained? Because—

It baffled all reason, Shaftesbury had thought as he followed his dear friend's coffin up the long nave of the Abbey, that he should ever call Lord Cupid his dear friend, that the insouciant, irreligious politician should feel for him—as he had obviously felt—warm affection and regard.

"Wonderful Pam!" he had written when his father-in-law was well past seventy. "Strong as a horse, lively as a kitten, laboring all day, sitting up all night in the House—vigorous, cheerful, ready."

His mind leaped clear of the hushing crowds, of the familiar vaulted dimness, and straddled the intervening years to recall his early impressions of the Parliamentary career which stretched sixty years back into his own childhood: Palmerston the Tory Changeling, the Canningite, the Whig recruit, standing for much that I detested, using methods that I deplored, predictable only on one count: that he would uphold the name and honor of England and Englishmen in any international situation, but also that he demanded from such exiles conduct not disgracing their name. It was not mere ripost when he answered the intended compliment of a Frenchman: "If I were not a Frenchman, I should wish to be an Englishman," with the quashing, "If I were not an Englishman, I should wish to be an Englishman." Yet from the day I married Minny, and later, since his marriage with Mum brought us into increased intimacy, he has shown towards my most awkward, unpopular, ridiculed concerns and projects a degree of understanding and defense and support which I have lacked from far more sober and virtuous politicians. A great and mighty door for good is now closed upon me, as far as I can see, forever.

It was typical of Shaftesbury that he attributed the understanding support to Palmerston's excellence, his reasonable and unvenal character, rather than to the powerful persuasion of his own dedication. He knew that many of their set considered Minny to be Palmerston's daughter, their belief confirmed by his unconcealed affection for her from a child. "Come in, come in, Minny," he had said a few days before his death. "You always seem to me like a sunbeam." But Ashley had always refused to entertain the idea. Lord Cowper, his wife's kind "papa," had been, in his quiet, undemonstrative fashion, devoted to Minny also. Nothing could be proved that way except the complete lovableness of his wife; attractive to every man, yet from the day of their marriage with eyes and heart for no one but him. The gossip which had assumed Mum as Pam's mistress for thirty years before her marriage to the notorious bachelor had been so long put out of his conversation with his wife that it seldom crossed their minds and—in the absence of certain knowledge or admission—was neither believed nor repudiated. Their personal standards of marriage had been (miraculously in Minny's case, unsourced in his) Puritanical, long before the late lamented Prince Consort had associated such standards with Victoria's Court; but, as children of the Regency, they had moved in circles where private immorality was public knowledge, flagrant yet discreetly unadmitted. Shaftesbury's eager hope for his friend's salvation rested on the dying man's ready acquiescence when his physician questioned him regarding his faith in Christ, and on his lack of dissent at the prayers uttered over him at the last; not on any indication of repentance for his amours or for a life spent in the pursuit of purely worldly affairs.

Yet there had been more; many indications in his later years that the faith he never disavowed influenced his conduct and attitudes. He had a very special dislike of every form of clerical assumption. "I have always endeavored," he stated, "in making Church appointments, to choose the best man I could find. If a man is a good man, I don't care what his political opinions are." Hence the Shaftesbury Bishops!

The procession had reached the chancel and Shaftesbury found himself able to scan the faces of a half-score of Deans, Bishops, even an Archbishop, who had been appointed on his advice. Good and proper men, all of them, he thought gratefully, sound members of the Church of England, active in their dioceses, acceptable to the working-people, moderate and decent in their language and personal intercourse with Nonconformists. Not all of them as good as those he would have recommended if the choice had been his own. He had been sensitive to the difficulties of a Prime Minister's position, and had recommended only those whose appointments could be defended on grounds other than the two considerations most important to himself: Scriptural faith, with the ability to communicate it, and a shepherd heart of concern for the flock of God.

Precious little credit he had gained by his abstentions! "Lord Palmerston's wicked appointments meet us at every turn," the infuriated Bishop of Oxford had written to Gladstone. Yet of Pam's thirty-eight appointments most were well received by the people and none was questioned, except by such baffled Tractarians. Palmerston's dislike of Romish doctrines and practices went even beyond his own.

Similarly Pam had consulted him or listened to his suggestions regarding secular honors to be bestowed. He had granted baronetcies to Baxter of Dundee and Crossley of Halifax in acknowledgement of their generosity to the people. He had appointed Dr. Payne-Smith Regius Professor of Divinity at Oxford, and Dr. Shirley Regius Professor of Ecclesiastical History. Without Shaftesbury, Palmerston would have had no idea of their abilities or worth.

Only when he had suggested a place in the Cabinet for his old enemy, John Bright, to let him demonstrate if he could use responsible power, Pam had refused sharply.

"No. He's too bad a man." Bright he considered really bad. "Haughty and envious, false, revolutionary, a mere leveller, without principle, without ordinary humanity" were terms the more striking because Pam rarely spoke severely of anyone. He had never forgotten the occasion during the changes of the Factory Act, when Bright had begged him not to allow the provision to pass commanding sheathing of machinery, as a protection to females and little children. It was too expensive for the manufacturers, he argued. It was far better that some of these accidents and mutilations occur than that trade be impeded by such regulations!

Gladstone, oddly enough, was the other public man—perhaps it was their mutual antipathy—about whose tendencies and hostility Palmerston was equally positive.

His death had curtailed, too, another opportunity of doing good, thought Shaftesbury. Almost all applicants for the Bounty Money made their approach to him through his son-in-law; and the busy Prime Minister, knowing that each case had been thoroughly investigated, confirmed his every recommendation.

"He will be a great loss to us," Florence Nightingale had written. "Though he made a joke when asked to do the right thing, he always did it. I shall lose a powerful protector. He was so much more in earnest than he appeared."

All would now be different, Ashley agreed. For many years he had been near the center of all action in politics, the fountainhead of all information. Now, not only Palmerston but the age of Palmerston was gone. The strong hand which had held the gates against a flood of change had been removed. "Gladstone will have his own way. We shall have," he gloomily echoed Pam's words, "strange doings."

XXXIII

"WILL I SAY A FEW APPROPRIATE WORDS at the unveiling of Lord Palmerston's statue in Romsey on the twenty-third?" Shaftesbury repeated aloud from the letter lying before him. He glanced at his desk calendar. July 14. Only three days since the end of the Waters litigation and he had not become accustomed to the sense of relief. "Come in, Lionel, come in. Yes, of course I will, though I abominate the hypocrisy of acquiescing in the ascription of the statue to the 'gratitude of Hampshire,' when I know that Mum has had to pay over half the cost! Sorry to subject you to a monologue, your Lordship." He was suddenly struck by something in his son's face. "You look like the bearer of news. Although I have not yet learned to read your expression under the disguise of that splendid moustache!"

"You *have* read it though." There was unsuppressed excitement in Lionel's voice. "Father, something has happened. I think you'll be pleased. I know you'll be pleased."

"Then I shall be pleased. A second piece of good news in a single week. Out with it, your Lordship. If this is a day of good tidings you do not well to hold your peace."

The Scripture was not lost on Lionel.

" 'Weeping may endure for a night but joy cometh' "—he riposted neatly. "With the ruin of the firm and my hope of a post dashed last month, I felt it was a long night." His father was standing now, an affectionate hand on his shoulder. The two dark heads were almost on a level. "Father, I know you are busy. But will you come and pay a visit with me—now? We can walk. It is just down Park Lane."

"I refuse to pay any visit unless I know why and to whom. And will it not be better when your mother returns? I expect, from her last letter, that she and Conty will cross next week."

"No, really. It cannot wait. I shall ask Mother to pay a call soon, of course. But it cannot be official until you consent. Father, I'm in love, really in love at last! And with the loveliest creature in the world."

"Who is—?"

"Fanny Hanbury-Leigh. 'Younger daughter,' as the Landed Gentry would describe her, 'of Capel Hanbury-Leigh, deceased, of Pontypool Park, Monmouthshire.' And just to prove her excellence she is in love with me, even though she knows I have no fortune and no title."

"A discerning young lady." Shaftesbury could not bear to dampen his son's enthusiasm, but he remembered his own months of suing for Minny, and had few illusions about the present attitude of parents towards almost penniless suitors. "Her father is dead. How does her guardian—is it her mother?—feel about the connections?"

"She wishes to meet you and to know your attitude, of course. I said I should try to bring you this morning. I am counting on your making a great impression. For my sake. . . ."

"Anything you say. Shall I wear my dress uniform complete with blue Ribbon? I am most imposing in it!"

Shaftesbury, still able to match his stride with his thirty-year-old companion, hoped, as Lionel raised the knocker at the Curzon Street house which Mrs. Hanbury-Leigh had taken for the London season, that his well-worn frock coat and neatly brushed silk hat were equally imposing. There was no doubt that his self-confident son had at last been reduced to the condition of humble suitor. Love had made him vulnerable. His father, recollecting his own youthful vulnerability, ached at the possibility that the tremulous eagerness, which made him look schoolboyish in spite of moustache and top hat, was doomed to disappointment.

For he had deduced, from the none-too-coherent conversation as they walked down Park Lane, that the family was wealthy. The hall and morning room into which they were presently ushered confirmed the impression of affluence. He was conscious that, while his name and connections were socially superior to the County families who possessed this wealth, the wealth enabled them to look higher than a third son for social advancement. Kind hearts might, according to Mr. Tennyson, be more than coronets, but neither kind heart nor coronet was at a disadvantage in the marriage-market if accompanied by a fortune; and it had been his observation of human nature that the value set upon such fortune seemed to rise in proportion to the evaluator's possession of wealth.

So he was not sanguine.

His wistfulness increased when Mrs. Hanbury-Leigh and her two daughters entered the room. Mrs. Leigh had passed from black to the violet stage of her mourning, and the color, and the small cap and veil were becoming. The elder daughter, whose betrothed, as Lionel had told him during their walk, had been killed at Cawnpore during the Mutiny, showed, in an intelligent, sensitive face, marks of sorrow still unforgotten after ten years. But in Fanny the evident exuberance of new love gave bloom to a complexion and features lovely enough without it. From her small-heeled shoes colored to match the crinoline dress of fawn-striped green silk, to the fair hair caught in a modish chignon, she was a model of youthful fashion. But the hazel eyes were honest; their glance was modest; and her greeting was so shyly warm that Shaftesbury's impressionable heart yearned to have her as daughter-in-law, and grieved at the possibility that worldly considerations might prevail.

The next few moments were uncomfortable for everyone. Small talk had never been one of Shaftesbury's accomplishments. Mrs. Leigh, in spite of obvious social competence, seemed little better at developing the spate of introductions, queries regarding Lady Shaftesbury's health and whereabouts, comments on the weather and channel crossings, into anything resembling easy conversation. Lionel's nervousness had increased pathetically with the excitement of his beloved's presence. The two sisters, trying to fill the gaps with appropriate girlishness, made remarks together, broke off simultaneously to let the other speak, and left the silence more awkward with each effort.

Shaftesbury, always quick to feel inferiority in social chat, inured to public criticism, and still smarting from his long and humiliating experience in the courts, was quite unconscious of the cause. It did not cross his mind that he was a figure of awe, almost a legendary name, or that there was anything in the experience of meeting him which could rob these affluent and easy people of their tongues. He felt that he was failing his son and was grateful when Lionel came to his own rescue.

"Mrs. Leigh Ma'am, Father, do you care if we leave you to talk? The young ladies usually take their spaniels to walk in the Park and I should like to escort them. We shall be back within the hour."

The diversion was welcome. By the time the three had returned in street clothes to take their temporary leave, a small green "pork pie" hat perched entrancingly above Fanny's chignon, and a King Charles tugging at the leash in her gloved hand, the atmosphere had lightened. Mrs. Leigh's comment when the door closed on them pitched a cheerful note for their interview.

"They are very much in love."

"Yes. I'm afraid Lionel is as unable to disguise his feelings as I was at his age."

"Then may I hope that you are not against the match? I have felt guilty to let it go so far without ascertaining your feelings. Believe me it was not intentional. Not until I realized how often we were meeting, apparently by chance, did I discover my daughter's preference. The change in your son's manner was equally evident. I am afraid young people are more impetuous— they have, of course, much more freedom—than in my day."

"I doubt if Lionel is more impetuous than I was when I met his mother," said Shaftesbury. "You ask me if I am against the match. Where my son's heart is engaged and the object of his affection so evidently worthy, why should I be? Frankly, I am only afraid that you may not find it equally advantageous."

He liked her responsive and dignified honesty.

"I was speaking of the difference in our families. You are referring to your son's lack of fortune, of which he has made no secret from the first."

" 'Family,' as you must be well aware, is of little practical value, especially for a third son when there is no expectation of coming into the title."

"In many cases, I should agree. In yours, Lord Shaftesbury, I do not hesitate to affirm that I consider a link with you, personally, an honor for my daughter which outweighs more worldly advantages."

Shaftesbury was speechless. His companion continued with some maternal pride.

"I shall not disguise the fact that there have been attractive offers. In confidence I may tell you that Lord Mahon has laid his wealth and future title at my child's feet. But she loves Lionel. I believe that they are suited mentally and spiritually to make each other happy. So I should prefer him, were he absolutely penniless, to any other. My dear Emma, whose attitude I find warm and generous in view of her own loneliness, agrees with me; and I have come to feel great respect for her judgment."

"I suppose you realize," said Shaftesbury with his rare smile, "that this is an epoch in the history of social life in England?"

"Then," said Mrs. Hanbury-Leigh gracefully, "it is appropriate that it should be connected with one who himself forms an epoch, altering the trend in thinking and action of our Kingdom. Believe me, Lord Shaftesbury, this is not idle flattery, but expression of opinion formed long before I had any idea our paths would cross, still less, conjoin."

"Madam, you overwhelm me," said the "epoch" frankly. "I cannot pretend that such words do not please me—more, perhaps, than they should. Especially as your high opinion of me is by no means universal! You may have read the recent statement of Mr. Cook, editor of the *Saturday Review*, that he hates all party of which I am the type and leader!"

"I am not dependent for my views," said Mrs. Leigh with fine scorn, "on Mr. Cook or others like him. And, since you quote, did I not read a report in the *Times* recently—you had been at a prize-giving I believe—referring to you as a 'nobleman by nature as by birth, drawing your rank from a higher Source than Royalty can command'?"

Shaftesbury spoke with difficulty.

"Then, not unnaturally, I esteem my son's choice—'like mother, like daughter'—even more highly."

In such an atmosphere the mundane arrangements to which they gave attention were easily made. Why should they not be, Shaftesbury asked himself, when he heard the size of Fanny's immediate dowry and her paternal inheritance. When he left Curzon Street after luncheon, with the young people radiant and a date set in December for the wedding, subject to Minny's approval, he thanked God for His wonderful and especial Providence.

XXXIV

"MAY I PRESENT TO YOU the future ninth Earl, if God will, of Shaftesbury."

Roars of applause, repeated cheers for the child, for his father and mother, for himself and Minny, cut short any further speech. It was as well, he thought, for the surge of feeling as he looked down at the baby in his arms swamped his powers of utterance. The christening party, emerging from the church porch, found the entire village population gathered to celebrate the occasion. The almshouses on their right, the Bull across the road, every house and cottage, was bright with flags and flowers. To their left over the great gates of St. Giles's House a triumphal arch had been set up; two others marked the entrance to the village from Cranborne and the gate of Mainsail Haul. Anthony and Harriet, apparently on an impulse as they moved down the aisle, had thrust the child upon their father and insisted that he present their heir to his people. They stood—for the first time in years as a family, Minny thought wryly—below the square church tower in auspicious sunshine, while the photographer, who had set up his camera obscura immediately opposite the Church porch, draped himself under mysterious black cloth, pressed bulbs, removed plates, and repeated the performance to the delight of the crowd, who had never seen one before. Anthony Ashley Cooper, his tiny pink face alone visible above the lacy frills of his christening gown, slept like a cherub while passed to his grandmother, to his mother, back finally to his father; slept even when, the picture-taking over, the crowd burst again into shouts that could never have been heard in Wimborne St. Giles since the first Lord Shaftesbury was born there in the early sixteen hundreds.

"Hurrah for our fellow-villager." "We have a lord of our own now." "Yes, one of us." "God bless the little lord."

191

"The tenantry have consulted me, Lord Shaftesbury, and wish to mark the event by a presentation dinner and a gift of plate to Lord Ashley, at which they would like you to attend," said the new incumbent of the living as they walked up to St. Giles's House in the lovely autumn weather.

"This is really gratifying. Is it not, my Dear?" Shaftesbury turned to Minny and was startled by the pallor of her face against the voluminous black of her mourning. He had forgotten, in the mingled emotions of the day, that it was scarcely more than a month since she had followed her mother's body to its resting-place by her beloved Pam in the Abbey. Poor dear kind Mum—he had not realized until her death how much he loved her. And to his wife's sorrow was added the shock of her abrupt summons when they had just reached Homburg, her enforced homeward journey alone, as he had to follow more slowly with Conty and the rest. A fierce gale had prevented their Channel Crossing and, by the time he could arrive, Minny had watched at her mother's death-bed, and made the necessary decisions for the funeral, without his support. And the long-thrown shadow of illness, which made Conty's girlhood health seem aeons past, was draining her vitality with that of their beloved, perhaps most lovable, child.

She had gamely insisted on accompanying him for this occasion from London. Suddenly he was aware of the memories that this christening would recall, not only of their dear unpredictable eldest who had lingered to bask in the congratulations of the villagers, but of Francis and Maurice and Mary.

She rose to the occasion now with one of her quick sunny smiles.

"Indeed, Mr. Harkness, it is. My husband has always striven to retain the old affectionate bond between landlord and tenant. He regrets that he foresees its passing. This may reassure him."

"I confess I was unprepared for such a show of feeling. It has something of former days. I know I am a sentimentalist but I doubt whether in many countries such respect and affection of peasant for proprietor can be found."

"The country folk are sentimentalists too," said Mr. Harkness smiling. "The idea that this is the first time in two-and-a-half centuries that a son and heir has been born in the village has immensely appealed to them."

"More than that, I think," said Shaftesbury firmly, "much is due to Anthony, who has lived among them and made himself deservedly popular."

That was true, thought Minny as she heard her husband repeat the words warmly to Accy, who with his wife and eleven-year-old Margaret joined them just before they ascended the stone steps to the triple arched entrance of St. Giles's. True, although his settling down among them might not have been entirely his own idea. Her blue eyes, candid, affectionate, but seldom deceived, passed from her son's handsome, excited face to her daughter-in-law,

192

whose manner, always vivacious, had seemed all through the ceremony—
what was the right word?—triumphant.

Ridiculous, my attitude, she reproached herself. Also cold and suspicious. Ashley—her Ashley—would think her very wrong in imputing motives. Still no one could deny that, after bearing Margaret that first reasonably pleasant year of her marriage, Harriet had seemed singularly uninterested not only in other children but also in the one she already had. Grandfather and Grandmother had yearned over little "Poppy," neglected while her parents became notorious for their flamboyant social excursions. They had been repeatedly rebuffed in their offers and attempts to take care of her.

It was seven years later, when Evelyn contemplated marriage, that Harriet gave birth to another daughter and, in well within two years, to another, at almost the same time that Wilfred was born to Evelyn and Sissy. Probably it was undesigned that Susan arrived the next year. Now, with her fourth daughter still in arms, she had finally produced a boy. Wilfred was no longer first in line for the title. Well, Minny, always fair, conceded that the feelings she attributed to her puzzling daughter-in-law were not unnatural. She remembered the veiled hostility of Lady Babs in the early days of their marriage. Her own feeling for St. Giles's was lukewarm because of early association and financial problems. But she could imagine how Ashley, with his atavistic affection for it, would feel if the inheritance had to revert to one of his brothers. It was all wrong, she knew, and their girls were as dear to them as their boys. But how could she, who had borne four sons in easy succession, put herself in Harriet's place?

"—to drink the health of my grandson, the future Ninth Earl, God grant it." They were gathered now in the Yellow Drawing Room and her husband's words recalled her and, the next instant, caused her acute discomfiture. "Perhaps the greatest temporal blessing I can pray for him is that he may have such a mother as his father had, unceasing, unsparing, unrivalled in her efforts for her children, in her affection, in her judgment."

"Of course I should have said it. I spoke with deliberation," said Shaftesbury, quite impenitent under her reproach. The company had left after a pleasant enough luncheon and Minny, with apologies for exhaustion, was resting in her room. "There was nothing that could be misinterpreted in paying a slight and very inadequate tribute to the child's grandmother. If Rita chooses to read more into it—"

"That will be exactly what you intended."

"I should rather say: 'If the cap does not fit, let her see that it does.'"

Shaftesbury sat down by the bedside, tucked the coverlet more warmly around her, and put a strong, cool hand caressingly on the aching forehead.

193

"Not that it ever can, perfectly. But it will give her a goal to aim at. Dearest of women, I know how often in my excitable temper I have said unjust and cruel things to you—"

"Have you indeed? I don't remember," said Minny, and her husband knew that it was true; she had a sublime power to forget. "But I should hate not to remember other things you used to say—lovely, extravagant, thrilling—"

"*Used* to say," said her husband indignantly. "I still say them: God never gave an earthly gift more in harmony with my early imagination, with what I ventured to think of and dared pray for. You are the accomplishment of all I asked or could have asked. And you are as captivating, as lovely, and as charming as on the day—can it be thirty-nine years ago?—when you became mine. Now what can be more moderate, less extravagant than that?"

"You are incorrigible." Her voice was never more silvery than with that hint of laughter in it, he thought. "I'm afraid your claim to moderate speech would meet some opposition—as from the lady who spoke about your Climbing boys."

"Immoderate!" Shaftesbury's eyes blazed. "*Her* words yes. 'A chimney sweep, indeed, wanting education. What next?' "

"And all you said—in the Lords too!—was—"

"I said, and I reiterate, that such a woman would cut up a child for dog's meat or for making manure."

"Ashley, Ashley Darling," but there was no reproach in her tone and she took his comforting hand in both hers and held her cheek against it. "I suppose you claim moderation also for your much quoted comment on *Ecce Homo?*"

"Now there I may have been wrong," said Shaftesbury, "although not at the time. An even more pestilential book—I still cannot remember adding 'ever vomited from the jaws of hell,' but in the heat of debate I probably did—is that foul thing you picked up in Paris, *Les Courtesans de l'Antiquite.*"

"About Mary Magdalene, wasn't it? I did not finish it. Remember I was called back to Mum."

"Unhappily it has literary merit, so it will have a wide circulation among the 'polite.' What Satanic imagination! Is this the first time that our most dear Lord has been charged with such sin? I have wondered that his enemies had abstained from that particular blasphemy."

"And this too when He died for us," said Minny simply.

There was a long silence. It was not the first time he had heard the words from her but they always shook him, spoken on that broken note of wondering pain.

When she spoke again it was to change the subject.

"Let us be thankful, Dearest. Anthony seems much steadier, and this display of affection from the village, together with little Anthony, may make the steadiness permanent. Evelyn and Lionel are happily established. Cecil has Cambridge at his feet, he tells me."

"If only our girls—"

Minny tried to toss her head on the pillow and winced with pain. "Serves me right, I shouldn't do that with a headache," she reassured him, "but I find a Christian spirit very difficult to maintain when I think of darling Vea. She has not yet recovered her spirits or confidence from that horrid affair last year with—I will not even name him. Creature!"

"I must admit," he agreed ruefully, "that I had never before felt any impulse to resort to a duel—I, a dueller! How Lord Mornington would have jeered if I had. When I think of the practical scorn with which I answered that foolish challenge of his! But it shows how far personal affront could take us, if we were not under Governance. I confess I yearned for a horsewhip! To lead that poor dear girl to believe that he cared for her—"

"When he was using her as a stalking-horse to pique his heiress into accepting him! I blame myself, Ashley. If we had been home I doubt if he would have dared. And Vea would have confided in us."

"You know you are not to blame. Conty was our first care. But how little Vea deserved it! And though we know that she behaved suitably she feels the insult terribly."

"Much more than the disappointment. And how can I enter into her feelings? At her age I had been married over ten years."

"Perhaps I can. I well remember my feelings of outrage when you kept me dangling."

"I am sure I did no such thing."

"Indeed you did. And all London knew it."

"Well," said Minny, cheering, "I doubt if all London knows of this. Society is less gossiping now, I think. Or perhaps I hear less. And I doubt our Hilda is likely to pine with unrequited love. Where are you going?"

"If you can spare me for an hour or so. I am grieved by a disingenuous report on this property by the Government Commissioner. I had hoped that he would say at least that we were making progress, that our wages were better than in former years, and our cottage accommodation vastly improved. Not a syllable. He pictures the County as it was thirty years ago. So I must acquaint myself with the facts. And Harkness is willing to ride over with me to Hinton Martell to investigate the agricultural gang which seems to be operating in spite of the law."

"My darling, cannot you ever rest? Must you do it today?"

"If not today, when?" asked her husband sensibly. "You say that you must rejoin Conty tomorrow. I have a dozen appointments in London. Else I should gladly stay down until Anthony's dinner."

"Then please be careful. I have always been anxious about your riding since you had that fall."

She had touched his one vanity. He turned from the door, came back to the bed, and looked down at her with a ludicrous assumption of offended dignity.

"How often must I tell you—and it is almost four years since the occurrence—that I did NOT fall? I was thrown violently when my roan swerved rapidly and reared. I do not believe a jockey could have kept his seat. Fall indeed!"

XXXV

"YOU'LL GET THOSE FINE BOOTS covered with clay, m'lord. Well, if you must, you must. But watch your step. It's slippy if you're not used to it."

Shaftesbury shook off the foreman's laconic effort to deter him from his inspection and ventured down the lane towards one of the worked pits, though with sensible caution. The place seemed deserted, a dun-colored featureless wilderness. At some distance he noticed eight or ten pillars varying in height from three to perhaps five feet. What could be their purpose, he wondered idly, unless they were left to indicate the depth to which the clay had been worked in their particular locations? Curiosity took him in the direction of the nearest of these phenomena and was suddenly, startlingly, satisfied.

For at his approach the small pillars, to whom six feet of morning-coated, top-hatted gentleman was an equally startling monstrosity, became mobile and vocal. Screaming as if something satanic were drawing near, they fled to the comparative safety of numbers. By the time he caught up with them, they were going about the work of procuring their next load in numb, tired indifference as if exhausted by their one burst of childish panic; and he was unable to elicit even monosyllabic answers to greeting or question.

196

For—or yet—they were children, even the stunted seventeen-year-old in charge of the little band; and the youngest, as he later found out, was not four. But they were so like the ground in which they worked, features, flesh, tatters of clothing—the younger ones almost naked—so covered with clay that they seemed like products of the earth, unimbued with spirit. By the time they had all acquired their load and tottered off under its weight to the next scene of labor, some carried clay on their heads, some on their shoulders, some little ones hugged the weight of it supported on their distended abdomens.

Shaftesbury plodded behind the procession, silent as they, save for his squishing boots as they were sucked by the clay. The children's bare feet, scarcely lifted, slithered almost noiselessly along. It was mid-afternoon. These little ones had begun work, he knew, at five that morning, and would not be released until at least eight in the evening.

"It is not because of his toils that I pity the poor," he quoted Carlisle between clenched teeth to give himself some release from the vicarious torment which was as usual striking him with enfeebling nausea. "I beg to differ from the sage of Chelsea in his noble, and undoubtedly sincere, reasoning. I too pity—chiefly, I suppose, pity—because the lamp of his soul is never enkindled, because without knowledge he lives and dies on the level of a brute. But, O my God, it is also *because* of his toils. Toils like these. Toils so severe that holidays, if any, are merely pauses of agony between labors; that night does not bring the poor man's slumber of which Carlisle writes so glowingly, but a punctuation mark of exhaustion to prolong exhaustion. These—if my estimates are correct—these brick yards employ thirty-thousand children and young persons. And the condition of men and women is no better—it is degradation and suffering far lower than the beasts of the field."

The grim little procession—they had met and passed several such straggling lines returning silent to the same pit—reached the long drab building and filed inside. The heat of a corridor struck Shaftesbury like a blow, but he followed them to their destination, a kiln where, one by one, they deposited their pitiful burdens beside the brick makers. These, stripped to the waist and working with ferocious steadiness, paid no attention either to their suppliers or to their visitor. He had determined to see conditions for himself; but after two minutes of the atmosphere which felt like a blast from the Inferno, he was forced to stagger from the inner room, make for an outer door, and lean against the building to recover. Leaning there, still weak, he saw the shuffling feet, clay crusted, press back on their relentless treadmill.

"No man with a sense of humanity or with the aspirations of a Christian," he told the Lords, with fervor that forced upon their coolness some realization of the scene he had verbally recreated, "could go through these places and not feel that what he saw was a disgrace to his country and ought not for a moment be allowed to continue. Therefore, my lords, I hope that not a day will be permitted to pass, until an Address is sent up to the Queen, praying Her Majesty to take the condition of these poor people into her gracious consideration, that such abominations may be brought speedily to an end."

So, officially, under protection of the law came the last group. It was just thirty years since he had instigated the Children's Employment Commission.

XXXVI

"This AREA MAY HAVE YIELDED finer produce in former days, but never produce more lovingly and anxiously tended." Shaftesbury paused at the south end of the Dean's Yard and turned to survey a sight which never failed to lift his spirits.

George Holland, who had come from Whitechapel to attend the Annual Flower Show Prize-Giving, looked up at him, puzzled. Dean Stanley explained.

"Lord Shaftesbury refers to the fact that this yard was the Abbey's Home Farm before the Dissolution of the Monasteries. We have just walked past the site of the granary. The Canon's residence here dates from the fourteenth century and was a Guest House of the Abbey."

"And even conceding that to all the monks 'laborare erat orare,' " said Shaftesbury, "I greatly doubt if Our Father, the Creator of all beauty, is not equally honored by these pitiful attempts to bring one of his works to perfection."

"If flowers could tell of their origins, we should be shown some strange surroundings," agreed Stanley. "The patients in Westminster Hospital have sent more exhibits than before, I notice."

"Look at this sad little geranium." Shaftesbury dropped his voice. "Last week I saw one very like it being tended in a cellar, by my little friend Tiny. And many a garret window has been robbed for this display."

"The interest at school has been at fever heat in the past few days. The children have talked of nothing else," said Holland, smiling the smile which had made Shaftesbury say: "He seems to live in the full light of God. It does me as much good to see George Holland's face as to hear a sermon" and again "I had rather be George than ninety-nine one hundredths of the great living and dead."

"Well, it is perhaps time to put them out of their suspense," said the Dean. "I shall see if the judges have reached their decision in every category. Fortunately, Mr. Holland, I can always depend on Lord Shaftesbury to present the prizes in such a way as to cheer the winners while making the losers feel equally estimable."

Shaftesbury shook his head.

"I have a prayer: 'May I die in harness; and may I, before I die, know when to desist from active share in public talking.' It is such people as you and such remarks as that which may delude me when I am no more than a twaddle.   'From Marlborough's eyes the streams of Dotage flow

And Swift expires, a Driveller and a Show.' "

"I can assure you the time is not yet—" began the Dean and broke off, shocked by the sudden change in his friend's face. At the mention of time, Shaftesbury's hand had gone to his waistcoat jacket and come away empty. He was staring down at it, his face bleak and forlorn.

"My watch is gone," he said hollowly. "My watch is gone."

Dean Stanley was suitably distressed. George Holland was frankly amazed. He had seen his illustrious friend break down at the hunger of children in his George Yard Ragged School. He had known him to provide for them in one winter ten thousand bowls of soup, made in his own kitchen and transported from Grosvenor Square. But that the loss of a trinket would affect him so strongly was not in character.

Shaftesbury recovered himself with an effort.

"You do not understand," he said simply. "This is no ordinary watch. I have never used, in fact never had, another. It was a bequest from the best friend I ever had in the world. You have surely, George, heard me speak of Maria Millis, who was a mother to me and who taught me in the things of God. I was eight years old when she died and this—"

"You lost it here? Surely no one. . . ?" The Dean surveyed the assembly with unwilling suspicion as it milled happily around the flowers. Young and old, poorly, disreputably, or neatly dressed, costers in their gaudiest array, ragged children, primly brushed poor folk, many of them looked quite capable of lifting a watch. But not on this occasion, nor from Lord Shaftesbury!

"I last recall pulling it out to check with the railroad clock when I was waiting for Mr. Holland at Charing Cross." Shaftesbury lifted his head at a recollection. "There was a crowd as usual. I remember, just as I caught sight of him, being jostled. That must have been when it happened."

"Then I greatly fear that you will not see it again," said the Dean sadly.

Shaftesbury distributed the prizes, treating each winner with personal and individual warmth, and singling out other entries for approval, until the whole gathering: domestics, laborers, costers, and children, was caught up in his delight and encouragement. Then his manner changed. He became a suppliant.

"My friends, I need your help. When I was a little boy"—he paused, beckoned, and held out his hand to a youngster in the crowd of youngsters who always edged close to him; the boy took it, surprised but confiding, and came up beside him,—"about the size of this young fellow, I had only one friend. She died and left me her watch. Some of you have seen it. In fact all of you who have ever asked me the time have seen it, for I have never had another. On the way to our Prize-Giving today I lost it. It is a gold watch, this size"—he made a circle with his hands—"but the value to me would be as great if it were tin. I beg you to make my loss known so that the finder may restore it to me. You all know where I live."

And they did. 24 Grosvenor Square was by this time far better known among the poor than, for instance, 10 Downing Street. There, at any time of day or night, came callers on strange errands: a well-to-do woman suspecting that a young acquaintance had been wrongfully incarcerated in an asylum (Shaftesbury had left the dinner-table and within fifteen minutes had been on his way to the railway-station to look into the situation and free the victim); a man about to leave the country, probably never to return, who gave a note for five hundred pounds for "Ragged Schools and other things," asking merely that the initials T. H. accompany the gift; the desperate man whom he discovered at his door late one night attempting to thrust a little girl into the arms of his bewildered servant because "I cannot trust myself to be its father; I cannot abandon it altogether; so I have brought the child to you—I don't know what else to do with it" (that little girl, adopted into a well-to-do home, was growing into a beautiful woman); parents begging him to find a runaway girl or boy among the dens and lodging houses to which he had entry; a flower-girl or laborer to be supplied with a basket or with tools for their trade; once a lady with the pitiful story of a Polish refugee (Shaftesbury, more than ordinarily impecunious on that occasion, had no cash in the house. "But the poor fellow must have something." Suddenly to his delight he recalled a five pound note which he had placed in a book as a nest-egg, and his perplexity was solved.)

The Dean's Yard was silent after his announcement. He added nothing to the appeal, made no suggestion of reward.

"I'm afraid he will never see his watch again," said the Dean to George Holland as the tall, erect figure stepped down among the now buzzing people, and a little girl held up her arms and put up her face to be kissed. Holland was sadly inclined to agree.

That was Saturday.

Two evenings later there was a loud ring at the bell in Grosvenor Square. The servant, opening the door, saw two men hastily disappearing into a hansom cab, which as hastily disappeared around the corner. Shaftesbury, leisurely descending the stairs, asked if there was a message.

"Nothing, my Lord. There were two men driving off in a hansom when I opened the door. But they have left a parcel." Long experience in the household had made his attitude stoical. The motion of his hand towards the parcel on the portico was eloquent but resigned.

It was a large canvas sack, firmly tied at the mouth and labelled. It was also animated and moving in squirming uncertainty away from the sound of voices. The two men hoisted it with some difficulty into the hall and closed the door. The label, crudely printed, read: "Eres the theef. Give im wot ee desarves."

The loosened rope discovered a crouching boy of perhaps ten years, Millis's watch clutched in one shaking hand. After a terrified glance around, he made no effort to move, only thrusting the watch forward with a dumb effort at expiation.

Shaftesbury took the hand and the watch in his own and lifted the boy to a standing position.

"Come, my little man. Step out of this sack. Take it away, please, Jimson. I shall call if I need you further."

"And glad I was to get away," Jimson proclaimed below stairs a few moments later. "How my Lord stands to touch these filthy creatures I don't know. Covered with vermin most likely. And smell! O my eye!"

The creature meanwhile had been taken, unwilling but unresisting, to the library. Shaftesbury told him to sit but he remained shrinking against a wall and obviously awaiting judgement. So he sat himself, behind his desk lest his towering presence add to the child's fear.

"Now," he said encouragingly, "tell me about the watch."

He had touched a deep sense of injustice. It welled from the boy in a torrent of words.

"Wot did they go for to do it for? I'd brung stuff before. Lots. Glad they was to get it and give me my bit. Ow was I to know this was different? Grab

201

me they did sif I'd stole the crown jools. Doncha ever touch Lord Shafsbry, they sez. Oo's ee, I sez. Eell settle yer hash, they sez. An popped me inter the sack."

Reading between the indignant lines, Shaftesbury was touched and amazed. The word had been spread. The "fences" had been informed. The young thief, appearing with his finest loot so far, had been instantly apprehended. Was their delivery of the culprit kind or ironical?

It did not make much difference. When, after patient questioning, he learned that the boy did not know how old he was and had only a disturbed memory of people who had "gorn off" and left him; that he slept in a huge iron roller in Regent's Park; when he felt the desolation under his cocky defiance and thought, with the watch in his hand, of a child's capacity for wretchedness and of what one friend had meant to him, he had no choice.

A bath—King, bless her heart, had bathed dirty children before; clothes long outgrown by Cecil, food, much of which they caught him attempting to stow away with squirrel-like providence; and a message to Mr. Weylland of the City Mission, who found a place for him in a Home for Little Boys: the small thief was sent to school with a special and kindly eye kept upon him; and another name was added to Shaftesbury's prayers.

XXXVII

DECEMBER TWENTY-SECOND, 1871.

I am seventy years of age and six months. My eyesight is very good, requiring glasses only for reading; I *am* somewhat deaf, I sleep well, walk easily, though not very far without fatigue. Am tolerably erect and have very few grey hairs. Whatever mind I ever had I think I retain. . . . My feelings are as vivid and as keen as in my youth—on all subjects, except in cases of neglect or affront. Here of course I am not pleased; but I accept the matter, as the French say, a '*fait accompli*,' and there the question ends.

December thirty-first, 1871.

Have been thinking lately of my past career and present position; and am astonished how I went through one and now stand in the other. In knowledge of all kinds behind my chief contemporaries, without pretense to literary attainments (though with an immense fondness for them); intellectually, not strong; over-anxious for success, over-fearful of failure, easily exalted, as easily depressed; with a good deal of ambition and no real self-confidence. Weak in debate, and incapable of any effort without some preparation; a poor and ineffective orator, though foolishly desirous of being a great one.

Yet I have had successes—great successes—successes for a time, the memory of which has passed away. How were they attained? I know not. The only qualities I can claim for myself are feeling, perseverance, and conviction. These, I suppose, have, under God, brought me to the position I now hold—a position of notoriety and even of reputation.

Shaftesbury paused in his personal stock-taking, stepped out on his little balcony, and looked away over the Ligurian sea, violet under sunset. Another winter's exile! He had hoped after last year's wasted months abroad that this year he could spend the precious time before the Session in much-needed work among the London poor and in preparation for forthcoming Bills: the Ballot Act, the Education Bill, the Ecclesiastical Courts—how often he wished that he had not allowed himself to become entangled there!

Below on the terrace Minny had pulled back a rug, and Cecil was helping Constance out of her long chair, as the sharp-slanting shadows announced the sun's departure. Hilda and Sissy, walking briskly up from the beach, joined them. They were greeted with loud squawks, which Hilda alone could interpret, by the parrot, recently acquired from a sailor at the Nice stage of their slow journey. They were stopping longer than they expected at Cannes while Conty recovered strength to go on to Mentone. Sissy looked up at him and waved affectionately. The sight and the sound of these reasons for his exile filled him with remorse at his complaint. After the preceding dreadful July he should feel nothing but gratitude that they were still alive. A scant two months back in England had brought about such a relapse that Dr. Gull prescribed another winter on the Riviera as Conty's only hope. Even more frightening had been Cecil's sudden illness. Was it brain fever? Meningitis? Infantile Paralysis? The doctors debated while he hovered between life and death and while Minny's anxiety for her "baby" drove her to unreasonable and inordinate effort. She watched over him day and night. Scarcely had he passed the crisis when she herself collapsed.

She had recovered—almost it appeared by an effort of will, so that attention would not be distracted from her children. But in spite of a journey to Scotland where their health was temporarily renewed, and in spite of sea-air at Folkestone, Conty was spitting blood again and the doctors counselled haste. They advised, too, that Cecil suspend his studies at Cambridge for the year.

So now—if Conty was well enough, they would go on to Mentone in a day or so. And if conditions there were favorable, he could return for the Opening in February. But he hated these partings, these increasingly long periods of separation from his wife. The see-saw of Conty's illness rendered him, as nearly as could be, without conscious preference for her future. Unless, of course, she could be completely restored! To linger through such pain as she intermittently experienced, and through such weakness as was her almost constant state, no one who loved her could wish. But they all loved her. No one of his children had maintained a more continuous loving relationship with all her friends. Without insipidity, with eager appreciation, she enjoyed life but did not seem to cling to it. Yet while she lived, as long as there was hope, he and her mother—what a mother! he thought, noting the slight limp from a knee which had caused her trouble for years—must do whatever was possible to prolong, to ameliorate that life.

As for the expense—he sometimes felt it a weary indignity that he, who cared nothing for money, should have to think so much about it. But it seemed base and unworthy, when a crisis brought a specialist from London to St. Giles's for Minny, that the fee of seventy-three guineas should cause him distress. It did. Not the money but the fact that he did not—in actual fact—have it, that it swelled again his slowly diminishing indebtedness. And even now he was accumulating bills, sent in with the leisurely assurance of the wealthy physician, for these last illnesses: sixty pounds from Sims, sixty-six from Gull, sixteen from Crosby, twelve from Potts, an estimated hundred from Ellis. He was—not for the first time—at his wit's end.

God is my only hope, he thought desperately, and, with customary adjustment of values, put worry below his surface thought—except, as always, to feel a deep pang for the many, the so many, who had to see their loved ones in pain, and had no means to provide for their relief.

But his darling wife! surely they would soon—he refused to face the how—be together and share the tranquillity of approaching age.

He stepped from the balcony into a darkening room. There was a candle on the table and safety matches in a small box beside it. He fumbled for the box and his hands found the open diary. He lighted the candle and glanced at his recent entry.

Then—he could hear Minny's voice answering Conty in the passage. They were almost at the door—he dipped his quill, wrote the next date: 1872, and left the book open to dry. The opening door blew a page up and left the year in shadow.

It began brightly enough with a safe journey to Mentone, where everyone fell in love with pleasant spacious lodgings in a sea-hung villa, with a pagoda for outdoor living. They acquired the use of two small donkeys, in whose hard, drab lives this brief period of petting and gentle usage by these mad English might have passed, if donkeys could transmit legends, as a foretaste of donkey heaven. They acquired a homeless mongrel, who with unerring instinct discovered them the day after their arrival. Lionel and Fanny and her sister joined them briefly. The newly married Marquis of Lorne and Princess Louise stayed nearby and came to luncheon. By mid-February Minny agreed wistfully that they could let him go in time to present the Bill which would, he trusted, free him from his Ecclesiastical Court's harassment for more important things.

So, in Grosvenor Square, the Lady Victoria Ashley acted as Chatelaine for her father, and foster-mother for Evelyn's five- and three-year-old during their mother's absence. But communication with Mentone must continue. His diary suffered while he sent Minny an almost daily commentary on events, interspersed for her entertainment with judicious gossip.

Feb. 23, 1872

"Dearest Min:

I have just received your letter of the 21st. No fault rests with me. The Newsman swears like the Gittite by all his gods that he has never failed to dispatch the *Times*. I have now told him to send you the arrears if he can find copies.

S"

February twenty-seven was a Day of National Thanksgiving for recovery to health of the Prince of Wales.

Feb. 27, 1872, ½ past 7

"Dearest Min:

The day has opened well, blessed be God. No rain, no special fog, and even a faint burst of blue in the sky.

I shall start from here at nine-thirty as the steamboat will leave the stairs at half past ten. The Press and the House of Commons may go "in plain clothes" like detectives. We shall have to walk from St. Paul's Wharf to the Cathedral but it will be short, easy, and safe.

Sydney gave me a ticket for Vea. She was indisposed to go. . . .

Tell Sissy that her brougham has been of mighty use to me. I have not yet been able to hire horses; and when I sent to East yesterday for a carriage to take me this morning, I learned to my horror that every vehicle had been pre-engaged for some weeks. Providentially Old Edy dined here and, with all the grace of condescension and the sense of obligation that property confers, offered his conveyance.

It is a spectacle for the whole nation not to be ashamed in these days to join in a great national act of religion. In the vast majority there may be no sentiment of the kind but at any rate there is a willing acceptance of it, and not as in Paris, a satanical rejection.

I must be off. God in His goodness protect you all."

Feb. 27, 1872.

"The day was fine, almost brilliant.
The sun shone repeatedly through the Church window.
Dearest Min:

I left my house at 9:30 and am back again at 3. It was, by God's blessing, a wonderful success. So far as we have heard not a single mishap. The whole of my passage was as easy as a walk from the villa to the Pagoda.

Yet there is a good deal of dissatisfaction that the Queen did not go in the State Carriage with the cream-colored horses. She is sure, if she can, to spoil everything.

The Duke and Duchess of M. came in and seated themselves among the rest. Later the Duke was perceived to leave, return towards the entrance, and consult some officials. I observed them, and I cannot say with what disgust, advance to the first seat and place themselves immediately under the Royal Pew as close as possible to the place where the Prince would be.

The gins, I see, are all laid, the traps are baited. Will the weak man fall into the snare? If he do Good-bye to the Ancient Kingdom of England!

God give him wisdom and strength. His little wife looked as lovely as a woman could. . . . May she be as good a wife and mother as you are. And may her husband be as faithful to her, as I, by His grace, have been to you.

Love to all. Respects to the parrot, the dog, and the donkeys. Remember me to Lismer, Sissy, Hilda, Conty and Anybody else that you think cares for me.

S"

XXXVIII

HIS FOUR VEXATIOUS YEARS for Reform of Ecclesiastical Courts ended in partial triumph in the Lords, final defeat in the Commons. "Never again will I interfere in Church matters. I have now, thank God, closed my Ecclesiastical career; nothing shall again stir me to move Bills in defense of the Establishment. All establishments are doomed and perhaps wisely," he had written three years before, and been overpersuaded to change his mind and pursue the attempt. Now it was over and with a "God's will be done" he refused to waste more time mourning what was, in his view, the greatest waste of time and effort in his long career. Few who heard it would forget the vigorous disgust of his summary:

"Ecclesiastical Reforms seem just as remote as they were before anything was said on the subject. I am not going to speak about such things any more, and I will tell you why. Two hundred years ago, an ancestor of mine was one day making a speech in the House of Lords. Behind him sat the Bishops and one of them, who disliked the Lord Shaftesbury of that day, perhaps nearly as much as the Bishops dislike the Lord Shaftesbury of the present day, exclaimed, 'When will that Lord have done preaching?' My ancestor turned around to him and said, 'Whenever your Lordships begin.' Well, I will not go on preaching about Ecclesiastical Reform, because it would be utterly useless, because I know their Lordships, the Bishops will *never* begin."

Much closer to his heart was a plan for Christian cooperation in matters of vital moment.

"I quite agree with you that in a crisis of the Faith, with untold myriads in complete ignorance even of the name of Christ, we are busy about external frameworks of secondary value," he wrote to Dr. Angus of the Baptist College, who expressed to him the need for joint action on the part of various branches of the Christian Church. "Can we find no common point, no subject of common appeal? I have one, ever present in my mind—the preaching of the Second Advent of our blessed Lord. Pay no attention to excited and angry critics who charge such a scheme with all the extravagances of the Fifth Monarchy and the Millennial inventions. The Second Advent, as an all-sufficient remedy, should be prayed for; and as a promise should be looked for. The mode, form, and manner of that event are not revealed, and therefore are no business of ours. The whole will become intelligible only by the issue.

"That such a tone of preaching would go to the very hearts of, especially, the poorest classes, I have no doubt whatever. . . . It would pacify both Churchmen and Dissenters," he concluded neatly, "as they would be laboring for an issue in which the one party would have no establishment to uphold, and the other none to attack."

In the proposed exclusion of religious education from the new Board Schools, he apprehended grave danger. So he renewed his efforts on behalf of his beloved children. As with his bold scheme for National Education in the factory legislation of thirty years before, his eloquent logic carried his hearers like a tidal surge. Again, as then, when the immediate impact had broken, prejudice, fear, and sectarianism—by no means without cause, though in Shaftesbury's eyes no cause was sufficient—came to the surface. Mr. Gladstone, whose Government espoused the present Bill, would, Shaftesbury thought, "rather exclude the Bible altogether than have it admitted and taught without the intervention and agency of catechisms and formularies." The Dissenters naturally feared this element of state interference.

"It is inevitable," he recorded, "that children who are objects of State care cease to be objects of private compassion. Where ten thousand are taught to read, not one hundred are taught to know that there is a God. The heart of England will become a great iceberg. Our nature is nothing, the heart is nothing, in the estimation of these zealots of secular knowledge. Everything for the flesh and nothing for the soul; everything for time and nothing for eternity."

"What we ask," he told the audience crowding St. James's Hall to capacity, "is simply this: that the Bible and the teaching of the Bible to the children of this vast Empire shall be an essential and not an extra. Take conscience clauses and time tables enough to satisfy the greatest cormorant for things of that kind. . . . I am satisfied that the people of England will never require them. . . . In this new Index Expurgatorius, as I understand it, the Bible is the only proscribed book! . . . There has just been granted to the people almost universal suffrage. Is this a time to take from the mass of the population that principle of internal self-control without which there can be no freedom, that principle of self-restraint which makes a man respect himself and respect his neighbor? Is this a time to take from the people the checks and restraints of religion? . . . to harden their hearts by the mere secularity of knowledge, or to withhold from them the cultivation of all those noble and divine influences which touch the soul?"

The successor to this speech brought an even greater ovation and he was very anxious for Minny to comment upon it, though his reference was casually inserted in the body of a letter.

March 5, 1872.

"Dearest of Women:
    Pray entreat Conty to conform to the opinion of her medical adviser, 'Lady Constance's doctor' as he is everywhere called—Physician-in-ordinary to Lady Constance Ashley, etcetera!
    Our day is beautiful. I am glad of it for I am going this evening to Greenwich to open some new schools.

I have dispatched a Record with a report of my St. James's Hall Oration. The success—*non nobis, Domine*—has been wonderful among all classes. Forster (the Minister I mean) is especially delighted and hopes it may aid towards a triumph in the House of Commons tonight.

Your account of Aberdeen makes one's mouth water. Is there a girl in England or Mentone who would not wish him to be 'my young man?' But is he, like the rest, a 'gay deceiver?' Take care!

Boo Leslie has invited us for dinner. I shall go for I am fond of Boo and we should encourage incipient Amphitryons.

Vea has charged me to say and to endorse what she says: that she is not depressed but really in good spirits; not *as* in good spirits as if you were all here, nevertheless in good spirits. Of "Willy" I know nothing. Though she mentions him sometimes it is never with any attention to 'his suit.' So I look, of course, both ignorant and indifferent.

Ellis has just been here. He is well-pleased with my pulse and says that it will last a long time, perhaps longer than my understanding. What a dreadful thing, an age of twaddle!

Really I have had nothing but interviews all this morning and it is now half-past two with a public meeting before me. I must conclude, praying God to bless you all!

S.

(This letter, though short, is twice as long as yours!)"

Letters of the seventh and the eighth contained the variety of comment, answer, intimate reference, and news, that kept the Countess of Shaftesbury in close touch with him and a world that, but for him, would have been her life.

March 7, 1872.

"The first thing is an expression of astonishment, joy, gratitude and all the emotions that Hilda has given signs of life and of life in Mentone! Is it possible? Three cheers!

I have sent you an extract from the *Morning Post*. It has appeared in all the Papers. This pretext for deifying John Brown will be seen through and the old story revived. J. B. had no more to do with this trifling affair than I had.

Boo Leslie gave us an excellent dinner. We had Henry Somerset and his wife—she is like her mother—Miss Thackeray—she is like her father and agreeable—Dick Charteris and his wife—I had only one word with her—Col. Probyn, Col. Riley, and a lady in black whose face I know, but I could not recall her name.

Vea is having such a levée. What with her chums and my visitors, the servants have enough to do to answer the bells.

Emberson's speech in the House on Tuesday denies in fact the existence of God. He is so used to his worship of Demos that he substitutes it for the worship of Jehovah.

The Government carried their points by a vast majority, I thank God. But the fiendish activity and hatred of our Lord will at last prevail. Coldness and indifference are universal. 'Leave us alone;' 'a little folding of the hands to sleep;' and 'it will last my time' are the words and sentiments of the day.

You've never told me if you received a copy of the *Record* containing an account of the proceedings in St. James's Hall. I *conclude that they were of no interest to you.*

I shall, I hope, have a horse to-day for the Brougham but I really do not care as my work is mainly house-work, letters, papers, interviews.

The other horses would have been no use. We had no footmen to go with them; besides East's bill was still unpaid, and I could not ask further credit and other horses without some modification of the bill.

London is thriving. Employment has not been, for many years, so abundant. This state enables the School board to make many experiments which will all fail in a time of no work and small wages.

Rover is watchful in the extreme. He barked last night as I went up to bed and *Gigas commented on it at breakfast. The vicinity of the Square in the Park is very convenient to the kids though Gigas always affects indifference when asked about it.

Vain to deny that a mighty change has come over the minds and hearts of the people. Thirty years ago no human power would have dared propose for Scotland such an Education Bill as the one before us. Every man north of the Tweed would have been in arms; now he continues in bed! 'The love of many is waxing cold.' "

*Gigas (Giant)—Wilfred, Evelyn's son

The pressure of business, chairs, speeches, investigations, was deliberately understated. Long experience had taught Minny to read beneath the chat of such letters.

March 11

"Dearest Min:

Your account of Conty distresses me. I had hoped that a real amendment of the chest had taken place—but she *must* be on the line of progress.

We dined with William and Georgina on Saturday. We had Llewellyn

Davies and his wife, she is rather a pretty woman. Lady Ashburton arrived late, detained by the drunkenness of her maid. Wm. with more kindness than sagacity advised her to keep the maid on the condition of her "taking the pledge!"

Protheroe Smith opened his heart to Pinkie and virtually, though not formally, cursed me by his gods for having been in the Chair of the Women's Hospital.

These doctors are foolish. If the women have merit they will succeed and they have a right to success. If they have none they will fail and the male physicians will be stronger than ever. I only want to give these women a fair chance and, as I said in my speech, "if they are found adequate they will be a grand addition to the practical sciences of society; and if the reverse, they will return to their position as the great ornaments and comforters of mankind." Now what could be prettier? Of course, my dear, I was, in the last part of the sentence, thinking of you as the perfect type of the perfect ornament of the sex!

Is Cecil going to Naples? I hope not. Surely he will stay with you a little and then come home.

The accumulation of business at the Saint is enormous. I hope, D.V., to go there on the twenty-third. Anthony who has been to Grosvenor Square but twice has requested me to support his Clubs at a feast in the Saint.

I am on the whole, thank God, wonderfully well but very stupid. I read letters, misunderstand them, and then mislay them. I am full of plans and can never reduce them to practice. I am as afraid of speaking as though I am sure of breaking down. But by God's blessing I shall go on as long as I can. When I can go on no more, may my end be Peace.

S"

XXXIX

BETWEEN THE SOCIAL OCCASIONS mentioned in his letters, he intervened to persuade the vestry of St. Luke's to rescind their prohibition of costermongers to trade in Whitecross Street; he distributed prizes at the Costers' donkey show (over the years of his Presidency of the Golden Lane Mission the condition and usage of those hardworking animals had improved beyond belief. Experiments had proved that with twenty-four hours' rest on Sunday they could do thirty miles a day without exhaustion; without it they could do no more than fifteen); he examined, or, more expensively, sent trusted agents to examine, reported cases of the violation of the Factory Acts, the Workshop Acts, the recently hard-won Brickfields Act. He was pressed to head a group of clergy and laity to consider Church Reform, and his home became an unofficial headquarters for their meetings. His letter in the *Times* on the public recital of the Athanasian Creed brought him a shower of abuse from furious enemies and "candid" friends. "I shall need a skin like a rhinoceros," he commented ruefully, "but a document, however sublime and true, yet human, must not be forced on unwilling ears." He examined the evidence and spoke in favor of Lord Buckhurst's Bill for the protection of acrobats and small children, a cause which, with characteristic tenacity, he did not abandon when it failed to pass that session. He visited, he arranged personally for adoptions, like that of the "little piece of stranded seaweed—a small, poor, parentless girl obviously entrusted by God's goodness to my care—" whom he sent to Canada with a Christian family. He gave prizes at a Ragged School where, as usual, the warm, sacrificial service of the teachers and the evident love and improved well-being of the children cheered him, in spite of his fears for the future of the Ragged Union under the new State system.

"Talk of the Real Presence?" his staunch Protestant comment horrified the Tractarian peer to whom he repeated it. "Our Lord was as much there last night as at any time or any place."

There were cases brought to him regarding treatment in Asylums, visits to his New Lodging House for Newsboys and his Refuges for little girls, calls for him to preside at a score of meetings, or contribute to a score of causes, each group considering him "the least occupied and the richest man in London."

But a day's omission of letter was noted and two days' caused concern. So. . . .

March 14, 72, ½ past nine.

"Dear Min:

Just had time to dine on my return from the House of Lords where I enjoyed four hours on the Ecclesiastical Courts Bill and I try to write you a short note.

Vea has gone to dine with Anne. I went to the Levée at Buckingham Palace. The Queen received us in person and was very gracious. She asked after you and then I passed on. The house was very full, very uninteresting, the rooms all had an air of bad taste and vulgar decoration that contrasted unfavorably with the palace at St. James.

Gigas was delightful. He came rusing into my room. 'Grandpa, I want to see you dressed. . . . Why do you dress so early?' 'Because the Queen tells us to come early'. . . then a thousand questions about the sword and the star which he insisted on lifting out of the case. 'Now you had better go upstairs. Your dinner will be ready.' 'Oh no, I must see you put on your hat.' And positively, he would not leave me until I passed through the street door. That boy, bless his heart, is too fascinating.

*The Dwarf was very gracious when I went upstairs to see her and allowed me to kiss both cheeks. You perceive that I have got into the fogrammic period and am passing rapidly into the regions of twaddle.

People cannot abuse me much more in my old age than they did in my youth. I am making enemies on all sides. Nevertheless I have the prayers of all the children of poverty and sorrow and I value them, I cannot say how much, beyond the opinions of all the literary, scientific, political, and social magnates that the world possesses.

Love to all.

God be with you

S"

*The Dwarf—Evelyn's daughter

He knew that she did not mind the twaddle, however.

March 15, 1872.

"Dearest Min:

His Lordship has just announced by telegram that he will be with us tomorrow.

That foolish dog Rover has thrown us all into a terror. He ran away in Regent Street and left the Giant in speechless dismay. Happily he ran to Cadogan Place and is now come back. . . . Gigas 'took on' very much, as the maids say, and refused his food. Dinnerless he started off to find him.

Meanwhile Rover arrived here. 'All's well that ends well.'

I am sleeping in the room of the great Cecil—tomorrow into your room. Vea then will surrender her 'suite' to the Lionels and take my place. She wants to go into the garrets but I will not hear of it.

Weather very fine, by no means cold. The Saint will be rather chilly.

Gigas was didactic this morning. Vea said to me: 'The Books are very high, twenty-four pounds.' Gigas remarked: 'That's a deal of money.'

With the boy going on in this way he will be a Solomon.

Love to all. God bless you

S"

March 18, 1872.

"Dearest Minny:

On Saturday could not find a moment to write to you, and indeed I shall have difficulty the whole of this week for I have much in hand.

Saturday, D. V., we go to St. Giles. Lionel and Fanny accompany us.

Cancel in your account book the fifty pounds you gave me. I have torn up the draft. You have many demands on your stores and I can do without for the present.

Dined at your brother's on Saturday.

Went, last night to Poplars—away off—at six to the special religious service. I had Waight, the converted Puseyite. He did some parts of the service very well, particularly the storytelling, a form the public liked exceedingly.

9 p.m.

The *Post* just arrived—no letter from Mentone. I conclude that your excuse is the same as mine—though I do not see well how it can be!

Letters overwhelm me complaining of the ultra-Montane principles and synodical tyranny of the Bishop. No doubt. But how is this sacerdotal flamen better than a pagan priest?

I called yesterday on *Julia. . . . Never saw I a woman so gorgeously attired—velvet and silk, silk and velvet, dark and blue. She looked proud as the apparel. Julia's finances will soon fall under such pressure. Why her skirt would have provided me with two coats, a dozen shirts, one neck tie and a pair of trowsers!

The Amphisbaena† had preceded me with her children. They are taken every place except Grosvenor Square.

I am glad you approved my speech. It was no proof of power but of decline. I never felt so much in my life the need of subsidiary notes."

*Julia, his brother's wife

†The Amphisbaena (two-headed serpent) refers to Harriet, Accy's wife.

There had been a reason for her silence.

March 19, 1872.

"Dear Min:

Your letter filled me with terror. God be praised for better intelligence sent to-day.

Sir Henry Holland has just been. . . .

Northbrook called on me to take leave. . . .

214

People began calls at ten o'clock. At ½ past I had not had time to shave. I write this hurried note and must go off to Chancery Lane. May God be with

you all
S"

March 21.

"Dearest Min:

God be praised that Conty is better. . . . Never mind causing me any distress. Tell me the whole truth and leave me to supplicate Almighty God.

It is now beginning to snow very hard. I am writing, at one o'clock, by the light of a candle, grateful that I have a roof over my head and a fire to sit by.

I had a very favorable meeting last night at the Artisans' Dwellings Company. . . .

But we had *such* a piece of music—sonata, a capriccio, a wild dream—on the pianoforte by a young lady! I thought it would never end; so great was its variety of roaring and mewing, enormous thumps on the keys and then almost silence, that we applauded in joy several times before it was over. . . .

I am going to have here, tomorrow, a regular tea-fight. I have invited sixty heads of missions, in the lower parts of London, to give me information respecting the progress of Christianity under those forms. Lots of sandwiches, tea, coffee, cakes, bread and butter, and plenty of speeches. The 'Invites' have made quite a stir: and Spurgeon has written for cards to be sent to two of his friends."

March 23

"Dearest Min:

The snow is falling fast. The damp wind from the North is very searching.

Just received your letter describing the visit of the Prince of Wales.

The tea-fight went off admirably. His Lordship trailed about sandwiches and toast but said nothing. Edy did not come.

10 o'clock.

An event! A letter has arrived from Hilda. The dear Frances has got it, dated Mentone. So we know where she is. The facts will be entered in my diary in red ink.

2 o'clock.

The weather is becoming worse and worse. Edy, however, has appeared and is in himself a light.

I will either see Gull or write and urge his passing by Mentone. I am sorry

215

the Prince of Wales is going to Rome. It is, I suspect, more unhealthy than ever.

Had a letter from Newman Hall to complain of the theatrical representations at Astley's. He says that wickedness and profligacy cannot go beyond it. And he wants me to go and judge for myself. What a pretty joke were I found sitting among the juvenile Astleians!

The *Daily News* remarks that English playhouses are now intrinsically worse than the French. And this is the time chosen to remove the Bible from the schools! Surely God will remove our candlestick out of its place.

God be with you.

S"

By mid-April he was beginning to feel her absence insupportable. The English spring had come and the recoveries in Mentone were so marked that even Minny began to think it safe to move Northward. "Sydney tells me," her husband held out as bait, "that the last Drawing-room will be on the sixth of May. Too early, I fear, for you? I want you back. The house needs a little stir. I hope you will have Azeglio to accompany you homewards. . . ."

April 13, 1872.

"Dearest Min:

I started at ¼ past 9 for Farningbrook to visit the Home for little boys—a beautiful institution abounding in God's work for the young and needy.

Your weather must be that of the Island of Calypso. Ours is bright but colder than yesterday. I do not oppose your journey by Paris, though somewhat grieved, for our communications will be less easy and I shall become fidgety. But if it please darling Conty, let her have her own way. Only don't make it longer than absolutely necessary."—it was an echo, he thought of a letter written forty years before when Mum's illness had kept her at Brighton. His eager longing was as great now as then.

"By the by," he continued, "you must request Cecil from yourself, not from me, to go with you if you go to Paris and other savage places." (The boy was at the independent stage, restive under the most delicately rendered command. That—and, of course, experience with his other sons—had been partially responsible for a recent entry in his diary: "No moral feature is so prominent and decided as the entire decay of parental influence. The utmost permitted the parents is to disapprove by silence; the utmost expected from the child is external civility. The complaint is universal in England and America in every class, on every lip. No one can assign a cause or devise a remedy.")

"I am amused," his letter went on, not irrelevantly, "if one ought to be

216

amused, by the discoveries that the infidel papers are now making of the moral condition of the country. 'Why is it,' says the *Saturday Review,* 'that the people no longer regard atrocious crime with the same horror as formerly? They seem to have lost,' says the sceptical editor, 'all moral sense of these frightful acts.'

People have ceased to feel, or express, the same degree of detestation as of old: thirty thousand children murdered every year is scarcely commented upon. 'Bad—don't talk about it.' Ah well—they have excluded God's word from education!

"Cecy must stay with you," he wrote emphatically on the eighteenth. "It is not right in Conty to dissuade him. A little self-denial is good and necessary for all, part of moral training.

"I am fighting hard for the Bible in the Schools. I have roused a strong feeling, God be praised. But church people are very cold, very stupid, and very self-indulgent.

I wish I had a little spare money. I could do a great deal more than now in this fearful conflict. . . . Let us, however, rescue whom and what we can and to God be all the glory.

S"

April 20.

"Dearest Min:

Hilda has arrived safe and sound, thank God. She got home yesterday by herself, looking wonderfully well and far from tired.

We have had no letter today, none dated later than Wednesday. You were then gloomy, having lost Sissy and Hilda. No wonder, Dearest, but such is life and the change is good. Even perpetual sunshine becomes tedious and unwholesome.

Pray do not stay much longer at Mentone. It must be relaxing, if not too hot. You had better prolong your visit to Paris by a few days than linger any longer where you are. The distraction will be beneficial and you will not see daily the empty chairs occupied by Hilda and Sissy.

I miss the children very much and Rover too, who walked with me every morning. Hilda was astonished with the growth and beauty of Gigas. He is certainly a noble boy, full of affection, kindness, generosity, and intellect, but proud as Lucifer. This must be watched and it may be overruled by God's mercy.

The Government are 'Catching it' on the Ballot.

Everyone now fears that the people do not care a fig, and though I fear we shall have a Bill, it will be in fact a pernicious Bill under which each man may vote openly or secretly as disposed. Were the House of Lords wrong to throw it out last year? The House of Commons have already introduced amendments which would never have come in if we had not rejected their measure.

God bless you and be ever with you.

S"

XL

YET HE PASSED his wedding anniversary still craving her presence. "Forty-two years ago was I united to that dear, beautiful, affectionate darling. What a faithful, devoted, simple-hearted, and captivating wife she is to me. Ah Lord, give me grace to thank Thee evermore. But she is still absent! God, in Thy mercy, bring her home speedily and safely."

He felt the need of her with particular keenness because of his speech on the Ballot Bill and its inevitable repercussions. The secret ballot, mooted in the Commons during the reign of Queen Anne, had been advocated in a bill by Mr. Grote forty years earlier during the first session of the Reformed Parliament. Frequently proposed, as frequently defeated, the movement had gained strength, and one leader after another, Lord Russell, now Wm. E. Gladstone, altered his views concerning it.

"It is a matter of principle with me, Haldane," said Shaftesbury simply, glad to talk the matter out with his Scottish friend who had dropped in to the Lords as he always did when a subject of common concern was pending. "Gladstone was as fervent against it as I. How can expediency justify a *volte-face?*"

You would not understand, thought Haldane. As if he had spoken, Shaftesbury continued with forensic defensiveness.

"I see the value of compromise. I have been attacked for it in my time. 'Half a loaf is better than no bread' was my expressed reason for taking the Government offer in '47 when there was no possibility of getting our straight Ten Hours at that time—perhaps for years. But there was nothing sacrosanct about two-hours-and-a-half a week, in view of our great gains. This is a *different* matter. As I said concerning the suffrage, I do not entertain any hostility to reform—very far from it. I should have wished, however, to

218

proceed more carefully and gradually. I should have wished to hold up the suffrage as a great object of ambition to the workingman; I should have wished to hold it up as the reward of thrift, honesty, and industry. I thought and said then, and I think now, that to lift by a sudden jerk the whole residuum of society to the level of the honest, thrifty workingman, dishonors the suffrage and throws the franchise broadcast to men who will misuse it. It was a trust—that entails responsibility. If it is a right, it entails none."

"Doubtless Mr. Gladstone considers the ballot inevitable. And certainly the widespread corruption discovered by Lord Hartington's Committee has affected—"

"It did not require Lord Hartington to discover bribery and corruption," said Shaftesbury scornfully. "Measures to deal with it could be devised and enforced—never, I am aware, for every case. But two wrongs do not make a right. As for the inevitability, I realize it also."

"You will not bow to the inevitable?" There was affection as well as amusement in the query.

"I must accept. I cannot pretend approval. It will, for good or for evil, produce serious and permanent effects on the constitutional habits, on the minds, thoughts, and feelings of the people of this country. I should not be consistent if I did not warn them of the principles involved."

"Forster will be coming to hear you speak; I met him at Gray's Inn yesterday."

"Good to know that two in my auditory are sympathetic. He was quick with an encouraging word last autumn when I came in for abuse on this very question. All the attacking papers and most of the anonymous letters struck at my 'Pharisaism.' Forster was in the throes of finishing and publishing his life of Dickens but he took time to give me my 'tonic,' as we call it between us. Have you read the book yet, Haldane? He sent it to me at Cannes."

"Yes. An excellent work."

"And what a subject! The man was a phenomenon, an exception, a special production. Nothing like him ever preceded. Nature isn't such a tautologist as to make another like him. God gave him a general retainer against all suffering and oppression."

And not him only, thought the barrister, Haldane, a few days later as, from the visitor's benches, he watched the tall erect figure rise and wait for the slowly-given mandate of the Assembly. That makes him a puzzle to temporizing politicians, an alternate idol and stumbling-block to the press. They flatter the people, humor the people, woo the people, and live in another world; he knows them, serves them and their children, visits them, has hundreds of friends among them, but has no illusions and tells them the truth.

"I have heard it said that the middle classes are not Conservative," he had told the Lords with delicate irony, "but that if you go deeper, you get into a vein of gold, and encounter the presence of highly Conservative feeling. I ask is that so? What do you mean by the term Conservative? Do you mean to say that this large mass that they call the 'residuum,' of which am I presumptuous if I say that, from various circumstances, few men living have more knowledge than I have, is Conservative of your lordships' titles and estates? Not a bit; they know little about them and care less. Conservative of the interests of the Established Church? Certainly they are not. Thousands upon thousands living in the vast city of London do not know the name of their parish, nor the name of the minister in charge. They are, however, very Conservative indeed of their sense of right and wrong. They are living from hand to mouth, and in consequence, are *very* conservative of what they consider their own interests."

The same candid appraisal was evident as he spoke now.

"I object to the Ballot, because it gives absolute and irresponsible power into the hands of those who, as yet at least, are most unfitted to use it. Again I object, because you are taking away from the great mass of the voters and all the working people, the noble sentiment of public responsibility. I have gone among the working people for some forty years; and the sentiment to which they responded most heartily was when I told them that they were responsible to God and man, and ought to discharge that responsibility in the eye of day and in the face of the whole community—"

"He believes it and made them believe it, bless him," murmured Haldane.

"And you can imagine how joyfully the Radical press will leap on him for it—'pious hypocrite' will be the mildest term," answered Forster out of his own forty years in journalism.

Below them Shaftesbury continued.

"That generous sense of responsibility you are now going to take away. You are going to do what will enable a man, indeed by your compulsory system, force a man, to slink away like a creeping animal. Just at a time when men are rising to a sense of their dignity, you insist that they shall not dare to declare their sentiments nor discharge their duty in the face of their fellow citizens. . . ."

"High doctrine though it sounds," argued Haldane as the two men waited for their friend to leave the Chamber, "he has lived by it, and suffered for it."

"True. But the general cry will be: 'Very well for him! He doesn't stand to lose his livelihood by it.' The ideal is good, granted, but—"

"In a sense he *has* often lost his livelihood by it," said Haldane.

220

"Ah but that the general public does not know."

"Nevertheless it gives him the right to speak. And surely it is evident that he is paying the so-called working man a far greater compliment than his governmental flatterers."

Forster shook his greying mane in humorous despair.

"Haldane, Haldane, come down to earth! It is with infinite regret that I declare the atmosphere too rarefied for me."

The other was unshaken.

"Perhaps. Lord Shaftesbury has spent so much of his time laboring to purify the material atmosphere in which these people are forced to live that he may well be excused for attempting to share his moral atmosphere with them. Yes, he is doomed to failure, like the prophet Jeremiah who is so dear to him. But, like Jeremiah, I think that future generations will acknowledge him to have been a true prophet."

"Well, here is our true prophet." Forster put a sudden hand on Haldane's arm. "Stay. There is a matter on which you might help me. Now that I have completed the biography of Dickens, I should like to write his."

"Have you consulted him?"

"Yes. Without success. If you were to add your persuasions . . ."

"I shall do what I can."

But when, after salutations and discussion of the proceedings, Forster renewed his request and Haldane supported it, they met with a courteous but firm refusal.

"I do not wish a memorial to remain," the proposed subject of it reiterated. And they felt that his answer had been rehearsed after much consideration. "If any good were to be served by allowing a publication I would assent. But, Gentlemen, simple philanthropy (unpleasant term!) without anything to back it such as wealth, connection, great gifts, is sufficiently feeble in itself, without the aid of my memoirs to make it ridiculous into the bargain. Now," he said firmly, as Forster was about to burst into impetuous argument, "I must ask you to excuse me. My wife and daughter return from Paris tomorrow and I propose to meet them at Folkestone."

And I shall have news of interest for her, he thought gratefully. Dear Vea, after hesitating at the discrepancy of seventeen years, has been assured by Templemore's considerate but ardent suit. He will be a happy man, happier I think than in his former marriage. May she be a happy woman! And my precious wife will be happy in her happiness. Also, though the prospect does not fill me with joy, in the bustle and wedding preparations!

The moment of meeting, of holding Minny close and safe in a realized

221

ecstasy of his prayers and yearning, passed. He later looked back on it as his last *happy* moment.

For when he turned to greet Conty he thought at first, with an instinctive clutching at alternative, that what he saw was blurred by the joyful tears in his eyes. Then, even as he met smile with smile and held the telltale ethereal face against his shoulder, he was aware of the presence of death.

XLI

HE LIVED UNDER ITS SHADOW for the next six months. Minny's response to Vea's news, her eager motherly interest, was as he had anticipated. But the doctors recommended an immediate departure for the invalid to a cure at Malvern. So the longed-for family reunion lasted only a few days and social matters were postponed. Heated sessions in the Lords while he labored against vituperating opposition to improve the clauses of the Ballot Bill; meetings for Church reform at Grosvenor Square; necessary businesses of his societies and philanthropies; the cornerstone laying of a workman's city called Shaftesbury Park; his duties as Lord Lieutenant in connection with autumn troop maneuvers in Dorset, and as host to the troops during their encampment near the Saint: all these he attended and performed in a nightmare atmosphere of dread and suspense. It mystified him. He had become resigned to the possibility of Conty's early death. In fact, he preferred it for her to prolonged debility and pain; and her parents did not have to face the distress of Mary's clinging to life and agonized struggles. Then why this depth of apprehension, this sense of a cold hand waiting to arrest?

Suddenly he knew. Minny's forced return to St. Giles's at the end of August, and her collapse there, gave substance to the shadow. Conty, whom he fetched from Malvern a fortnight later, was mercifully better; but all other anxieties seemed trifling, as his earthly mainstay fluctuated between frightening exhaustion, temporary strength, feebleness, and unprecedented depression.

Fragments only remained when, after the fatal day, he tried to put together the six weeks' actuality: annoyance and loss of confidence in the local physician; loneliness in a full house where only five-year-old

Wilfred—his Gigas—and two maids attended family prayers ("of influence I have none, authority I will not resort to"); return to London where Sir William Gull, the Prince of Wales's physician, baffled by the "grave case," called in Drs. Andrew Clarke and Sir Spencer Wells for consultation; the writing of a letter to the *Times* concerning a climbing boy suffocated—thank God, he could still be stirred to action by the sufferings of others! a letter to Orsman asking for the prayers of his brother Costers and their children; the comfort of Mr. Spurgeon's sermon when he stole an hour to go to hear that "blessed servant of God;" anger at a report in the *Times* of "a wicked, false, hardhearted, and un-Christian attack on Ragged School children by a Church of England clergyman;" Minny's brave rallying; her attempts to reassure him in the brief periods when she became almost her sunny self again, and what he held at dread arm's length seemed suddenly absurd; her repetition of the phrase "none but Christ," almost like a refrain, when she was too weak to say more. October fourteen: the dreamlike quality of a brief ride with her in Edy's brougham when a week's renewal of strength gave her a desire "to take the air;" and on their happy return her collapse in his arms, as though felled by an unseen blow; that night's watching. . . .

"Heart rending to see poor Minny's suffering. . . . Will God 'take away the desire of mine eyes at a stroke?' If so, surely He will not, as with Ezekiel, forbid me to weep. O Lord, if—if—μη γενοιτο—may it also be true of me 'In all this Job sinned not nor charged God with folly.' "

How indistinct his handwriting had become! yet he clutched his diary while he sat or paced the room, jotting disjointed sentences as a buffer against wild primitive impulses: to seize and hold the beloved tossing figure, as if he could impart his life to her; failing that, to cry out, to fling himself on the floor in a paroxysm of protest at the vulgar indignity of death, her death.

And when it was over, when he had done his duty to the stricken family as a father, as a Christian, when at last he could be alone, his diary received the bitter cry which his voice suppressed, the thoughts which he must not utter to add to the children's grief:

"Minny, my own Minny is gone. God took her to Himself at about twelve o'clock this morning. She has entered into her rest and has left us to feel the loss of the purest, gentlest, kindest, sweetest, and most confiding spirit that ever lived. O my God what a blow! . . . What do I not owe her and Thee, O God, for the gift of her! But now tonight will be a terrible event. For the first time, I must omit from my prayers the name of my precious Minny."

Strange how that thought distressed him! He thrashed out his beliefs and feelings in the days that followed until he achieved a comforting equation. "We cannot pray to the Saints in heaven. Both Scripture and reason forbid it.

But neither forbids me to believe that the blessed in heaven may pray for the struggling on earth. Our Lord is ever interceding for those He loves; why not, in a far lower degree, the departed spirits for those they have left on earth?"

The funeral at St. Giles; the deluge of letters all to be answered, from the Queen's kind personal missive to the misspelled, cherished scrawls of his costers; prayers, torn between newly urgent "Come, Lord Jesus, Come quickly," and desperate petitions for strength to labor for the outcast; attempts to comfort his family; business at St. Giles; and a few moments peace in the cold and lonely church near her dear resting place: "To the Memory of a wife, as good, as true, and as deeply beloved as God in His undeserved mercy ever gave to man"—the words engraved themselves suddenly on his mind as he prayed. That would be her epitaph, understated, but what statement could approximate the truth? "O Lamb of God, I come"—again God's undeserved mercy to bring to his mind that almost last cry of his "sincere, sunny and gentle follower of her Lord," as he described her to Lady Gainsborough, adding "an increase and no abatement of love on either side in over forty years." Scarcely a wonder that people thought he should not grieve at his time of life! He could not help it; he was astounded and dazed to find himself without her.

"You are to me as meat and drink and the air I breathe. I cannot do without you," he had written in the glad early years, and had never ceased to feel it. In a sense, then, Ashley too had died—a man cannot live without food and drink and air. Shaftesbury was left, left with work to do and will to do it. Strange, though, that he could feel neither the peace of the grave nor the joy of the life to which, he was assured, his darling had passed. Faith he continued—by the grace of God alone, he knew—to exercise. It was enough to walk by, as long as he had to walk. He continued to live; but his personal world was empty, dry, airless.

Meanwhile there were preparations to take Conty back to the Riviera—her only hope, agreed the doctors . . . and the harassment of the long, tedious, sorrowful journey . . . and the sorrow of a Mentone haunted by Minny's absence . . . then Conty's inflammation of the liver, weakening her so that she could fight the consumption no longer . . . the unexampled radiance—"if it were written in a novel no one would believe it," said Hilda, awed—of her death-bed: the renewal of strength so that she sat up exulting, her thanks to him for his teaching, her joyous conversation with Cecil and Hilda, her last words, "I know that I am going to die, I feel so happy."

Surely, thought Shaftesbury, this was a striking and special mercy vouchsafed by God, not only to mitigate their sorrow but positively to raise them into joy. It carried them back to England where the entire family gathered at the year's ending to lay daughter beside mother in the vault at St. Giles.

Almost as though closing an era and before returning, though stricken, to the fray, he opened the New Year with the note:

January, 7, 1873. To London yesterday for Vea's marriage to Lord Templemore tomorrow. It will be very early, very private, and for a wedding-day very sad—yet, he added whimsically, it may be accompanied by Hallelujahs in heaven.

In the interval his hair had grown quite grey.

XLII

"I HAVE READ YOUR MEMORANDUM, in fact your memoranda, of '67 and '75 and '79, and am not convinced." Evelyn looked up from the manuscript on his knee and smiled to soften his dissent. "Your second—or third, or fifth thoughts in this regard were certainly your best. Having given as much encouragement and help to Mr. Hodder as you have done, you would, I feel, be most unkind to forbid him to proceed with the biography now. It is not like you to waver, Father."

His eyes rested fondly on the long spare form, draped with a rug against the September wind. Shaftesbury's bath chair was turned towards the Folkestone coast, and his heavy-lidded eyes were fixed on the sea or on the faint outline of French cliffs beyond it. He brought his gaze back to his son, and the two men measured each other with mutual affection across the small table placed between them on the lawn.

Not for the first time, the father thought with mild amusement that the new-style, heavy, Prince of Wales beard and moustache gave his son, at forty-nine, an air of portentous solemnity which he himself lacked at eighty-four. The son, looking at his father's face as he had always known it, clean-shaven except for still-curling, iron-grey side-whiskers, thought what a gentle face it was, in spite of harsh lines, deep-seamed by sorrow at the forehead and mouth.

"What has made you think of altering your decision?" he persisted to break the silence. "I can understand your feeling in '67, when you were an

225

open target in the Waters' litigation. I can understand to a degree your writing as you did in '75, so soon after losing dear Mother and Conty. I cannot concur with what you add in '81, that the Guildhall celebration of your birthday was of mere local and parochial interest—or the Freedom of the City two years before. Surely you realize what a national figure—and international—you have become. 'Incomparably the Peer of Peers and the noblest Englishman of our time or any time.' That was said twenty years ago by one man, but it is a general opinion now. The public craves news of you."

"The poor, yes. The newspapers have been kind—recently. Any comments by critics would vary between compassion and contempt. Come, Edy. You know in how many circles I am regarded as inaccessible and morose, a very Maw-Worm."

"And since you are exactly the contrary, it is in the interests of religion and philanthropic work that the fact should be made known," said Evelyn stoutly. "You thought that my biography of Palmerston did only justice by showing a side of him little known to his defamers. Edwin Hodder seeks to do the same for you. May I say without prejudice, and knowing the love we shared for Pam, he has a much worthier subject."

"I do not wish adulation," said his father almost sharply. "I should like the reality to be told, be it good, be it bad, and not a sham. Nor do I wish my unpopular religious views toned down or explained away. Yet you know, Evelyn, that these, more than anything else, have brought me opprobrium."

"Yes, I know." Evelyn suddenly recalled an incident of his adolescent years. He had entered his father's study, one evening cf holidays, to find him shaken and unnerved before a desk piled with over a hundred letters. The mere thought of answering them, in addition to his father's other labors, had appalled the youngster, whose power of communication at that time was taxed by brief token letters home from school.

"Why must you answer them all, Father? Particularly the ones from people you don't know. They have no right to bother you."

He had never forgotten his father's tormented face.

"Because of my Order and my profession, Edy. Because these people take for granted that, as an Earl, I have unlimited ease and money to pay secretaries for such work. Because what they consider a discourtesy they will use to feed hatred of the landed aristocracy. But that I could endure. What is terrible to me, what I cannot willingly incur, is the reflection on my Christian profession. 'You are no Christian.' 'You call yourself a Christian' is the accusation made repeatedly if I fail to answer one of their requests."

"But *you* know it isn't true, Father."

"I know. Yet I am causing my good to be evil spoken of, and my Lord's

226

name contemned. The next cry of 'pious hypocrite' in the papers will have a new endorsement through my neglect. That I *cannot* endure."

He had broken off abruptly, his face beaded with perspiration, his whole frame vibrating as one of his mysterious "ear noises" struck with fury. The young Evelyn had stolen away. The older Evelyn, The Honourable Evelyn Ashley, M.P. for the Isle of Wight, ex-Parliamentary Secretary to the Board of Trade, Under-Secretary of State for the Colonies, spoke now to efface the memory.

"People have only to meet you informally to have any notion of dourness dispelled," he said. "I saw Drummond-Wolff in London as I passed through. He said that he had never known Lord Randolph listen to another raconteur with such pleasure as the night I had him to dine with you. It was the most pleasant dinner he had attended, Churchill agreed, and your witty reminiscences were the cause."

"Careful. Praise has always elated me unduly," said his father. "Fortunately there has been enough blame to restore the balance. Has this periodical come your way at Davos? The copy is three years old but I read it only recently. Some anonymous 'friend' thought I might not have seen it."

Evelyn took the copy of "The World," open at a feature article by one, Kosmos. He glanced down the page entitled Open Letters, his initial puzzlement giving place to mounting fury.

"You, my dear Lord Shaftesbury," Kosmos had written with disarming sweetness, "can look back on an existence, blameless, beautiful, beneficent, beyond all precedent. I say what most thinking men believe: that you have done more than any man of our time to invest religion with a halo of humanity and kindness. You have not only elevated the Christian faith in the eyes of multitudes and the judgment of not too friendly critics. You have given that particular school of Christian doctrine with which you are identified a certain aristocratic cachet, made Evangelicalism a popular, even patrician creed, stamped religion with well-bred modishness. The Lord, according to you, was a cadet of the Great House of David at the head of a group of country gentlemen of Judaea, who happened to be, like so many today, in reduced circumstances."

Evelyn winced. He was aware of the pain that his own deviation from orthodoxy and his youthful period of fashionable scepticism had caused his father. He could imagine what exquisite pain that last stabbing sentence had inflicted, particularly because of its specious cleverness. His father always had a nice appreciation of wit even at his own expense; but at the expense of his Lord—!

"Were it not," the writer continued with barbed delicacy, "for the

227

ennobling spectacle of your good pure life, religion would never be almost as highly approved a fashionable pursuit in country houses as aestheticism now. There would be no preaching peers or psalm-singing chancellors, apart from your sanction. Missionaries were once regarded with distrust and contempt. Melbourne said he would like to crucify every one of them. Palmerston condemned them to a severer fate—and jauntily changed his attitude under your influence."

Well into his subject, the anonymous journalist drew the sword farther from its bland sheath.

"You have shown society how to combine in decorous fashion the worship of God and Mammon. There does not live in England a prouder peer. You love the atmosphere, surroundings, trappings, with a devotion only second to that for the Christian revelation."

How brutally untrue, thought Evelyn, of a man who has spent the greater part of his time outside the House, day and night, in slums, dives, arches of bridge or viaduct, pottery yards, factories, lunatic asylums, children's hospitals, Ragged Schools, so that he was rarely seen in the fashionable world. It was almost thirty years ago—he remembered it very well because he had gone on a visit to America and it was part of the news in his mother's first letter: "Your Father and I went to hear the Messiah in the Crystal Palace. It was good to see his enjoyment. The effect was like that of the music of Revelation, he said. And he would have rejoiced to hear the evening performance of Judas Maccabeus and Israel in Egypt with me but—you know your father. He had to attend a Mothers' Meeting in Westminster." So typical—and as for "trappings," had there ever been a less ostentatious Great House in the country? And was it not this same proud Peer who had advised, urged, and prevailed upon, prime ministers to elevate worthy men in trade to the peerage?

"Christianity," he resumed his reading, "exercises no levelling effect upon you. Poverty of spirit is not one of the Beatitudes you have ever exemplified. The scriptures assert that those seeking heaven must be humble and meek as little children. You have demonstrated in your own person that this state of mind is not essential for the supreme ordeal! Is it very difficult to pass through a needle's eye? My lord, you have convinced me that it is not. Your enlarged concept of the Christian church has made it plain that in books of devotion there is a place for Debrett and Burke as well as the Old and New Testaments."

What on earth is behind these rotten slurs, these plausible, but provably false insinuations? Evelyn asked himself. He knew that his father was watching him. He did not trust himself to comment aloud. Ah, here it came!

"When one contrasts the philanthropic part you have played in great measures of national reform"—that at least the writer could not deny—"with the attitude you adopt towards any move for changing Sunday—now a day of wretchedness and gloom for the bulk of the laboring class—into one of healthful enjoyment, I begin to understand what 'the complacent religiosity of the prosperous' means."

From consideration of his father, Evelyn restrained the expletives, which might have relieved his indignation more than the gesture of contempt with which he hurled the offending paper across the lawn. It fell to the ground at a little distance and he went to retrieve it, glad of the excuse for action. Shaftesbury's voice, he was grateful to hear, came to him, serene.

" 'Fret not thyself,' Edy. I gave you the article so that you might see my point when I suggested that, though I have no reason to urge why I should not go down to posterity as a hypocrite or as a fool—or as both—the better line is that which leads to utter oblivion."

Evelyn had recovered his temper.

"That is impossible. And therefore the biography Hodder has in mind—in execution rather—is a debt that you owe."

Shaftesbury groaned and turned it into a laugh.

"Not that word, Edy, I beseech you. My old wound! Any word but debt."

"Then I beseech you, Father. Let him complete it. Even such foul misconstructions as this scribble will be robbed of effect when the facts are fully known."

"You are more sanguine than I. But be it so. I should like you to know, Edy, that I realize how difficult it has been for you children to have me for a father. For the girls and their prospects I realized it long ago, but for you boys also."

Evelyn was deeply touched. The occasions on which he had felt the same rose to accuse him. A certain amount of obloquy was the price paid for public life by public men and their families. The breadth and compass of his father's interests, the fearless expression of unpopular opinions, the disregard of self which made him incapable of neutrality in a question of right or wrong, had brought him misunderstanding and vilification at one time or other from every group or party, even those benefitted by his efforts. His occasional errors in judgment, as in his mistaken use of Lady Canning's name during the furor over the Sepoy mutiny and massacres, were seized upon with glee and magnified with ridicule. Evelyn and Lionel did not share their father's aversion to legalization of 'marriage with deceased wife's sister,' or to the Revised Translation of Scripture. They regarded the ubiquitous Salvation Army without his reasoned, though only privately expressed, abhorrence.

229

Yet he had, his sons now frequently admitted, an uncanny faculty of seeing beyond a specious good to the end result. And no amount of unpopularity or misrepresentation could silence his opposition. Yet no sooner was he tagged as a sentimental opponent of scientific progress because of his opposition to vivisection, than he showed himself in advance of public thinking as the champion of women in the field of medicine and hospital administration; or again as the espouser of cremation against the objections of many, clergy and laymen. But the criticism hurt. How much, Evelyn had come to understand in these last years when he had drawn close to his father and tried to fill the place of an eldest son which Accy had never filled.

And perhaps no other course had so lent itself to subtle ridicule and outright abuse as had his strong, undeviating warfare against every attempt to encroach on the sanctity of Sunday. Evelyn had been at Harrow when Lord Ashley became the most roundly denounced man in the kingdom for carrying the motion which stopped the postal service on Sunday, though because of pressure it was renewed three weeks later. Then there had been the issue concerning Government appointment of military bands in the parks on Sunday, and the attempted opening of the Crystal Palace. "During two successive Sundays our house has been in a state of siege, windows closed, blinds down, and mobs expected," his father had written. Much had been threatened and, though nothing untoward had happened, the experience had been unnerving.

What his detractors, and such contemptible journalists as the anonymous Kosmos, refused to consider, thought Evelyn, though his whole career made it evident, was the basic principle behind his opposition to all unnecessary Sunday labor: his passion, his lifelong concern for the workingman's right to a day of rest. Their crocodile tears for the "wretchedness and gloom" of the workingman's Sunday! Evelyn knew—his mother had explained to the awed children one memorable Christmas—of the real tears which had spoiled his father's enjoyment of untold Sundays and Christmasses at the knowledge of enforced and illegal labor in mills and mines and factories. He thought of the long, determined fight to ensure one day in seven, and the equally tenacious struggle for Early Closing and the Saturday half-holiday. He thought of the exhausting "chairs" of various societies to promote parks and healthful recreation for Working-people. The boys had gone through a period when they secretly considered their father a crank in the matter of Sunday observance, classing his concern with his disapproval of their cigars. Evelyn dated the change in his own attitude from his trip down to Scotland a dozen years earlier when the Lord Provost had conferred on Shaftesbury the freedom

230

of Glasgow. The moving enthusiasm, the informed, outspoken gratitude, with which they were greeted at a large meeting of the Glasgow Working Men's Sabbath Protection Association, gave the lie to the bogey of Sabbatarian oppression.

"Once make this day a holiday," the chairman, Robert Mackintosh, had boomed to vigorous applause, "and it will be impossible to rescue it from the grasp of mercantile rapacity. One man's pleasure involves another's labor. If the master ride, the servants drive. One goes by rail, others keep books, stoke, drive engines. You fasten a yoke of labor on the necks of unwilling workmen who dare not refuse." The speaker had gone on, to Evelyn's surprise, to quote Lord Macaulay's vivid comparison: " 'the natural difference between Campania and Spitzbergen is trifling compared with the difference between men full of bodily and mental vigor and men in bodily and mental decrepitude. Therefore we as a nation are not poorer but richer for resting one day in seven.' "

After this introduction, his father's speech—fully reported in the local papers—had been warm, humorous, colloquial. Evelyn, long accustomed to speeches from the hustings and at public meetings, was again impressed by his effortless communication with his listeners. He never descended, he never apologized, he never flattered. His acceptance of social distinction, as a fact but an almost incidental fact, established a relationship much more honest than the uncomfortable efforts of most politicians to ignore or deplore it. He could refer to the platform people as fine folk and to the audience as workingmen without offense because those were their own terms; but also because they realized that he loved them, and loved them without sentimentality or illusions, as one who had pursued their interests through their support and their desertion, and would not cater to their new and growing power.

"I have had threats of popular indignation thrown at my head," he had told the Lords a short time before. "I know well the power of the people. I am prepared, when it is proper, to conform to their opinions. I am not going to tell them that wisdom and truth dwell with them and with none other. I do protest against this House being treated like a set of lacqueys in an antechamber, waiting in idleness till it please their master to declare what work shall be assigned them!"

At the Glasgow meeting he had begun by a wry reference to an article in the local paper. "I don't complain of the tone; it is rather friendly than other. But it speaks as if I had come to Glasgow to put a restriction on the ordinary pleasures you enjoy—to limit poor people in their walks on the Sabbath." His

231

intention was quite the reverse he explained; and dilated on the social intercourse, the little innocent joys, the time for families to disport under the open canopy of Heaven, which the day of rest permitted and encouraged.

"All in toil of brain or hand call out for repose. Our opponents admit the necessity of a holiday in principle, but lose sight of it in religious argument. If ever there was a period in the history of the world when rest was needed, it is at the present hour. We are living with immense rapidity, crowding into a year the events of a century. The mad competition of trade keeps everyone on tenterhooks and the nervous system is frightfully shaken. The moral and intellectual system is also more disturbed than ever, because of wild competition in every department of science, trade, and art.

"I do not want," he told them, "to impose on others any ascetic observation; I do not choose to be deprived of my own privilege. I am not calling them by Act of Parliament to attend places of worship, but I am demanding that they do nothing to prevent workingmen from attending worship or devoting, if they are so minded, the whole day to the refinement of moral life. The Act which interdicts labor on Sunday is the charter of the workingman."

Suddenly returning from his excursion to the past, Evelyn realized that he had made no answer but a deprecating murmur to his father's statement. He was on the point of making some attempt to voice his feelings when his elder sister joined them. Lady Templemore had found or made her marriage a state of happy tranquillity. Her only child, a daughter, born when she was thirty-seven, compensated for later miscarriages. Her husband, secure in heirs by his first marriage, delighted in her companionship and family and accompanied her or, as now, lent her to nurse her father. She was acting as his amanuensis also, and her hands were full of letters for him to sign. Her brother, appraising the tall, graceful figure in its close-fitting morning-dress of mauve alpaca, thought that she combined the Ashley features with her mother's basic joyousness.

"These are all you have dictated so far," she said, setting a small writing case on his knee, and an inkwell on the table. She dipped the pen and was handing it to him when she saw him shiver. "Father dear, have you caught another chill? These letters can wait. Evelyn, I think he must come in and lie down. He will never spare himself."

"Nonsense, Vea. Just tuck the end of the rug around me if you please. Having Old Edy here is as good for me as the sea air. Remember how your blessed mother always yearned for it—the sea air, I mean, Edy—not you. But you must go back to Davos, Darling Sissy needs you."

"Then, when she is well enough to travel we shall go to Cliffoney and take you with us, Father. If you like this view, think of that one."

"Yes, indeed. Classiebawn is the closest I have ever been to America. Awesome to think that there is nothing between us from that cliff but the Atlantic."

"Well the place is yours," but you will never see it again, they all knew. "Vea is right. You must take more care of yourself. Lionel wrote in May that you had to return from St. Giles's in an invalid carriage. Why on earth did you stay in London, working all through July, when you had been ordered away for rest? Taking the May chairs was bad enough. Going to distribute prizes, and meetings at Flower Girls' missions and City Mission, and visiting the Home Office forsooth. I don't know what we are going to do with you!"

Shaftesbury looked at him, surprised.

"Hasn't Vea told you? A Mrs. Douglas—no, her name was not familiar to me either until mid-June—left me sixty thousand pounds for distribution among the charities of London. I had to attend to that."

"Very well. The distribution could have waited your return."

He stopped, reading the incredulous look on his father's face. A month's delay, it said, perhaps two, when children were starving and homeless and victimized by crime, when the sick could find no beds in his beloved hospitals, when the poor were existing in foul conditions and slept under bridges for lack of shelter? Evelyn capitulated.

"I understand. 'Bis dat qui cito dat' I suppose."

"Exactly." The moment of emotion over, he became Shaftesbury, the meticulous, conscientious administrator. "With such a trust it was necessary for me to be more precise and careful than with my own money. So I drew up a memorandum—Vea dear, I had a copy of it somewhere? Never mind. In brief, I determined to keep the distribution to London. Make an exception and every town has an equal claim. Then to make no purely religious or sectarian grants; to except Social causes, however worthy like the Y.M.C.A., the Victoria institute (for grants to them would take up much of the bequest and leave the poor out in the cold); to avoid my own special interests where controversial, not knowing the lady's opinion on Anti-Vivisection, Homeopathic-Hospitals, the Working-Men's Lord's Day Association; similarly to omit all Missionary Societies. In fine, to keep as closely as possible to the needy institutions connected with charity. But it took time and not a little labor to receive all applications, take the best advice, and apportion the money—Hilda, my dearest child! When did you arrive? Vea, was this your surprise?"

233

Lady Edith Florence Ashley, now in her thirty-ninth year, still had, with her athletically slim figure, the girlish manners, the youthful face, which often characterize the youngest, made much of in an older family. Since Conty's death she and Cecil had been a decade removed from their brothers and sister, and, petted by them, had enjoyed an extended, pleasant social life. Shaftesbury might blame himself for her unmarried state, but neither she nor her younger brother showed more than a mildly flirtatious interest in any one. She mothered him, nursed him in bouts of sickness, fretted about him during his absence in Cape Colony and the Transvaal on the staff of the Governor-General, Sir Bartle Frere. Since Fanny's untimely death ten years before and Lionel's return to his father's home, she had grown closer to him also. He found her an excellent partner for tennis. Cecil taught her the rudiments of yachting.

She was, Shaftesbury thought, very like her maternal grandmother, without the latter's amorous proclivities. She played games—tennis, battledore, billiards—where Mum had played politics; but both were ebullient, kind, and irrepressibly sociable. Like Lady Pam, if Hilda had any serious thoughts she kept them to herself. She kissed her father warmly now, kissed her brother and, disdaining his offer of a chair, sat on the lawn at their feet, gloved hands clasped around her knees, the bustled drapery of her green merino travelling dress spreading behind her.

"I had the cabman approach the house stealthily. I am the bearer of many greetings. Lionel will be down tomorrow. Cecil sends love from St. Giles's and will see us as soon as he can get your bridge repaired. Margaret says Anthony and Harriet are on their way back and send love. And now that I am here you will have to eat up and grow strong. Remember when you were taking the waters in Homburg, we decided that you have the digestion of an ostrich, and that only two things upset you: overwork and Rhine Wines. Any Rhine wines, Vea? No? Then I diagnose overwork. And I don't need that ass of a doctor of yours to tell me. I was eavesdropping and heard all."

"What was it you called the doctor, Hilda?" asked Evelyn, amused.

"Well—he cannot tell us anything about Father that we don't know already. Oh, Edy, did Sissy ever tell you how socially impossible he was at Homburg—and how we all blessed him for it? I'm sure I wrote her about it."

"You haven't told me at any rate," said Vea.

"What is more important," said Shaftesbury, "you haven't told me. Socially impossible indeed, young lady! I spare the retort."

"Well let us say—what is that Latin phrase you quote, Edy? Means 'I am the King of the Romans and above the laws of grammar.' No, I shan't

234

remember it if you do tell me. But Father is like that, above the laws of society."

"Instance, instance." Evelyn was glad of his father's diversion.

"Of course I can give an instance! When we were at Homburg Princess Mary was there also, taking the waters by order of her physician. Protocol was strictly observed. And after dinner she did not like to go walking but sat on forever. So, of course, we had to sit. We dined at six and at nine we were still sitting, everyone casting desperate looks and swearing inwardly. Finally our hero, to the horror of her aide Colonel Greville, but to the amusement of everyone else, got up, wished Princess Mary who sat beside him Goodnight, and walked off. According to Lionel, Papa had been giving hints, pulling out his watch, saying it was very late."

"No heroism about that," said her father. "It was the sensible thing to do. High time some one made a move."

"Talking about a move," said Vea firmly. "You are coming in and going to lie down. I let you out here on the plea of an hour and it is nearly tea-time."

There was no demur. Goldsmith, the valet, was summoned. In reaction from talk and laughter their father seemed suddenly to wilt before them. As he was being wheeled away, he raised his long thin hand to Evelyn.

"You will see me before you leave, Edy."

"Surely, Father."

They watched him go in silence. Then Hilda spoke as if to ward off impending depression.

"Of course what Papa did was sensible. But how many people *do* the sensible thing?"

"It's typical of Father," Evelyn agreed. "What really enrages me in these slurs is the suggestion that he is stuffy, dull, conventional. He never made a dull speech in his life and he found it hard when others did. That was what made him a good chairman. You felt you had to be on your toes if you were speaking for him. Otherwise, you might get a sharp tug at your coat-tails and hear that urgent voice—he was too kind to check a novice or men whose self-esteem would be badly damaged—'My dear fellow, are you never going to stop? We shall be here all night.' "

"How awful!" said Edith. "But would there were more like him. You have all the luck, Edy. I'd give anything not to have missed that time when he cheered—"

"When he what?" asked Vea.

"Oh," said Evelyn. "You mean at the hospital dinner? That was sheer inspiration on Father's part. You see, old Gadsby was there. He had given a

235

large contribution—his heart is in the right place; unfortunately his head dictates his speeches—but he had to be asked to reply to a toast. He mistook his few remarks for the speech of the evening, which mistake could have been forgiven if he had had anything to say. Since he hadn't, the audience was suffering agonies of ennui. He went on indulging in unbelievable platitudes about each member of the hospital staff when, by a stroke of amazing luck, he said: 'But what shall we say of Dr. M?' and paused for effect. Father positively leaped into the breach, that is he leaped to his feet—or so it seemed to us—with: 'Three times three for Dr. M.' I led the cheers vigorously you may be sure, and the old boy was so overcome that he forgot what he was going to say and sat down. Yet Father always had a horror of being boring himself. Ages ago I remember his telling Mother that when he took one of his chairs he felt like saying: 'Ladies and Gentlemen, the mixture as before' and sitting down."

"Remember when the Costermongers presented him with Coster?" said Vea. "And after it was led off the platform Father asked the gentlemen of the Press please to state 'the donkey having vacated the Chair, its place was taken by Lord Shaftesbury.' "

"He has always had a flair for the right word. Remember his summary of a sermon 'Revelation frappée,' or the 'Gospel on ice'? And he appreciates style in anyone else. But he has never built up an immunity to the Press," said Evelyn meditatively. "And the Press is both remorseless and incalculable. I doubt if any public man has been so praised, so blamed, so adulated, so misrepresented, so misunderstood. Of course, how can you expect them to understand a man in his eighties who proposes a factory act to give the women and children of India the rights he won for them in England? Who founds a colony for persecuted Russian Jews in Cyprus? Who has founded hospitals and raised funds for them; yet who opposes most medical science on vivisection, on the grounds that, whether or not it be conducive to the advance of science, we have no authority in Scripture to subject God's creatures to unspeakable sufferings?" he broke off, realizing that he was becoming oratorical.

It is because they cannot bear to acknowledge greatness, he thought an hour later, looking down at his father's sleeping face. They wish to label a man, to fit him into their approved or disapproved pigeonhole. They have no objection to idolizing—so long as a man agrees with their personal or party prejudice and they have the right to pull the idol down and put another on the pedestal. When they cannot deny his work—for it faces them at every turn—or uncover venality or self-aggrandizement—or counter his logic in debate—they resort to ridicule. God knows I've done it myself privately, to silence my conscience. A man who feels intensely and expresses himself intensely is always fair game for the cynic who risks nothing. I have had to acknowledge him right so often, in his shrewd unpopular judgments, that—who knows? I may not live to see it, but a later generation may find him a true prophet in his fear of God-less schools producing educated devils, of democracy resulting in mob domination, of trade-unions enslaving and dehumanizing the workingman.

He was suddenly aware that his father's eyes had opened.

"Edy." His hand came up to meet his son's in a strong grip. "You must leave, my dear boy. I could gladly have your company but your place is with dear Sissy. You say Wilfred will be down? I shall be glad to see the Giant. Give Sissy my love. She has been another daughter to me."

"I will." Evelyn could find nothing further to say. He was afraid of words. He bent to kiss his father and on an impulse knelt beside him.

"God bless you, Edy, you and yours. You know that I shall not probably see you again? The doctor is reasonably sure that this time I shall not recover."

Still Evelyn could not speak. The surge of emotion amazed and confounded him. The hand that held his tightened with understanding. Yet his father's words, when they came, were unexpected.

"To live is Christ and die is gain. I know it and have always thought death would be welcome, especially these years since . . . But now that I know I must soon die—I hope it is not wrong to say it—I cannot bear to leave the world with all the misery in it."

The agony in his voice on the last words shocked Evelyn to answer. Incredible—that instead of being comforted, he should have the task, the privilege of comforting. He raised his head.

"Father, do you remember, years ago you taught us to pray for the Second Coming? You explained that, no matter how much you or any one or all of us together could do, it was little weighed against the collective misery of the world. *That,* you said, only Christ in the restoration of the whole creation could alleviate—and would. So you taught us to pray: 'Even so. Come, Lord Jesus.' "

There was a long, full silence. Shaftesbury's voice, when it came, was broken but tranquil.

"True, Evelyn. Thank you. He is wise and I am a fool."

But a fool for Christ, his son thought, still shaken. Many times in their seldom broken association he had been taken into his father's confidence, had supplied him with firsthand information, as on the American slave plantations, offered sound advice, as with regard to subsidies for the Jews in

237

Cyprus, applauded or withheld comment on controversial speeches, asked his aid, in general passed under the aegis of the paternal name. But in matters of faith—in the tremendous relationship of his father with his God—he had never aspired to be needed or to be of use. To the end of his days, the experience with which he still tingled, as at a shock of electricity, would be awesome and humbling. He wished to apologize, to state his unworthiness, to try to put into words something of his indebtedness.

Not now. In writing. Yes, that would be best. In a letter.

His father had gone back to sleep.

September 18, 1885
Davos Place

"My dearest Father:

This is a line of love and greeting from Sissy to whom I gave your message. It was a sore trial to leave you but, as you said, my duty was to come and look after my wife. I had my heart too full when with you to say all I wished, but you know well how grateful I feel for all you have been to me and how ardently I wish I could in any way repay it.

May our Father above bless you as you deserve. This is the daily and fervent prayer of your son,

Evelyn."

Epilogue

SLOWLY THE ABBEY EMPTIED. Through the West doors past the corner where his statue would soon stand in symbolic isolation, Lord Shaftesbury was carried by eight friends, long his co-workers among the poor, surely the strangest group of pallbearers ever to attend an earl to his grave. Behind the mourners—but everyone was a mourner—together with representatives of Royalty, the Peerage, Parliament, and diplomatic circles, walked deputations from two hundred religious and philanthropic societies, many of his founding, most of his influence, all of his connection. Among the flowers massing the plain coffin of the man who hated funerary show, a wreath from the Crown Princess of Germany lay beside the "Loving Tribute of the Flower-Girls of London." The peal of the great organ died to the throbbing of the Dead March, laboriously and earnestly played by volunteer representative bands as they fell in behind the undecorated hearse. The crowd which had filled the Abbey augmented the crowd standing in the rain outside.

Thousands had lined the route of the cortege from twenty-four Grosvenor Square, along Piccadilly, past the drawn blinds of clubs and houses on St. James's and Pall Mall, down Whitehall and Parliament Street. Uncovering heads, and symbols of mourning which dwindled from crape-hung banners: "Naked and ye Clothed Me," "A Stranger and Ye Took Me in," to scraps of black cloth displayed on coat sleeve or bonnet, paid mute respect; and no mere ceremonial could have called forth the tear-wet faces, the sobs, the myriad broken, individual comments.

Now the last stage of the last journey of his much-journeying began. The Abbey, where he had witnessed the crowning of three sovereigns and attended generations of dignitaries to their rest, was not to hold him. "Surely there is a natural feeling to be buried with one's fathers," he had written at twenty-five; and the Dean's letter urging a resting-place in Westminster had met with the firm repetition: "No. St. Giles's. St. Giles's." It was bad enough, he implied, though with resignation, to die in a "lodging house."

In other respects his wish for his death had been realized: "May God

239

grant," he had written the previous year, "for Christ's sake, that to my last hour I may be engaged in His service, and in the full knowledge of all that is around and before me!" The first of October had been a day of bright sunshine. At noon, soon after his last words—typical that they should have been "Thank-you," and to his valet—he went, awake, to the awakening.

So now—since his body must rest somewhere—it was to "the Saint" that he was taken and to his own tiny church at the Great House gate.

The inscription under his statue in the Abbey, the plaque at Harrow, the tribute composed by Gladstone for Gilbert's winged Love—Agape, misnamed Eros—burying its shaft in the street named by his name: these laud the man. With exquisite rightness, not he but the Holy Scriptures, which he loved and by which he lived, are exalted in his plain epitaph:

Antony Ashley Cooper
Seventh Earl of Shaftesbury
Born April 28 1801   Died October 1 1885

| "What hadst thou that thou didst not receive?" | "Let him that thinketh he standeth take heed lest he fall." | "Surely I come quickly. Amen, even so come, Lord Jesus." |

Chronological Table

Events in the life of Anthony Ashley Cooper	Contemporary events in British (and world) history
1801 April 28. Born at 24 Grosvenor Square, London.	Act of Union with Ireland. Bonaparte destroyed Second Coalition
1802	Beginning of gas lighting.
1804	Napoleon Emperor of France Pitt the Younger again Prime Minister of England.
1805	Trafalgar. Death of Nelson. Battle of Austerlitz.
1806	Death of Pitt.
1807	Abolition of the slave trade in the British Empire.
1808 Maria Millis, the family house-keeper, died.	
1808–1813 Spent at Chiswick School.	
1810	Beginning of the regency (George III's mental failure; his eldest son made Regent).
1811 Fifth Earl of Shaftesbury died. His brother Cropley succeeded as Sixth Earl. Anthony became Lord Ashley.	
1812	Britain at War with U.S.A. Liverpool's Tory Ministry begins. Napoleon's Moscow campaign. Napoleon defeated at Leipzig.
1813 At Harrow.	
1814 At Harrow.	Napoleon exiled to Elba. Congress of Vienna opened.

1815	At Harrow.	Battle of Waterloo. Napoleon banished to St. Helena. Economic depression in England. The Corn Law.
1816	At Harrow.	
1817	From Harrow to board with clergyman-relative in Derbyshire.	Riots. Suspension of Habeas Corpus Act. Elizabeth Fry begins her work in Newgate prison.
1819–1822	At Christ Church Oxford. Graduated with a First Class in Classics.	The "Peterloo Massacre."
1820		Death of George III; accession of George IV.
1822	Set out on grand tour of Europe.	Canning Foreign Secretary. First Eton v. Harrow cricket match.
1824		Death of Byron in Greece.
1825		Stockton-Darlington Railway.
1826	Returned as M.P. for Woodstock. Visited Paris.	Ampere's electrodynamics.
1827	Declined post in Canning's government. Travelled in Wales, learned Welsh.	Canning succeeds Lord Liverpool. Prime Minister until his death in August.
1828	Appointed by Wellington as Commissioner of Indian Board of Control. Seconded Bill to Amend Law for Regulation of Lunatic Asylums.	Wellington Prime Minister. Repeal of Test and Corporation Acts. Bentinck Governor-General of India.
1829	Appointed Chairman of Commission on Lunacy (office held until 1885).	Roman Catholic Emancipation Act passed by Peel and Wellington. Metropolitan Police Force founded by Sir Robert Peel.
1830	June 10. Married Lady Emily Cowper. Elected member for Dorchester.	Death of George IV. Accession of William IV. Dissolution of Parliament. Lord Grey's Whig government formed. Palmerston Foreign Secretary. Recognition of Greek Independence.
1831	Elected member of Dorsetshire	Rejection of Reform Bill.

242

	(County Member).	Dissolution of Parliament.
	Eldest son, Anthony, born.	Defeat at the polls of Sadler, who had inaugurated the Ten Hours Bill for factory children.
1832		Great Reform Bill.
1833	Undertakes the Ten Hours Bill. After initial success, his bill defeated by the government's Factory Act.	Abolition of slavery throughout the British Empire.
1834	Accepts post in Peel's government as a Lord of the Admiralty (until fall of Peel's government four months later).	Poor Law Amendment. Melbourne Prime Minister. Houses of Parliament burnt. Melbourne dismissed. Peel's first ministry.
1835	Forms Indigent Blind Visiting Society (President until 1884).	Melbourne's second ministry (until 1841).
1836	Formed "Pastoral Aid Society" composed of clergy and laymen to reach the vast number of larger poor parishes. Active regarding abuses of the Factory Act of 1833 and the dangerous new Factories' Regulation Bill, proposed by Poulett Thompson.	South Australia founded.
1837	Death of Lord Cowper, Ashley's father-in-law.	Death of William IV. Accession of Victoria. Rebellions in Upper and Lower Canada.
1838	Continued effort for the Ten Hours Bill. Defeated 119–111.	Coronation of Queen Victoria. Appointment of a Vice-Consul to Jerusalem. Outbreak of Chartism. Lord Durham Governor General of Canada.
1839	Visit to Scotland. Visit from Daniel Webster. Reconciliation with his father (the Sixth Earl). Marriage of Lady Cowper to Lord Palmerston.	Melbourne's resignation. Peel's three-day administration. The Bed-chamber Crisis. Melbourne re-instated. The Durham Report on Canada.
1840	Lord and Lady Ashley among the	Marriage of Queen Victoria to

few invited guests to the Queen's wedding.

Vigilant efforts to obtain evidence and to participate in debates regarding chimney sweeps (climbing boys).

Undertook law-suits on behalf of climbing boys.

Prince Albert of Saxe-Coburg-Gotha.

Beginning of Opium War with China.

Annexation of New Zealand by Britain.

Act of Union of Canada.

After efforts in 1788, 1804, 1807, 1809, 1817, 1834 to improve the condition of climbing boys, the Act for Regulation of Chimney Sweeps and Chimneys became law.

1840 Rescued a climbing boy from a brutal master; arranged for his education.

Persisted in efforts for factory workers and silk-mill workers.

Proposed and obtained an inquiry into the operation of the Factory Act.

Obtained an inquiry into employment of children in mines and collieries (later referred to as Children's Employment Commission).

Wrote article on Infant Labour for the *Quarterly*.

Penny postage.

1841 Elected the fourth time as County Member for Dorset.

Refused office in the Royal Household.

Began investigation of housing conditions in London.

Began work, with co-operation of the King of Prussia, for the institution, under the Church of England and the Lutheran Church, of a Protestant bishopric in Jerusalem.

Melbourne's government overthrown.

Peel's Tory ministry begun.

Appointment of Dr. Alexander, a Hebrew convert and scholar, as Bishop of Jerusalem.

1842 Opposed growth of the Tractarian party (Puseyites, Ritualists, Anglo-Catholics).

Worked strenuously, opposed by his own party leaders, for the Ten Hours Factory Bill.

Made a notable speech for the colliery workers.

Visit of the King of Prussia to stand godfather for the future Prince of Wales.

Passage of the Mines Act.

Persisted in struggle for passage of Mines Act through the Lords.
Assisted in founding The Labourers' Friend Society.

1843   Proposed a motion on national education.
Proposed a motion against the opium traffic.
Espoused the Ragged School movement.

1844   His appeal for the Society for the Improvement of the Labouring Classes (formerly Labourers' Friend Society) interested the Prince Consort to accept the presidency.
Espoused the cause of Milliners and Dressmakers.
Proposed a motion on behalf of the Ameers of Scinde, involving indictment of the Indian government.
Strenuous efforts for the Ten Hours Bill defeated by the opposition of Peel and Graham.
Made report of the Commission on Lunacy.

The Bill for Regulation of Labour in Factories.

1845   Secretaryship of Ireland suggested as a bribe.
Opposed (with Disraeli) to Maynooth Grant.
Brought forward condition of children in the Calico Print Works.
Brought forward and passed two bills for the improvement of Lunatic Asylums.
Wrote his Dorset electors stating his change of attitude on the Corn Laws.

Potato disease in Ireland.
Admission of J. H. Newman and other Anglican clergy to the Church of Rome.
The Maynooth Bill.

1846   Reintroduced Ten Hours Bill.
Resigned as member for Dorset (i.e. applied for the Chiltern Hundreds).
Made president of the Ragged School Union.
Pressed project of Model Lodging House.

Repeal of the Corn Laws by Peel's Tory government.
Defeat of Peel's government.
Split of party into Old Tories and Peelites.
Lord John Russell Prime Minister, Palmerston Foreign Secretary.

245

(Out of Parliament for almost two years.)

1847 Wrote articles on Elizabeth Fry and on Model Lodging Houses.

Ten Hours Bill passed.
Famine in Ireland.
Responsible government in Canada.

1848 Worked for relief of the English dispossessed in France.
Consulted by Victoria and Albert re condition of the working people.
Chairman of Central Board of Health.
Planned emigration of Ragged School "graduates" to the colonies; obtained a grant of 1500 pounds for the scheme.
Held meeting with 400 thieves.

Year of Revolution: France, Austria (Louis Philippe and Metternich took refuge in England).
Last outbreak of Chartism.
Public Health Act.
Manifesto—Marx and Engels.

1849 Proposed Motion for Subdivision of Parishes (to ensure better care of the needy).
His second son, Francis, died.
Worked incessantly on Board of Health.
Tried (and failed) to obtain annual government grant for emigration scheme.

Cholera epidemic in England.
Conquest of the Punjab complete.

1850 Inquest of water supply for London.
Opposed Papal aggression in England.
Prepared Interment Bill.

Death of Sir Robert Peel.
The Don Pacifico incident.
Issue of a Papal Bill dividing England into districts governed by two archbishops and twelve bishops.
Publication of *Uncle Tom's Cabin*.
Secession to Church of Rome by Archdeacon Manning and other clergy.

1851 Made President of British and Foreign Bible Society.
Introduced Lodging-House Bill in Commons.
The Sixth Earl (Ashley's father) died.
Took seat in House of Lords as Seventh Earl of Shaftesbury.
As his first work in the Lords he

Louis Napoleon's coup d'etat.
Palmerston dismissed.
The Great Exhibition.
Gold discovered in New South Wales and Victoria.

brought through his own bill for the Inspection and Regulation of Lodging-houses.

1852 Successfully intervened with the Grand Duke of Tuscany to save two Florentines sentenced to the galleys for propagating their religious beliefs.
Composed address from the Women of England to the Women of America on slavery.

Derby-Disraeli Ministry.
Death of the Duke of Wellington.
Napoleon III Emperor of France.
Invasion of Syria by Mehemet Ali.
First Tory *minority* government.
Whigs and Peelites combine to form government.

1853 Brought through the Second Common Lodging-houses Bill.
Moved the Juvenile Mendicancy Bill.
Held anti-slavery meetings in honor of the visit of Harriet Beecher-Stowe.
On the Board of Health produced:
(1) Act to amend the laws concerning Burial of the Dead in the Metropolis.
(2) Compulsory Vaccination Act.
(3) Smoke Abatement Nuisance Act.

Extinction of the Board of Health.

1854 Wrote an answer to the Czar's Manifesto against England and France.
Wrote letters to the Emperor of the French protesting the lack of religious freedom in his empire.
Brother-in-law, Lord Jocelyn, died suddenly of cholera.

Cholera Report.
Outbreak of the Crimean War.

1855 Successfully introduced a Liberty of Religious Worship Bill, which annulled the Conventicle Act and other repressive measures, still on the statute books and recently invoked.

Palmerston Prime Minister.
Responsible government in all Australian colonies (except Western Australia).

1855 Suggested and took charge of the Sanitary Commission to the Crimea.
Brought forward legislation on behalf of the chimney sweeps and

dressmakers and milliners.
Death of his third son, Maurice.

1856   Exerted himself to prevent
secularization of Sunday; also to
obtain early closing hours and a
Saturday half-holiday.

End of Crimean War with the Peace
of Paris.
Responsible government in New
Zealand.

1857   Launched second attack on the
opium trade.
Accy (now Lord Ashley) returned
as M.P. for Hull.
Commencement of Sunday evening
religious services for the masses
in Exeter Hall; opposition led to
his proposal for Religious Worship
Act Amendment.

The Indian mutiny.
The "Arrow" incident at Canton.

1858   Censured the Tory government
for their policy in India.
Worked on behalf of the Social
Science Congress.

Second Derby-Disraeli ministry.
End of East India Company's
rule in India.

1859   Supported Sardinia (Cavour and
Garibaldi) in opposition to
Austria.

Palmerston Prime Minister again;
Gladstone Chancellor of Exchequer.

1859–1860   Supported special evening
services in seven theatres (average
attendance 20,700) against clerical
opposition.
Presentation made to him as
President of Ragged School
movement by Ragged School
teachers.
Presentation to Lady Shaftesbury by
the Factory Operatives.
Culmination of eight years of
effort in erection of the State
Criminal Asylum at Broad-
moor.

The Unification of Italy.

1861   Moved to provide treatment
for the insane of the middle
classes.
Worked for irrigation and
internal navigation to combat
famine in India.
His daughter Mary died.

Death of the Prince Consort.
Civil War (1861–1865) in the
United States.

1862	Acceptance of the Order of the Garter (refused in 1854).	Bismarck in power in Prussia.
1863	His repeated speeches against the Russian treatment of Poland led to protest by British government to Russia.	Insurrection in Poland. Ruthless Russian (and Prussian) subjugation of Poland.
1864	24 years after his espousal of the climbing boys' cause, all existing acts having failed, he achieved the Chimney Sweepers' Regulation Act (later disregarded in practice). Addressed the Pastoral Aid Society. Addressed the Y.M.C.A. Entertained Garibaldi. Made proposal for examination of "organized labor" known as "Children's Agricultural Gangs." Proposed bill for regulating the labor of juveniles in workshops.	
1861–1864.	Advised Palmerston on ecclesiastical appointments "The Shaftesbury Bishops").	
1861–1868	Litigation with his unfaithful steward, Waters.	
1865	His mother, the Sixth Countess, died.	Death of Palmerston. Assassination of Lincoln.
1866	The frigate *Chichester* established as training ship for boys (later the *Arethusa* also). The farm and Shaftesbury schools at Bisley and Twickenham established to train boys in agriculture for colonial life. Also girls' refuges at Sudbury and Ealing and The National Refuges for Homeless and Destitute Children. Chaired inaugural meeting of Victoria Institute. Refused the Duchy of Lancaster. President of Social Science Congress.	Third Tory minority ministry, under Derby and Disraeli.

1867	Opposed proposals of the Reform Bill. Carried out work ("right and hopeless") on Vestments Bill.	Disraeli's first Ministry. Second Reform Bill. Publication of *Das Kapital.* British North America Act (Canadian Confederation).
1868	Suggested to Gladstone a peerage for the Jewish philanthropist, Sir Moses Montefiore.	Gladstone Prime Minister.
1869	Wasted much distasteful work on Ecclesiastical Courts Bill. Lady Palmerston died. Accy's son, the future Ninth Earl, born.	Irish Church Act. Opening of Suez Canal.
1870	Opposed "Godless schools," i.e. exclusion of Biblical teaching in the new National School system. Founded National Society for Aiding Sick and Wounded in Time of War. Supported Married Women's Property Bill.	Franco-Prussian War. Education Act.
1871	Opened a lodging house for news-boys. Made successful application on behalf of children working in the brickfields. Granted freedom of the city of Glasgow.	
1872	Still at work on Ecclesiastical Courts Bill. Worked to prevent violation of Workshop Act, Factory Acts, Brickfield's Act. Supported Bill for Protection of Acrobats and Small Children. Made final speech against the Ballot Act. Laid memorial stone of a Work-men's City ("Shaftesbury Park"). His wife, Lady Shaftesbury, died. His daughter, Constance, died.	The Ballot Act. France's Third Republic.
1873	Founded the "Emily Loan Fund" to aid the Watercress and Flower Girls' Mission.	

Espoused cause of temperance.
Supported Plimsoll's efforts to
obtain a Protection Act for
Seamen.
Busied with amendments to Public
Worship Bill.

1874   Opened new house for London   Disraeli's second ministry (to 1880).
        City Mission.
        His fourth son, Evelyn Ashley,
        returned as M. P. for Poole.

1876   In opposing Queen's adoption of   Vivisection Act.
        title Empress of India, he moved   Turkish atrocities in Bulgaria.
        Amendment to the Royal Titles
        Bill.
        Founded Society for Protection of
        Animals from Vivisection.
        Worked (since 1868) for Coster-
        mongers.
        Paid off ruinous mortgage on St.
        Giles's Estate.

1877   Called to give evidence before
        committee appointed to enquire
        into operation of Lunacy Laws.
        His sixth son, Cecil Ashley,
        posted to staff of Governor of
        Cape Colony.
        Appealed for relief of Bosnian
        and Herzegovinism refugees in
        Austria.

1878   Saw completion of work on   War in Afghanistan.
        behalf of Factory Operatives in
        Factories and Workshops Act,
        consolidating 45 existing acts.
        Received freedom of Edinburgh.
        Continued interest in George
        Lane Ragged School, and in
        Spurgeon's almshouse and
        orphanage.

1879   Carried through the Lords the   War with the Zulus.
        Habitual Drunkards Bill.   Dual Alliance of Germany and
        Carried the Factory Workers in   Austria.
        India Bill.
        Spoke on behalf of Lord Truros'
        Bill for Abolition of Vivisection.

251

Refused to allow the writing of his biography.

1880   Presided and spoke at celebrations of the Sunday-School Centenary in Gloucester, on the Isle of Wight, at the Thames' Embankment. Spoke on Employers' Liability Bill, Hares and Rabbits Bill, Irish Registration Bill.

               Gladstone's second government (to 1885).

1881   His 80th birthday celebrated in the Guild Hall. Second resolution condemning the opium trade (40 years after he first voiced opposition). Continued work for Costers and Ragged Schools.

               Married Women's Property Act. Boers defeated British at Majuba Hill. Second Irish Land Act. Death of Disraeli. Democratic (later Social Democratic) Federation.

1882   Protested persecution of Jews in Russia.

               Gladstone intervened in Egypt.

1883   Protested futility of operation of Children's Dangerous Performance Act (1879). Round of charitable organizations and services.

1884   Freedom of the city of London. His speech in response: "If I cannot aid any lustre to the citizenship, the time for me is so short that there will be little opportunity to tarnish it. If anyone ever writes my biography, will he have the goodness to say that I died a citizen of London." Speech at Y.M.C.A. opening in Brighton. Head of deputation to beg G.N.R. for trains and cheap tickets for working commuters. Chair of Bible Society. Unveiling of Tyndale's statue on the Embankment. Chair of Jews Society. Jubilee of London City Mission. Wycliffe Commemoration. Speech to 7000 at commemoration of Spurgeon's 50th birthday.

               Third Reform Act. The Fabian Society.

| 1885 | Speech on the housing of the poor. Public espousal, against religious objections, of cremation. Help to Society for Promoting Female Education in the East. Resignation of Chairmanship on Commission of Lunacy in protest against Lunacy Amendment Bill— resumption of office when the bill was shelved. Efforts to establish Jewish exiles from Russia first in Palestine, then in Cyprus. Died on October 1. | Death of Gordon at Khartoum. Lord Salisbury's Act: Housing of the Working Classes. |

Memoranda

An attempt has been made to list by year the outstanding or the new endeavors in which Lord Shaftesbury was involved. But his work for these causes extended in some cases for over fifty years, and the demands on his time, means, and energy were unceasing.

It is fashionable to pillory as "bigot" anyone who has strong convictions on moral or religious issues; Lord Shaftesbury in his lifetime and since, has been a target for the term. Few men deserve it less. He was a convinced and unrelenting opponent of the Ritualist or Tractarian movement, which he believed to be undermining the Church of England; yet he sustained criticism for cooperating with the Roman Catholic Mrs. Chisolm in her work for children, for his unstinting praise of Dr. Pusey's personal piety and Pusey's commentary on Daniel, for his public collaboration with all branches of Dissenters. His friendly correspondence with Cardinal Manning, his approval of Moody and Sankey, his friendship with Charles Haddon Spurgeon, are not the reflection of a bigoted nature; nor his refusal to countenance the deposition of scholars like Jowett from their university appointments because of their neological views.

Finally: Members of Parliament were unpaid in the nineteenth century. Only twice in his lifetime—once before his marriage for a period of two years and later again for a few months—did Lord Ashley occupy a government position with remuneration. He could never afford a secretary; his voluminous correspondence and all his speech notes were written by his own hand. More, the material for his speeches and bills—the data and research—was assembled by personal first-hand investigation, and the expense of the necessary journeying paid out of his own pocket.

Truly, a Man for *this* season!

Bibliography

Airlie, Mabell, Countess of. *Lady Palmerston and her Times*. London and New York: Hodder & Stoughton, 1922.

———. *Thatched With Gold*, J. Ellis ed. Leicester: Ulverscroft, 1962.

Ashley, Evelyn. *The Life and Correspondence of Henry John Temple, Viscount Palmerston*. London: R. Bentley, 1876.

Best, G. F. A. *Shaftesbury*. London: B. T. Batsford, 1964; New York: Arco, 1964.

Bready, J. W. *Lord Shaftesbury and Social and Industrial Progress*. London: Allen & Unwin, 1926.

Briggs, Asa. *Victorian People*. Chicago: University of Chicago Press, 1970.

Cecil, David. *Melbourne*. Indianapolis: Bobbs-Merrill, 1954; Westport, Conn.: Greenwood, 1971 repr.

Creevey, Thomas. *The Creevey Papers*, a selection from the correspondence and diaries of the late Thomas Creevey, ed. Sir Herbert Maxwell. London: J. Murray, 1903, 1904, 1912, 1933; New York: E. P. Dutton, 1904, 1923; rev. edition, ed. John Gore, London: J. Murray, 1948, 1949; New York: Macmillan, 1963.

Foot, *Eleventh Shaftesbury Lecture: Lord Shaftesbury: His Achievement and His Legacy to This Generation*. London: Shaftesbury Society and Ragged Schools Union, 1936.

Fulford, Roger, ed. *Dearest Child*, letters between Queen Victoria and Princess Royal. London: Evans Bros., 1964; New York: Holt, Rinehart & Winston, 1964, 1965.

Granville, Harriet Elizabeth (Cavendish) Leveson-Gower, *Letters of Harriet, Countess Granville 1810–1845*, ed. F. Leveson Gower. London and New York: Longmans Green, 1894.

Greville, Charles. *Greville Memoirs*, ed. Roger Fulford. New York: Macmillan, 1963.

Guedalla, Philip. *The Hundred Years*. London: Hodder & Stoughton, 1936; New York: Doubleday, Doran & Co., 1936, 1937.

Hailsham, Quintin McGarel Hogg, 2nd Viscount. *Shaftesbury, A New Assessment*. London: Shaftesbury Society, 1958.

Hammond, J. L. and Barbara. *Lord Shaftesbury*. London: Constable & Co., 1923, 1925; New York: Harcourt Brace, 1924; New York and London: Longmans Green, 1936.

Hibbert, Christopher. *The Court at Windsor*. New York: Harper & Row, 1965.

Hodder, Edwin. *The Life and Works of the 7th Earl of Shaftesbury*, 3 vols. New York: Barnes and Noble, 1971 repr. of 1886 edition.

Holland, Elizabeth. *To Her Son, 1821–1846*, ed. Earl of Ilchester. London: J. Murray, 1945.

Jaeger, Muriel. *Before Victoria*. London: Chatto & Windus, 1956; New York: Fernhill, 1956.

Leader, Barbara Blackburn. *Noble Lord*. London: Home & Van Thal, 1949.

Longford, E. *Victoria R. I.* New York: Harper & Row, 1973.

Martineau, Harriet. *A History of the Thirty Years' Peace*, 4 vols. New York: Barnes & Noble repr. of 1877 edition.

News from the Past, newspaper acounts, 1805–1807, ed. Yvonne French. London: Victor Gollancz, n.d.

Pearson, Hesketh. *The Smith of Smiths*. New York: Harper, 1934; Havertown, Pa.: R. West, 1973 repr. of 1934 ed.; St. Clair Shores, Mich.: Scholarly, 1972 repr. of 1934 ed.

Pemberton, William Baring. *Lord Palmerston*. London: Batchwork Press, 1954.

Perugini, Mark Edward. *Victorian Days and Ways*. London: Jarrolds, 1964.

Pollack. *The Poor Man's Earl.*

Ridley, Jasper. *Lord Palmerston*. London: Constable, 1970.

Rowse, A. L. *The Later Churchills*. London: Macmillan, 1958. American edition has title: *The Churchills: from the Death of Marlborough to the Present*. New York: Harper, 1958.

Seeley, Sir John Robert. *Ecce Homo: A Survey of the Life and Work of Jesus Christ*. London: Macmillan, 1866; Boston: Roberts Bros., 1866, 1867; London: J. M. Dent, 1920; New York: Dutton, 1932.

Shaftesbury, 7th Earl. *Speeches of the Earl of Shaftesbury upon Subjects having Relation Chiefly to the Claims and Interests of the Labouring Class*. London: Chapman & Hall, 1868.

Sitwell, Osbert and Barton, Margaret. *Brighton*. London: Faber & Faber, 1925.

Strachey, Lytton. *Queen Victoria*. New York: Harcourt Brace, 1949.

———. *Eminent Victorians*. New York: Putnam, 1963; New York: Harcourt, Brace, Jovanovich, 1969.

Wyndham, Maud Mary (Lyttleton). *The Correspondence of Sarah, Lady Lyttleton*. London: Hodder & Stoughton, 1924.

Genealogy of the Ashley-Cooper Family

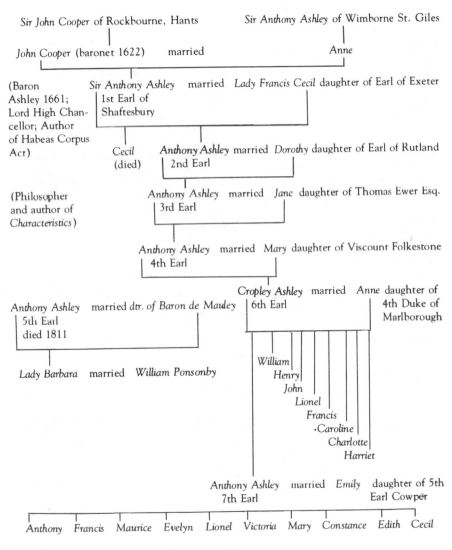

Sir John Cooper of Rockbourne, Hants   Sir Anthony Ashley of Wimborne St. Giles

John Cooper (baronet 1622)   married   Anne

(Baron Ashley 1661; Lord High Chancellor; Author of Habeas Corpus Act)

Sir Anthony Ashley 1st Earl of Shaftesbury   married   Lady Francis Cecil daughter of Earl of Exeter

Cecil (died)

Anthony Ashley 2nd Earl   married   Dorothy daughter of Earl of Rutland

(Philosopher and author of Characteristics)

Anthony Ashley 3rd Earl   married   Jane daughter of Thomas Ewer Esq.

Anthony Ashley 4th Earl   married   Mary daughter of Viscount Folkestone

Anthony Ashley 5th Earl died 1811   married dtr. of Baron de Mauley

Cropley Ashley 6th Earl   married   Anne daughter of 4th Duke of Marlborough

Lady Barbara   married   William Ponsonby

William
Henry
John
Lionel
Francis
Caroline
Charlotte
Harriet

Anthony Ashley 7th Earl   married   Emily daughter of 5th Earl Cowper

Anthony   Francis   Maurice   Evelyn   Lionel   Victoria   Mary   Constance   Edith   Cecil

257

Genealogy of Emily,
Seventh Countess of Shaftesbury

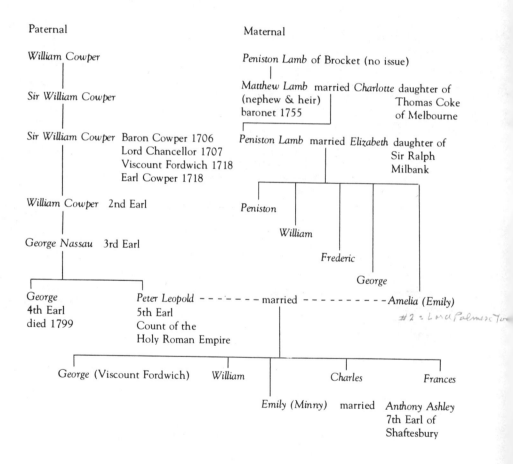

Paternal

William Cowper
|
Sir William Cowper
|
Sir William Cowper Baron Cowper 1706
| Lord Chancellor 1707
| Viscount Fordwich 1718
| Earl Cowper 1718
William Cowper   2nd Earl
|
George Nassau   3rd Earl

George   Peter Leopold
4th Earl   5th Earl
died 1799   Count of the
                    Holy Roman Empire

George (Viscount Fordwich)   William

Maternal

Peniston Lamb of Brocket (no issue)
|
Matthew Lamb married Charlotte daughter of
(nephew & heir)   Thomas Coke
baronet 1755   of Melbourne

Peniston Lamb married Elizabeth daughter of
                            Sir Ralph
                            Milbank

Peniston

William

Frederic

George

- - - - - married - - - - - - - - - Amelia (Emily)
                                     #2 = Lord Palmerston

Charles   Frances

Emily (Minny)   married   Anthony Ashley
                          7th Earl of
                          Shaftesbury

258

Maternal Genealogy of the Seventh Earl

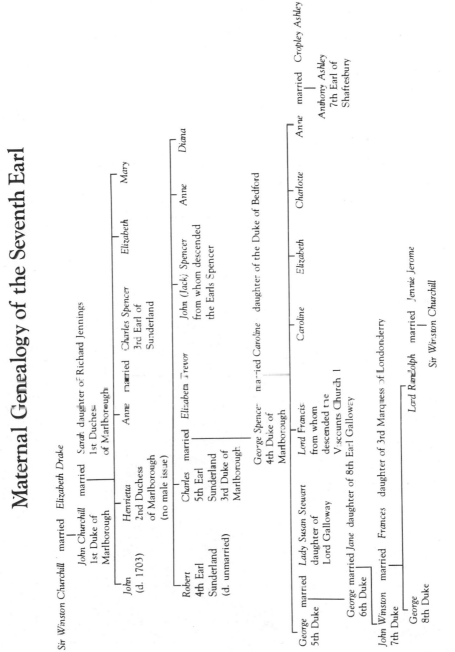